*She surrendered
to passion...
and discovered love!*

UNEXPECTED PLEASURE

"Pledge me your hatred, my lady," Piers challenged, looking down at her.

Vivian's lips parted, revealing her tightly clenched teeth. She aimed a sibilant hiss at him.

He laughed. "A tiger cat with fangs bared. But a small tiger. Much overmatched, I fear." He took another sip of brandy, then slowly inclined his head, bringing his lips nearer and nearer to hers. His eyes were so close to her own that she could now see they were not a single opaque dark color but brown, floating, shifting shades of brown with a golden radiance around the pupil.

His lips touched hers. And something happened. Something swift and hot as lightning streaked through her limbs. It made her curl her hands into fists and draw her breath in sharply. She could not help herself. The need to taste more of him and heighten this fiery sensation drove her to pull him even closer.

A wave of unsought passion swept over him. Suddenly, there was nothing but the sweetness and warmth of her mouth. . . .

Deana James

Speak Only Love

ZEBRA BOOKS
KENSINGTON PUBLISHING CORP.

Again for Rachel Andrea—
who is just beginning to know
the power of words.

ZEBRA BOOKS

are published by

Kensington Publishing Corp.
475 Park Avenue South
New York, NY 10016

Copyright © 1991 by Mona D. Sizer

First printing: July, 1991

Printed in the United States of America

Prologue

December 1809

The coach slid sideways on the icy highroad, bumping crazily as its wheels dropped into the ruts frozen solid by the harsh December blast. The coachman, muffled to his eyes, swung his long whip over the backs of the horses and cursed his mistress viciously. Lady Marleigh was seven kinds of a fool. No one should have started a journey on such a day. Christmas bedamned! The weather was too bad; the roads, too dangerous. A heavy fall of snow had turned to sleet the previous night. On either side of the dark road, trees and hedgerows bowed their limbs to the white earth in arcs of shimmering ice.

The near impassability of the road had made the journey last far into the evening. With an angry scowl at the darkening sky, he cracked his whip again. One gray wheeler neighed shrilly as the coach bumped in and out of the frozen ruts of the crossroad with a series of bone-jarring jerks.

Within the coach Lady Marleigh rubbed her elbow tenderly before wrapping her hand more firmly around the leather strap beside the window. The tightly drawn curtains and windows provided maximum protection from the elements. Unfortunately, they contributed to a feeling of disorientation as the coach tipped crazily in every direction as if it were being shaken by a giant's hand.

Around her was a sad welter of cushions and rugs originally bestowed amid the leather, wood, and metal of the coach's interior to shield the occupants from the cold. Now they did yeoman's service as protectors from the bruising jolts of the road's rough surface.

Lady Marleigh swallowed before looking disgustedly at her maid. The girl's tear-streaked cheeks were greenish pale. She had been wretchedly ill throughout most of the journey thereby adding to the unpleasantness of the coach's interior. Even as Lady Marleigh frowned at her, the maid bent over her knees pressing a handkerchief to her mouth in an effort to control her nausea. "Really, Maud," Lady Marleigh said with a sigh.

"Sorry, milady," came the wretched gasp as the coach caromed to the left and then to the right.

Alarmed at the roughness, the gentlewoman wound her arms protectively around the body of her sleeping daughter Vivian. With the complete relaxation of innocent youth, the nine-year-old girl slept soundly against her mother, blissfully oblivious to the tortuous way.

A wave of love swept the mother as she caressed the small thin arm and shoulder. Gently she pressed a kiss against the pale silvery hair curling softly on the smooth forehead.

With incredible swiftness the coach slewed viciously to the side of the road. A loud crack accompanied by the hoarse shout of the coachman was the last sound Lady Marleigh heard. She was flung violently against

6

the opposite side of the coach. Her temple struck the cast brass lamp bracket, stifling her scream of terror forever. As the broken wheel shattered on the curve and threw the coach toward the ditch, the harness bar snapped loose from its fittings.

The terrified horses, freed of the weight and maddened by the whip broke free, pulling the coachman headlong from the box by the reins wrapped around his wrists. His body struck the icy roadbed face down snapping his neck beneath his falling weight.

Caught with her head bowed to her knees, Lady Marleigh's maid struck the door of the coach headfirst. It burst open flinging her body outward. Knocked unconscious by the blow and the fall onto the frozen ground, she lay in a crumpled heap in the snow. Teetering for only a moment on the side of the highroad, its broken wheel collapsing beneath it, the coach toppled with a crash onto its side into the deep ditch. With a heavy thud, the door now turned upward toward the stars slammed shut. Icy silence closed round as two wheels parallel to the ground spun uselessly, slowed, and ceased.

For several minutes the silence prevailed. Then a shrill wail, a child's high-pitched voice, penetrated the icy dusk.

"Mother! Mother! Help! Help! Please, somebody, help!" The screaming became muffled as more snow began to fall on the still bodies. Screams gave way to hysterical sobs. Small fists pounded on the sides of the coach. "Please, God! Please, Jesus! Help! Somebody! Mother! Oh, Mother, don't die!"

Not for several hours did the shivering, shuddering team find its way into the yard of a posting inn. The sleepy hostler turned over several times before rousing sufficiently to hear the animals stamping and blowing. Almost another hour passed before a party had been grudgingly organized to follow the fast-disappearing tracks back along the road. Finally, the searchers neared the wreck.

One man turned over the distorted body of the coachman dragged several hundred feet down the road, before the reins broke free from his wrists. "Coachy's dead," he reported laconically.

The leader grunted as he led his party stumbling onward through the white night. He had expected little else when he had seen the team.

"Woman dead here," another reported, bending over the mound of snow that covered the body of the maid.

Slogging to the side of the road, the leader of the party pounded on the bottom of the overturned vehicle. "Anybody there?" he called.

Silence greeted his question.

"They be all dead, froze most likely," one man said irritably. "Told ye there'd be none left. They'd ha' been just the same in the mornin', and we'd ha' saved ourselves a walk in the dark."

"Up on the coach, Tim," the leader ordered. "Open the door and shine your light in."

A youth scrambled up with some difficulty and stood on the side, tugging manfully to lift the door. Laying it back, he lowered his lantern into the interior.

"Sweet Jesus!"

The swinging light revealed the body of a woman, her mouth agape and blood frozen in a ghoulish mask down one side of her face. Obviously, she was dead. Pressed against her body was the smaller body of a girl. Tears streaked the little face that blinked owlishly in

8

the light. The child's mouth opened and closed, but no sound came from the blue lips.

Hanging the lantern from the interior door handle, the boy dropped clumsily into the coach and gently began to pry the little stiff fingers from their grip. Only with difficulty could he loosen the child's hold on her dead mother and lifted her in his arms. When he did, her mouth opened and closed silently. Wildly she struggled, reaching backward in terror for her mother.

"What'd you find?" came the call from outside.

"There be one alive," the boy replied. "One of you climb up and help me get her out. She be scared to death, and that's a fact."

Another man scrambled up onto the coach and peered in. "What about the woman?" he asked as he held down his arms.

"She be dead." The boy held up the struggling girl who twisted in his grasp, trying to avoid the hands of the man reaching for her through the coach door. Her little mouth moved futilely, as her lips formed words, but no sound came.

Chapter One

"Follow me. I'll show you directly to the patient." The housekeeper's mouth drew into a tight pinch-purse, as if the idea of a patient in the household were somehow a reflection on her own industry.

Sister Grace Hospitaler's rubicund face twisted as she pressed her hand against her chest. "If you please, my good woman. We would like to be shown directly to our rooms to wash before we enter the sickroom."

Rusty black skirts swirled as the other woman pivoted at the foot of the stairs. "Rooms? I received no instructions about *rooms*. One room will certainly be all that's needful."

The nun glanced nervously over her shoulder. Her companion, a much younger woman, shook her head quickly. Perspiration trickled down Sister Grace's wrinkled cheek into the groove made by the starched wimple. Her expression betrayed her frustration. "One room won't do," she told the housekeeper crossly. "We must have two rooms. We'll be taking turns beside the bed and need our sleep."

The pinch-purse mouth tightened impossibly. "If

11

one is in the sickroom and one is in the bed, then you don't need two. Besides, I don't have any instructions for two."

"Prepare two." The voice carried a raspy authority that brooked no argument. All three women started and looked toward the sound. "See to it, Mrs. Felders."

To the right of the stairs, a door had opened silently. In its archway stood the bent dark figure silhouetted against dim light.

"Sir—"

"Two rooms. One for the old one—and one for the young." He laughed once, a single staccato sound.

"Very well, sir."

As the three women watched, he closed the door. As if mesmerized, they waited until they heard the faint click of the latch mechanism slipping into place.

Mrs. Felders moved first shrugging her shoulders. "If you'll follow me, I'll take you to the room that's ready. You can wash there and leave your things. While you're seeing your patient, I'll have another room prepared."

"Good," the older woman replied. The younger one remained silent, her head humbly inclined.

The countess scarcely seemed to breathe in the big bed. Her head drooped to one side on the single pillow. Her mobcap had slipped allowing locks of wispy-silvery hair to trail down the side of her neck.

On the far side of her bed, a man climbed wearily to his feet as the women entered the sickroom. With a groan, he arched his back and pushed his hands into the small of it. " 'Bout time you got here. She's failing fast I'm thinking. A couple of days more and you'd have wasted your trip."

The housekeeper hushed him with a frown and a

finger to her lips. "Better keep your ideas like that to yourself, Mr. Watkins. She might hear you."

"Poor lady doesn't know a thing," he replied with a shake of his head.

The older nun advanced to the side of the bed. "You can't know that. The hearing is the very last sense to go. She might be hearing everything you say and planning to turn you off the minute she wakes up. So be off with you." She made a shooing motion with her hands.

With a shrug he drifted toward the door.

The younger nun stepped aside to let him pass.

"She wouldn't be letting me off in any case," he muttered. "He's the one who says who goes and who stays."

"Mother." The man leaned over the sickbed. A lock of dark red hair, a most unusual color, worn unfashionably long, had escaped from the black riband at the back of his neck. It swung forward bisecting his temple and sharp cheekbone. "Mother."

The countess's brows drew together. She sucked in an unsteady breath and released it on a sigh. "Piers?"

"Yes." He pressed his lips gently to her forehead.

Her lids fluttered upward. Eyes that took their color from the mauve shadows surrounding them focused on her son. "Piers, why are you still here?"

He did not miss her meaning. Tenderly he leaned forward to kiss her forehead. His face only inches from hers, he said, "Mother, I can't leave you."

"You must." The words were only a breath of sound. Her eyes drifted closed, then opened again and sought the nurse. "Go away," she whispered.

Still bent over his mother, the gaunt face turned toward her. The lock of wine-red hair brushed the pillowcase beside his mother's head.

The young nun rose. Instead of leaving like a noiseless ghost, she came to the bedside and lifted the blue-veined hand. The pulse fluttered and skipped in the emaciated wrist.

The countess made a weak attempt to pull herself away. "I said, 'Go away!'" she breathed. Faint color spread across her cheekbones.

The young woman returned the hand gently to the coverlet and raised her own hand with fingers spread wide.

"Five minutes." The man nodded his head impatiently. "Very well. Very well. I won't tire her. Just be gone."

Only as she closed the door behind her, did she recognize the odor of brandy on his breath. Outside in the hallway she hesitated. Should she remain in the room? Better to fetch Sister Grace, an expert at rousting intruders from sickrooms.

The old nun sat up too quickly and fell back down. One pudgy hand fluttered to her enormous bosom, the other to her forehead. "I—I'll be all right in a moment, milady," she whispered.

The young woman hurried to pour a glass of water and hold it to Sister Grace's mouth. The nun's close-cropped iron-gray hair stank with perspiration. She emptied the glass greedily and dabbed at the moisture on her forehead with the corner of the sheet. Her hand trembled. She stared at it, then at the pale smooth face hovering anxiously above her. "I'm not well," she said slowly as if admitting a fault. "But someone had to come. Bring me some of my medicine and then leave me alone for a few minutes."

The younger sister nodded grimly. She brought

more water and held the glass while the nun swallowed the tincture.

Grimacing at the taste, Sister Grace handed the glass back. "Thank you, milady. Now go on. Go on back. Don't leave your charge. I'll be right behind you. Just give me a few minutes." She swung her swollen limbs over the bed and sat up carefully. "I'll be right behind you."

The one called "milady" looked doubtful, but the old nurse reached for her veil. "Go on. Go on. I'm right as rain now. Just sat up too fast."

"—nothing to keep you here," the woman was saying as the door opened.

The young man had seated himself on the side of the bed. One knee was drawn up. His hand draped languidly over it, his fingers trailing beneath a fall of lace. "There's you, m'dear," he replied, and then he flashed a mocking grin. "And my own bad habits."

The countess smiled slightly. "Bad boy, Piers." She sighed. "And you will persist in going to the devil."

"I'm afraid so, Mother."

She turned her head into the pillow. Her voice quavered. "God forgive you. And me." She began to cough weakly. Tears spouted from her eyes. She fumbled and found a handkerchief and lifted it to her mouth. The cough deepened.

The young nun hurried around to the other side of the bed.

Piers leaned forward to take his mother's hand. "He probably won't forgive any of us. He's forgotten we exist."

"Ah, Piers. Piers." The paroxym became more violent. The spasms jolted the countess's body. The

15

young nun slipped one arm under the thin shoulders and thrust first one pillow and then another behind them.

The young man rose to his feet alarmed and angry. "Can't you do something more? She's choking."

Her patient's head elevated, the nurse began to unbutton the high-necked gown and clear the area of the throat. Still the choking continued to grow worse and worse. The countess's face reddened. The thin lips turned blue.

"Mother!" Piers caught hold of her hand. "Mother!"

"Here. Let me through." Sister Grace Hospitaler brushed him aside. She poured a measure of syrup from a dark brown bottle and held the glass to the woman's lips. "There, there, milady, just try to keep calm and drink a little of this."

The countess managed a weak shake of her head. Her eyes were starting from their sockets, as her cough grew more agonizing. Blood flecked her lips.

Sister Grace wiped the woman's chin and presented the glass again. "Steaming hot water and towels. Quickly. Let's try to clear the sinuses."

The young nun dashed from the room.

Piers took her place across the bed. "What are you going to do?"

"Open her head with steam so she can breathe. Just like a poor dear croupy baby." She held the liquid to the old woman's lips. "Swallow, dear lady. Swallow. That's a good baby."

The countess coughed again violently. The liquid spewed into the nun's face. She blinked and shook her head, but persisted. "That's all right. You couldn't help it. Poor, dear girl. Swallow. Swallow."

"You'll strangle her," Piers cried. He reached for the pudgy wrist.

Sister Grace shook her head. "Soothing syrup. It'll

16

ease the throat. It'll—" She broke off with a smothered cry. Her fingers clenched, then flew apart. The glass spilled its liquid onto the coverlet.

"Here. What are you doing?" Piers grabbed the glass as the nun stumbled back.

Her hands mashed into her bosom, clutching, kneeding. She wheeled away from the bed and stumbled blindly across the room. One step. Two. The door opened. The young nun hurried in just in time to see Sister Grace sink to her knees, her face twisting in agony. "M-milady," she called, reaching out toward the woman in the doorway. "Oh, Milady Viv—"

"Here," Piers called. "You can't—"

Too late the young nun tried to catch her older sister as she fell forward striking the floor face downward with a horrible crunching sound. Piers gasped and stepped away from the bed, then returned to his mother whose spasms seemed likely to tear her throat out.

With trembling hands the young nun turned the body over. The skin of the old woman's nose and forehead had been split by the fall. Blood welled from the wound. Sister Grace could have made no effort to save herself when she struck the floor. She had been dead even as she fell.

The young sister opened her mouth, then clasped her hands together in front of it as if to stifle a cry. Horror and terror mixed in equal parts and twisted her face.

At last the countess's coughing ceased. She subsided on the pillows, her eyes were closed, her head drooped to one side.

Piers smoothed a tendril of hair from her cheek and returned her hand to the coverlet. Satisfied that she would rest for a moment, he flung himself at the door. His voice boomed in the hall outside. "Felders! Watkins! Rot you both! Get up here!" Turning back, he threw another glance at his mother, then dropped to

17

one knee beside the body of Sister Grace. He fumbled beneath the sleeve of her habit, found her wrist and checked for a pulse. "She's dead."

The young nun pressed her hands to her mouth. Her eyes pleaded silently over the tips of her fingers. She gave a quick shake of her head.

He looked down at the mutilated face. "I doubt if she knew when she hit the floor."

The valet stumbled in first, his eyes on the bed. His gaze dropped in amazement to the tableau around the body on the floor. "Milord! What's happened here? What happened to the poor woman?"

Piers rose to his feet with a resigned air. "She looks to have had some sort of a fit." He shrugged wearily. "Anyway she's dead."

The valet murmured unintelligibly as he lifted his eyes from the dead face to the stone white one above it. "Miss—that is, Sister, you have my sympathies."

Again Piers went to the door. "*Felders*! Damn it. Where are you?"

"Probably getting the hot water and towels." The valet nodded toward the young nun. "That was what was wanted, wasn't it?"

Both men stared as she lowered her head to rest on the old one's chest. Her eyes were closed as she listened desperately for a heartbeat.

"You're wasting your time," Piers returned and came down on one knee beside the body. This time he turned the back of his hand beneath the nostrils. "No breath," he muttered. "What an ungodly mess!" Not the faintest stirring of warmth could be discerned. "She's dead. Damn it! Right here on mother's carpet."

The young woman's head snapped up. Blue eyes, so pale they were almost colorless, glared at him with cold fire. He raised a quizzical eyebrow and started to speak.

18

At that moment Mrs. Felders burst through the door, her eyes on the figure drooping on the bed. "Oh, sir, has the end come?"

Piers's head snapped round at the eagerness in her tone. He rose angrily. "No, the end has not come. At least not for Mother, but for this poor creature. For God's sake, Mrs. Felders. Could you not have hired someone healthy?"

For the first time, the housekeeper glanced at the two nuns one lying, the other kneeling on the floor. Her eyes narrowed; her mouth puckered as if she had bitten down on a sour pickle. With a disgusted grunt she bent to inspect the body of Sister Grace. "Wasn't my doing that brought them here to begin with, milord. They've been more trouble than they're worth, making all the extra work of two rooms. Are you sure she's not just fainted?"

The young nun, tears trickling down her cheeks, lunged to her feet. Her fingernails arced like talons toward Mrs. Felders's face.

The housekeeper stumbled back throwing up her arms to protect herself.

"Here now." The valet Watkins thrust himself between them and caught the nun around the waist. "Easy now. Don't take offense." He held her while the housekeeper ran out the door. "She don't mean a thing by that. She just sees everything from her own angle. Is it going to mean more work for her, don't you see?"

At that moment the countess uttered a terrible pained cry and began to cough again.

"Mother." Piers jumped to her side. "Mother, it's all right. I'm here. Mother."

The old woman's face turned red from her efforts to clear her throat. She raised one hand trembling pathetically. Her eyelids fluttered.

"For God's sake, get yourself over here," he snarled.

19

"What was that stuff the old one was going to pour down her throat?"

Shifting the terrible death aside with visible effort, the nun's eyes flew to the bottle of syrup on the bedside table. Retrieving the glass from among the bedcovers, she poured another draught and held it to the old woman's lips. While Piers held his mother's head and shoulders, she managed to get the countess to drink some medicine between the spasms.

Almost immediately, the syrup began to take effect. The next bout was much less severe. The countess again sank back on the pillows with a piteous moan.

The moment past, Piers eased back and looked around him. His mouth relaxed slightly as he watched the young nun smooth his mother's hair back and straighten the lace-edged mobcap where it had slipped. He exchanged a glance with Watkins, who waited anxiously at the foot of the bed. At last he looked at the body of the old woman where it still lay stiffening on the floor. Mrs. Felders had not returned. A shocking expletive burst from his mouth.

"Milord?" Watkins said uncertainly.

"That damned Felders couldn't even bother to send the footmen up to carry out the body." Piers strode to the door. "Damn and blast!"

"I'll take care of it, milord." The valet raced him to the door and darted out.

"Can you care for my mother while I get this properly taken care of?" Piers tossed over his shoulder. When no answer came, he looked irritably in the direction of the bed.

The young woman nodded, her face white as the white linen around her neck and shoulders.

He raised one eyebrow. "I think the vow of silence much overstrained, ma'am. Surely the situation here allows a bit of latitude."

20

A slow flush rose in her cheeks. She turned back to her charge who coughed fitfully.

A couple of footmen appeared at the door. He motioned them into the room and then snorted in disgust as they looked helplessly at him awaiting direction. "Pick her up in the carpet," he snapped. "It'll need a good cleaning anyway. Roll her up and be gone."

When the nun would have left his mother's side in protest, he motioned her back mockingly. "Only as a means of carrying her, Sister. We won't bury her in an expensive carpet. Rest assured."

At that moment the housekeeper appeared in the doorway, her composure intact, though her face was white. Piers's eyes narrowed. "Mrs. Felders, was something said about hot water and steaming towels?"

She lifted her chin and came on to the foot of the bed. "Yes, sir."

Even as she spoke, a footman appeared in the doorway, a yoke over his shoulders and two buckets hanging from the ends. Turning sideways he could not keep his eyes from the body of Sister Grace—her poor mutilated face turned upward to the light, thin streams of blood running down her cheeks and across her forehead. He dropped the yoke off his shoulders. The buckets thudded to the floor, water splashing as he bolted for the door.

Piers cursed again, disgust and anger in his tone. Hefting one of the buckets, he carried it to the bedside. Watkins came in with towels. At Piers's signal, he passed them to the sister, who stared at the water helplessly.

"Get on with it," Piers snapped. "My mother could die while you stand thre like a dummy."

Again her anger flashed from beneath the habit.

"I've never heard such confusion." A raspy voice

21

froze them all in their tracks. "I can only presume it is all over."

"No, your grace." Mrs. Felders folded her hands under her apron. Color stained her cheeks. "The commotion is because one of those stupid nuns has fallen down and broken her head open. Clumsy, useless bead rattlers."

The young nun turned from the bedside. Her fingers clenched around a steaming towel. She drew back her arm, but before she could fling it at the housekeeper, Piers caught her wrist. One corner of his mouth curved upward in a humorless smile. He held her stiff body back and tried to turn her to her patient.

The earl looked with some interest at their muted struggle. The corners of his mouth twitched. He cleared his throat. "So I am safe in assuming that the body hustled out so unceremoniously past me was not that of my beloved wife. I rather thought as much." He glanced at the figure in the bed. "I rejoice in the news."

"And now you are come to bid her good night." Piers's voice was equally ironical.

The earl shuffled forward to the foot of the bed. There he rested, hands crossed over the top of an ivory-headed walking stick. "Of course. Good night, Georgina."

A spasm crossed the countess's face. Her eyes flickered open. Illness and exhaustion blurred the sharp edge of her hatred. "I'm not dead yet, Larnaervon."

"So I see."

They stared at each other in silence. Then her eyes slid to the housekeeper hovering at his shoulder. "Get out."

Mrs. Felders did not move though her mouth drew tighter than ever and her nostrils dilated.

22

"Get out," the sick woman repeated, her voice rasping in its intensity. She coughed.

Still Mrs. Felders did not move.

"Get out!"

The paroxym gathered strength. Piers came to the end of his mother's bed, forcing the housekeeper to retreat. Her pinch-purse mouth straightened. She might have smiled had she not turned and left the room.

The earl moved across his son's path. Almost breast to breast the two men faced each other. One tall, broad-shouldered, his disarranged hair glowing burgundy red in the lamplight. The other bent, his once tall figure crookbacked, his long white hair spread over the shoulders of his black velvet coat. He cocked his head up to his son. "Georgina has always played 'dog in the manger' about Felders," he confided with a smirk.

Biting down hard on his temper, Piers stepped back and returned to his mother's bedside.

The earl shuffled nearer, passing the end of the bed and coming up behind the nurse. While he watched, she draped a sheet over the head of the bed and poured aromatic oil into the steaming water. For a time everyone was silent except for the countess's labored breathing. The odor of camphor filled the sickroom.

When the countess began to breathe more easily beneath the makeshift tent, the earl looked to his son. "Thanks to this young woman's good work, the crisis has been averted, wouldn't you say, Piers?"

"I'm sure you're pleased, Larne."

"Why, yes, as a matter of fact I am." He moved slowly around the end of the bed, his cane tapping on the bare floor. "As a matter of fact, I am very pleased."

The son's jaw set stonily. "You have paid your obligatory call, Larne. I'm sure you want to be off to—er—bed."

23

Larnaervon chuckled. "Perhaps. Perhaps. Indeed I might go 'off to—er—bed' in a little while. On the other hand I might not. After all, my wife is very ill. Perhaps I should stay here in the sickroom. Perhaps do the watching thing beside the bed. What do you say?"

"I never believed you were a hypocrite."

Again the short humorless chuckle. "No?"

"No."

"Well, perhaps you're right. Besides, if Georgina were to awaken and find me beside her, she might be moved to use her tongue on me again. I find I have had quite enough of that over the long years." His black eyes followed the nun's black-clad figure as it moved past him, retrieved the other bucket, and set it up on the other side of the bed under the sheet. The odor of camphor again permeated the room.

The earl coughed affectedly. "The whole house will need to be aired."

A muscle leaped in the viscount's jaw. "Good night, Larne."

The earl managed to look remorseful. "Ah, Piers, 'tis a fact of life that sickrooms develop the odor of the disease and the medicines that are required to cure it. You shouldn't be so sensitive. I assure you that if I were lying there and Georgina were standing here, she would be saying the same thing."

Piers ran a distracted hand through his hair. "God damn you," he whispered. "Ah, Watkins, returned at last. How fortuitous. The earl needs your strong shoulder to escort him to his room."

"Ah, not at this hour of the evening." The knobby, brown-spotted hand lifted in protest. "But I will let you lead me down the stairs and into the library."

"Milord." The valet bowed obsequiously.

"After which I shall expect a spot of brandy, suitably warmed." The earl allowed himself to be led to the

24

door. "I leave you to your watching, Piers." He paused, one hand on the valet's shoulder. "And you, Sister. Good night to you both."

With Watkins supporting him, he made his way slowly out. When the door had closed behind them, Piers sank down in a chair. "God, what a mess. What a damnable mess!" He cast a glance at the nun. "I beg your pardon if I offend your delicate ears, but I'm quite certain that God has consigned this house and its occupants to eternal damnation long ago. He wouldn't pay attention to His name on our lips if we shouted it to the skies."

He watched the nun's face for some sign that she disapproved of what he was saying, but there was none. "God, you're a cool one. The only time I really saw you forget your humble pie was with Felders."

The nun bowed her head.

"Damned witch. She'd try the patience of Saint Simeon Stylites himself. Never leave her alone in this room with my mother, do you hear? Never." He leaned his head back on the chair. His breathing evened after a time and his head drooped to one side.

"Remarkable job, Caleb. Truly remarkable." The earl turned a ledger page, skimmed down the column of figures with his finger, then leaned back in his chair.

"Thank you, milord."

Eagle eyes studied the solicitor approvingly from under tangled white brows. Thin lips quirked. "You weren't somehow responsible for that timely demise on Georgina's carpet, were you? If you say you were, I will believe you because I see before me the proof of your cleverness."

"No, milord." Caleb Pross's face was an emotionless

mask. "I did not seek to name the companion who came with her. My assignment was only to see that she came."

The earl laughed—a humorless staccato sound. "And these—" His knobby hand slid across the page in front of him. His stained nail underlined the notation at the top of the page. "How did you come by the estate accounts from Stone Glenn? Or should I want to know?"

The solicitor raised one sandy eyebrow. "I assure you, milord, they were acquired through the most appropriate channels. Audits. Excises. Taxes. All these things must be looked into regularly. The firm of Pross, Davey, and Fieldstone regularly exchanges such activities and arranges to perform duties of these types with other reputable firms. Favors for favors, you understand. Barnstaple and Rowling is a reputable firm. Quite unexceptionable. I assure you."

The earl laughed again. "For months?"

"The mills of the gods grind slowly—"

"You are a pirate."

"No, sir." Pross allowed himself a small smile. "I am simply a man of business."

Someone was shaking him by the shoulder. He woke disoriented and stiff. The fire had gone out on the hearth and the room was chill. He pushed aside the blanket that had been draped over his body and stood.

The nun led him to his mother's side. He heard her draw a faint breath. For what seemed forever she did not move again. At last another tiny movement of the chest.

"She's dying," he murmured, his voice breaking. "Mother. I love you. Take that with you wherever you go. I love you." He bent to touch his lips to her

26

forehead and cheek and to whisper at her ear. "I love you."

A whisper of breath. A tremor of facial muscle at the corner of the mouth.

"Always, Mother, I love you." He waited for the next breath, but it did not come. The body seemed to settle in the bed, its functions ceasing, its muscles relaxing in death.

Piers's head sank to the pillow beside it. He could feel the tears on his cheeks. Even though death was a blessing and a release for her, his mind could not command his heart to stop hurting nor the emptiness to fill.

At length he rose. His muscles seemed to cramp with every inch of height he gained. Brandy. Suddenly his mouth felt parched. He licked his lips. His face felt tight particularly across his cheekbones where the tears had dried. He was glad that his father had not stayed to see him at the end.

The nun stood across the bed from him, her fingers moving through the beads of her rosary, her lips moving silently.

He arched his back and rolled his shoulders. "Will you share a brandy with me, Sister . . . I beg your pardon. I don't believe we've been introduced."

The nun shook her head.

"Oh, for God's sake! Please. Out of the goodness of your heart, answer me," he begged wearily. "I assure you, Sister, God does not know. And if He does know, let it be my sin. Tell Him I forced you." He had poured two glasses of brandy from the decanter in the small cabinet. Now he returned with them and pressed one into the nun's hand. "I thank you for your faithfulness." He toasted her.

Accepting his accolade with a nod, she lifted the glass to her lips

27

He put his hand on her wrist. "Before you drink. Tell me your name."

She shook her head. Her teeth caught the edge of her lower lip.

He tossed the brandy down. Her obstinacy irritated him. "Damn it. I am a suffering human being. Don't I need a benison? Tell me."

Trembling with strain, she took a sip of the brandy shuddering at its potency. She shook her head.

"Damn you. I'll have no more of this. Speak to me." Swiftly, roughly, he reached out and caught her face in his hand. His thumb pressed into her cheek. "Put that ancient superstitious nonsense to rest," he commanded.

She clawed at his wrist.

"Ah, evil. Evil. Scratching me." He tipped more brandy down his throat. "You'll have to spend hours on your knees to get rid of that mark against your immortal soul. Hours of penance. So have two. Speak. And I'll let you go be about it."

She twisted and turned, without success. The brandy glass shattered on the floor as she clawed at him with both hands. His thumb sank deeper into her soft cheek. Her mouth was inexorably opened by the pressure on her jaw. Her frightened breathing filled the room. Tears started in her eyes.

They were beautiful eyes, he realized suddenly. Drowned eyes. Crystal blue, blue ice, shimmering and shifting like water. Wide with panic, the dark lashes swept up onto satiny skin below the brow. And her lips were palest pink. Her lower lip trembled, surprising him with its sensual appeal. He could feel the blood pulsing through the vein beneath her jaw. "Why, Sister?" he asked, softly. "Why won't you speak to me?"

She held herself stiff against his hand, refusing either

28

to confirm or deny. Crystal tears welled over her lids and slipped down her cheeks.

And the wimple and veil disappeared, leaving only a hurt beauty that he could not resist. He bent his mouth to hers and kissed her, tasting her lips, caressing their softness. Feeling them open in a voiceless protest, he slid deeper into the kiss, tasting her sweetness.

She clawed at his wrist, but her short-clipped nails made little impression. Then she drew back her sturdy shoe and kicked his shin with all her might.

"Damn!" He tore away, staggering back a step.

She twisted out of his grip and sprang across the room. Her mouth was open, her hands out in front of her to ward him off. Her eyes showed only too clearly her terror.

His jaw tensed. Then his hands dropped to his sides. "You didn't have to kick me," he said mildly. "You could have told me."

She shook her head desperately. The black veil flapped round her shoulders.

"You can't speak? You really can't speak?"

Free, her only thought was escape. She sprang across the room, hands reaching for the latch. Flinging the door open, she fled down the hall.

He stared after her for a moment, his face twisted. Then with a shrug he lifted the brandy to his mouth and drank it all. The shards of glass crunched beneath his half boots as he walked back to his mother's side.

Chapter Two

On wooden legs Vivian tottered to the narrow cot and sank down. Delayed shock set her body to trembling. Gingerly she touched the spot on her cheek where the viscount's hard thumb had pressed into her flesh. What sort of monster was he? She shook her head remembering the hatred that had blazed between the dying countess and her husband. What sorts of monsters were they all?

Her lips burned. She tasted his brandy on them. He had kissed her despite the fact he believed her to be a nun. She shuddered. The habit was sacred. All men recognized it and respected it. Except him.

She looked around her despairingly. She should pack her things and leave immediately. She hugged her arms around her trying to stop shaking. Her feet ached to the knee from standing beside the countess's bed for almost twenty-four hours. Her back felt permanently bent. Her hands were blistered from wringing hot water out of the towels and holding them close to the countess's face, in the hopes that the steam would clear the ulcerous throat.

In the end all her efforts had been to no avail. All the energy she had expended had put her in the way of the humiliation she had endured at the hands of the viscount. His mother had died. Only one consolation had arisen out of the horrible scene that had taken place in the sickroom. The countess's passage had been relatively peaceful and painless, just a gradual stopping of the breath. Vivian could not doubt that the old woman had sunk into a deeper sleep, exhausted by the anger swirling around her. Probably in some deep inner consciousness, she had been relieved to go.

No more relieved than Vivian would be herself. Heaving a sigh, she rose and began to undress. The wimple and veil slipped off together, and her hair fell down her back. Inclining her head, she swung the skein around to the front to comb it through and through with her fingers. How good to be free of the weight of starched linen and heavy black wool!

Next she untied the lacings on the habit pulled it away from her neck. Of all the garments she had adopted at the behest of the order, it was the most constricting, the most uncomfortable. She hung the habit on a peg in the wall, unlaced the stout shoes, and rolled down the thick woolen hose.

At last, clad in a simple cotton shift, she sank back on the bed. For a few minutes the chill of the room felt good to her overheated skin. Eyes closed, she combed her fingers through her hair allowing the gentle tugging at her scalp and the silky feel to soothe her shattered senses. At last she shook it back over her shoulder where its ends swept against the coverlet on which she sat.

If the countess had died peacefully, how terrible by contrast had been the death of Sister Grace. Vivian could not rid herself of the old nun's poor mutilated face. With it came consciousness of the humiliation of the footmen rolling the body up in the carpet and carrying it away—as if the wise and dedicated woman

31

were part of the soil that would be cleaned from it.

Shivering suddenly, Vivian tucked her feet into bed and pulled the covers up around her. Wearily, she recognized the mistake she would end up paying for all the long night. Her bed was dank and cold, and she had allowed her precious body heat to escape. Teeth clenched to still their chattering, she pulled the feather pillow around her ears. To surround herself with softness was a trick she had learned over the last nine years. She drew her knees up to her chest and tucked her shift over her toes. The bed was so cold.

Silent tears began to trickle into the pillow. In the chill darkness she struggled against self-pity.

The silence. The damnable silence! The frustration of being unable to communicate her ideas, to answer questions, to object to injustice. If she had only been able to speak, he would not have put his hands on her. Neither his father, nor the obnoxious housekeeper, nor the viscount himself would have treated her as they had done. She gritted her teeth in anger. Her hands slid round her throat; her thumbs pressed bruisingly against her Adam's apple.

Make a sound! Any sound! Something!

Her doctor had held some hope once upon a time that she would regain her speech probably when she suffered some shock such as the one that had robbed her. Or, he had added sagely, when she forgot the reason why she could not speak. Of course, he was a fool. Every doctor she had ever seen had earned her like estimation. She could not remember what had happened to her at all, much less forget the reason.

Certainly this evening had been full of shocks. Most shocking was the viscount's mishandling of her person. She had been coldly furious. Why had she not been able to answer the bastard?

Bastard!

Pressing her lips together to form the first letter, she willed the word to come. Air exploded from her mouth, but not a single sound came from her. Not a sound.

Not a sound!

She clenched her fists until her nails cut into the palms of her hands. How did she get this way? Her earliest memories were of herself speaking. She knew words. And how they were formed. She understood everything that was said to her. But no matter how hard she tried, when she opened her mouth, no sound came.

She could remember her mother as a beautiful, loving person from her childhood. Her father she could not remember at all. They were both dead now. And somehow their deaths were associated with her condition. Had she witnessed their deaths and been struck dumb with horror? More terrible! Had she caused their deaths and been struck dumb with guilt? Why could she not remember when everything else about her life seemed so clear? She rolled over on her back. Staring into the darkness, her jaw clenched, every muscle tense, she asked herself again and again.

Why?

Piers Gaveston Maximillian Larne sat in a deep wing chair with his booted feet resting on the fender of the fireplace. He had given up drinking from the glass once he had emptied it for the first time. Now he lifted the bottle to his lips, letting the fiery French brandy roll down his throat. With a sigh he let the bottle fall into the space beside his hip.

His mother. He thought of his mother. The awful stillness of her face and hands, of her whole form appalled him. One minute she had been moving. Her chest lifting and falling, her eyelids fluttering ever so faintly as if she were dreaming. The next she lay still. The very blood had stopped and fallen back down the tubes of her veins giving her a terrible white shrunken appearance.

He had stayed beside her for hours watching the swift change from life to death. When they had lifted her to bathe her body, the thin skin on the backs of her arms and shoulders looked as though it had been bruised where blood had run back down to pool in the lowest parts of her body.

He took another swallow of brandy. Why did he allow himself to think such thoughts? They only made him nauseated and could do his mother no good.

Felders! There he could do some good. He had expressly forbidden her to come into the countess's room. Never mind that he had called for her when the old nun had dropped dead. She had disturbed his mother's dying moments with that hateful smirk on her face. He sucked air sharply in through his nostrils. He would see the bitch turned off without a farthing if it was the last thing he ever did.

He took another swallow of the brandy. Usually he could laugh at life, snicker at the catastrophes as examples of his sure and certain sense that the world was a mad, godless place. If not, why had the old nun just spun around and fallen over dead? He had heard of such things happening, but for the first and hopefully the only time, he had witnessed one. He took another drink of brandy and this time he did manage a ghoulish chuckle. Just fallen over dead, like a black statue knocked off its pedestal. He kept the corners of his mouth turned upward in a travesty of a smile.

His father had offered to join him in a watch beside the bed. Hypocrite! Lying, smiling hypocrite. His parents had hated each other almost from his earliest memories. To pretend at the deathbed made him nauseated. He took another burning swallow.

The other nun was a voiceless half-wit by all appearances. But she had at least put up with no insults. He had to smile at the memory of her drawing back to throw that hot towel in Felders's smirking face.

He should have let her throw it. What harm could she do? He gave a soft bark of laughter. God! The sickroom had resembled a madhouse in those few minutes. His mother had probably been glad to die to get away from the mess.

Tristram Alexander George Lorne, Earl of Lurnuorvon, lifted the sheet of paper, turning it so the light fell more fully on it. His dark eyes scanned it closely. A tobacco-stained finger, its nail long and ridged, led his eye back and forth across the page.

He chuckled softly. "So, Vivian Marleigh. There you are. Under my roof at last."

He laid the paper to the side and took up the one that had been beneath it. This time his finger ran down a column of figures then leaped back up to the top to trace another column. His breathing quickened as he came to the bottom of the page. As it began to vibrate, he let it fall and leaned back in the chair.

Suddenly, pain lanced through him. With a grunt he spread his hands against his mounded belly and stared downward in pain and disgust. He hated the crumbling, aching thing he had become, hated his son for having the vigor that he had enjoyed in his youth. Hated the copy of himself that insolently lounged around the house, wasting time and substance. God! To have his body straight and fit again.

The pain intensified. He gasped. His face contorted.

35

Reaching over his shoulder, a movement that caused him to wince and clench his teeth, he found the bell cord and tugged it feverishly.

While he was still tugging, Mrs. Felders came hurrying through the door. "Larnaervon!"

"Emma," he croaked. "P-pain." His face was gray. Sweat trickled down his temples.

"Oh, my dear." She swept around beside him and put her hands over his belly. He turned his face into her bosom shuddering. "There," she whispered, kissing the top of his head. "There. There. Don't take on so. It'll go away in a minute."

"It better." His comment was muffled. "Damn dyspepsia."

"Yes, yes. I know." From the pocket of her dress, she fished a small bag of horehound candies. "Here. Suck on one of these."

He turned slightly and she slipped it between his lips.

For a long time they remained silent and still except for the gentle rhythmic movement of her hands. One massaged his belly; the other combed through his sweat-dampened hair. Occasionally, he shivered. When he did, she pressed him tighter against her.

At long last he pulled away. "Bring me some brandy."

"I don't think—"

"Bring me brandy. It'll help. At any rate it won't hurt."

She moved some books aside in the bookcase and withdrew the bottle hidden there. Pouring two fingers into a water glass, she brought it to him.

He accepted it with both hands and turned it up to his lips. The liquid sloshed against the sides of the glass, so shaky were his hands. A generous swallow and he sat back with his eyes closed. At long last he spoke. "I don't think this is dyspepsia, Emma."

36

She frowned. "Of course it is. It can't be anything else. The cook's just putting too much pepper in the food. I'll let him know about it as soon as I leave you. With the loss you've suffered—"

He raised one white eyebrow. "Suffered?" he mocked. "Oh, of course. How I suffered! To be sure."

Mrs. Felders did not answer. Color rose in her face. "You'll feel more the thing in a few days," she insisted.

He shrugged and yawned. "I'm tired now. I think I can lie down."

She smiled coyly. "I'll help you to bed, sir."

He watched the lowering and raising of her eyelashes over her dark eyes. He managed a smile in answer as he rose and put his arm around her shoulder rather than reaching for his cane.

She put her hands on his back and chest. Moving together as one, they walked to a recessed door between the bookcases. The library opened into a small room made up into an ornate bedroom suite. "Call Mackery," Larne said.

She took a deep breath. The action rubbed her breast against his chest. "Do you really want Mackery?"

He looked down at her, one corner of his mouth lifted. "I thought you might be tired."

Emma Felders's fingers slid the buttons of his vest out of their holes. "Oh, Mackery is the one who's tired. And Watkins, too. They've taken turns in that hot, smelly sickroom rolling and shifting and fetching and carrying."

"Poor beggars!"

She pulled the end of his stock. It came untied and she tossed the end over his shoulder. "I can take care of you."

He lowered his head, his voice a rumble in her ear. He could smell her female scent. Georgina had been fond of bathing. He had not found her nearly so stimulating as Felders. Unfortunately, he was in no state to perform the man's part for her. Still, he led her on. His hot breath played along the tiny hairs at the base of her scalp. "Yes?"

She slid his shirt off his shoulder. Her lips moved across the thin blue-veined skin. Above the collarbone she bit him gently.

He winced. His voice dropped to a breathless whisper. "Vixen. How dare you show your teeth to me."

She pulled the shirt off his other shoulder. His chest was wide, the hair on it a mixture of white and gray but crisp. Her lips traced a path down through it until they came to the pale flat nipple.

He moaned softly, then groaned as she coaxed it delicately with her tongue, until it erected. Then she bit him gently. "Emma! Beware!"

"Never, milord. I know I've nothing to fear."

He put his arms around her pressing her against him. "Proud vixen."

She pressed body, breasts, and belly, against his side, so he could feel the jointure of her thighs along his hip. They walked together to the bed where he stretched out to allow her to pull off his shoes, his small clothes, and his hose. When he was naked, she covered him with a quilted spread and then a fur. His eyes narrowed to slits as he enjoyed the feel of her hands on his body. His voice became a rumbling purr. "Ah, Emma."

She tucked a blanket around him. "I'll return, milord. Just let me give the instructions to Millard."

When he sighed, she stooped to kiss his mouth lingerly. His hand came up to caress her shoulder. Then he waved her away.

When she returned, he was snoring softly, his head turned into the pillow, his long hair blending with the whiteness of the linen.

38

"Sound asleep, old man?" she muttered. With a quick shake of her head, she calmly stripped and climbed into the bed beside him. She pressed her buttocks spoon fashion into the curve of his belly. Barely disturbed by her intrusion, he mumbled something and put his arm over her waist.

Her teeth ground together in helpless frustration as she lay surrounded by his warmth, his masculine scent, the shape of his male body. Her own needs disturbed her mightily. She pushed herself back against him, butting him in her frustration.

He grunted. His white eyelashes fluttered. Then he muttered something. Angry, she pulled at the knobby, spotted hand, but he merely tightened his grip. A prisoner in the darkness, she stared outward with burning eyes.

"I don't have time to take care of this now, you foolish woman." Mrs. Felders scarcely glanced at Vivian's request. She thrust the slip of paper back into the girl's hand and continued on her way.

Vivian stared aghast, then hurried after her, catching her arm. Determined not to be put off, she thrust the paper back in the housekeeper's hand. The woman looked her full in the face, her eyes hard as flint. Her thin lips gathered in a pinch-purse, she wadded the note up and let it fall to the floor.

Vivian sucked in her breath, striving to control her frustration. She had never counted on her carefully devised request being discarded. She glanced at the floor, then at the retreating back. The housekeeper swept to the end of the hall. With her hand on the doorknob, she looked back. A smirk curled the usually tight mouth.

Vivian could feel her cheekbones burning as her

anger mounted. Unaware that she had clenched her fists, she took a step toward the woman. The smirk disappeared as the housekeeper hastily opened the door and whisked around the edge of it.

Pride demanded that Vivian leave the note crumpled on the floor, but practicality triumphed. Letting her breath out in a sigh, she bent to scoop it up.

"Bravo."

The mocking voice almost toppled her over. She tipped sideways, put her foot on the hem of her skirt, and had to brace her hand against the wall to aid her to her feet.

"And again bravo."

Embarrassment adding to her anger, Vivian spun to face the viscount lounging in the shadows at the end of the hall.

"What grace. What agility." He inclined his head and swept a half-empty bottle of brandy by him as he executed a mockery of a courtly bow. Pushing his long body away from the wall, he strolled toward her. "I would say, my dear sister, that although you lost the battle, you remain unbowed."

The paper rustled against her skirts as she lifted them away from her feet. Frissons of alarm skittered up and down her spine. The faint slurring of his words, the dark circles under his eyes, the unshaven cheeks all bespoke, if the bottle did not, a night of heavy drinking. Did he mean to harm her? Never taking her eyes off him, she backed another step.

"Now don't run," he sneered. "Don't spoil it all. Here I thought I was seeing a bit of courage."

Pride made her straighten. She planted her feet and lifted her chin.

He grinned and came on until he loomed over her, casting his shadow in the dimly lit hallway. His wine-red hair was no longer cut back in its old-fashioned cue but spread over his shoulders in the same manner as his father's. Vivian wondered if his father's had been red as well. He wore no stock. His shirt hung open almost to his waist, its drawstrings dangling.

Her eyes dropped to the dark red whorls of hair on his chest, coming together in the center and arrowing down to his pants. She swallowed convulsively. He was so close she could catch his scent as well as the brandy on his breath. Her heart stepped up its rhythm. Her skin prickled. Her eyes flew to his face.

He chuckled. "Ah-ah, Sister What's-Your-Name. Carnal feelings aren't allowed beneath that black wool."

She flushed.

His teeth flashed white, the front one on the left a little out of line. "Do you like my chest, Sister? Poor little nun. Never seen one before, have you?"

She could not help herself. She fell back a step from his piercing eyes. They were dark eyes. She could not be certain of their color. Were they black or brown? They seemed to lock on her own and read her secrets. She tore and to her horror dropped her eyes to his chest. She took another step backward into a piece of furniture.

He followed her, bringing his chest closer to her eyes. Less than a foot separated them. She felt dizzy. Tension built into unfamiliar pain in her belly.

"Poor little sister." His voice was soft, slurring liquid. It made her shiver.

Desperately, she turned her face aside, presenting him her profile.

"A silent woman," he mused. He put just the tips of three fingers under her chin. "Ah, do I detect a bruise on your cheek? *Mea culpa,* my lady."

She shivered as he applied just the tiniest bit of pressure. It was enough to turn her face to him. His

41

eyes looked deep into hers. "And all untouched. Until I touched you last night. But I don't think you enjoyed that kiss. Again *mea culpa.*"

She took a deep breath. It was a mistake. He filled her senses. Sight, scent, sound, touch. Only one remained. And she was no longer afraid. Why, she could not say. Why did she want—

He bent his wine-dark head. His hair fell forward. Their lips met behind its dark silken curtains.

His lips were firm and sweet. Sweet. The sensation tantalized her. Unable to stop herself, she pushed the tip of her tongue between her lips. Just to taste a little more, she excused herself. Just a little more of that exquisite warmth and sweetness.

He growled. The sound rumbled out of his chest, startling her. She drew back, but he put his hand to the back of her head and followed her mouth with his own.

She pushed her hands ineffectually against his chest and twisted to no avail. Why had she let him? What in heaven's name had compelled her to kiss him? His thighs trapped her against the furniture, a heavy table of English oak.

His tongue thrust into her mouth, hot, demanding. It pushed her own aside and drank with a deep caressing motion. She was drowning, she was fainting. Her heart pounded, blood roared in her head.

"For God's sake!" He stepped back as she slipped from beneath his hand, leaving her veil in his fingers. Bonelessly, she crumpled to the floor. Her silvery-blond hair rippling around her.

He stared from veil to girl in amazement. She had fainted. His kiss had terrified her, or overcome her so that she had lost her senses. Down on one knee beside her, he touched the back of his fingers to her neck. The pulse was steady. The thought of kissing a virgin until she fainted tickled him. He raised the brandy bottle in a silent toast. As he turned it up to drink, his father's voice brought him around.

"Not enough maids to dally with, Piers? You must assault a nun?"

He pivoted and came to his feet with a little laugh. "She dared me with her chin in the air. And then—By God! She kissed me back."

The earl smiled slightly. "Kissed you back. Imagine that. Not a cold, shrinking virgin at all."

Piers took the drink he had been intending to have when his father interrupted him. "Oh, she's virginal enough. Never been kissed. Till now. Never been held. Till now."

"But daring," the earl reminded him. "Kissed you back."

"Right. New breed of girl in the nunneries these days."

"You're very drunk, my boy."

"You're very right, *my father.*"The emphasis on the words made it a curse. "But I intend to get much drunker. Too drunk to be in the same room with you when you put Mother's body into the icy church vault."

Vivian stirred, pushing herself up on one elbow, staring around her dazedly. Piers dropped the veil in front of her and stepped back. "I would offer to help you to your feet, Sister, but I fear the touch of my ravaging hands would send you off into a fit from which you might never recover."

Her hands flew to her head, then reached for the veil, flaring it around her as she covered her hair.

"Too bad," he mocked. "It really is a sin against your God's creation to cover such a beautiful color. Don't you agree, Larne?"

She pushed herself to her feet, swaying, embarrassment reddening her cheeks.

"Oh, I agree, Piers. Wholeheartedly."

43

She swung around at the earl's voice so close behind her. The oak table, once her nemesis, now braced her hips. Still like a doe caught in the hunter's net, she stared from one to the other, her eyes enormous.

"And such a sweet mouth, and such a delicate color to the skin," he continued. "Was the mouth sweet?"

Piers raised the bottle to his mouth and drank again. "Sweet as . . ." He swayed back on his heels. "Oh, sweet as any one of a number of sweet things. I would have to be Shakespeare to name them."

Vivian pushed herself away from the table. Too embarrassed to meet their eyes, she inclined her head and took a step to move between them. Something crackled beneath her foot. She lifted it and stepped back.

The note!

Too frightened to maintain even a semblance of pride, she stooped for it and handed it to the earl. Her head remained down while he read it. But her eyes never left his gnarled, stained fingers.

He sighed before folding the note and slipping it into a pocket of his velvet coat. "I'm sorry that you want to leave us so soon, Miss Marleigh."

She started at the sound of her name. How had he known?

He smiled thinly, revealing teeth stained yellow and brown like his fingernails. "However, I beg your indulgence. As you must realize, my house is in confusion. People coming and going offering condolences. A gathering here for the funeral. All our carriages are at this moment being hung with crêpe to show the proper respect as we ride to the church."

She shook her head. Desperately, she pointed to his coat pocket where the note had disappeared.

"Ah, my dear, I would do much to help you, but I cannot do so at this time. May I suggest that you return

44

to your room and—er—offer up prayers for the souls of the dead. I will appreciate your efforts. My countess's passing has left a great void in my life. I am all but overcome with grief."

Behind her Piers uttered a name so foul that Vivian jumped. Fury blazed from the old man's eyes directed at his son, who strode back down the hall and slammed the door behind him.

With an avenue of escape open, Vivian too backed away down it.

"I cannot set you on the road for several days, Vivian Marleigh." His breathing was faster than normal. The lines around his mouth and between his eyes seemed deeper than before. "I ask you return to your room and assume the virtue of patience. In good time you will be taken care of."

Her spirits sinking, Vivian gathered the remnants of her dignity around her. Inclining her head in acquiescence, she walked back down the hall.

He watched her with a smile on his face until she had disappeared. Not until he was alone, did he allow himself to pull a linen kerchief from his sleeve and wipe his face with it. As he took his hand away from his face, he studied its violent tremors dispassionately.

He had not much time. And so many plans to effect.

Chapter Three

Through the window Vivian watched the carriages winding their way back up the snowy road. Black crêpe streamed from the carriage lamps and fluttered from the sleeves and hats of the drivers.

Was the viscount slumped in one of those carriages? Or had he been able to drink himself into insensibility as he had wanted? Somehow she doubted that he had been able to do so. He had been too steady on his feet, his speech too sensible, his anger too real. Anger so bitter would be hard to drown in sweet brandy.

She shivered and came away from the window to huddle in the wing-back chair. A fire burned in the grate, just barely large enough to create a circle of warmth. The coal scuttle on the hearth was nearly empty. She would have to go for more. And for food as well. No servant had appeared with a meager tray, for the house had not broken fast before the countess's funeral.

Vivian tipped the remaining lumps into the grate and arranged them on top of the glowing bed. She would wait until the last of the coal was consumed, and the carriages had begun to drive away. Her stomach rumbled a faint protest, but she patted it and leaned forward in the chair to warm her hands.

Someone knocked at the door. "Milady."

Vivian hesitated, last night's confrontation making her wary. The knock came again and the handle turned. With a sigh she rose to unlock the door and open it a couple of inches.

The valet Watkins bowed respectfully. "The earl has requested your presence for the cold collation."

She stared at him then shook her head. Not for anything would she go down into the midst of the gloom.

Watkins put his hand on the door to prevent her closing it. "He is most insistent, milady." He hesitated. "Best come on. He'll just send someone else who'll bring you, if you know what I mean."

Vivian did not know, but she could imagine. She gestured for him to wait. Behind the door she smoothed the heavy wool garments and arranged her veil. Although she had not taken the vows, she would not disgrace the habit that protected her.

Putting her most placid expression on her face, she opened the door.

Watkins broke into a smile. "Very good, milady. Soft and easy and butter won't melt in your mouth. That's the ticket."

They had a bit of confusion as to who should precede whom down the hall. In the end Vivian went ahead because Watkins begged her to do so. "The earl might not take kindly to me walking into the room first."

The murmur of voices and the discreet clink of silver and glassware guided her. Watkins swung open the door, and she stepped into a long room, the Larnaervon portrait gallery. Two tables were spread, one at each end with food and beverages.

The hum of conversation dropped momentarily as the guests became aware of her presence. The earl smiled urbanely and came to meet her. Before he reached her, she caught a glimpse of Piers slumped in a chair, his hair a dark flame in the gray light from the tall window. Mrs. Felders, clad in black, stood at the end of one of the tables, her sharp eyes following the two footmen where they passed trays among the guests.

All these impressions registered, then her gaze was concentrated on a heavyset man, part of a group at the far end of the room.

Larnaervon followed her stare. "I believe you know each other."

Vivian's eyebrows rose as she recognized Sebastian Dawlish, her cousin thrice removed and her guardian. As if feeling her scrutiny, he looked in her direction. At first he saw merely the figure in the nun's habit. His eyes moved on, then flashed back. He gaped as he recognized her. His heavy jowls reddened. Hastily, he set down his plate of food and hurried across the room to meet her.

At her shoulder the earl chuckled. One gnarled hand closed gently but firmly around her upper arm. She could feel the perpetual tremors of his infirm body through the thick wool.

Dawlish halted in front of them, his brows drawn together in a frown. His eyes flashed angrily as they fastened on the earl's hand. "Vivian. What—what are you doing here?"

"She came as a nurse from that convent you put her in, Sebastian." The earl's fingers squeezed her arm as if sending some sort of signal. A warning to be cautious?

"A nurse. But why? She's not a nurse."

Larnaervon's smile peeled back over his teeth like an old wolf's. "I must confess a little plot here. It was I who

48

requested that she come to my wife's bedside. Perhaps you did not know that you had a connection with my dear Georgina, Vivian. You were so young at the time of the accident."

"She was ill," Sebastian stammered. "Very ill."

"To be sure. Nevertheless, your grandmother, dear girl, was the countess's godmother." He heaved an affected sigh.

"Vivian!" Sebastian's jowls turned a vivid puce.

"I'm sure you had no idea, but at the time of the accident, I tried to have myself and my dear wife named your guardians, Vivian," the earl continued smoothly. "Alas, my request was denied."

Sebastian stiffened angrily. "I was her blood relation. You, sir, professed a connection that was suspect at best."

The earl assumed a martyred air. "I assure you that the connection was very real. And my dear Georgina so wanted a daughter."

Vivian cast the earl a startled sidewise glance. His repeated references to his "dear Georgina" belied the hate-filled scene between the two of them just before the countess's death.

Sebastian tried again to take her arm. "You shouldn't be here at all, my dear. How dare those people send you out into the countryside? You were in the quiet and seclusion of the abbey to rest and recuperate."

Shoulder hunched against the grappling fingers, the earl continued as if Dawlish had not spoken. "Although my request to be your guardian was denied, my dear, I have always maintained a close watch on your interests. When my wife became mortally ill, I determined to grant her anything at all that would help her to her eternal rest."

Vivian could not repress a shiver. By inference he

painted a picture of a peaceful and loving end. The countess's death had been horrible. Horrible.

The earl smiled down into her face. "I hope you appreciate how important your presence was to my dying wife. Yet to arrange for you to be at her bedside required the efforts of my people. Surprising, I must say."

"Vivian, don't listen to him."

The earl's voice carried a note of triumph. "Imagine my surprise when I was told that you, her guardian, had forbidden her to leave the abbey."

The words were spaced for emphasis. Vivian looked swiftly from the earl to Dawlish, who shifted uncomfortably. "Oh, now, really. That's not so. I wouldn't have said anything like that. They must have misunderstood. You must have misunderstood."

"Perhaps I did," Larnaervon agreed. "Strange. They were so determined that she should not leave. I had to use quite a bit of influence to get permission for her to come. So fortunate that the bishop and I have an understanding."

"The bishop? Ah, the bishop." Dawlish's jowls shook as he nervously cleared his throat. "To be sure. So—er—Vivian, you're—er—looking well."

What had been said, as well as what had *not* been said, burned in Vivian's mind. She was scarcely conscious that Larnaervon had signaled to a footman. The man hurried forward bearing a tray with glasses of hot mulled wine. Automatically, she accepted the drink.

"My dear, come this way." The earl's velvet-clad shoulder brushed against hers. "I know you must be hungry. Felders, fix a plate for Miss Marleigh. Some of that salmon there. And a slice of bread. Plain food, my dear," he added with a suggestion of an apology, "but filling."

She nodded absently. *Forbidden to leave the convent. Imprisoned!* Her stomach clenched at the thought of remaining for the rest of her life behind those cold stone walls. She was no nun. Never had she had the slightest intention of taking holy orders.

She had been taken to the sisters as a patient. In the winter of last year, she had been so close to death from double pneumonia that she barely remembered the trip in the coach. She had spent her eighteenth birthday in the convent hospital.

Dawlish had come to see her with some regularity at first as she slowly recovered. Helplessly, she had watched him assume more control over her life. First, he had dismissed her companion explaining that the woman was unnecessary with the nuns to wait on her hand and foot. Then he had decreed an extended stay. Whenever she gave him a note mentioning leaving, he had always made some excuse. In the spring he had informed her that he was having Stone Glenn, the home seat of the Marleighs, redecorated for her return.

But when summer had come, the project was taking longer than necessary. ("Incompetent workmen, my dear. Shocking.") Worse, an epidemic of scarlet fever had broken out in the vicinity. She could not return to such uncomfortable and dangerous conditions.

In the fall? She could not remember what had happened in the fall. Ah, yes. He had been in London and the house was locked up.

The nuns had been very kind to her always treating her with the utmost deference. Why should they not? If she were going to be their paying guest for the rest of her life, they would not stint to make her comfortable.

With clear eyes, she remembered the summons to the Mother Superior's office. No wonder the lady had looked unhappy when she had explained an imaginary emergency situation and asked Vivian to accompany poor Sister Grace. Suddenly, Vivian wondered how much the Mother Superior had known about Dawlish's plans. Had the two conspired to keep her there? She tightened her hand around the glass, taking comfort in its warmth.

The earl led her across the room to a chair beside his son. "I'll leave you here, Vivian. To eat and think about what you have learned. I must say farewell to my guests, many of whom will want to begin to depart soon. I trust you *will* think about what has been said."

She looked up into his dark eyes and nodded. Again her inability to communicate frustrated her. She set the plate down on a small table and laid a hand on his wrist.

He looked down at it and smiled coldly. "We will speak later, my dear. Rest assured. And you will have your pad and pencil in hand so that you may ask me any questions you wish. Piers, Miss Marleigh has just received a rather nasty shock."

The wine-dark head turned slowly. The viscount stared at her, his eyes glassy.

Drunk, she diagnosed. *He was able to drink enough brandy after all.*

A heavy body dropped down in the chair on her other side. "Vivian," Sebastian whispered tugging at her sleeve. "Vivian, I must get you out of here."

She looked him up and down, her outrage obvious.

He pulled his hand back as from a flame. "I know. I know. You are upset. But you mustn't condemn me without hearing me out. Believe me when I say I did what I did for your own good. We'll straighten all that out later. To your satisfaction. I promise."

Her head snapped around to look straight ahead.

Again he reached out, his fat fingers tugging at her sleeve again. "You don't understand. You are in danger here. Grave danger." He looked beyond her, then

52

leaned forward until his face was only inches from her own. His jowls quivered. "Grave danger."

She swayed away from him, distaste and anger evident in her eyes, in the curl of her mouth. Realizing she was beginning to shake, she raised the wine to her lips. Bitter it might be to her taste, but she craved its steadying effect.

"Vivian." Sebastian would not be put off. He pushed aside the veil so he could put his mouth close to her ear. "You don't understand. You have to let me get you out of here."

"Why?" came a familiar mocking voice. "Why, Sebby, old boy, should she be in danger?"

"Sssh!" Sebastian sprang away from her, his hand pawed the air.

"But really, Sebby." The viscount pushed himself off his chair, listed to one side, but managed to straighten and stand erect. "You know she's in no danger here. You know all about everything, old boy. But what are you going to tell her?"

Vivian looked from one to the other, anger blazing in her pale eyes. Abruptly she rose, pushing the viscount aside. He staggered back with a drunken laugh. What a fool she had been to come down without any means of communication! Never had she dreamed that any of the mourners would speak to her in her nun's habit.

"Vivian," Sebastian called.

"Let her go, Sebastian. I expect she doesn't want to listen to you right now."

On winged feet she fled from the gallery. Tears of anger and frustration were already coursing down her cheeks. She was helpless. *Helpless!* Outside, she picked up the skirts of her habit and ran.

"Vivian."

She had locked the door and put a chair in front of it while she tried to think. Hunger was giving her a headache. She had had nothing to eat in nearly twenty-four hours. Before that she had eaten only light meals, trays brought to her room with niggardly portions no doubt spooned up at Mrs. Felder's express orders. She had lost flesh during her stay.

"Vivian!"

Sebastian had locked her up in a nunnery. The words rang stark through every cell in her brain. How had he accounted for her disappearance? What had he told her solicitor? her banker? her friends?

The answer was altogether terrorizing. Her solicitor would have asked no questions so long as Sebastian reported to him. Her banker likewise, since Sebastian's name appeared on the drafts. Her friends? What friends? She had none. How easy it had been for him! She supposed she was lucky that he had not murdered her. Unable to communicate with anyone except on a very limited basis, she was the perfect victim.

Perfect.

How easy to imprison her for the rest of her life while he lived off her money. And she could not speak to defend herself. Fear sank its claws into her heart and belly. Gasping, she crossed her arms about her chest and tried to think. Where could she go? Not with him. She knew without asking that he would take her back to the nunnery. To her own home and barricade herself in. But was it her home? Or had he taken it for his own?

"*Vivian!*" His voice was near the middle of the door. He must be kneeling at the keyhole. This time he accompanied his call with a light knocking. "Vivian. I know you're in there. A footman pointed out your room. For God's sake, come out. You don't understand. You're in grave danger."

Hastily, she scribbled on a piece of note paper and

passed it under the door.

He picked it up. A tiny silence followed during which time she heard the paper crackle. When he spoke again, his voice had changed, become calmer, more pleading. "Of course, you can see your solicitor, Vivian. I'll take you directly to London. But you must come with me now."

She wrote again.

"Now, Vivian." He sounded slightly exasperated. "You don't have any need for money. Be sensible. You know I'll provide whatever you need. I promise. At any rate you can't travel unattended. Be reasonable." He paused. "You don't understand what's happening here, my dear. If you'll just let me in, I'll explain everything to you. You don't understand how the earl—damn him—has been lying to you for his own reasons."

She hesitated. Could the earl have purposefully defamed Sebastian? He did not strike her as a particularly honest man. Indeed quite the contrary. Again she sent a note under the door.

"Vivian, I'll tell you everything if you'll just open the door."

She wiped her trembling fingers on her skirt and stared at the doorknob.

"Please, Vivian. You're upset—with reason. But you don't know why I did what I did. I had to do it to protect you."

Even as her fingers touched the knob, a thump, a cry, and the sound of a scuffle reached her ears. Hastily, she opened it to find Sebastian sprawled on the floor, his hand to his derriere. And standing over the prone body with a smile of malicious pleasure on his face was Piers.

"Sebby," he mocked, "I can't say I'm surprised. Peeking through keyholes does seem a likely way to learn about the opposite sex. But a nun." He made a scolding sound with his tongue. "Not a lot of opportunity there, old boy. Probably wears a lot of wool next to the skin and never takes it off. And besides this one's too skinny." He grinned at Vivian, whose face flamed with embarrassment.

Sebastian scrambled to his feet. "I wasn't peeking through the keyhole, damn it all." His face flushed with anger because he had bothered to deny the accusation. "Why don't you go finish drowning yourself, Piers? There must be some brandy left to drink."

Piers face darkened, but his tone when he spoke remained mocking. "He who is without sin *et cetera,* Sebby. Just what were you trying to do here?" Piers stooped and picked up a crumpled note from the floor. Spreading it open, he read it. He quirked an eyebrow at Vivian, his smile widening. "'Money?' Why, Sister, you do surprise me. Somehow I hadn't guessed you were so—er—modern. Perhaps I ought to avail myself of your services."

"Damn you," Sebastian sneered. "That note has nothing to do with that sort of transaction. Your mind's a sewer, Larne."

"At least I don't peek through keyholes at nuns. Was she adjusting a garter, old man? Looks to be completely dressed."

"Damn it! I was not peeking at nuns."

"Ah, but you were, Sebby. Remember I caught you with your whole face practically glued to the paneling." He regarded the oak critically. "Looks as though you left a greasy spot."

Sebastian's face turned puce. He sputtered frantically.

Vivian caught at the door. Exhausted, starved, her head pounding, she could not deal with them and their embarrassing wrangling. Moving carefully as if a sudden movement might shatter her into a thousand fragments, she turned back into her room and closed the door behind her.

"Vivian," Sebastian's voice sounded even more muffled than the oak would have accounted for. She tottered toward the bed. Another step. Another. The room sccmcd much larger than she remembered; the floor, uneven.

She did not make it to the bed.

"Coming round at last, are you?"

Vivian raised her hand toward her head only to encounter a warm wrist sprinkled with springy hairs. Opening her eyes, she stared up into the face of the viscount. Instantly, she closed her eyes.

"Oh, come now. What is it the Americans say? No playing possum. You've given away that you're awake." A wet cloth stroked her temple and cheek.

She opened her eyes again. He was still there, leaning above her, his face impassive. Not a muscle moved beneath the tanned skin. His eyes mesmerized her. They were velvet brown, so dark they probably appeared black to all but his closest friends. His face was all bones, cleft chin, strong jaw turned upward at a sharp right angle, high cheekbones, the skin stretched tautly over them. His mouth.

It curved into a mocking smile. "Planning to draw me from memory at some later date?"

She turned her face aside. A little color came back into her cheeks as she realized he had caught her staring.

"No need to turn away. I don't mind." He sat back.

The movement made her suddenly aware that he was sitting on the side of her cot. His hip was actually pressed against hers. His presence in her room was bad enough but his presence in her bed alarmed her. She tried to push herself away but found she could not

57

move. He was sitting on her skirt. She tugged harder, but he put his hands on her shoulders and pressed her down.

"Don't start thrashing around," he advised her. "I only despoil nuns on Mondays and Tuesdays. Since this is Wednesday . . ." He reached behind her and pulled out her pillow, fluffed it up, and doubled it. "Rise up now and I'll put this behind your head. Don't act surprised. I used to do this for M-Mother." His voice wobbled, then went on affecting a bored drawl. "Come on now. Think of me as the old woman who came with you."

She shot him an incredulous look.

He shrugged. One side of his mouth lifted in a mocking grin. "Get yourself set up here and then you can have something to eat."

At that bit of information, she boosted herself up on her elbows. Sure enough. He had brought a plate with a couple of slices of rare beef draped over the top of a small round loaf of bread with a dollop of mustard on the side. Her mouth began to water. Her expression brightened.

"Drink first," he advised her succinctly, holding a tankard to her mouth. It was ale and bitter, and she shuddered as she drank it. "Ah, not to your taste, but you'll find this goes down better." He handed the plate to her and watched her as she ate. "'Plain food,' my father says. And Felders sees that he gets what he wants. I doubt he can taste anything anyway. Why not have a bit of pepper now and again?"

He held the tankard for her to drink. "A bit dry?"

She nodded but took another bite.

He stared at her face while she ate. Clear white skin, fine-grained as silk; pale blue eyes with gray smudges of shadow beneath them; lips pink, delicately tinted and shaped; and a firm little chin. Her eyebrows and eyelashes were soft fawn-gray like a baby's. He remembered the color of her hair, silver-gilt. She really was a little beauty. Very, very Anglo-Saxon, without a trace of darker Celt. Unusual so far west in Devon.

She had finished her beef and bread and now looked at him over the top of the tankard.

He cleared his throat. "What do you want to do?" he asked gently. "I'm here to do more than feed you. If you need to go somewhere, I'll send you."

She set the tankard down and reached for her pad and pencil. She stared at him for a minute and then wrote, "Please put me on a stage for London."

"London?"

She nodded anxiously.

"What will you do in London?"

Back her answer came. "Solicitor."

His expression mocked her. "And how would you find one? Good ones are not thick upon the ground."

"Mine," she wrote.

Piers shook his head. "Probably not a good idea. Sebastian has undoubtedly told him all about you. His version, of course."

The thought chilled her to the bone. Her face twisted. She stared at the pad, then wrote. "Must try."

He rose and went to stoke up the fire. "Have you no relatives? A maiden aunt tucked away somewhere? Surely there's someone with whom you could live."

She shook her head.

Still he hesitated, staring narrow-eyed into the glowing ashes on the hearth. "The earl went to great trouble to bring you here. For the life of me, I don't know why. Perhaps he did it as a joke to intimidate Sebby. I don't believe he had any thought of easing Mother's passing."

She threw him a calculating look.

"Oh, I heard most of what was said. No matter how I

tried, I couldn't get drunk enough. And Larne—damn his eyes—wasn't trying to be discreet. Quite the contrary. He pitched his voice so that even the ancestors on the walls could hear."

She smiled slightly and swung her legs over the side of the cot. With deft hands she straightened her habit and picked up her bag. The color had returned to her face and with it her determination.

The viscount shrugged. "Wait here. I'll send Watkins to you in about an hour. Go with him. He's trustworthy. He'll take you to Exeter. You can catch the Mail. It's a hard journey and long, near two hundred miles. And when you get to London, then what?"

She wrote again. "My solicitor."

He tried once more. "You shouldn't ought to be traveling alone."

She grinned slightly then wrote. "My habit will protect me."

The offices of Barnstaple and Rowling were on a side street behind the Old Bailey. Vivian was practically staggering when she opened the door. Whitefaced with weariness, she nevertheless had her notes ready. The time sitting in the posting inns had not been spent idly.

The secretary stared at her in disapproval. "We do not allow charitable solicitation in the offices."

She had made her first mistake, but she could not help her habit. She had no money to buy a suitable dress and no place to stay while it was being made. She advanced, her skirts and veil flowing around her, like the Mother Superior in full sail. From a large black bag, she pulled a leather-bound Bible and whipped out her first communication from between its leaves. She

60

presented it to the secretary, who eyed it distastefully, no doubt believing she was presenting him with a plea for money.

As he read it, his face changed. Still he passed it back to her. "Mr. Barnstaple will not be in the office until two."

Vivian did not even flinch. She had not expected to get an appointment so easily. She turned the page and extracted a second note from her Bible.

"Mr. Rowling is in conference at the moment. I might be able to make an appointment for you at the first of next week."

Frustrated, but determined to remain calm, Vivian pulled out a third note.

"Miss Vivian Marleigh," the secretary read aloud. He eyed the habit skeptically. "Would that name mean something to him?"

She nodded firmly. Her pulse beat a tattoo. She would not leave this office until she had seen one of the two men. She would have preferred Barnstaple because she remembered him. But Rowling would do.

"If you'll come back later," the secretary continued, "I'll take the note in to him when he's free."

She nodded. It was the best she could hope for, but she would not leave. Neither Rowling nor Barnstaple would walk through this office without her confronting them. She lowered herself onto the bench against the wall.

The secretary frowned heavily. "You're liable to have a very long wait," he told her. "Sometimes these conferences go on for hours." He paused. "And Mr. Barnstaple is frequently late."

Pointedly ignoring his suggestions, she arranged her skirts around her. For the better part of an hour, she sat on a slat bench that hurt her thin posterior more with

61

each minute. She tried shifting to a more comfortable position, but each movement increased her discomfort.

She was aware that the secretary kept glancing up at her each time she stirred. His sly regard irritated her. He was waiting for her to give up.

Her intense discomfort fueled her resentment. What was she waiting for? Rowling would surely see her. She had been informed that the firm had represented her family for many years before her birth. Perhaps her own father had employed them.

She took a deep breath. Rising, she strode across the office and opened the inner door.

"Here! Wait! You can't go in there!" Too late, the secretary sprang to his feet to prevent her passage.

In a musty book-lined office, two men, one behind a desk, one in front of it, stared at her in amazement. The man behind the desk started to his feet. "What's the meaning of this? Clarence!"

"I couldn't stop her, sir," the secretary apologized, his voice quivering. "She's been sitting there quietly and then suddenly, she bolted across the office."

Vivian pulled another note from the Bible and offered it to Rowling. He looked at her, then opened the note. She watched his eyes as he read it. They changed from angry to puzzled to incredulous.

He laid the note down and stared at her. What he saw was a gaunt, anxious face, almost as white as the wimple that framed it. One blue-veined hand braced itself on his desk. Its fingers looked incredibly fragile. Every tendon created a ridge in the procelain white skin.

The solicitor turned to his client. "If you will excuse me for just a minute, Wyman, I'll just see to the comfort of this lady."

Wyman had risen, too. He now bowed politely.

"If you'll come this way," Rowling said, leading her

through still another inner door. "Clarence, fetch some tea and perhaps some scones from the bakery. My dear, you must be very tired after your journey."

In a matter of minutes, Vivian was seated in a comfortable leather chair, a pot of steaming tea in front of her. She lifted the pot and suddenly, her hand began to tremble. The tea sloshed onto the napkin that lined the tray, and into the saucer. She bit her lip at the mess.

Abruptly she set the teapot down. Helplessly, she stared at her shaking hands. Then, unable to control herself any longer, she began to sob.

Chapter Four

"Oh, Miss Marleigh, I didn't have the least idea that I was deserting you. Your cousin, Mr. Dawlish, told me that you didn't need me anymore. Paid me so handsomely, he did. How could I doubt him? He said you'd decided to stay in the abbey and take holy orders. And with you bein'—well—the way you are. How could I know?"

Frances Eads was bleating her excuses for the third time as she poured greenish black tea into a china cup. Admittedly, she had become less shrill, but still Vivian looked at her with a pained expression.

Frances chose at that moment to look around her appreciatively. "This is a real nice set of rooms. So pretty. And comfortable. Mr. Rowling's not one to pinch the penny for them that he likes."

Vivian, still clad in her nun's habit, looked around her as she was bid. She had to admit that in the forty-eight hours since she had forced her way into his office, Rowling had done much to make her comfortable. He had installed her in a fine hotel. He had found and engaged her former maid servant. He had ordered sumptuous meals to be served in her room and sent a seamstress in to measure her for new clothes. When she looked back, Frances passed her the tea. She sipped it, then drew back, grimacing at the taste.

Still he had not granted her the long desired interview. She looked again with dissatisfaction at the beautifully appointed suite. The damask draperies and Turkish carpets delighted her eyes as did the silk cushions on the chairs and the linen and silver on the tea table. Then she thought about the bare hard furniture in her apartments in the abbey. A shudder coursed through her.

Frances saw the movement. "Oh, are you cold, milady? Have a little more of that good hot tea, and then maybe you'll want to lie down for a nap?"

Vivian shook her head. Instead she added more milk in an effort to kill the taste. It was a fermented tea, not her favorite. As she stirred, the green-black color stained the milk. It made her faintly nauseated. She started to set the cup down.

"Oh, do drink it, milady," Frances begged. "It'll do you good. It's just the right temperature. It'll be such a shame to waste it."

Frowning again at the taste still not entirely disguised by the milk, Vivian drank it down.

Frances took the cup and saucer from her. "That's a good girl," she said in a peculiar singsong voice.

Vivian glanced at her sharply.

Frances smiled tenderly. "Will you have anything else, milady? These scones are ever so lovely—with raisins. Mr. Rowling said you was to have anything your heart desired."

Vivian took a deep breath. She reached for the pad and pencil.

Frances read the note and shook her head. "Send for him at this time in the evening, milady. Oh, I don't think that would be a good idea. He's probably gone home to his wife and family."

Vivian glared at the companion, who was beginning to irritate her more by the minute. Why had she ever engaged her?

Then she remembered. She had not engaged her. Sebastian Dawlish had. On the excuse that Vivian needed someone younger and more her own age, he had pensioned off her old governess. Frances Eads had appeared the next day and had taken over. Thereafter, Vivian had hardly left her apartments by herself.

A cold sweat broke out on her palms. She swallowed hard against a rising nausea. For the first time, she suspected the magnitude of her danger. Had she come to London thinking to win justice only to put herself into the lion's mouth?

Was everyone against her? Why had Piers Larne been so eager to help her? Had Frances been conveniently "found" because Rowling had known just where to look? Why was Rowling refusing her an interview?

Forty-eight hours was a long time for a lawyer not to have any free time for one of his clients, especially one whose situation was so grave. In such a long time a message could reach Sebastian Dawlish and summon him to London.

She pushed herself to her feet. Horrified, she realized that her head was swimming. She tried without success to focus her eyes. The tea! The damned tea that Frances had insisted that she drink.

"Ready for bed, milady." Frances was by her side in an instant, firmly taking hold of her arm.

Vivian shook her head vainly. *Concentrate,* she told herself. *Concentrate! Keep your head. Fight the drug.* She straightened, pushing at Frances. The effort toppled her sideways making her stagger.

Frances threw an arm around Vivian's waist and pulled Vivian's other arm across her shoulder, clamping the wrist tightly. "Now, milady, let's get you lying down, so you won't hurt yourself. You're just feeling sleepy right now. And that's as you should. You'll have a nice sleep. But when you wake up, you'll be just fine. No headache nor anything. You'll be ever so much happier. You won't have any worries."

Stupid woman. Stupid. Stupid. She actually believes she's helping me. Vivian clawed with numbed fingers at the woman's thick wrist.

Frances dragged her resisting charge into the bedroom. Vivian could not keep her balance when Frances tipped her over onto the bed. "Now you just let me lift your feet up and make you comfortable. No need even to undress. Believe me, milady, it's for the best. You'll be—"

Vivian could not understand any more. Could not feel Frances's hands lifting her by the ankles. Her tongue felt too heavy and thick to protest. Her eyes closed of their own volition. She could not fight the whirling, resonating blackness that dragged her down.

"—taking her to Dr. Moorstead. He'll certify her with no problems." Rowling grated. "But I don't like this, Dawlish. Not above half. What if Barnstaple finds out she's not at the abbey anymore? He won't stand for it."

"Old fool. He's sharing in all this without getting his fingers dirty."

"He won't stand for it," Rowling repeated.

"Silly bitch." This from Frances. "Helpless as a baby. Putting her somewheres so she can be taken care of proper's the best thing for her."

"How easily you salve your conscience, Miss Eads." Rowling's voice dripped sarcasm.

The woman uttered a disgusted grunt. "Just pay me

my money and let me go. I've wasted enough of my time on the quality and their doings."

Paper rustled. Coins clinked. A door closed with a sharp slam.

Vivian jumped. Or at least she thought she jumped. Pain lanced through her head. Her nerves jumped. Her muscles might have twitched.

"Will she keep her mouth shut?"

"Oh, yes, Rowling. No question about Frances's loyalty. It's cast in stone—prison stone if she—"

Vivian could no longer understand their words. Their voices faded into nothingness.

"Who are you? You're not the one. Here, you can't come in here?" The cry of outrage changed to one of pain.

Vivian barely managed to open her eyes. The room seemed to be floating in dark gray mist. The bed on which she lay swayed gently back and forth.

"Settle down, fancy man. I've come to pick up a bird."

"You get the hell out of here. You're not—"

The thwack of a rod striking flesh cut off the protest followed by the thud of a falling body.

Vivian pushed herself up on her elbow. Desperately, she bit down on her lip. The pain helped her focus on the dark silhouette in wide-skirted coat and tricorne.

"Easy, lady-bird. Don't make this hard."

Fear sent a surge through her muscles. She managed to roll across the bed and stagger to her feet on the opposite side.

"Here now, settle down." He caught her by the shoulder.

She swung wildly away. Her arm caught the side of

his head, but he did not let go. Instead, as she sprawled forward, he was left with her veil hanging from his hand. She fell to her knees and tried to crawl away from him.

He cursed her mildly as he tossed the garment onto the bed and planted his boots on the skirt of her habit.

Her hands slipped out from under her and she fell on her side.

He bent and caught her by the wrists. Lifting her up by them, he spun her around and twisted them behind her back. "Some gels like it the hard way," he mused coarsely as he caught her wrists together and wrapped a leather strap round twice and buckled it.

The gesture was unnecessary. By the time he hoisted her to his shoulder, the drug had closed in again and she was unconscious.

The whistling wind carried snow mixed with rain to pelt against the windows of the coach. As Vivian struggled up out of the nightmare, she weakly flexed her numbed hands. No nightmare this. The stiff strap that bound her wrists behind her was terribly, painfully real. She was in a closed coach galloping at breakneck speed through the night. Mindless terror sank its claws deep into her.

The thunder of the horses' hooves and the rumble of the coach merged with the thunder of the winter storm. Lightning flashed, sliding in from the tiny slits between the leather curtains and the glass windows. Where was she going in such a storm?

She could barely remember a fight between two men. Dawlish certainly. And someone else. And who had won? She twisted her hands behind her, feeling the hard leather weal her wrists. Who held her captive now? She lay in the floor between the leather seats, her cheek scratched by straw and grit. Struggling around to her hip, she managed to sit up.

Her hair fell in a tangled snarl over her shoulder. Her veil. She had lost her veil. Its absence bothered her disproportionately. Without the veil she felt vulnerable. She became just another woman in a black wool dress. A helpless woman, alone, without support. At that moment the coach swung wide on a curve. Its speed slung her against the door. Her temple struck the hard wood with a punishing thwack.

The next time she awoke, she was nauseated. Her stomach rolled and heaved and gave up its contents into the dirty straw. Disgusted but a little stronger for being rid of the last of the drug, she drew up her legs and waited for her chance.

In a few minutes the coach started up a hill. Its slower pace plus the angle of the interior enabled her to push herself up onto the seat. Though the penetrating cold tormented her, her head was beginning to clear. Somehow she knew she was not with Dawlish. She remembered his voice protesting. She remembered his cry of pain. But who? Who had her?

Convulsive chills racked her as vicious draughts whirled up through the floorboards under the hem of her habit. Frances—the traitorous wretch—had left her dressed but had thoughtfully removed her shoes. Uselessly, she rubbed one stockinged foot against the other. Her feet and ankles were like ice as were her poor bare hands.

Suddenly, she became aware that the coach was slowing. Hastily, she squeezed herself against its padded side and tried to see behind the curtain.

The storm seemed to have moved off, or perhaps they had outdistanced it. She heard the noises of other

70

horses and coaches, the sounds of men's voices calling instructions, cursing, objecting. They had halted to change teams. She felt the coach sway as her driver left the box.

Desperately, she slid off the seat onto the floor. Drawing her knees up to her chest, she drove her stocking feet with all her might against the door. If she could just break it open, or at least attract the attention of some passerby to her plight, she might cause some delay. But no one came to the door. In the hurly-burly of a busy inn yard, her few feeble thumps went unnoticed.

Next, she tried to hook her toes under the handle of the door. With teeth sunk into her lower lip and her hands and arms crushed beneath her, she struggled until the handle actually came down, the mechanism clicked. She pushed with all her strength against the door. It would not move.

Tears spilled over and ran down her cheeks. Her abductor had undoubtedly locked the coach from the outside. Anger sparked through her tears. *Damn him!* She would get out of here. She pushed herself to her feet, bent over in the coach and caught the edge of the leather curtain with her hands.

Just at that minute she felt the coach sway. He was climbing onto the box.

No.

But the coachman called to the leaders. The whip whistled and snapped. The coach lurched forward. The curtain ripped away in her hands as she was thrown off her feet. Her face smashed against the leather seat; her knees cracked against the floorboard. Tumbling helplessly, she ended up in a heap on the dirty floor.

The coach gathered speed, the coachman calling to the fresh team in a hoarse voice. She was too exhausted to pull herself back onto the seat. A cold, miserable figure, she huddled in the filthy, musty straw.

Morning came without sun. Merely a grim gray sky, scarcely less dark than the night. She could see it through the window where she had torn the curtain away, but she had neither strength nor spirit anymore.

Her tired brain refused to function. Limply, she lay on her side, her knees drawn up to her chest for warmth. Occasionally a faint twinge reminded her of her numbed hands. Her belly had long since ceased to cramp with hunger. Whenever her eyes flickered open at some particularly hard bump, she focused dully on the gray rectangle of the sky.

At last it began to blacken again. The horses seemed to be slowing. With a lurch forward and a sway to either side, the coach drew to a halt. It tilted as the driver dismounted from the box. His boots echoed against stone as he moved away. Vivian heard the sound of voices as light shone through the window. She tried to lift her head, but she was too ill.

Footsteps approached. A lock rattled, a bar slid back. Someone yanked open the door and the light streamed in, blinding her.

She could not see the face of the man who reached in, grasped her upper arm, and dragged her unceremoniously out. Still without a word, he twisted her around, pulled her out headlong, and put his hard shoulder in her middle bruising her ribs.

Then she was being borne up the steps into a lighted building. Beneath her dazed eyes she could see the dull tiles of a parquet entrance hall.

"This way," came a strangely familiar voice. "Bring her this way."

Confused, she tried to lift her head, but her captor was carrying her along at such a clip that she could only bob helplessly, her eyes on his flapping greatcoat.

Up a flight of steps, he carried her, panting now. "How much farther? Gawd almighty. She's gettin' heavy."

The light here was dimmer. Dark red carpet spread beneath her eyes as the man carried her down the length of a hall, turned right, stepped up two steps and continued. She was being taken into another wing of a house. At least it was not another abbey. No abbey would have dark red carpet on its hallways.

Her captor halted in front of a door and tilted her farther back, in an effort to reposition her weight. The movement brought him no relief because Vivian's hipbones bruised his shoulder. He cursed again and dragged her forward.

This time her ribs received the punishment. Her extreme hunger and cold, the traces of the drug still in her system, the painful pressure on her abdomen, and the blood pounding in her head were too much for her to bear. As if someone had blown out a light, all feelings ceased together.

Her captor removed her body from his shoulder and deposited her on the carpeted floor before a blazing fireplace. She lay on her side, her silver-blond hair a tangled mess, her face pale as the crumpled white cloth about her neck.

"Well, here she is. And I hope she's worth it. Gawd almighty. I'm tired enough to die where I stand."

"Then go on to bed. You don't need to wait around. Your job's done."

"Want I should untie her hands?"

"No," a woman's voice replied. "Just leave her to me and get on your way."

"Them hands 've been tied up a long time," he suggested.

73

"Let her blame him," came the cryptic reply. "She's not my idea anyway."

Vivian moved slightly. Her hands twitched, the fingers flexed. The voice. She recognized the voice.

"Remind him that he owes me extra for this job."

"I'll remind him."

"An' he better come through." The boots thudded away from her. A door opened and closed.

Her eyes flickered open and rested on the orange blur that was the fire.

The man's boots thudded away, and Vivian heard the sound of a door opening and closing. She turned her head, but her eyes refused to stay open long enough to focus.

Hands gripped her by the shoulders and pulled her over on her back. One arm slid under her shoulders. A glass touched her lips.

"Here now, Miss Marleigh." A woman's voice, very familiar, sounded next to her ear. "Drink this."

Brandy trickled its liquid fire down Vivian's raw throat causing her to cough and choke. She struggled feebly, rolling her head from side to side, but the woman was inexorable. "Don't waste it. It's good French brandy." And then under her breath. "Clumsy slut."

Opening weary anguished eyes, Vivian focused with difficulty on the face of the woman who supported her. *Ema Felders.*

Sharp gray eyes stared back at her from a sallow face. The firm jaw and pinch-purse mouth offered no sympathy. "Can you stand?"

Vivian shook her head. She could not sit up, let alone stand. The brandy was burning in her stomach.

"Like lying here like a pile of dirty linen, do you? Suits me fine. But his lordship wants you up." She shifted her position, got her legs under her, and lifted with surprising strength. Without a wasted motion Vivian felt herself dragged to her feet and steadied. "Now stand up there and we'll see about getting you loose."

Once on her feet, Vivian felt the woman's hand at the back of her neck. Again Felders raised the glass to Vivian's lips.

Vivian swallowed obediently, then again. The fiery liquor spread from her empty stomach to all her parts. She blinked and took a deep breath. The room swam around her, then righted itself.

Satisfied that her captive would not collapse, the sharp-eyed woman caught Vivian's arm above the elbow and forced her back several stumbling steps. Vivian felt the seat of a chair behind her knees.

The woman's other hand pressed down on Vivian's shoulder. "Now just sit down here. Don't make any fuss."

Vivian tried to twist her arms around to remind the woman of the painful strap.

"Oh, did I forget that? Fancy that." Mrs. Felders allowed herself a humorless grin. "Well, all right. So long as those hands have been tied up, you can bet you're going to feel the life coming back into them."

Vivian bit her lip and twisted still farther around. She would suffer any pain just to get her hands back in front of her again. The frustration and agony of the coach ride would remain with her—she was certain— for the rest of her life. Doubly so, because with her hands tied behind her, she was doubly helpless.

A couple of efficient twists and the strap came away from Vivian's wrists. As if she were ninety years old, she brought her strained arms around to the front of her body. Immediately, a thousand burning needles attacked each hand. She thrust her hands between her knees and squeezed as hard as she could. But the pain intensified as warmth and circulation returned simultaneously. Tears spilled down her cheeks.

Hands tucked beneath her white apron, Emma Felders watched Vivian's efforts. When the pain began to abate, she cleared her throat. "If you're ready, I'll tell his lordship."

Vivian swiped the sleeve of her habit across her cheeks. She pushed her snarled hair back over her shoulder and sat upright. With a trembling hand she pointed to the brandy bottle.

Mrs. Felders snorted. "Best not get too drunk, Miss Marleigh. You'll need all the stray wits you might have about you. Just sit up straight and pay attention to his lordship when he speaks to you."

With that she left the room. Vivian shot a look of unmitigated fury at the smooth oak panels. Mentally, she recited the various torments she would inflict upon the housekeeper when she would have the opportunity. The exercise did not stave off despair for very long.

How could she do any of those things? She had just been abducted from one of London's fine hotels. Her abductor had carried her more than halfway across England by coach with about as much ceremony as one would deliver a parcel. She had been drugged and tied up and starved. She was helpless. Helpless. And raging with impotent fury.

Defiantly, she shot out of the chair and strode to the side table. Jerking the stopper out of the bottle, she poured herself a stiff tot of brandy and drank it down. She was setting the glass down when the door opened.

A cold draught of air played round her ankles reminding her that she was standing in her stocking feet outside the magic circle of the fire. Still she was determined not to scurry back. She turned to face the earl and the viscount with her chin held high.

"Ah, my dear, what an ordeal you have been

subjected to. Please, come back, sit by the fire." Larnaervon came toward her in his usual black velvet, his white hair spread over his shoulders, his cane tapping.

She had an insane impulse to throw herself into his arms and burst into tears. A younger Vivian Marleigh might have done just that. An innocent, trusting girl who lived alone with her books and her horses at a country estate called Stone Glenn.

Ironically, Vivian Marleigh had gone away forever in this very house. She had dissolved into her present frightened self the night the earl had revealed the machinations of Sebastian Dawlish. In doing so he had taught her more than he planned. She did not trust him either. Over his shoulder she saw his son, the viscount, staring at her with a quizzical, calculating look. And behind him Emma Felders closed the door and planted her body in front of it like a guardsman.

Heart pounding, breath short, Vivian waited.

"My dear, please." The earl had softened his rasp to a pleasant purr. "Piers, help the lady to the chair. Felders, I think some refreshments are in order. Perhaps a cold supper."

"Cook's asleep, sir."

He swung his white head in her direction. "Well, wake him up. Or fix it yourself. I'm sure you can find something that will—"

Vivian put the glass down so hard it cracked. Her anger, clearly transmitted by the sound, drew their eyes. She shook her head and made a motion as if she were writing.

The earl shrugged, his smile a little thin. "Well, Mrs. Felders, Cook's sleep will remain unbroken. Miss Marleigh does not care for food. Am I correct in this assumption?"

She nodded and repeated the writing pantomime.

He ignored her request. "Please sit down. Piers, take her arm and lead her to the chair. The poor child is swaying on her feet."

"Larne, what sort of nasty game are you playing?" The viscount made no move toward Vivian.

"How well he knows me," the earl commented. "Please, my dear child, do me the favor of sitting down. You look sick to death. And I have trouble standing for long."

She touched her fingers to her aching forehead.

"Please."

With a sigh she moved to the chair and lowered herself gingerly in it. Her black stockings stuck out from beneath the skirt of her habit.

The earl's sharp eyes missed nothing. "Why, my dear, no shoes?"

She shook her head and made again the writing motion.

His face serious, he took the seat across from her, his own feet and legs stretched out to the fire. "My dear, you shall have everything that you desire in the morning. For right now I want you to listen to me carefully without thinking about anything except what I'm saying to you."

Her stare was bitter, but she had no choice.

In the background Piers helped himself to the brandy.

"You sit there blaming me for your present condition, when in point of fact you brought this all on yourself." When she glared at him, he chuckled. "Oh, I will admit that my dear son helped you to it. For reasons of his own which I have been informed of in an alcohol soaked but nonetheless triumphant voice. To 'put a spoke in my wheel' was I believe the clever way he put it. Right, Piers?"

No answer came, but Vivian could see the black

scowl on the viscount's face. He raised his glass and drank deeply.

"Consider, if you will that I wanted you to stay here until I had sufficiently recovered from grief at the death of my beloved wife."

Here he was interrupted by a mocking snort from his son.

"—my beloved wife," he insisted in a flat voice. "Yes, my beloved wife, Georgina, countess of my heart, is dead."

"Damn hypocrite," Piers snarled, coming to stand between them and glare down at his father.

Larnaervon shrugged, a mere twitch of the bent shoulders. "Would you believe that once—? Ah, but no. Suffice it to say, that we had you, Piers." He smiled thinly as the viscount cursed viciously and turned back to the brandy.

Vivian leaned her head against her hand. She was becoming dizzy with the brandy, and exhaustion was making her a little sick to her stomach.

The earl observed her drooping. "Now, my dear, try to pay attention for just a few minutes longer. I want you to understand that I am an old man. My hair is white, my skin wrinkled, my shoulders shattered by a riding accident, my spine crooked, one leg shorter than the other."

As he catalogued his ills, she stared at each one in turn.

"Not a pretty sight," he mused, "and not a one of them can be changed. No, I'm forced to admit with my wife gone and myself locked within this old body, I must look to others."

A small silence hung in the room as the earl stared into the fire. Drooping with exhaustion, Vivian had almost ceased to care what he said.

Then he roused. "If you remember, my dear, I was

responsible for rescuing you from your snug Catholic prison. Admittedly, you did not know that you had been imprisoned, but I think only a few more weeks, perhaps days, would have elapsed before you would have begun to suspect that something was not well." Here he looked at her a little contemptuously. "Poor chit."

She stiffened at the insult.

"I hope your ill-conceived visit to your solicitor made everything clear to you. Sebastian Dawlish is not nearly clever enough to carry this plot off by himself. He had to have a confederate, and Rowling does like his comforts. You were a coney, my dear, ripe for skinning. And your soft fur would have lined their nests for many long winter nights."

Vivian shuddered. She could not doubt that the earl spoke the truth. The conversation she had overhead among the three conspirators had told her as much.

"Had my man not taken you away in the night, you would have found yourself on the morrow in a very private institution where the rather mild drug administered by the treacherous Mrs. Eads would have seemed like a cup of tea. The fair Frances, by the way, is quite a good hand at slipping those kinds of potions into drinks. She works most of the time for press gangs desperate to acquire bodies to man the ships for His Royal Majesty's fine fleet."

They could hear the gurgle of brandy as Piers poured another drink. However, instead of drinking it himself, he offered it to Vivian. She accepted it with a flash of gratitude.

The earl smiled. "So you see, my dear, you really owe me your freedom, your health, and probably your life."

She swallowed a portion of the brandy and looked him straight in the eye. What he said now was the point of the whole exercise. Instinctively, she knew that he

80

had gone to all this trouble and expense for reasons.

He tipped his head to one side. "Ah, I can see you are alert enough to ask me the right question with your eyes. Bring me a brandy, Piers, and pour one for yourself. We mustn't keep the lady waiting too long. She wants to know what this is all about so she can retire to her chamber and sleep to rid herself of this harrowing experience."

Piers came with two brandies and stood between their chairs. A heavy frown creased his brow. Larne never did anything without a very good reason. He much feared that the silent Miss Marleigh was in for a very unhappy time. Perhaps the drugs that she would have been given at the "very private institution" would be preferable to what lay in store for her. Grimly, he stared at his father.

"My dear." Larnaervon leaned forward. "I really am not such a terrible ogre. I've brought you here to ensure your future. To keep you safe from harm. I would like you to become part of my family. In that way I can look out for your interests."

"My God," the viscount interrupted. "You can't mean it. Larne, she's only nineteen. You can't marry her."

The older man canted his head up, his smile flashed briefly. "No, Piers, I can't. But you can."

Chapter Five

Piers's face whitened. A muscle ticked in his jaw. His eyes widened then narrowed as they looked from his father to Vivian, who stared at Larne as if she could not believe her ears. "Marriage," he gasped. "To her!"

"Hardly a flattering reaction," Larne remarked dryly.

"What kind of reaction do you expect?" his son snarled. "How in hell do you expect me to—"

Like a judge demanding order, Larne struck the floor with his walking stick. "That will do. Your behavior is insulting to your future bride, Piers. And I might say to me as well. I went to a great deal of time, trouble, and expense to arrange this marriage for you both."

Vivian catapulted herself from her chair, but Larne swung the end of his stick up and drove her back into her seat. "Keep your place, my dear, and listen. You will learn much. And"—he swung the stick back and forth before her outraged eyes—"do not perform that writing pantomime. One of the reasons why you are so suitable for my son is your unfortunate condition."

"Larne!" Piers cried angrily.

The stick swung toward him. Like a tamer in a lion's

cage the earl kept the two at bay. "One man's meat, as they say. You will both subside into those comfortable chairs before this warm and pleasant fire and you will listen to what I have to say."

"Not for my life!" The viscount tossed down his brandy in one gulp and crashed the glass down on the table.

He strode to the door but found the way barred by Mrs. Felders. When he raised his arm to brush her aside, his father called after him. "The door is locked, Piers. From the outside. And my good and faithful servant, Jack Beddoes, is standing guard behind it. We shall not be disturbed."

Piers turned back into the room, fists clenched. "You go too far."

"Sit down." The earl swung the walking stick toward a wing-back chair on the other side of the fire. "Good God, she is the one who has been kidnapped, bound, and brought here against her will. And she behaves better than you."

The look Piers threw her made Vivian want to cringe. "She has no choice," he grated, contempt palpable in his tone.

"Sit down!"

Piers flung himself into the chair, slinging one long leg over the chair arm. His booted foot swung viciously back and forth.

The earl nodded, a mirthless smile flicking the corner of his pale lips. "I shall remain standing. It gives me a commanding presence." He planted the end of the stick on the floor between them and leaned his upper body weight over it.

"Now, to begin. Regard her if you will, Piers. Good height, good straight bones. I'm sure she has good teeth. No indulgences since childhood. Very important that." He nodded sagely. "Not set on going up to

83

London and spending your money. Your mother—Ah, but I shall not resurrect old and unpleasant memories. Suffice to say. This one will not spend your money."

Vivian sank back in her chair staring at the old man with furious incredulity. Rage whitened her skin and widened the pupils of her eyes. His appraisal of her person insulted her so that she curled her fingers into talons on the arms of her chair. He was serious. She might have been a half-wit for all he cared for her good opinion. She could not believe that such an anachronism existed in the nineteenth century.

Piers's scowl was thunderous. "That makes absolutely no difference to me. I have none to spend except—None to spend."

Larne's mouth spread in a wolfish grin. "Indeed, but now you will have. Hers. Why did you think Dawlish had her locked up in the first place? He could spend her money unrestricted. Lovely old money. Lovely old house."

Piers's angrily swinging foot slowed. His eyebrows rose as he studied the unprepossessing figure clad in the bedraggled black habit.

Vivian pushed herself indignantly from the chair. Larne thrust the end of the walking stick into her chest. She caught the end trying to wrench it away, but he whipped it out of her hand. When she started up again, he raised it above his head threateningly. "Here I was criticizing Piers for acting like a barbarian, and you start up. If you move one more time, my dear, I shall order Mrs. Felders to tie you to that chair. And, believe me, she will take great pleasure in making the knots as tight as possible."

Faced with the three-foot stick with its lethal gold knob at the top, Vivian subsided. She shot a sulfuric look at Piers, who shrugged and slouched back in his chair, eyelids drooping.

"Now." Larne drew a deep breath. "You will both pay attention and learn the real economics of marriage. You, Piers, have had a bride carefully selected for you since you made no move to select one of your own."

"I have had other things to think of. Mother was ill for—"

"To be sure. To be sure." The earl callously brushed aside mention of his wife's very recent death and burial. "Very laudable of you. But now life goes on. And I am particularly set on life going on." He added the last with particular emphasis. "Did I mention that this young lady, the Honorable Vivian Marleigh, is an heiress? Yes, I believe I had been allowed to say that much. To a considerable fortune and a fine country house and estate with several very productive farms and a mill as well as a town house. I don't believe I have omitted anything of importance, have I, my dear?"

Vivian refused to grant him a nod of approbation. At the same time, she realized that the earl probably knew more about her business than she herself knew. The knowledge galled her. She should have learned her business. While she could not speak, she could read and write. She should have demanded that her solicitors inform her. All too late. She had contributed to her own disaster.

The earl turned to his son. "All this will be yours after you shall have wrested it from the unsurping hands of her cousin Sebastian in your wife's name, of course. Think of it, Piers. You have the chance to steal a fortune legally, an act which could give you no small pleasure."

"Poor old Sebby," the viscount murmured without a trace of sympathy.

"Exactly." The earl's smile was feline. "Furthermore, since you cannot take the farm without the livestock, look at what you will be getting."

Vivian's expression of outrage would have slain a lesser man.

Larne merely chuckled. "Of course, the nun's robes are somewhat disagreeable, I will admit, but look closely. Skin like velvet. Hair, truly amazing, a silver-gilt color. Why, I have known women who would kill for hair that color. And the eyes, Piers, the eyes. I've never seen that color anywhere else. Moon on water."

Piers snorted rudely. "Much more of this and I may be sick."

Larne's smile disappeared as if it had never been. "What a disappointment you are! Fool. You sit and sneer at everything." He pointed his stick at Piers's crotch. "Are you a man? Or perhaps it is that you can't work up an interest in anything female? Did I leave you with your mother too long? Have I raised a daughter instead of a son?"

Piers's eyelids narrowed to slits. "Larne," he said steadily, "another word, and Felders and Beddoes be damned. I'll break through that door and be gone."

The earl's veined nostrils quivered. With a monumental effort at control, he swung the stick toward Vivian. In a flat voice he continued. "Good straight bones, good teeth. The grandfather and grandmother Lord and Lady Casterbridge—both most unfortunately carried off by influenza—were nevertheless of long-lived stock. Her father, a younger son, was killed at Talavera. Her mother died in a coach accident the same year."

The mention of her mother's death cast a chill over Vivian. Exhaustion and depression weighted her back into the chair. She closed her eyes.

The earl droned on. "Alone in the world, an heiress, of good family." He dropped the stick to the floor again, to put a period to his speech. "Altogether suitable. She'll bear strong, healthy sons."

Piers's face darkened angrily, but his expression did not change. He stared at Vivian, then his eyes shifted back to his father. "Except that she's a freak. Her children might be like her."

Vivian's eyes flew open. Her nails ripped the material of the chair arms.

Larne shook his head. "You thought of that possibility, did you? Very good. Let me assure you that will not be the case. No, not at all."

"You can't be sure."

"Ah, but I am. She didn't lose the power of speech until her mother was killed. I've read all the family records. I've investigated the story thoroughly." He scowled at his son. "Do you think I'd take a chance on my own posterity?"

"Family stories could be lies," Piers scoffed. "Besides, maybe she's half-witted. How long ago was the accident? Perhaps she got her brains bashed in?"

The earl shifted irritably. His body was rebelling against standing so long. "I tell you she is not half-witted nor a freak."

"I don't want her."

"Damn you. You will take her. She is the best that can be found for you." Larne's complexion darkened. A trickle of sweat ran down his hollow temple. "We have no friends in all this end of England among suitable people. I will not have my heir dropped by some farmer's ill-bred sow or some poxy whore from the streets."

"Larne."

The old man swung his stick. The heavy wood whistled through the air like a saber. "Not another word more. Not one! I have gone to great lengths to provide her. You will do as I say. Or I will make you very, very sorry that you did not. Remember, my arm is long and a cell in a French prison would be easy enough to arrange."

Piers leaned forward in the chair. "Why go to so much trouble? Simply have Beddoes drop me overboard some dark night."

The earl's face twisted in rage. "Don't think the thought has not occurred to me."

"But, of course, when I'm gone, then your heir is gone also!" Piers's voice rose defiantly.

"You will do as I say!"

Vivian pressed her fists to her temples. Her expression was frantic as she shook her head.

The earl drove his stick into the floor and pivoted to face her, showering her with his wrath. "And you, my dear Miss Marleigh, will marry him! Or go back to Sebastian Dawlish and the prison cell in the madhouse he has reserved for you."

His pronouncements made, Larne hobbled to a chair across the room and dropped into it with a groan. Pulling a handkerchief out of his sleeve, he mopped at the sweat that trickled down his face and stained his neck cloth. Slowly lowering her fists, Vivian caught Piers staring at her in the red light from the hearth.

Mrs. Felders remained immobile at the door. Her burning eyes watched the earl. A silence settled over the room.

At last, lids drooping to conceal the expression in his dark eyes, Piers pushed himself out of the chair. An insolent twist to his mouth, he strolled over to Vivian's chair.

Closer he came, and closer. So close that his knee actually nudged the side of hers. Vivian could keep her head bowed no longer. From near sleep, she managed to push her way through veils of exhaustion and tip her head back to meet him.

88

As he returned her half-defiant stare, he noted the dark mauve circles beneath her eyes, the deepened hollows in her cheeks, the colorless lips. She was near the end of her tether. Still his eyes betrayed not a jot of feeling. Silently, he stared down at her, peeling away the rumpled, filthy habit and seeing the shape of the body beneath.

A frisson of alarm wracked her. She sucked in her breath in apprehension. A faint color rose in her cheeks as her bosom swelled.

He focused on the movement. One dark eyebrow rose. Behind him, the earl chuckled lecherously. Piers shrugged and returned to his study of her, letting his eyes move critically from her toes to the crown of her disordered head.

Her fear and distaste could not sustain itself against her body's total exhaustion. She had had neither food nor rest in over twenty-four hours. Before that had been the days of nursing a dying woman, of traveling alone except for her own fears. Vivian dropped her eyes and bowed her head.

Trembling, she stared dazedly into the flickering flames to avoid noticing how the dove-gray buckskin covered the muscular thighs with never a wrinkle, to avoid staring at the soft material stretched taut over the hard bulge at the bottom of his flat belly. When she tried to take shallow breaths, she only succeeded in starving herself for air; so in the end she was forced to gulp.

A log broke in the fire. The flames sprang up and died back as quickly. Then long brown fingers slid under her chin and turned her face back to his. Dispassionately, he studied the play of expression across her pale mouth. When she tried to twist out of his hand, his grasp tightened painfully.

With the other hand, he brushed the disordered

silver-gilt hair from her forehead and cheek. Tangled and snarled as it was, its beauty was extraordinary. His hand smoothed down the long skein and brought it to lie over her right shoulder.

The unexpected tenderness of his touch brought tears to her eyes. Her color came and went. Her scalp prickled at the feel of his fingers in her hair. She shifted uncomfortably as a peculiar heat built and curled between her thighs. Her fine dark brows knitted together in puzzlement.

He grinned stiffly and tilted her face back to the fire observing the purity of her profile. Anger rekindled signaled by a flush of color. She clutched at his wrist to pull his hand away.

He bent closer until his lips were only a few inches from her ear. He might have been a lover bestowing a kiss, but his tone made a mockery of his gentle touch in her hair. "How do you feel about this, milady in nun's clothing? What do you think of the prospect of being my suitable wife and mother of my heirs?"

Sagging with weariness, she pantomimed writing.

The earl chuckled. "I'm sure you see the beauty of this entire scheme, Piers. She cannot object. She was in the coach, the night her mother was killed. How old were you, my dear? Nine or ten? She was marooned for hours in a snowstorm. When they found her, she couldn't speak. Not a word. And not a word since. Without a pad and pencil, she's helpless. And even were she to write a protest, who would believe her?"

"Sebby might." Piers straightened only enough to rest his long arm across the back of her chair. One hand still tangled in the skein of hair at her shoulder.

"Oh, to be sure. He would indeed. But what could he do? He wants to keep his skin whole. He's the one who had her locked away to begin with."

"What about the solicitor she was trying to reach in London?"

"Thick with Dawlish. If Beddoes had gotten there a couple of hours late, she'd have been long gone."

They were doing it again. Talking in front of her as if she were not there. Despairing, she huddled in the chair. Yet even as she collapsed, the earl surprised her. "Am I right, Miss Marleigh?" His hoarse bark aroused her. "Nod your head. You can do that much."

Vivian roused to look up at the man who claimed her. Obediently, she nodded.

Piers shrugged. "So you rescued her. Why not send her on her way? Take her under your guardianship? Get control of her money. But don't breed her to me. You talk about strong, healthy heirs. What kind of mother would she make? My God, Father! A good colt needs a strong mare to follow. This one may be simpleminded. If she hasn't taught herself to speak in ten years—"

Vivian clenched her hands. She swallowed again, willing herself to speak to utter a refutation. Nothing happened. Her throat could not produce a single sound. Not even a groan.

The earl's face darkened. For a moment he hesitated, his smile fading. Then he shook his head. "I'm satisfied with her. She was perfectly normal until the accident. I have proof incontrovertible of that. The family doctor was a fund of information. His theory was that women are simply not capable of withstanding the stress to which she was subjected. But as for her children, they'll be normal."

"But—"

"We won't allow her around them, if that bothers you. They can be just as carefully reared by nannies and nurses and later tutors and governesses. You will have

91

the money to hire any number of servants. Three-quarters of the aristocratic families of England never see their children except when they're cleaned up and brought downstairs for holidays."

"And what about my wife? Will I clean her up and bring her downstairs only on holidays?"

The earl slammed his stick against the floor. "Damn you, Piers. I don't ask that you associate with her. Take a mistress when your duty's done. Society has never meant anything to you one way or the other." He motioned to Mrs. Felders. "Pour drinks for everyone. We'll toast the bride and groom."

The housekeeper moved silently across the room. The earl took his brandy with pleasure, his smile affable, now that he saw his plan nearing completion. Piers took the glass, his face a mask of self-disgust.

Vivian waved the woman away. She would not drink with her enemies. Furthermore, she was sure that her stomach would refuse the drink. The final humiliation of this wretched encounter would be if she vomited and further befouled herself.

The earl rose. "To my son and daughter-in-law."

As Vivian watched, Piers's expression changed. He tossed the brandy into the back of his throat and held out the glass for more. As Mrs. Felders silently refilled it, he laughed mirthlessly. "To the Earl of Larnaervon, Tristram Alexander George." He pitched his voice and spaced each word, so the high beams of the room resounded. "Whose special attention is incalculable. What a future he has contrived for his son! Wedded to a wife that hates the sight of me."

Piers signaled to Felders. "Fill her a glass." When Vivian shook her head, he stooped and dragged her to her feet clasping her hand tightly in his own. "No fainting and fading away, my dear. The end of the evening is nearing. The long ordeal, about to be finished. Just one drink and you can be escorted to your penitential lying. And remember just before you sink into exhausted slumber that at least it will be better than the restraining straps at an institution. But only just."

Felders pressed the glass into Vivian's hand. She stared at it stupidly.

"Drink," Piers prodded softly. "Believe me, this is better than any watered wine in the nunnery. And a thousand times better than any foul substance pushed into your mouth in an institution. Good French brandy." He clinked his glass against hers. "Drink."

"Careful, Piers," the earl suggested. "She's had a long day and night."

"Why so she has, but can she complain?" He spun her halfway round.

The black nun's skirts flew out. Vivian staggered, and he caught her against his body. She was aware of his arm clasping her, of the scent of his body. The brandy slopped from her glass, wetting the front of her dress.

Piers drank again, his strong fingers massaging her shoulder, holding her pressed against him. "Can she complain? No. Can she question? No. Can she rant and rail? Not those either. Can she beg and whine and whimper?"

Vivian rallied for a single instant, though her head was spinning. He was supporting almost her full weight leaned against his chest. Her head fell back on her shoulders. Her silver-blue eyes flashed up into his own. Pain almost too severe to be borne pounded and clawed at her temples. Her mouth was so dry that she could not have spoken in any case. Only her eyes lived in the pale mask of her face.

Piers looked deeply into them, then up to his father. He took another drink. "No," he said softly. "She can do none of these things. She can only hate. And hate. As Mother hated you."

The earl's amused stare dropped. He drank his own brandy, then glanced back at his son with a halfhearted shrug.

"Pledge me that hatred, my lady," Piers challenged, looking down at her.

Her lips parted, revealing her teeth tightly clenched. She aimed a sibilant hiss at him.

He laughed. "A tiger cat with fangs bared. But a small tiger. Much overmatched, I fear." He drank again, then slowly, he inclined his head bringing his lips nearer to hers; his hand tilted her head to one side. His eyes were so close to her own that she could now see they were not a single opaque dark color, but brown, floating shifting shades of brown with a golden radiance around the pupil. Closer they came, their color richer, until it lost focus and became unclear.

His lips touched hers. She tasted brandy first and foremost, then his tongue caressed her teeth begging admittance. She was not aware she had opened them until she felt him slide into her mouth. His breath mingled with her. He sought and found her own tongue.

Then something happened. Something swift and hot as lightning streaked through her limbs. It made her curl her hands into fists and draw her breath in sharply. It set the muscles along the tops of her thighs to quivering and clenched the secret places between her legs. She could not help herself. The need to taste more of him and heighten this fiery sensation drove her to suck at his tongue.

Startled, he froze, then locked his tongue with hers. Remembering belatedly that they were not alone, he turned her so that his body shielded hers. His other hand sought and found her breast covering it gently, warming it through the prickly wool. A wave of unsought passion swept over him. Anger at his father, disgust at the scene faded. Suddenly, there was nothing but the sweetness and warmth of her mouth. Without removing his lips from hers, he shifted his grasp to her shoulder to lift her toward him. The feel of her smooth skin stimulated by her compliance excited him unbearably. His kiss deepened.

The earl's hoarse laugh rang out, destroying the moment between them. Vivian's passion turned to remembrance and rage. How dare he laugh at her helplessness in the hands of his horrible drunken son. She brought her jaw champing down.

"My God!" With an exclamation of pain and rage, Piers jerked away from her, clapping his hand to his mouth. Incredulously, he stared as she blazed her rage and momentary triumph.

The earl laughed. And this time Mrs. Felders allowed herself a small smile.

Piers heard and saw them both. His own hair-trigger temper exploded. He pushed her from him and she stumbled, falling clumsily to the floor. She sprawled helplessly on her side, her senses fainting.

He stared down aghast at his own bad temper. The sight sobered him instantly. He went down on one knee, to touch her shoulder.

Witness to the tableau, the earl shook his head. "Nasty tempers both of you. Not a good thing for my heirs. Not a good thing. But at least you both give as good as you get." He signaled to Mrs. Felders. "Open the door and let Jack Beddoes take me to bed. Take Miss Marleigh back to her bed she vacated so impulsively. By the look of her, she could lie here, but the fire will die down and she might take a chill."

When Piers hesitated over her, the earl clapped him on the shoulder. "Help yourself, my boy, to the brandy.

We'll have the minister in tomorrow. I took the trouble of procuring a special license shortly after I saw her." He looked down at Vivian's prone body. "She'll be a fine breeder. A lady of spirit."

"I'll not marry her," Piers murmured.

The old man laughed. "You'll marry her and consummate the marriage. You can't fool me. I saw what happened between you. You kindled a blaze. You won't be able to keep your hands off her. Nor she you."

They were the last words Vivian heard before her head sank to the cold stones of the hearth.

Chapter Six

Piers waved Felders back when she came to rouse Vivian. "I'll see to her. You take care of your master." As he stooped to the unconscious girl, his eyes met those of the housekeeper. Low and vicious, his voice reached only her ears. "I'm surprised he can find his way to bed without you."

Felders stiffened in midstride. Her nostrils pinched and angry mottling darkened her neck as she absorbed the insult.

"Just ring for Watkins on your way out the door."

When her black skirts had swished around the corner, Piers slipped his arms under Vivian's body and gathered her up in his arms. Her head tipped back and her silver-gilt hair swung like a banner as he climbed to his feet. His eyes slid over the graceful line of her white throat. He caught his breath.

Watkins appeared in the door. "Milord?"

"Make up the room next to mine."

"Milord?" The valet hesitated, his eyes on the rusty black habit. "Perhaps the other wing—"

"Don't object, Watkins. That miserable priest hole Felders had her stored in won't do. She at least needs something more comfortable than a cot."

"Very well, milord."

"And bring the brandy. She'll need a restorative when she comes to herself." He shifted her head to his shoulder. "And so will I."

When Piers lowered Vivian to the feather bed, she did not stir. While Watkins built a fire, the viscount lifted her wrists one at a time. His jaw tightened. A band of dark purple encircled each where Beddoes's straps had left bruises. Piers's thumb was not broad enough to cover the width. A soft curse slipped from his lips causing the valet to throw an inquiring glance over his shoulder. "It's a wonder her hands didn't turn black and drop off."

His task complete, Watkins rose and came to the bedside. He shook his head at the sight. "Only if he'd wanted them to, milord. Beddoes knows his trade. Knows just how tight to make them. Probably the lady fought them all the way from London."

Piers nodded solemnly. "Probably so. I would have. But somehow one doesn't expect a female to do so. Maybe weep and wail, but not hurt herself like this!" He gently touched the bruise with his index finger.

"No, sir." The valet hesitated. "Will that be all, sir?"

"Yes."

Piers raked his fingers through his wine-dark hair. He had sent Mrs. Felders and Watkins away. He now faced the problem of making the woman comfortable. A year ago, even six months, he would not have given such a thing a thought. But as his mother's illness had grown in virulence, as her pain and discomfort had increased, he had learned to perform kind offices for her—acts that none other had been there to perform because his mother would not have Mrs. Felders in her rooms.

98

The female body was no stranger to him. With a shrug he sat on the edge of the bed, rolled the unconscious girl onto her side, and began to undress her. He dropped the bedraggled white cloth to the floor. Efficiently, he unfastened the neck and tugged the habit up over her body, replacing its covering with a sheet and blanket. As he bared her torso, he shook his head in wonder. Why would any woman become a nun? The coarse wool had chafed the tender skin on her neck and the inside of her elbows.

While he undressed her, he became aware that she was altogether too thin. Her breasts were spare mounds with no more than a pale shadow of nipple beneath the linen shift. Still the shape was altogether womanly. A light sweat broke out on his forehead. He covered her quickly.

Sliding his hands beneath the covers, he pulled off her stockings, arranged her limbs, and then straightened. When the covers were tucked up around her chin, he stood beside the bed looking down at her.

His future bride.

The irony of the situation brought a self-mocking grin to his lips. He—of all people—to wed a woman whom he had never seen dressed any way except in a nun's habit. He laid the backs of his fingers against her cheek. She felt a little warm to the touch; perhaps she might be running a slight fever. However, except for the circles under her eyes and the dark eyebrows and eyelashes, her face was as pale as the sheet. He grinned a little wearily. Many more patients to nurse, and he could open a physician's practice.

As he watched her, she moved. A frown knitted her eyebrows together. She turned her head in negation on the pillow. One hand fought its way up to clutch the sheet, then relaxed.

His grin changed to an amazingly tender smile.

Probably she was trying to escape in her sleep. What a rude entry into society she had endured! From the quiet haven of the nunnery, she had moved into a company of villains the likes of which she had never dreamed. She had found treachery and lawlessness, pain and death. And no love at all. He stroked the small hand and tucked it back under the cover. No love at all, he reminded himself.

Vivian awoke to pain; her wrists, arms, and shoulders ached abominably when she stirred. Denying her struggle to orient herself, her mind refused to form intelligent thoughts. She stared blankly at the canopy above her. She had never seen the dingy draperies before.

A gusty wind rattled a window. She turned her head in time to see another dingy drapery billow outward. Beneath her cheek, the pillow smelled musty. She lifted the edge of the sheet and stared first at the material and then beneath it. A slow flush crept up in her face as she saw her body clad only in her shift. Someone had undressed her before putting her in this bed.

She raised her head as far as her aching back would allow and stared downward at the thick mattress pressing up on either side of her. This was not her bed in her almost forgotten room at Stone Glenn. Nor was this the barren hospital at the abbey. The bed, unlike her hospital cot with its thin mattress, was big, warm and very comfortable, albeit the linens were dreadfully stale as if they had been made up months ago.

The curtains of the bed were tied back giving her a good view of the room. A lamp turned low on the bedside table and a flickering fire in the fireplace drove the shadows back into the corners. The furniture was oak, heavy and ornamented. The legs of the table and chairs were ornately carved relics from a bygone era.

Only then did she remember where she was. Her breath slipped out of her chest as she sank back on the pillows. Could she keep herself from drawing it again? Could she will herself to die? Death seemed the single control she maintained over her existence. Otherwise, she was shuttled from place to place like a poor relation.

The leaden panes rattled again. The fire flamed briefly then began to die. Her chest ached until she could not help but breathe. With weary acceptance of life, she stared at the flickering red tongues until they rose no more from the glowing heart of the coal.

Woozily, Piers tilted the brandy decanter over his glass, then tilted it up until it was perpendicular to the table. "God," he whispered. "Empty and I'm still upright and sensible."

He set the decanter down and wove his way toward the door. "Can't let this happen," he murmured. "Can't go to bed sober."

The hall outside his door was fifty degrees colder than his room. A gusty draught blew down it fit to freeze any uncovered part of a body. It drove him back inside with a shiver and a curse. He would never be able to make his way downstairs without sobering still more. Clearly he was caught. Trapped. Doomed to stare unhappily into the fire, his thoughts moiling around in his brain.

Suddenly, he remembered himself telling Watkins to bring the brandy. Where? To the room next to his. Easy enough to slip in there and retrieve it. He opened his door again and sprinted for the next room.

Vivian shot straight up in bed as her door swung open. The fire flared up and the curtains billowed. The viscount stood on the threshold in his shirtsheeves and woolen stockings. Instantly, she jerked the covers up to her chin.

"I beg pardon, madam." He bowed unsteadily. "But I left something in your room."

Her eyes widened impossibly. She clutched the coverlet tighter.

He closed the door against the draught puffing at his back and started for the bedside table.

She all but vaulted from the bed. The instant that her foot touched the floor, she fell back. Piers had removed her stockings, and the icy polished oak sent its shock throughout her system.

"Cold, eh?" He grinned as he picked up the decanter, holding it up to the light, and noting its contents with satisfaction. "My room's none too warm. And the hall—" He made a mock shuddering noise. "It doesn't bear contemplating."

Vivian stared at him, common sense warring with terror. Obviously, he had come for the brandy, but had he come for something more?

She had her answer when he moved closer until his thighs touched the edge of her bed. One long arm slid along its head, the hand with the bottle knocking against the carved wood. "Just settle down now under the covers." He leaned over her, interest kindling in his eyes as they scanned her face and hair. "Damme, if I can recall your name. And you my bride-to-be."

She hesitated, then reached for his free hand.

He allowed her to take it all the time grinning with satisfaction. "Please feel free with my person. Maybe I'm not so drunk as I thought. The night may not be so long after all." He leered suggestively at her. "Were you lonesome, er, Mary. No Elizabeth."

She gave him a disgusted look, then stabbed the hand firmly down on the coverlet. Turning it palm up,

102

she began to trace letters upon it with her index finger.

"What the deuce are you up to?" He tried to pull it from her.

She grasped it tighter and began again.

He looked from her face to his hand, then back again. Then leaned over his own hand staring at it. "V-I-V-I-A-N. Vivian." She released his hand, but he did not remove it. "So that's how you carry on a conversation." Their faces were very close.

Too late she was aware of him, his arm behind her shoulder, his hand in her lap, the scent of him.

"Vivian," he murmured persuasively. "Tell me more."

She tried to slide away, but the arm behind her settled on her shoulders drawing her back. Her eyes searched his face, struggling with her fear and something else—the strange heat that contact with him seemed to generate.

"Ah, Vivian." His mouth came down on hers. His tongue slipped between her parted lips.

Her fists struck at his shoulders, as the bed sagged beneath the weight of his knee. He bore her back onto the pillows. She was locked in his embrace before she could draw breath. Alarm streaked through her. She pounded on his back, but he paid no attention, only went on kissing her, his mouth moving over and over hers. His tongue filled her, thrusting in and pulling out rhythmically.

His hand shaped her hip, her narrow waist, the curve of her ribs, her breast. Wherever he touched, she burned. Her body burned and quickened. She drew up one of her legs involuntarily, and when it fell, it no longer lay tight against the other. A strange weakness invaded her muscles. Her heart beat faster.

"Vivian," he murmured again against her mouth. He trailed kisses down the side of her face to her ear. His thumb and finger found her breast, the nipple hardened into a nub. "Such a responsive bride."

At the word, light flooded her mind. Clear as crystal she could recall a scene as she had seen it from the stable loft not two years ago. The big Shire stallion lumbering into the paddock. The mare squealing. The kicks and bites. The blood trickling down the mare's thrashing neck as the stallion held her between his yellow teeth. And then his grunting while the mare shuddered and braced her legs beneath his weight.

With the memory came determination. Her fists unclenched; her fingers arched into talons that she brought raking down across his back. Her nails had grown in the past week. She used them, ripping at the linen of his shirt, hooking her hands in the back of the neck and pulling with all her strength.

He swallowed and gasped as his air was cut off. "Damme!" His hand left off fondling her, to pull at the front of his shirt.

She bucked up and twisted beneath him, succeeding in shifting halfway out from under him. When he tried to follow and hold her, she hit him in the jaw with her doubled fist. It was a short blow that really hurt her more than it hurt him, but he cursed and drew back.

They stared at each other warily.

After a couple of seconds, he grinned placatingly. "Now, Vivian, don't get so upset over a little kiss."

The remark galvanized her into action. She twisted around in the bed and kicked and pushed at him with her feet.

He sat up, too, rubbed his jaw, and held up his hand. "No more. I'll leave. I can tell when I'm not appreciated." He adopted an aggrieved tone though a devil was dancing in his eyes. "I was just giving you a little goodnight kiss. After all, we're going to be married."

She drew both knees up to her chest and let fly. Her heels thudded against his chest.

He slid off the bed and came to his feet, a mocking grin on his face. "No need to get so violent. I'm leaving." He waved the brandy bottle at her. "I only came for this after all." He backed away from the bed. "But later, Vivian, I shall expect a warmer welcome." He paused at the door to stare at her consideringly. "You have lovely legs, my dear. And lovely breasts."

Her mouth dropped open. Her face flamed. She clapped her arms across her chest.

With a mocking laugh and a bow, he was gone.

Defying the cold, she sprang from the bed and ran to the door. Opening it a crack, she watched him lope down the hall and enter his room. As he closed his door, she closed hers and pushed herself against it.

Dear God in Heaven! His room was the next one to hers.

Vivian's stomach growled. She patted it comfortingly, but it only growled louder. With a sigh she realized she could bear the gnawing ache no longer. She held no hope that someone would come in and light a fire, bring her chocolate, and hold her robe. Those days seemed gone forever. Her breath fogged in the air as she sighed.

Despite the protest of her back and shoulder muscles, she pushed herself to a sitting position. The cold air rushed in around her lightly clad body. One shivering hand pulled the covers up to her throat. Her head swam dizzily, and she almost sank back against the pillows in weakness. The temptation to do so was strong, but her stomach growled again.

Steeling herself and gritting her teeth, she thrust her slender feet out of the bed and gingerly touched the floor. The shock of the cold polished wood beneath her soles made her shiver and draw back. Drawing a deep breath, she resolutely gathered the sheet around her and stood up. Dragging it from the bed and wrapping it around her shoulders, she hurried to the thick fur rug thrown down in front of the hearth. A coal shuttle stood by the fender. Clumsily she tipped its contents onto the grate. A cloud of gray ash shot up, but beneath it live coals glowed red.

Then with her toes curled in the rug, she looked around the walls for the bell cord.

None was in evidence. Mentally cursing, she spied her nun's habit tossed on the chair beside the bed. Again gritting her teeth, she started toward it but stopped in midstride. Toes curled under her feet, she realized she was staring at her own trunk placed at the end of bed. Flabbergasted, she blinked at it twice, certain she was mistaken.

Her hunger and cold momentarily forgotten, she crossed to it and ran her hand over its leather-bound surface. Wonderingly, she fingered the brass handles, traced her initials in gold above the lock. Its presence passed all understanding. It had gone with her to the nunnery but had remained unopened when the abbess had insisted that she wear a habit. Undoubtedly, the habit had been donned according to Sebastian's orders.

And undoubtedly, the trunk had been brought to her by order of the earl. She shuddered. *From one prison to another*. But at least she could wear her own clothes.

Eagerly, she flung back the lid. Inside was her clothing, neatly folded, smelling familiarly of lavender and the camphor wood press in her own room at Stone Glenn. Her eyes filled with tears. Over a year had passed since she had done more than look at these clothes in the privacy of her room.

Wool and cotton day dresses, her fine merino-trimmed spencer; in the tray drawer her silk undergarments, so long given up when the nuns furnished her with their own clothing. Allowing the sheet to drop, she held each familiar garment up, then laid it aside. One and all they seemed fragile and unsophisticated. For now she needed armor.

Even the hated nun's habit would be preferable to a dress of fine rose wool with deep lace collar and cuffs. Shivering with chill, she pulled out more garments until she came across what she sought—her royal blue velvet riding habit. In a moment she had found undergarments and her riding boots and had begun to dress herself with fumbling haste. Never had buttons and laces resisted so obstinately. Her fluttering fingers trembled as she clumsily secured her skirt, blouse, and jacket.

Drawing on her boots, she ran to the window and cautiously parted the heavy draperies noting with distaste the dust clinging to the fabric. The panes were fogged over. She wiped away the dampness to stare outward at a bleak cloudy sky. Still it dazzled her eyes accustomed for so many hours to partial darkness. Blinking rapidly, she pressed her hands against the panes of the window in frustration.

Beneath her, gray stone walls sheered straight down from her window to a flagstone terrace at least thirty feet below. She was in the second story of one wing. Across the terrace stretched another wing, probably identical. Windows gray as the day and the walls in which they were set, stared opaquely back at her.

A grim smile fleetingly curved her lips. She was a captive in this grim, gray house. *How Gothic!* was her thought. *A Castle of Otranto*. With herself as Isabella.

She turned back into the room. *Does anyone even know I'm here? Does anyone care?*

A mirror glinted on the door of the wardrobe. Allowing the draperies to fall closed, she peered into its grimy surface. Her reflection shocked her. Her blond hair was wildly disheveled, hanging in locks and snarls tumbled about her shoulders. Deep mauve shadows hollowed her eyes and made her white skin all the whiter. She raised her hand to push at her hair. For the first time, she saw her wrist in the mirror. In horror she looked at it, looked at both of them. How had she gotten those bracelets of bruised skin?

The leather straps.

How could she forget the nightmare ride in the jouncing coach, a ride that seemed to stretch into eternity? She rubbed her wrists tenderly, her mouth twisting. Not only was the skin tender, but the flesh beneath felt bruised to the bone.

She lifted her eyes to the mirror. Surrounded by a witch's snarl of hair, a haggard face stared back at her scarcely recognizable as her own. She looked infinitely older than when she had last seen herself in a mirror. Old and bitter. Her mouth lifted in a sneer as she pulled a tangled snarl down over her left shoulder. Her pride and joy. She felt a pain deep inside her. Her eyes burned and a sheet of tears sluiced across her eyes.

She knew herself to be a commodity. An heiress with land and money to be fought over. And a body to bear children. The drunken viscount who had come for his bottle of brandy last night had not even remembered her name. Yet he had been ready to make love to her. Like the stallion with the mare, he was ready to mate with her. And he, like the stallion, cared nothing for the mare except as a receptacle of his lust.

He had kissed her. Her empty stomach turned over and she swallowed, tasting again the brandy in his mouth and the indefinable something that must be him. It had made her head swim, her muscles weak.

And that, she supposed, was lust, too. Her lust. She flushed. *God bless you, Hewes Attewater.* Her old groom's weathered face rose in her memory. The single person who had been her friend since babyhood, old Hewes had been her mentor and teacher as well. A pragmatic Cornishman whose salty conversations about men and animals she had been allowed to overhear, although he had been angry and frightened at the same time when he had discovered her hiding in the loft to watch the stallion put to the mare.

Thanks to dear Hewes, she had not totally surrendered to the desires of the flesh. At the most crucial moment, her mind had triumphed over her body.

And so it must continue to do, if she were to survive in this unhappy house. She would need to wear armor on her body and in her mind.

In the top of her trunk was a box of her toilet articles. Carrying it to a chair beside the hearth, she sat and took out her brush, her comb, her hand mirror, and small bottles of scent and lotion. Whoever had packed her things at the abbey had gotten everything. Eagerly, she opened the lotion and began to rub it gently on her wrists.

Then she raised her aching arms and brought the brush down through the mass of tangled hair. Her scalp smarted as the bristles caught in the snarls. Tears started in her eyes. Swinging the skein over her left shoulder, she began again by brushing the tangles from the ends.

A tear escaped to trickle down her cheek. Her agitated breathing and the occasional hiss of the coals were the only sounds in the dim room. In frustration she flung the brush onto the table and sprang to her feet.

A wave of dizziness swept her, forcing her to brace both hands flat against the table top and hold on for dear life. After drawing several deep breaths, she stared again at her own face. It gleamed whiter than before with a pinched look about her mouth; only her eyes showed a trace of color. Weakly she swayed as her knees threatened to give way. She must have food before all else. Beyond that she could not think.

Behind her she heard the door open. Her scalp prickled and she turned swiftly to face her adversary.

In the doorway stood Emma Felders, her hard mouth pursed tight. Her eyes were cold with hatred that she made no effort to conceal. A small tray in her hand held a silver pot and a china cup and saucer.

At the sight Vivian almost smiled. How the housekeeper must have hated to carry them to her. Vivian raised her chin and forced herself to walk calmly across the room and seat herself before the fire.

The older woman set the tray down on the table side. "Your tea, milady."

Vivian stared pointedly at the tray. The pot sat naked on it, no cozy holding its heat in. Nor did it set on a stand with a warming candle underneath it. Even if the water had been boiling when the housekeeper left the kitchen, it would be only tepid after its trip through the draughty halls. She touched the side of the pot with her fingers. Stone cold. Her eyes found Mrs. Felders, their accusation clear without words.

Spots of color appeared on the woman's cheekbones. She shifted uneasily. Then a muscle jumped as she tightened her jaw. "It's late in the day. People are about their accustomed duties. I myself had to leave a task unfinished."

Vivian pushed the tray back and rose, conscious that everything she did was a test of wills with this woman. Ignoring the hunger clawing at her, she left the fireside for the dressing table.

The housekeeper's face was a study. Uncertainty flickered in her eyes as she watched.

Vivian picked up her brush and extended it.

Mrs. Felders shook her head. "Lord Larnaervon requires your presence downstairs, milady. I was sent to bring you as soon as you'd had your tea. Since you don't want it, I suggest you come immediately."

Vivian stabbed the brush at the housekeeper.

The woman laced her hands together under her apron. "If you know what's good for you, you won't keep his lordship waiting. When he says 'do,' everybody around here does. He's not a man to cross. As many have found out to their sorrow."

At the reminder of the earl's ruthlessness, Vivian felt her stomach twist and the color drain from her cheeks. Her arm trembled.

Mrs. Felders's sharp eyes detected the movement. "If you'll follow me quickly," she suggested silkily, "he might still be in a good humor."

Vivian's slender figure seemed to droop. The arm lowered, then lifted. She fixed her sternest expression on her face. It was an expression borrowed from the Mother Abbess and guaranteed to make strong men quail. Determined to have herself made presentable, she extended the brush.

Drawn against her will by years of servitude, the housekeeper took a step forward. Her hand reached for the brush, then drew back. Her lips tightened. "You don't have time for that, milady."

Vivian thrust the brush into the lax hand and twisted round on the dressing stool. From her box on the table, she drew a wide blue velvet ribbon. She tossed one end

111

over the shoulder. In the mirror her eyes met those of the housekeeper.

In the seconds that followed the air between the two women was charged. Then Mrs. Felders succumbed. With poor grace she took the proffered brush. "Oh, very well, milady, but you'll come to regret this. If not this time, then the next. You'd best be warned. He'll make you sorry you were ever born."

Chapter Seven

Piers stretched gingerly in his big bed. His head pounded from the brandy he had consumed the night before. His mouth tasted foul as an unclean stable. Carefully, he opened one eye only to moan softly in pain. A long rectangle of dim light managed to slip between the draperies. It struck his eyes eliciting a grimace as he slowly rolled over on his side away from the window and levered himself up onto his elbow.

The excruciating agony of such an ambitious movement wrung a hoarse curse followed by a groan from his parched throat. Clearly, he had succeeded in rendering himself unconscious last night. Gently, he pulled the pillow over his pounding head.

Waiting on cue for the curse and groan, Watkins entered with morning coffee. The china rattled as the valet set the tray down on the table.

Piers groaned again. "Lord Jesus and all the angels, Watkins. Do you have to crash crockery?"

"Sorry, sir. It slipped."

"Well, you slip away, won't you—that's a kind man—and leave me in pain. I don't want any of your damned coffee."

The valet poured as if the viscount had not spoken.

"Milord, I think you'd better drink this."

At the stern tone, Piers eased the pillow down from about his face. "Why?"

"Because his lordship requires your presence in his study as soon as possible." The valet took the pillow from Piers's slack hands and shook it out. "Let me just slip this behind you, sir."

"To hell with that!" Piers pushed himself halfway up until the pain between his eyes struck him with stunning force.

The valet dropped the pillow against the headboard and guided the coffee cup into Piers's hand. "Best drink it, sir, while it's hot."

Piers swallowed some, finding it laced with brandy. He drew down his dark eyebrows and squinted at the valet. "My father, you say? What time is it?"

"Barely noon, milord."

"I don't like the sound of that."

"No, sir." The valet moved to the wardrobe and began to lay out Piers's best suit.

Preferring not to know what lay ahead, the viscount sipped the brew, sighing in relief as the alcohol numbed the pain, and the hot coffee washed away some of the debris in his mouth. At last he felt able to rise.

His agonized growl brought Watkins back with a robe. Piers listed to one side, clutching at his head with one hand, the bedpost with the other. Watkins slipped himself expertly beneath the taller man's arm and supported him.

For a moment while his stomach churned, Piers swallowed hard, ducking his head and transferring his grip to the smaller man's shoulder. When he had mastered his rebellious disgestive track, he shakily manuevered his way across the bedroom and into the hot bath already prepared in the small adjoining chamber.

Stripping naked, he sank gratefully into the steaming water. Sweat broke out on his skin as the poison of the night's drinking rolled from his body. He was beginning to feel almost human, when an ill-conceived shake of his head set his temples to throbbing with renewed fury. Pressing the heels of his hands against them, he cursed foully.

"Milord?" the valet inquired.

"Bloody hell, Watkins! Why do I do it? I can't remember anything of what happened last night. Whole evening's a fume."

"Yes, milord." The valet imperturbably soaped the broad back and shoulders, massaging the knotted muscles and nerves of the spine and neck.

Piers let his hands slide limply into the water. "That's why I do it," he murmured. "So I won't have to remember."

Watkins hesitated, not because he feared to speak. He was privy to all the viscount's secrets. Neither did he fear reprisal. Piers had never acted less than a kind gentlemen to him. Nevertheless, he cleared his throat delicately. "Perhaps it would behoove you to recall—"

"—my bride-to-be," Piers finished.

"Exactly, sir."

Again the viscount cursed. His father had gone too far this time. No question but that the man was mad. The whole Gothic scene last night had been like something out of Monk Lewis. Marrying his only son to a mute nun! Piers laughed loudly and painfully.

"Sir?"

"My bride, Watkins. I'm contemplating my affianced bride."

The valet cleared his throat. "A very kind lady, sir. Very well-bred."

Piers let his head drop back against the curve of the tub. "Too well-bred I'm afraid." He closed his eyes as

115

he muttered, "An attic to let."

The sponge halted in its rhythmic circles. "I did not find the lady so, milord. She nursed your mother with great kindness and efficiency."

"Oh, she can do small things like that, Watkins, but only God knows whether or not she's an idiot."

The valet lifted the linen towel. "I don't believe she's an idiot, milord."

Piers's eyes remained closed. He sighed deeply. The piercing pounding had retreated to a faint dull ache and a bad taste in his mouth. With a return to physical health, he began to regain a measure of charity. He really had no objection to the girl. One girl was much like another. A casual acquaintance, a passing affection, an heir or two and then he would be on about his business. The part that rankled was that his father had selected her for him.

He opened his eyes to see the valet waiting with the towel draped over his arms. "Bloody hell, Watkins! Can't I even enjoy my bath?"

"His lordship was most insistent, sir."

"What difference will a few more minutes make to him? To me a bit more brandy and anything would be bearable." *Even marriage to an idiot.* He stared morosely at the smoke-blackened wall of the bathroom. What bloody difference did anything make?

At the valet's pleading expression, he rose and stepped into the warmed towel. While he dried himself, Watkins began to mix the soap for shaving.

Of course, he was only babbling. She was not exactly an idiot. After all, she could write her name in his hand. Of course, that was a slight thing, no real measure of intelligence. Still she did have an air about her. And she was beautiful. He grinned slightly as he dropped down on the stool and allowed Watkins to drape a hot towel across his face and begin to strop the razor.

116

He had told her she had beautiful breasts. And so she had. He shifted and tugged the towel more securely across his legs. When his cheeks and chin were smooth, he looked up into Watkins's lined face. "What does Larne want with me?"

The valet dabbed a tiny fleck of lather from the viscount's chin, then stepped back to avoid the explosion. "I believe he has brought a priest to the house, milord."

Piers did not change expressions beyond a short nod. "Ah, well. 'If it be not now, yet it will come. The readiness is all.'"

Not understanding the valet merely bowed. "Will you wear the blue superfine, sir?"

"As good as any for my wedding finery."

With poor grace Emma Felders accepted the brush and touched the bristles to the crown of Vivian's head. "I can't do any more than brush it out," she warned. "There's a girl below stairs. Matilda. She has a way with hair. She can really fix it. She's the one you'll be wanting, milady."

Vivian sat stonily enduring the long sweeps. Tears started in her eyes at least twice as the snarls caught. The housekeeper glanced in the mirror from time to time. Each time she dropped her eyes after briefly meeting Vivian's.

When at last all was smooth and shining, Mrs. Felders leaned over and placed the brush on the table. "You'd best be going downstairs," she muttered direly. "His lordship doesn't like to be kept waiting."

As the housekeeper drew back, Vivian proffered the blue velvet ribbon.

"I don't know that I can—" She met Vivian's eyes in the mirror. Tightly pursing her mouth, she gathered the bright skein of hair together at the nape of Vivian's neck and clumsily tied the ribbon. The bow did not lie flat and the ends hung down unevenly.

Vivian shook her head as she lifted the hand mirror behind her to view the result. She looked at Emma Felders in the mirror. The two women stared at each other, the older one daring the younger one to complain.

Considering that she had tried the housekeeper enough, Vivian nodded briefly. Calmly, as a queen proceeding to chambers of state, she rose and crossed to the door where she paused, waiting for Mrs. Felders to open it.

For the first time Vivian walked through the earl's house with her head erect. No longer was she clothed in nun's garb, her vision bound by the blinding wings of her veil. For the first time she looked around her with an interested and observing eye.

The hall ended on a long landing that joined the two wings of the house above a double staircase. Her new room was in the wing occupied by the viscount rather than the wing where the countess had died. At the bottom of the staircase were the parlor and dining room and presumably the earl's study.

She looked about her critically. The red Turkish carpet was practically threadbare. Dust grayed the carvings of the banisters. Spiders had long ago draped their webs between the scounces—so long ago that the webs were gray and fuzzy with dust. She frowned at the housekeeper's stiff back. Threadbare carpet was a thing no servant could help, but dust and neglect were undoubtedly her responsibility.

With Mrs. Felders leading the way, they descended the wide staircase and crossed the scarred parquet floor in the lower hall. Soil had worked into the indentations and scratches left by hundreds of boot heels. Vivian

118

shook her head at the sight of such inexcusable neglect. In front of the dark double doors of the study, the housekeeper stopped and rapped with her knuckles on a richly carved panel.

By the light seeping through dingy panes on each side of the massive front door, Vivian could study with some distaste the evidence that neglect was not relegated to the floor. The walls were smoke-stained and dull. The windows were filthy. A large painting in a tarnished gilt frame hung beside the study door. The colors had darkened with age and dirt until the subject was uncertain. Gazing up at it, Vivian noted spider-webs spun from the edges of the frame to the walls behind.

The countess's illness had been of long duration. Given the precarious state of the earl's health, he probably noticed nothing beyond his own creature comforts. Somehow that thought was reassuring. It embodied him with a weakness where he had hitherto seemed invincible. Vivian shuddered, dreading the confrontation.

Mrs. Felders knocked again more loudly to be rewarded by a peremptory summons to enter. She turned the handles back on the doors, swung them inward, and stepped aside.

Vivian quelled an overwhelming desire to run. Her legs were unsteady under her as she crossed the threshold.

"Ah, the bride. Good morning, my dear. Blue velvet," he remarked, surveying her clothing. "An excellent choice."

As Mrs. Felders closed the doors behind her, Vivian hesitated, unwilling to approach him.

"Come closer, my dear." He sat behind a huge block of furniture. As her eyes grew accustomed to the dimness, she realized he sat behind a desk where papers were stacked in several neat stacks. At the same time she wondered how any room so dark could be called a library.

Heavy draperies covered the windows from ceiling to floor. Shelves filled with leather-bound books lined the walls from the windows to the hall doors through which she had entered. The only light in the room came from a standing candelabra behind and to the side of his desk. The candles gilded the long white hair spread over his shoulders but kept his face in shadow. The Earl of Larnaervon sat in a cell. But it was a cell of his own choice, she reminded herself.

"Don't be shy, my dear—Vivian?" His voice lifted her name at the end as if requesting permission to use it. She stiffened at the courtesy in the light of his treatment of her body.

He detected the movement and shrugged, twisting his crippled shoulders slightly. A pool of silence filled between them. Then he pushed several pages of foolscap toward her with his knobby fingers. "I promised you your chance to write your protest. Have at it now."

Taking a leather chair beside the desk, Vivian stared at the blank sheets. She had forgotten her demands of the night before. Her thoughts whirled. Even if she had had the power of speech, she doubted at that moment she could have formed coherent statements.

"Pen and ink, my dear." He pushed the stand toward the edge of the desk.

Fingers cold, she dipped the pen and scratched a couple of words on the paper. "Stone Glenn."

He rose with the aid of his cane and limped round the desk. "Your home. It will be restored to you, my dear." He placed one hand on her shoulder. It hooked over her, the fingers hard and knobby. It might have been a skeleton hand for all the warmth that penetrated the layers of material, and the tremors in the arm rattled the old bones against her.

"Sebastian."

The fingers squeezed. "Ah, thirsting for revenge, are you?" He chuckled. "I like your spirit, Vivian. Leave your erstwhile guardian to Piers and me. We'll see that every shilling, every tuppence is accounted for."

She looked up into the earl's withered face. His eyes blazed with the heat that his fingers lacked. His scrutiny made her more uncomfortable than his touch. She barely managed to control a shudder as she dropped her eyes to the paper again.

"Lawyers."

"Shylocks, everyone of them. Aiding him to swindle you." Muttering something unintelligible, he released her shoulder and leaned across his desk. He staggered slightly, unsteady on his stiff legs, and cursed as his hip bumped against the edge.

For a minute or two one hand, heavily spotted on the back, paddled in the papers. Finally, he found the one he sought, extracted it, and passed it to her. "I didn't go to bed last night," he continued, clearing his throat noisily. "Now that you are safe." He smiled at her and dipped his head. His white hair swung forward. "I was consumed with the desire to set this business to rights."

She glanced at the candelabra, noting that the yellow tallow had indeed overrun the drip pans.

"Too damnably much work to do," he continued, "and too little time left." He shifted so that his bony shanks rested on the edge of the desk. His shoulders hunched over the cane braced between his legs. He stared at her while she tried to make sense of the paper. At last she looked up into his face. His white hair and unshaven white stubble on his blasted cheeks gave him an appearance like nothing human. The sunken eyes glittering so close above her made her ill. Their whites were bloodshot and yellow as tallow.

In the back of Vivian's mind a memory stirred, a book she had read, or a fact she had heard. Disease of the liver, she recalled. Jaundice.

He stared back at her. Like antagonists they sized each other up searching for weaknesses. "Piers should be up and at work. But he drinks. He needs—" The man glanced at the paper, back at her, then focused his eyes on the candle's heart. He muttered again, then expelled his breath in a shuddery wheeze. "He needs the weakness beaten out of him," he told her confidentially.

Vivian curled her nails around the arms of her chair. This man talked of his son as if he despised him.

Lord Larnaervon shook himself as if he had said too much, coughed harshly, and tapped the paper she held. "Your guardian was robbing you blind, Vivian Marleigh, with the consent and aid of those high-priced London solicitors. My dear, don't think that I have kidnapped you. You should be falling on your knees in gratitude before me for taking you into my care."

She wrote again on the foolscap. "Home, please."

He shook his head. "After all the trouble and expense I've taken to rescue you. My girl, you can't take care of yourself in this cruel world. You may be intelligent. I think you are. I think that you may be more than even I am aware of. But the odds are too great against you. That's the thing you have to face."

"Hire honest men," she wrote.

He read the words and shook his head. "These are unfortunate times. And your wealth would tempt anyone but a saint. You can't fight greed. It corrupts. And you are a very wealthy young woman. Read that account."

As he bade her, she tilted the paper into the candlelight. It was a report of rents collected from

122

Marleigh Court tenants. The rents were dated months in advance and paid into the account of her guardian. Furthermore, they were exorbitantly high.

When she had finished, he handed her another. It was a statement of monies paid by the London firm of Barnstaple and Rowling to Sebastian Dawlish for expenses incurred as executor of the Marleigh estate. She gasped at the figures.

Larnaervon snorted. "That's a niggardly statement. Some are twice and three times that."

Unbelieving, Vivian reached for papers on the desk but was stopped by his hand grasping her wrist. When she glared at him, he grinned.

"Think of this, my dear. Piers and I will have our own interests at heart when we take care of your property. After all it becomes ours. We won't be trying to rob you blind or shut you up for a Bedlamite. It's to our best interests to keep you happy and healthy." He gradually released his grip on her wrist. His long fingers still encircled her skin without touching it. She might have been a small bird that he was testing to see if she were tame.

For her own part she did not move, fearful that if she did, she would be ensnared again.

He heaved a deep sigh. "From now on we'll manage the revenue from Stone Glenn as if it were our very own. Because it is. And all you have to do is sit back and enjoy the life it provides." His face assumed a crafty look. "And in due time you'll have a son or two to look after. That should please you. Good women are pleased to be mothers."

She could not help herself. She jerked her wrist out of his hand. A babe was one thing, but the process by which it was gotten, to lie with his drunken son, was quite another.

Biting her lower lip to control a rising tide of angry

123

resentment, she stabbed the pen into the inkwell and began to write.

He leaned over toward her but could not read the hastily scribbled words until she stabbed a point at the end, reversed it, and thrust it beneath his nose.

He read her words, grinned sardonically, then read them aloud. "'Let me return to Stone Glenn, or I will turn you over to the authorities.' And what authorities might that be, my dear? Can you name me one? A sheriff, perhaps. Or a justice perhaps? Perhaps you'll go to London again and demand an audience with the old mad king?" His expression turned menacing. He pushed the pad toward her. "Write the name of the one you'll turn me over to."

She ducked her head. He had called her bluff. She knew no one. No one at all. And she could not ask anyone.

He pushed the top of his cane up under her chin and forced her face up. "You'll do as I tell you. And as Piers tells you. You don't have a choice. So the faster you learn that the better."

"Is that how you persuaded Mother to come to you, Larne? No wonder your relationship was so loving!"

Neither member of the tableau moved. Vivian found she could not turn her head. The thick gold knob at the top of the cane pressed tightly into the hollow beneath her chin. Larne, determined to wring submission from her, held her in painful durance.

"If you keep that up, she'll be dead before she can marry me."

With a malicious grin and a twist of his wrist, Larne pulled the cane away. Vivian slumped back in the chair. "Her, dead. Never. Can you imagine another woman up on her feet after being driven at breakneck pace across the south of England? She's something, isn't she? A fine strong mother for my heir—through you, of course, Piers."

"How thoughtful you are, Larne. Planning lives when your own is a pathetic ruin."

The earl hefted his cane. "You dare to say such a thing to me."

Vivian looked from one man to the other. Their voices rose. The older man's withered cheek was suffused with red. The younger stood with clenched fists at the ready.

"The days when you could swing that cane and make me cringe are gone. Do it now and see what happens." Piers's jaw was set, his chin tucked into his chest. He looked at his father from beneath dark brows.

"You—" The earl raised the cane above his head.

Piers's fists came up. His left one rose to shoulder height. "Try it."

Vivian sprang from her chair and backed up against the bookshelves. Her movement distracted them both.

The earl followed her flight. Then he visibly relaxed. Again his shoulders twisted in the strange motion that passed for a shrug. "Not worth the trouble. She'll have me a real heir soon enough."

Piers let his fists drop to his sides. He, too, glanced at Vivian, a mirthless grin curving his mouth upward. "Don't be too sure. A few words don't make a marriage."

Larne's lips pulled back in a snarl. He shot a look of obdurate hatred at his son, then turned slowly to limp around the desk. Suddenly, a cackling laugh burst from between his withered lips. Like a snake he struck.

Vivian saw the movement as a blur. Her mouth opened in a silent scream. Piers barely got his forearm up to partially deflect the blow before it connected with a solid thud on his shoulder. Another inch to the right and it would have grazed his temple. Two inches and it would have rendered him unconscious.

Piers dropped back a step and caught the cane even as it rose to strike again. He jerked at it and twisted, but the taloned hand would not release the weapon.

"Damn you!" he panted, the pain streaking down his arm and across his chest.

"Damn you!" the earl shouted. "You'll not laugh at me. I'm still master here in this house." The old man's other arm flailed about. The inkstand went flying. Books and papers followed it.

The chair where Vivian had sat went over with a crash as Piers closed with his father, one fist locked round the cane, the other grasping his father's neck piece and ramming it up into the wattled throat.

Vivian darted to the bellcord hanging over the desk. As she yanked it, she heard the drumming. Someone was banging on the study door with imperious fists.

"Milord! Milord."

Neither man paid the slightest attention.

Piers bore his father back over the desk, his face suffused with blood, his eyes wild. "Give over, old man. Otherwise, I'll hurt you."

"You'll—not—" Larne was panting now, his white hair whipping out around his impassioned face. He still struggled to wrest the cane from his son. His feet had been lifted off the floor and now kicked impotently in the air.

"Milord! Larne!" Mrs. Felders called. The knocking became a steady pounding.

Vivian dashed around the struggling men and flung open the door. Watkins, Mrs. Felders, and Millard, the butler, burst into the room.

"Help him!" Mrs. Felders screamed. "Help the master." The two men sprang forward to part the combatants. Watkins grabbed the viscount by the arm

126

and dragged him back as Millard flung himself between the two. "Milord," he cried to the earl. "You mustn't."

As if the wind had gone out of his sails, the earl dropped back onto the desk. His empurpled face contrasted shockingly with his stark white hair. The veins throbbed in his temples with every beat of his heart. "Dared—me—"

"You'll do yourself an injury, Larne." Emma Felders hurried to his side and slid her arms around his twisted shoulders. "Please, milord. You must calm yourself."

"He—"

"Don't think about it." Over her shoulder she ordered Millard to pour some brandy.

While the butler obeyed, Watkins made a show of straightening the viscount's clothing, patting him with hands that fumbled what they sought to set to rights. "Are you injured, milord?" he muttered through his teeth.

"Not to speak of." Piers massaged his shoulder. He grinned reassuringly at his valet. "He's slowing down."

Vivian, hovering at the door, stared in consternation. What kind of man could sustain such a terrible blow and come away grinning? No one had ever lifted a hand to her. When she had entered into this house with Sister Grace such a short time ago, she had stepped into a different world. Here even natural death was unnatural and hate-filled, and fathers and sons regarded each other as adversaries. They even played violent games with each other. She could not doubt, the entire incident had been a game, a terrible contest with one taking great satisfaction in scoring off the other.

Larne downed the brandy that Millard had thrust into his hand and endured Mrs. Felders soothing with good grace. He held out the tumbler for more brandy and

127

drank it, too. His eyes never left Piers and Vivian, who stood poised on the threshold.

Millard moved between them, very much on his dignity. "Milords. The priest has arrived."

Larne gave a short bark of laughter. He pushed himself off the desk and shook off Mrs. Felders's hands. The gold-headed cane slid down in his hand and became once more a walking aid. "Then by all means let the wedding commence. I long to see these two happy people united in wedlock."

Chapter Eight

Sebastian Dawlish arrived just at sunset. With him were the solicitor Rowling, the Justice of Assizes Thomas Penstaff, Captain Rory McPherson of the local garrison with four of his men, and Mrs. Frances Eads.

Sebastian stomped into the hall, his face frostbitten, his eyes searching feverishly. "We've come for my ward. Vivian Marleigh. Where is she?"

"Sir," Millard stood firm in front of him as he strode toward the staircase.

"Out of my way."

"You can't just come in here," the butler began.

"Let him come, Millard." The Earl of Larnaervon opened the door of his study and stepped out.

"There he is, Captain," Sebastian cried. "Do your duty."

The young man hesitated uneasily. The earl cut an imposing figure in his black velvet coat, his long hair spreading over his shoulders.

"Do your duty, Captain MacPherson," Sebastian repeated, coming to a halt in front of the earl. His normally plump face was pinched with cold. A fever blister had popped out on his mouth and his lower lip was misshapen. "You have a warrant. Serve it."

The earl smiled unpleasantly. "I should be very sure that I was doing the right thing, Captain. Otherwise, you may be very sorry indeed before this business is over."

MacPherson needed no second warning. He was already thoroughly unhappy at being included in the expedition.

"Now, Mr. Dawlish." The justice sidled forward to put out a timid hand and pluck at Sebastian's sleeve. "Surely there is some misunderstanding here. Let's all keep our tempers and allow his lordship to explain. I'm sure it's a mistake that he can easily explain. You can, can't you?" He looked hopefully at the earl.

Rowling stepped in front of the timorous justice. "Misunderstanding indeed," he declared in his best oratorical style. "Kidnapping is not so easily explained. The lady was abducted. We have every reason to believe she was brought here."

"Oh, my sweet lady," Frances keened. "Kidnapped. Kidnapped right out of her hotel room. Right from under my eyes." She joined the group surrounding the earl, who stood stiffly, his hands folded over the top of his cane, his mouth twisted wryly. "You monster." She brandished her gloved fist. "What have you done with my lady?"

The earl's look would have melted chilled steel. "What lady might you have the presumption to call yours, madam?"

A real lady's maid would have cowered, completely intimidated by the earl's fierce demeanor, but Frances Eads had long ago rid herself of timidity and shame. "Why, Lady Marleigh, that's who! I've taken care of the sweet helpless child since she was a wee one."

"You lie," the earl declared. "Sebastian Dawlish hired you within the year before Miss Marleigh's

130

illness. Before that, you had never been close to a lady, let alone served one." His dark cold eyes stared at Frances until her fist wavered and she flushed and stirred uneasily. "'Tis strange to think how the illness came upon her so shortly after your arrival."

The statement had the effect of a lightning bolt striking in the room. Thomas Penstaff gasped and covered his mouth with his hand. The garrison captain stiffened. His keen eyes shifted from the earl to Dawlish, whose face reddened. The solicitor cleared his throat noisily and rocked back on his heels.

Frances's composure slipped. Her eyes darted to Dawlish, then dropped to the floor. Her mouth set in a sullen line. "I'm sure I didn't have anything to do with her catching pneumonia."

The earl did not deign to make her an answer, instead he signaled to Millard to escort them through to the downstairs parlor, a gloomy, dusty room, with no heat whatsoever. Emma Felders came from the foot of the stairs. "Tell Vivian that her guardian is here with an army to take her prisoner. Be particularly sure to tell her that they have brought the Eads woman with them."

"Yes, milord."

The quick look Frances Eads shot the lawyer was not lost on the garrison captain.

The earl remained standing in the hallway as the quintet looked round them in dismay, their breaths fogging before their faces. "Please to make yourselves comfortable," he invited, his smile a mockery. "I have sent Mrs. Felders to summon my son and new daughter-in-law, so you may confront them together."

"New daughter-in-law!"

"Oh, my precious lady."

"See here!"

"She can't marry without my consent."

131

"You will understand when I do not remain with you. My health is frail and the draughts of this room do an injury to my limbs." Larne stepped back over the threshold, and Millard closed the door on the storm of protests.

"They've come for you," Emma Felders said, her pinch-purse mouth spread in a malicious smile. "You'll be going with them I expect. Back where you belong."

Vivian did not pretend not to understand. A chill ran up her spine. Dawlish, of course, but who else? She wrote the question on the pad and thrust it under the housekeeper's sharp nose.

"Larne said to tell you that the Eads woman was among them below. And a couple of gentlemen, official by the look of them. There's a garrison captain in his full dress uniform, poking his nose into everything. I told his lordship the minute you bead rattlers walked through the door, you'd be trouble. But he wouldn't let his wife go off without a show. What did he care if the old bitch died? They'd hated each other for years."

Not waiting to listen to more of Mrs. Felders cruel and indiscreet remarks, Vivian picked up her skirts and hurried from the room. Halfway down the stairs she halted and clutched the banister with cold fingers.

The earl stood in the hall, his white hair overspread his black-clad shoulders. His black trousered legs and his gold-headed cane planted to form a triangle for balance. He looked immovable and infinitely menacing. "So," he said, "Sebastian calls and you come running."

She shook her head faintly; her mind spun in confused circles. *What am I doing?*

"You choose Dawlish and Rowling and Frances Eads," he sneered. "You must really believe that marriage to my son is a fate worse than death."

She shook her head again.

"I won't stop you," he sneered. "Come right down. Walk right into the parlor like a foolish fly into the spider's web."

Vivian took a step backward, then another. Her own sense of helplessness made her ill. Her voice. Her voice. If she could only find her voice. As it was she could not utter a single protest.

Behind the earl, the door to the parlor opened. Sebastian Dawlish stuck his head out. "Vivian!"

She backed another step.

The earl did not turn his head. He merely looked up at her, his mouth curved in a malicious grin.

"Vivian! Come here! The marriage can be annulled!" Sebastian called. He dashed to the foot of the stairs.

Behind him came Rowling, his voice quavering slightly with anxiety. "My dear Miss Marleigh, I'm sure you've put a wrong complexion on the whole affair."

The earl laughed nastily. "I'm sure she put exactly the right complexion on the whole affair."

"Vivian!" Sebastian started up the stairs, but the earl's cane shot out.

"No man goes up these stairs except by my express invitation."

Frances Eads came up on the other side, a seraphic smile on her face. "Shall I come up and help you get dressed, milady? The way I used to?"

Vivian retreated shaking her head.

The young captain of the guard stood in the threshold of the parlor taking in the scene. She caught his eyes, warm with sympathy. But he did not know whom to believe. He could never help her.

"Vivian!"

"Miss Marleigh."

"Please, milady. Let me help you."

All were lying. All of them. But she could not return with Sebastian. That way was sure disaster.

"The way you did before." The earl sneered at Frances. "Drugs in her tea. And how did she suddenly become so ill? Near to death, so I was informed, when she was taken to the abbey?"

"She had a bout with pneumonia," Frances insisted doggedly. "It just weakened her. I didn't have nothing to do with makin' her sick." Her cultered accent began to slip in her confusion.

"Frances, shut your mouth," Sebastian ordered. "Of course, you didn't have anything to do with making poor Vivian sick. She's always been sickly."

At his words Vivian turned and fled. Fled for her life, certain that if she fell into their hands she would be put away forever. At least here with the earl, she might have some chance. Some chance however slim was better than none.

Sebastian wheeled on the earl. "I have a warrant. The court has ordered her to go with me. She's my ward. You have no right to marry her to your son. The marriage isn't legal anyway."

"Ah, but it is. I assure you," the earl rejoined. "She was married today at noon by the good priest from St. Anselm's. I have the papers."

"Then the marriage hasn't been consummated." Sebastian seized upon the point immediately. "It can be annulled. Isn't that right, Pikestaff?"

"Er—Penstaff." The justice came forward. "I don't think . . . That is, I don't know that—"

"The marriage hasn't been consummated," Rowling finished for him in disgust. He started up the stairs. "Bring her down here and let's be on our way."

"Do you have a warrant to go up those stairs?" the earl demanded. "What say you, Captain MacPherson?

134

Are they in possession of a warrant?"

The captain shook his head. "I haven't seen one so far."

Dawlish shot him a scalding look. "Penstaff, do your duty."

"But—I—"

"For the lord's sake!" Dawlish was practically dancing up and down in his fury. "Take this idiot some place where he can sit down and tell him what to write."

Rowling took the little man by the shoulder and turned him back into the parlor. Dawlish and the captain followed them. Frances Eads put one foot on the first riser, but the earl hissed so viciously in her ear that she jumped back and scurried after them.

In her room Vivian wrapped her arms tight around her body. She had only minutes before her guardian would take charge again. Minutes while a timorous little man wrote a document dictated by her own solicitor. And taken to a madhouse. She shuddered. Her teeth chattered. Her knees threatened to give way. The earl had given her the very briefest of respites. She had only minutes to save herself.

A terrible idea took shape in her mind. Like a drowning person clutching at a single spar in a maelstrom, she embraced the thought.

The viscount was in his room. He had to be. Throwing the trailing blue velvet riding skirt over her arm, she bolted down the hall. She knocked at the door, but did not wait for him to answer. Instead she slipped inside and closed the door behind her.

He was sitting in his chair before the fire, a brandy glass in his hand. Watkins had helped him off with his coat, vest, and shirt and was dabbing at the hideous bruise on his shoulder. A single trickle of dark blood

135

ran over his white skin. The bicep of his muscular arm bulged beneath that skin.

Vivian swallowed, pressing her fists against her waist. Fear and heat, surprising in their intensity, curled in her belly. His chest was so wide; the dark hairs, thick in the center, emphasized its flat planes. The bicep jumped beneath Watkins's hand as the valet started at her unexpected entry. With strength like that, he could take hold of her—

A hideous embarrassment drained the color from Vivian's cheeks. She had come here in her desperate need. Yet how could she convey it to him? The idea of writing, of committing to paper what she wanted, what she wanted him to do to her drove the breath from her body.

Conscious of the sharply disapproving looks from both him and the valet, she opened her mouth to suck in air. She took a deep controlling breath and let it out slowly. Dropping the skirt of her riding habit, she allowed it to trail behind her as she crossed to Piers's side and took the cloth from Watkins's hand.

Piers stared at her white face. He took a swallow of brandy. "What the hell do you want?"

Vivian made a dismissing gesture to Watkins.

The man looked to the viscount for confirmation. When Piers nodded, he bowed slightly and left the room. Lifting the brandy to his lips again, Piers stared at her curiously.

His scrutiny making her more nervous than ever, Vivian washed the blood from his skin, conscious that this man was her husband. Dipping her fingers into the jar of salve, she smoothed it on, feeling the heat in his skin.

"Your fingers are cold," he observed without inflection.

She lifted them away, then shrugged helplessly.

136

"What did you come for?"

She shook her head, her eyes haunted.

Throughout the entire process, his eyes never left her face. As she was screwing the lid on the jar, he raised one dark eyebrow. "To what do I owe this 'wifely' concern? Don't pretend with me. Begin as you mean to go on."

Drawing on steel deep inside her, she managed to plaster a tentative smile on her stiff lips.

His dark eyes narrowed. "What are you up to?"

Her kiss answered his question. She had never kissed a man of her own volition. But she pressed her lips clumsily to his. His mouth was open to question her, a startled exclamation turned to a gasp. She pursed her lips against his and his tongue slid between them. The intrusion startled her. She jerked her head back.

His eyes were still open. His tongue slid provocatively over his lower lip. "The amateur wife?"

Tremors began deep in her belly. Her knees were close to buckling. Yet she could not pull away. She must somehow do what she had come to do. The alternative was prison in a hell too terrible for her imagining. Lowering her mouth to his again, she brushed his lips.

He grunted shortly and pushed her away. "What the hell are you about?"

She smiled and reached for the strip of linen that Watkins had laid by. Her fingers trailed across his skin as she placed the pad tenderly on the wound. She lifted his arm, so she could pass the strip under his armpit and bind the pad in place. Her fingers touched his chest, so near the aureola of his nipple that it tightened. Her eyes flew to his face, fearful of the tiger she was rousing.

He gasped, his nostrils dilating as his blood began to heat. In the firelight his pupils glittered beneath the dark fan of his lashes. "What have you come for?"

She finished the knot, tucked the ends under the edges of the bandage and lifted his hand. While he watched, she hesitated. Her index finger trembled. Then she pressed it down into his palm. "Love."

"Write that again," he ordered gruffly.

She flinched. "Love."

"You love me?" He snorted. "Permit me to doubt that."

She shook her head slowly. Again she wrote, "Love."

He stared at her, suspicion darkening his eyes, cynicism curling his mouth. "You want me to make love to you?"

She nodded. Her hands began to tremble. Her fingers felt icy. She longed to thrust them into her skirts, hold them out to the fire, anything to break the terrible contact with his.

He set the brandy glass down. "Now? Here?"

She did not nod. Instead she wrote, "Yes."

Rage so fearful flamed in his face that she tried to fling herself backward, but he caught her wrists and dragged her down to her knees in front of him. Her face was white with fear as she twisted to free herself.

"You! Come to me here in my room and try to seduce me?"

She struggled impotently against him. Her eyes burned as tears threatened to overflow.

"My father must have been deceived in you. He said you were a frightened virgin. But you're not frightened."

She shook her head, trying desperately to free her hand. She could not answer him unless she could write.

Effectively as a gag, he gathered her wrists together in one of his hard hands and caught her chin. Their faces were inches apart as he studied her. Contempt blazed in his dark eyes. "Are you pregnant with someone else's child? Sebby's perhaps?"

138

How could he guess at such a thing? She had never considered that her coming here would lead him to assume something so horrible. She tried to shake her head against his hand.

He felt the movement. "Not Sebby's. Not foolish, pitiful Sebby's."

She managed to wrest one hand free. Her nail scratched at his wrist.

"She-devil!" He let her go abruptly.

She caught his wrist and scratched.

"Damn you! Get a pencil and paper if you want to tell me something."

Her fear made her awkward. She tried to rise, fell back, tried again. Her feet slipped, her ankles twisted, tangled in the heavy folds of her velvet skirt.

He groaned and held up his hand. "Stop. Just calm down." He picked up the brandy glass. "I'll try to ask the right questions. Just nod your head if I'm right, and shake it if I'm wrong." He looked down at her floundering in the folds of her dress. "You can do that, can't you?"

At that moment she hated him with all her heart and soul. He had dragged her down there, then mocked her clumsiness.

He took a long drink and rubbed his bruised shoulder gently. "First." He pointed a long finger at her. "And tell me the truth on your life. Are you trying to foist someone's bastard off on me?"

She shook her head and grabbed at his hand.

He caught it back out of her reach. "None of that. I'll ask the questions, and you'll answer me without clawing me to ribbons."

She subsided, clenching her hands in the folds of her skirt.

He took a sip of brandy and regarded her steadily. She dropped her eyes to a spot of the floor beside his

139

boot, then shifted them abruptly to the blazing hearth as she realized she was staring at a spot of his blood. Her flaming cheeks whitened. "Did the earl send you?"

She shook her head.

"You came of your own free will? This was your idea?" he asked incredulously. "Pull the other one."

She nodded hastily.

"No."

"Yes." Her lips formed the word, then breath passed between them, but no sound came.

"But why?" he muttered. She moved restively. "Don't try to answer," he hastened to add. "This was your idea. But why did you decide to do it? Good lord! You can't have fallen in love with me?"

She shook her head violently.

"No need to be quite so adamant about that," he said sarcastically. "A simple shake or nod will be sufficient." He took a sip of brandy while he stared at her with knitted brows.

A knock sounded before he could frame the next question. Watkins came in and closed the door behind him. "Beg pardon, milord, but they're beginning to search for her."

Vivian struggled to get up, the skirt of her riding habit holding her down and threatening to send her toppling over backward.

"Here, be careful." Piers caught at her and assisted her to stand. "Who is going to search for her?"

"Mrs. Felders told me, rather gladly I might add, that they've come for her. Her guardian, her lawyer, old Judge Penstaff, and the captain of the local garrison."

"Good lord. MacPherson."

"Yes, sir."

Vivian buried her face in her hands. She could not think what to do. Her guardian would find her. He would take her away. No matter how much she resisted him, fought him even, she would lose. In the end she would have to eat, and her food would be drugged. Even a simple cup of tea. She stumbled away toward the door. Better to run. The place had a back stairs. Better death in the cold, clean snow.

Piers followed her and caught hold of her shoulders. She was breathing hard, her body shaking. He turned her toward him and forced her to look up at him. "Is this why you came to me? For help?"

She nodded. Her eyes tried to communicate her terror and her desperate need.

"Mrs. Felders took a lot of pleasure in telling me they're in the parlor now," Watkins put in, his tone worried. "The lawyer's telling old Penstaff what to write down and he's doing it. MacPherson's men'll be searching the house soon."

Piers let Vivian go and swung round. "They can't do that. My God! If they look in the cellar—"

"Yes, sir."

"Damn nuisance." He shot her an angry look, then flashed an ugly smile. "Looks like Larne's outsmarted himself this time. Oh, this is rich."

Watkins's face remained bland. "It would seem so, sir. Perhaps the best thing for all concerned would be for me to escort the lady downstairs and let them take her away."

At his words, Vivian twisted out from under Piers's hands and dashed for the door.

"Hold on there, damn you." Piers leaped after her to catch her shoulder and drag her back. Clapping one arm across the front of her body under her chin, he held her against him while he stared at Watkins. "They can't take her away. She's my wife."

Vivian shook her head violently and stabbed her finger into the back of his hand. "No."

141

"Stop that clawing, damn you."

Watkins too shook his head. His eyes skittered up to a spot somewhere near where the wall met the ceiling. "You haven't made her your wife, sir. They know that, and they mean to have her out of here before you have a chance to—er—"

The viscount's arm fell away. He stared at his valet, a slow red creeping up his neck. Whether from anger or embarrassment, Vivian did not know. She only knew that too much time had been wasted. She caught up the trailing skirt. If she could slip down the back stairs and reach the stables, she could ride for her life.

"Stop trying to run out of here." He caught her a second time and pulled her back against his naked chest. His voice was harsh in her ear. "You came here for that, didn't you?"

Shocked color flooded her cheeks. She was terribly conscious of Watkins's having left off studying the wall to gather up the towels and screw the lid on the jar of salve.

"You came here to seduce me to make yourself my wife. You came to consummate our marriage."

She closed her eyes. The embarrassment was enough to kill her. She felt his chest heave.

"Then consummate it we shall. Leave us, Watkins. And try to lead them everywhere but here."

"Yes, sir." The relief was patent in the valet's voice. He moved to the door, then paused seeking direction. "Not the cellar, of course, milord."

"No, not the cellar. But everywhere but the cellar and here."

He held her against him till the door closed behind the valet, then he turned her in his arms and stared down into her face trying to read her thoughts. "You must be very afraid."

She nodded. Her eyes were dry and aching. Her

142

throat swollen. Tears were not far away, but she could not let them fall. They might have only minutes. *How long did it take!*

He looked her up and down, feeling the tremors wracking her body. A door slammed somewhere below. She jumped. His fingers tightened. "When this is all over, you shall write me a long letter about what happened to you in London."

Suddenly, she was very aware that she was in the arms of a half-naked man. Excitement flushed her cheeks and she lifted her hands to his chest to push herself away.

"Don't do that," he murmured. "Don't push me away. Let it happen."

She bit her lip, a shiver running down her spine as the huskiness in his voice caressed her.

"Push your arms up around my neck," he suggested just before he bent to kiss her.

She slid her hands as he directed. The palms rasped the hair on his chest.

His arms tightened fractionally as one of her nails encountered his erect nipple. He groaned softly into her mouth and flinched. "Lord, that's sweet."

Her hands paused at his shoulders, lightly brushing over the bandage. She wondered if the wound were aching badly, wondering if he were too hurt to make love. Then her arms went round his neck.

His arms tightened around her. He tilted his head and deepened his kiss. When she took a deep breath, it lifted her against him. Womanly breasts under velvet rubbed against him. He could feel himself grow hot and hard, could hear his blood humming. Even if her brain was defective, the rest of her was certainly better than normal.

Never taking his mouth from hers, he shifted her slightly in his arms and unbuttoned her jacket. Even as

143

she stiffened, his hand dived between the lapels, found the buttons of her shirtwaist and opened it, too. A single layer of sheer linen separated him from her beating heart.

His hand cupped her breast, then squeezed it.

She twisted. Her right leg bent, her knee involuntarily nudged him.

He pulled his mouth away from her and looked down. "Good lord. Who taught you to do that?"

She looked at him dazedly. He squeezed her breast again. She shuddered so powerfully that her whole body vibrated against him. Unable to control herself, unconscious of her own sensuality, she moved against him. Her knee slid up between his thighs.

He heard the thud of footsteps on the stairs. "They're coming." She threw a frightened look at the door, then back at him, her eyes pleading. Stooping, he slid one arm beneath her knees and lifted her high on his chest. "Keep your arms around my neck," he commanded. "And your mouth on mine."

She closed her eyes and complied, her body trembling.

A couple of quick strides and he laid her on the bed, her legs hanging over the side. He drew back from her, staring down into her pale face. "Are you sure this is what you want to happen?"

She swallowed. Another door slammed somewhere. She nodded.

He grinned mirthlessly. "I've never made love on demand before. Nor have I ever had to rush. You will remember that this is not the best way?"

She nodded. Feet thudded, a man's voice called out, demanded, too muffled to be understood.

He stepped back and lifted her skirts and petticoats. His hand reached for the drawstring and then found the opening in her thin linen drawers. "God," he murmured. "What an initiation."

He unbuttoned his own breeches. His eagerness surprised him. Instead of feeling offended and outraged, excitement sang in his veins. He had not known himself at all. She was a desperate girl besieged on all sides. He should be sympathizing with her.

But sympathy would do her no good. "Spread your legs," he commanded, surprised at the hoarseness in his voice. He found her opening. "Damn. You're as dry as a desert."

She looked at him fearfully, then closed her eyes. Her fists clawed up double handfuls of the spread beneath her.

He eased two fingers into her tiny opening. Her eyes squinched shut and a frown creased her forehead. She was tight. So tight. And undoubtedly a virgin.

"Stop. You can't go in there." Watkins protested vociferously in the hallway.

"Do your duty, Captain MacPherson." Sebastian's voice mirrored his triumph. "We've run the prey to ground."

They burst into Vivian's room next door.

She opened her eyes. Her unspoken command came to him as clearly as if she had shouted the words.

With a short nod he placed himself at the entrance to her body and leaned. It was too tight. Too damned tight. No, it was giving. He could feel his own excitement throbbing, throbbing.

She clawed at the spread. Sweat broke out on her forehead. The excruciating pain mounted. Surely there could not be more. Surely. She could stand no more. No more! But it mounted.

She opened her mouth. A scream built inside her. She pushed it out of her lungs. But nothing happened. Nothing at all.

And then suddenly, he burst through the gossamer

shield. His long thick length slid into her virgin passage.

Behind him the door swung open, but he did not hear it. His own body reacted to the pressure, and the slickness, and the heat. He exploded. A cry of triumphant release burst from his lips.

In the doorway Sebastian Dawlish gave a groan and then cursed violently. He took a step toward the couple on the bed, but Captain Rory MacPherson caught him by the arm and dragged him back. "Looks like you got here too late, sir. The marriage has been consummated. And that's plain for all to see."

Chapter Nine

"Have I killed you?"

Vivian opened her eyes. The canopy of the bed swam through a veil of tears; the folds of the material wavered. Never had she experienced anything so painful. *I've been raped,* she thought, irony keeping the tears at bay. *And I begged my ravisher to do it.* And hard on the heels of that thought, came the next. *I should have killed myself. Death would have been preferable.*

Piers lifted himself gingerly from between her slender thighs and slid to the side. As the bed sank beneath his weight, she lolled slightly, her shocked muscles flaccid.

He, too, stared at the canopy, his heart slowing, his breathing steadying. A wry smile curled on the corners of his mouth. Love on demand. And just in the nick of time. He was still pumping into her when he felt the rush of chill air on his buttocks. God! Sebastian must have been furious when he pushed opened that door. A minute more. So close.

In flagrante delicto had never had a truer interpretation. His sense had been blazing indeed.

Flexing the muscles of his arms which had borne the

147

weight of his upper body above her, he grinned. He would have given much to see the expression on Sebby's face. But then he would not have been able to show Sebby his backside. Chuckling, he rolled over lazily to stare at his wife.

The girl beside him stirred.

He ran a hand over his chest, scratching reflectively. She lay almost as he had left her, except that she had thrown one arm across her eyes. In profile, she looked like a pile of clothing, her skirts and petticoats wadded around her waist. Her jacket and shirtwaist unbuttoned. One side of her linen chemise was pulled down to expose a small perfect breast peaked with a rosy nipple. He moistened his lips, wondering what she tasted like. Hastily he slid his eyes down to the froth of her petticoats. From beneath them he stared at a slender, curving thigh.

Propping himself up on his elbow, he saw that her feet still dangled over the edge of the bed. She still wore her hose and boots. He groaned and sank back. What an initiation! Would she ever let him touch her again?

She shuddered. Her fist clenched. Then she resolutely lowered her arm and pushed herself up on her elbows. He watched the slowly dawning horror as she stared at the lower half of her body. At the base of the flat plane of her belly, her pale hair was matted. Bright red blood stained it and smeared her thighs.

Her movement had the effect of tilting her pelvis. Hot liquid trickled out of her. Hideously embarrassed, she clamped her legs tight together and pushed clumsily at her petticoats.

"Don't." His voice rasped in her ears.

She shuddered. Her body swayed as her vision swirled and wavered.

He caught her by the elbow, tugging gently. "Lie back. This is not how we should leave this."

She shook her head. The movement seemed to drive out some of the nauseating dizziness.

"Don't go." He tried again, his voice a deep velvet sound. "We can make this right."

She looked at him, horror and disbelief in her face. Catching hold of the bedpost, she pulled herself to her feet. Her skirts fell down arond her legs and more liquid coursed down her thighs. She stepped away from the bed. A quick agonized look over her shoulder drove the rich color into her cheeks. She had bled onto the spread.

He followed her look. "Don't be concerned about that. It's natural enough. It'll stop. It's probably stopped already."

Her eyes flickered, drawn against her will to his body. He still lounged naked with his pantaloons and small clothes crumpled around his knees. His limp organ nestled in the bush of dark red hair at the base of his belly. The bright red blood glistened on it. Against the stark white skin of the true redhead, it looked as if it curled on a bed of glowing coals.

Sick to her stomach, she swung around and staggered to the fire, holding out her shaking hands to warm them.

Behind her, he hastily struggled to his feet and pulled his clothing into place. When he had put himself to rights, he poured two brandies and pressed one on her. "Now, there's no need to run," he soothed. "Drink this."

She accepted it gratefully and tossed it down. Another shiver and another.

He went to pour another tot. "Another drink and then I'll carry you into your room where you can lie down. As I said, this is not the way to leave this."

She shook her head, turning away from the fire. With stiff fingers she buttoned her blouse and the

149

jacket over it. Neither was enough. She felt vulnerable, helpless, exposed. Even a suit of medieval armor would never be enough.

Between her legs the torn edges of her flesh burned. The single glass had rendered her light-headed and swaying slightly on her feet.

Piers took a sip of his own brandy, regarding her narrowly, waiting to reach forward to steady her.

In the silence the knock on the door startled them both. The liquid sloshed in Piers's glass, and Vivian flung out a hand to clutch the back of a chair.

Her face was white but composed. She nodded to him.

"Come in."

"Begging pardon, milord, milady." Watkins's face was impassive. In no way did he betray his part in what had taken place only minutes before. "Lord Larnaervon requires your presence downstairs. The guests are departing and wish to make their farewells."

Piers gave a short bark of laughter. "I'll bet a monkey they do." He laid a hand over her cold one. His eyes met hers. "You don't have to go if you don't want to. I can make your apologies."

She threw him a hopeful, grateful look.

He smiled encouragingly. "On the other hand, if you would face them with a smile, you'd never have any trouble again. Rowling would skip back to London with his tail between his legs. And Sebby—" While he spoke he slipped into the clean shirt that Watkins selected for him. "Come on, m'dear. Don't you want to throw a spoke into old Sebby's wheel?"

She shuddered.

The valet and the master exchanged knowing glances. Piers continued, his voice soothing and encouraging. "Actually, you don't ever have to see either one of them again, but you would do us a great

150

favor if you'd present the happily-married-woman-act to that garrison captain. MacPherson is fast becoming a trial. Ambitious and honest. He just might take what he suspected to be your plight as his own crusade."

While he was speaking, he allowed Watkins to finish dressing him and to catch back his wild wine-dark hair in a black riband. He ran his hand across his chin. "I could do with a shave, but I don't suppose there's time for that."

Watkins shook his head. "I'm afraid not, sir. Mr. Dawlish was most belligerent. He was threatening and cursing when I left the room."

Piers laughed again. "And well he might. Bad enough if he'd just seen it himself. He could have lied about what he'd seen. But to have MacPherson see it too—It's rich."

Vivian thought she would faint from embarrassment so profound that it made her breath catch in her throat. At least three men had actually seen her beneath a man, in the act of fornication. Only by taking deep breaths could she control the ringing in her ears. How could he laugh? He was actually enjoying this whole thing hugely. While she had destroyed her honor and her reputation, he saw the whole affair as nothing more than a chance to score off her guardian.

Words bubbled in her throat, bubbled and boiled like a hell-broth, and fell back unsaid. Frustration with her disability made her ill. An all-consuming rage swept her. It drove away the dizziness and brought a little more color to her paper-white cheeks.

Piers saw it and nodded. "Ready to go down, wife?"

She lifted her hands to her hair and smoothed the errant strands back from her temples. Pulling the long skein over her left shoulder, she combed her fingers through it until it was smooth and she could swing it back.

151

"Very attractive," he murmured. "Now?"

She would have liked to tell him no. But above him, above all else, she hated and despised Sebastian Dawlish. Her guardian's greedy machinations had brought her to this pass while Piers had only done what she had asked him to. Moreover, she had agreed to the marriage. Struggling between honesty and revulsion, she allowed her new husband to lead her from the room.

The downstairs parlor fairly steamed with the exhaled breath of rage. Sebastian Dawlish strode up and down the center of the room, his comments to Rowling interlaced by curses. The London solicitor sat straight in a brocaded French chair, his fingers curved tightly over the arms. His face had a distinct gray cast around the mouth. Thoughts of his reputation, even his position with his father's firm skittered about in his head as he wished himself anywhere else but in this cold, inhospitable house.

Frances Eads, looking hideously discomfitted, perched on a chair on the opposite side of the room, her traveling cloak drawn tightly around her against the chill. Penstaff had sidled to the door which he kept eyeing with unsuppressed longing. He clasped his hands behind him and rocked back and forth on his heels.

Leaning against the wall, one polished boot crossed over the ankle of the other, Captain Rory MacPherson regarded Dawlish and Rowling. His quick mind noted all the heavy man said to his solicitor. More than once, Rowling shushed Dawlish, but the man's rage was too great to bottle up. Forth it spewed, and with it the information that the lady was possessed of a considerable fortune which Dawlish had managed as if it had been his own.

Suddenly, the door opened. The butler ushered in

the earl, his cane tapping, his white hair lifting in the fierce draughts that rushed from the room. "Will you gentlemen be joining us for an extended stay?"

At the unmistakably ironic tone, Penstaff blanched. "No, sir. Not at all. I must be leaving. I hate being on the roads so late. But I came with, that is, I was brought by Mr. Rowling." He looked anxiously at the solicitor. "I really must be leaving."

Rowling looked at him, then back at Dawlish. "Shall I send him in the carriage?"

"No!"

"I shall be happy to lend Mr. Penstaff the use of one of our vehicles," the earl said smoothly.

"Very good. Oh, very good. I do hope this unfortunate incident . . . that is . . . precipitant visit . . . that is . . . awkward . . . um . . ." Penstaff bowed and then bowed again before either of the men could protest. As the butler was closing the door, he slipped through.

"Would anyone else care to leave now?"

Frances Eads half rose out of her chair, but a look from Rowling dropped her back into it. The corners of her mouth curled in a sneer.

"My son and daughter-in-law will be down in a minute. Being newly wedded, they were naturally drawn upstairs." The earl smiled silkily. "May I suggest that you not plan to stay past tomorrow when they will be departing on their honeymoon?"

"She's a prisoner here," Dawlish declared angrily. "He was raping her."

"Did you hear her scream for help?"

"She can't scream," Dawlish pointed out instantly.

The earl nodded. "Ah, you are right. I forget." He turned to the captain. "The dear lady is so remarkably self-sufficient. She nursed my late wife, you know? Had much to do with making the countess's last days easier.

153

I assure you if she had wanted to impart any information to you, she would have done so."

"Nonsense," Sebastian interrupted angrily. "I shudder even now to think of her helpless body. Kidnapped and abused. A tragedy. I shall not leave here unless she goes with me."

"Ah, but she retreated up the stairs away from you. Strange that she should not have run down to you to rescue her." The earl made the statement directly to the garrison captain.

"She misunderstood what happened to her in London. She is not what she should be. That is why I have continued to be her guardian. I would have set her down and explained everything to her slowly and carefully in a way she can understand, but she was kidnapped." He turned to MacPherson. "You hear that, don't you? Damn it, man. She was kidnapped. She's being held here against her will. What we witnessed was the torment of a poor helpless girl."

"A girl whose life you have been guiding with such vigilance," the earl remarked ironically.

"Well, of course. She couldn't be expected to manage—"

"—the huge estate—unentailed, I might add—and the accounts by herself," the earl continued for him. His lips peeled back from his teeth in a wolfish grin directed pointedly at Rowling. "Of course, she did have the help of a very old and reputable London law firm. Although her account was not handled by one of its senior members."

The solicitor bridled, his face red, his breathing pumping as MacPherson and the earl both scrutinized him. "I—My father—"

His explanation was forestalled when the door swung open again. Vivian, dressed in her blue riding habit, walked into the room her hand laid formally on Piers's arm.

154

MacPherson straightened away from the wall.

Within arm's reach she passed him, so close he could see the faint trace of a blue vein throbbing in her temple. Her back was as straight as a lance; her skin, as pale as her hair and fine-grained as silk. Her mouth was set as if she would never smile again. In that moment the captain fell in love.

Dawlish sprang forward. "Vivian, my poor dear child. What an ordeal! You were never meant for this life at all." He signaled to Frances. "We'll take you away from this ravisher." He glared at Piers. "Monster. These are modern times. You can't treat a woman like that. Even if she is your wife."

Rowling stepped forward and bowed low. Hot color flamed across his cheekbones. "My dear Miss Marleigh, I assure you that whatever misunderstanding may have arisen in London can be easily clarified."

"I doubt that will be your problem from now on," Piers spoke coldly. "Lady Polwycke's affairs will no longer be handled by Barnstaple and Rowling."

The color drained from Rowling's face. He actually stumbled in his haste to stretch out his hand to Vivian. "No. Miss Marleigh, I beg you to let me explain. You mustn't allow that. You know we have always handled the Marleigh estates."

Her look was arctic ice, but desperation made him bold. He reached out and clasped her free hand to draw her away from Piers's side.

Furious at his presumption, Vivian jerked out of his grasp.

Even as she turned, Sebastian too lurched forward. He threw a heavy arm around her shoulders and pulled her against his corpulent body. "Vivian. Vivian. Poor child." He glared at the others. "She doesn't know what she's doing. Poor sick thing. She needs the care of the good sisters."

Quick as thought, Vivian spun away. Rage, frustra-

155

tion, helplessness, the agony of betrayal all combined in one burst of violence that shook her whole slender frame. Teeth bared, she swung at Dawlish, not with an open palm, but a double fist. She swung with all her might and caught him full on his lying mouth. His lips smashed against his teeth, his head snapped back, and he staggered. With a muffled cry of pain, he clapped his hand to his face and, rubber-legged, dropped to his knees.

The earl gave a triumphant bark of laughter. "Bravo, Boadicea!"

"Miss Marleigh!"

At Rowling's cry, she spun and came at him fists flying. Frances Eads sprang shrieking to her feet and dodged behind the chair.

The earl laughed again.

Captain MacPherson shook his head, an admiring grin spread over his honest face.

Only Piers moved. He caught Vivian around the waist and lifted her back off her feet. "Easy," he murmured in her ear.

She kicked back and jabbed at him with her elbows. The skein of blond hair lashed around and sprayed across the dark superfine of Piers's coat. Rowling hastily backed away.

"Easy," Piers chuckled in her ear. "You've made your point."

"I suggest to the three of you that you are no longer welcome here." The earl's voice soared in triumph. "Perhaps, Mr. Rowling, if you will assist Mr. Dawlish—"

Sebastian staggered to his feet. "You haven't heard the last of this. She's not in her right mind."

Vivian clawed herself out of Piers's grasp and sprang at her erstwhile guardian again.

When Dawlish cringed, Captain Rory MacPherson

stepped between them. Vivian stopped, brought up short against the broad chest covered in coarse blue wool and brass buttons. "I think 'tis time for us to be leavin'."

Piers came up behind her and put his hands on her shoulders. "I couldn't agree with you more, Captain. Glad you could come by though. Nice to know that our shores are safe, so to speak."

MacPherson shot him an intense look over the top of Vivian's head. "I try to do my duty, sir." His eyes dropped to Vivian's. His gaze was warm and admiring. "Would you like to speak with me, milady?" He paused meaningfully. "Alone."

Every person in the room tensed. Sebastian shot Rowling a frightened look. The earl's eyebrows rose. Piers sucked in his breath.

Vivian drew in a deep breath and pushed automatically at a lock of fine hair that had tossed across the front of her riding habit. With one hand she smoothed it while she tugged at the bottom of her jacket disarranged where Piers had held her. She was conscious that Piers had dropped a proprietary hand on her shoulder.

"With your permission, sir?" The captain inclined his head.

Piers's fingers clenched. He shook his head. "I don't see—"

Rory MacPherson was adamant. "Perhaps I can just satisfy myself that the lady is really where she wants to be."

Even the cold air seemed to freeze between them. A half-dozen pairs of eyes trained on Vivian.

She stepped out from under Piers's hand to a point apart from everyone.

"Milady?" MacPherson bowed formally to her.

"That won't be necessary, Captain. She is where she

wants to be," the earl asserted smoothly. "She has made her choice and recited her vows of her own free will. Isn't that right, daughter?" He gave a peculiar emphasis to the last word.

Depression and unhappiness drained the strength from her body. The burning ache between her legs reminded her of what had occurred hardly an hour before. She could barely think, certainly not clearly. This handsome young captain with the kind eyes offered her an escape. But to what?

She was not living in a fairy-tale world. She lived in a world where men ruled—by laws made by them for their convenience. She was trapped by them—as they had meant she should be.

She shuddered. Her eyes swept the group of men. The earl's face was grim. Piers waited, his face resigned.

Sebastian Dawlish grinned, his smashed lips peeling back. His expression set off warning bells in her mind. A swift glance at Rowling showed her that he was leaning forward expectantly. If she left this haven— surely a strange and hellish place to find a haven—they would find a way to get her back under their control.

Too late! Too late for her to save herself. When all was said and done, she had never really had a chance. Ill luck had turned her into a prize, a succulent bone thrown down between savage dogs. She had just as much chance as that bone. She tipped her head back in her effort to keep her tears from falling.

"Miss Marleigh?" MacPherson asked softly.

If only she had met him sooner—known that he might be her friend. She put out her hand to him. The earl's stick tapped as he took a step forward, but Vivian was already shaking her head. She put her hand on the captain's arm and looked up into his blue eyes. Gently she pressed her fingers into the coarse cloth, then stepped back.

Behind her Sebastian's curse covered up the relieved expulsion of Piers's breath.

"A toast to the new bride." The earl raised his glass to Mrs. Felders.

She knotted her mouth into a purse. "You've made a bad mistake," she predicted direly. "That girl's already brought trouble. We've had too many visitors. You should have let me shove her out the door when that captain rode up the drive."

"Nonsense. They went away without suspecting a thing about the business."

"They'll be back. She'll draw them back again and again, until they'll come at the wrong time."

"She's an heiress," he pronounced gleefully. He leaned forward and held out his hands to the glowing coals on the hearth. "My son now controls her estate. If anyone comes snooping around, we'll simply pay off the men and send them away."

Behind his back the housekeeper scowled. "Beddoes won't like that. This is a sweet business."

"Beddoes will do as he's told." The earl turned his head. The long white hair swung down, glowing red in the reflected light. "He's made more than any man of his station can expect to make in three lifetimes. If I say quit, he'll quit."

"He won't like it. And he won't see the point of it. We've got a sweet arrangement. It's not fair to a man who's risked as much as Jack has to tell him to give it up and walk away."

The earl straightened and reached for his stick. The high spots of color on his cheeks were not from the heat of the fire. "He'll do as he's told!"

"It's not—"

"Emma! He'll do as he's told. And so will you." The

159

earl stalked forward and caught her upper arm in a punishing grip. "Get busy and serve dinner. Although it's probably inedible by now."

In his corner of the lurching carriage, Sebastian Dawlish glared at Rowling. "I should have insisted that they search the cellar."

"The cellar?" Rowling had pulled his hat over his eyes. He slouched in the corner, his ankles crossed in the seat on which Dawlish sat. Desperately, he courted sleep to still the thoughts that raged in his brain. Old Barnstaple would have his head when the request came for the Marleigh papers.

The estate was a plum, a long-standing trust of the firm. It accounted for several hundred pounds a year in legal fees and required almost nothing but the most minimal administration. For this reason he had been given it. And when Dawlish had approached him with this scheme, he had seen a chance to make extra money. He shifted uncomfortably as he thought of the incoming bills he would have to find a new way of paying.

"The cellar," Dawlish snarled. "We might have been lucky. There might have been something stashed there."

"Like what?" He would have to put off his plans to make the improvements on the town house. He would have to stave off the carriage maker for the new coach. He would have to refuse to take the order of the new boots.

"The stuff from France."

"France?" Good God! He would probably lose his position. Barnstaple could easily decide to boot him right out of the firm. Perhaps they would keep him on as a clerk as a favor to his father's memory.

Dawlish drove his fist into the side of Rowling's thigh. "Pay attention, you idiot. In the old days, the Larnes were smugglers. That's how they kept up that moldering pile and the dirty acres around it. Land's not worth tuppence."

Rowling sat up, dropping his feet onto the floor. He stared through the dimness at Dawlish's face. How had he ever been led into anything by this man? He had taken a garrison captain of the coast guard into the house of a known smuggler and kept the man searching the upper bedrooms. "Are you sure about this?"

"Of course. Damme." Dawlish scrabbled for his cane on the floor. "We'll go back. I'll set MacPherson on them."

Rowling stayed his hand. "You fool. The chances are we won't find anything now. They were probably moving it out while we were clambering around in the bedrooms. Besides, it's the middle of the night. Spend the night at the next inn and make our plans."

"Right." Dawlish struck his cane on the roof of the carriage and bawled the new instructions.

Rowling frowned heavily. "The best thing might not be to catch them with the goods in the cellar."

"Why not?"

"The stuff's got to come into land. Set a trap. Bring the viscount out of the house where he can be killed. He's no good to you alive in prison. She'd still be married to him. But dead. She's a widow."

Dawlish grinned. "Very smart, Rowling. Very smart indeed."

Chapter Ten

Vivian's hand trembled against the heavy oak as she closed the door behind her and leaned her forehead against its cool surface. Somewhere in the house a clock began to chime. She counted nine strokes. Nine o'clock. And she could not remember when she had eaten or drunk. Real pangs shot up from her belly.

Turning back into the room, she stiffly crossed to the hearth and bent to poke up the fire. It had burnt out long ago and now the ashes were scarcely warm. She straightened with a sigh. When had her life passed out of her control? When had she lost warmth and food and freedom from pain?

She stood on her wedding day in an old riding habit, in a room she did not recognize as her own, her hearth cold, her stomach empty.

She could not live like this. She would not!

Even as she formed the defiant thought, a knock sounded at her door.

She stiffened warily.

"Vivian."

Her husband had knocked at her door. She shrank back against the mantel. *Oh, no. Not now. Surely to heaven, not now.* The sudden movement reminded her

162

forcibly that her nether parts were still tender.

"Vivian." He opened the door. His smile faded. "No need to cringe trembling like a frightened rabbit," he said brusquely. "I'm not a monster come to have another go at your tortured body."

Embarrassed, she drew herself up and lifted her chin.

"That's better." He came to her and held out his arm. "Lady Polwycke, I've come to escort you down to dinner."

At the mention of food, her stomach rumbled so loudly that they both heard it. His eyes met hers and he grinned. "And just in time, too. Shall we?"

She held out the skirt of her riding habit and looked down at it ruefully.

He shrugged. "Under the circumstances a perfectly acceptable garment. The lateness of the meal, don't you know? Not even time for a whisky. And I've been dry for hours. Indeed, I think our dress will be excused. My own attire looks a trifle like it's been slept in."

She glanced down before she could stop herself. His pantaloons were badly creased. She lifted her eyes quickly, her expression agonized. A blush rose into her cheeks.

He laughed. "There you go again. You spent too long in the nunnery, m'dear. But that's all over. You'll have to get used to my humor, such as it is. We'll make an entrance together. My lady." He caught up her hand and bowed low over it, holding her fingers in the manner of the minuet of another era. His lips brushed her skin, then he twisted his head around to shoot her a playful look.

She hesitated only a brief moment, then nodded. As he straightened, she sank down in a regal curtsy befitting a presentation at court.

"Delightful. Shall we go then?" He drew her up.

"Mustn't keep the culinary masterpieces waiting. They should be viewed in all their blackened splendor. Especially considering how long they've been held. Unfortunately, Cook has limited abilities at the onset." He chuckled with more gallows humor. "The food will undoubtedly be a unique experience."

Together they descended to the dining room. Murky gilt mirrors on either side of the doors reflected their images side by side. He halted them. "Not too bad, considering the circumstances." He ran his free hand over his chin. "I need a shave."

She took his key from him. With her free hand she caught her long hair.

"You do need a hair style," he agreed. Then he shrugged. "We'll get better. Tomorrow."

Critically, she studied first their reflection and then his face turned to the light. To her eyes he had a very handsome face with fine chiseled features, yet somehow he was pitiable. Despite his one or two humorous sallies in her bedroom, his mouth had set in stern lines as they descended. His skin looked almost unnaturally pale. His eyelids drooped in affectation of ennui that she perceived was not entirely assumed. Beneath his eyes swollen pouches bespoke last night's drinking.

Perhaps enhanced by his wrinkled clothing and shadow of a beard, the tainted air of dissipation clung to him. What had she married? Then she remembered that he had recently lost his mother. Perhaps she was mistaking grief for cynicism. After all he had helped her to get to London on that most disastrous of all trips. She smiled slightly and shook her head at his reflection.

"You do not agree?" He pretended astonishment, turning his head from side to side and studying his face. "What, pray tell, about m' face displeases you, madam?"

Rather than answer, she smiled and drew him gently away from the mirror and in through the double doors.

Faintly irritated, he scowled at her. "You must tell me later."

They entered the dining room where he led her to the sideboard. An array of decanters and glasses gleamed dully in the light from branches of smoking candles. "Will you have a drink?"

She shook her head.

As the lone footman hurried from the back hallway to pour a glass for Piers, Larnaervon entered the room, followed closely by Mrs. Felders. Their arrival was a signal for the meal to begin. The footman set the decanter down with a clink and hastened to hold the chair at the head of the table for the earl. With a glare of disapproval at the two young people, Mrs. Felders bustled out.

Tossing down the drink as if it were water, Piers set the glass on the sideboard and conducted Vivian to the chair halfway down the long table on the earl's right. When she was seated, he walked around the table and seated himself opposite her on his father's left. The footman placed his drink beside his service.

The earl stared at one and then the other, noting their white faces and rumpled clothing. He signed to the footman to pour a pale French wine into their glasses. His voice raspy, he lifted his in a salute. "To the future countess of Larnaervon. My dear, you do us proud."

Vivian looked at him in some amazement.

"Didn't she do us proud, Piers? Like Boadicea. Warrior queen of the Britains. Magnificent. My grandsons will be fighters everyone. I couldn't be more pleased with you both. Especially since you've already got to work on begetting them."

The footman splashed the ladle into the soup.

Surreptitiously, he dabbed at a spot on the tablecloth. Vivian's eyes flew from father to son and then down to her lap. Her cheeks flushed bright red in embarrassment.

His face impassive, Piers reached for the glass beside his plate and drank deeply. "Larne," he replied, carefully setting the glass down. "You must learn to moderate your language from now on. We will be having a lady present at our table."

The earl laughed again. "A lady. Ah, well, perhaps I have forgotten." He leaned forward, his silver hair swinging. "Do you find my language offensive, daughter?"

How to answer to convey her shock and embarrassment? Vivian looked to Piers.

"She doesn't say a word," Larne went on gleefully. "Not a word. The perfect wife. That's what I've arranged for you, you young fool, and you don't appreciate my efforts."

"Larne."

"Hell and damnation, boy. I'll say what I want at my own table and I advise you to do the same. Begin as you mean to go on. I never changed my way of living for any woman."

"Perhaps you should have."

"Bah! Georgina never acted as if she minded. But if she did, and if I'd changed, she'd still be dead," he snarled heartlessly. "And you'd still be the only son of my body because she couldn't have any more after that one time."

Vivian twisted nervously in her chair. The footman had finished serving the soup and had moved silently to the sideboard. She could tell by the very stillness of his body that he was listening and taking in every word that was being said.

Larne dipped his spoon into the soup and sipped it

166

noisily before raising his head. "I really didn't expect you to come down tonight. I was sure you'd want to take her back to your bed."

"Larne," Piers warned. "That will do." He held his glass for the footman to fill, but the earl waved the man back.

"Don't drink any more, fool. Wine mars the performance."

So overset she could not think, Vivian picked up her spoon with a trembling hand. She must eat. On a full stomach this whole conversation would undoubtedly gain a proper perspective. When she took a spoonful of soup, she almost gagged. It was barely lukewarm and the consistency of gummy sauce. Its taste was appalling. Setting the spoon down hurriedly, she reached for the wineglass at her right. Over its rim, she caught Piers's mocking gaze. Raising his glass, he toasted her.

The servants ate much better food than this. She knew for she had eaten with them while she had nursed the countess. She looked to the earl, but he seemed to notice nothing wrong. She frowned.

The second course was no better. Cold, overcooked cabbage lay limply gray beside a white sliver of fish without a sauce of any kind.

The Earl of Larnaervon appeared to ingest everything with no trouble whatsoever, and Vivian began to suspect that he had no sense of taste. She stared at him from under her lashes. Was he merely eating from habit? Her eyes shifted. And was his son merely drinking from habit?

Throughout the meal, the old man joked and laughed. For Piers he had advice, shockingly sexual. Vivian found she could not swallow. Another footman had joined the first at the sideboard.

From time to time, Larne directed remarks to her

concerned Sebastian's anger and the solicitor's discomfiture. When he laughed heartily, he did not mind that he laughed alone. He spoke of Frances Eads. "How could you have thought she was a suitable companion?" he asked. "Why she fairly reeked of the cribs and stews of Cheapside."

Vivian clenched her fists. Words rose in her throat, words to explain her helplessness, her naïveté, her misplaced faith in Sebastian, who had always presented such a kind face and always brought her thoughtful gifts. She wanted to scream them out. She framed them with her mouth, twisted her tongue around them, pushed against the back of her teeth, but no sound came.

Piers made no remark. The old man moved on to the subject of Captain MacPherson and for the first time the virtual monologue seemed to take a serious turn. "I quite believe he was satisfied with everything. Do you agree?"

"In-Indubitably, Larne." Piers lifted his glass and drank to his agreement. "He wash shatisfied that S-Sebby wash a crook. He probably thought we were, too, but my dear—my esh-timable wife wouldn't go out of the room wi' 'im." He looked at Vivian, his eyes blearing. "Why?"

She stared at his plate, noting that he had eaten almost nothing. A bite of the fish, none of the vegetable. Instead he continued to drink steadily from the wine which he did not allow the footman to water. Both men looked at her as if waiting for her to suddenly make a statement.

Then the earl laughed. "Why because she's your wife, you fool. And she knows which side her bread's buttered on. Don't you, daughter dear?" He leaned forward. "I promise you this, Vivian Marleigh. You give me a grandson and you can have whatever is in my power to give you." He sank back in his chair as the footman cleared the food away. Lifting his glass, he regarded its color in the light. "You'll never be shut up in a nunnery or locked up in a cell in an insane asylum either. I promise you that. Just give me that boy."

Another course was brought, this time a roast of beef charred black on the outside. A dry, gristly slice was placed on Vivian's plate. Privately, she thought it looked like nothing so much as a pile of burnt matchsticks as she pushed at it with her fork.

The earl at that moment took notice of her riding habit. "I would think a bit more formality in your dress, daughter dear."

She shot Piers a quick look.

"I do not mind your riding. In fact exercise is good for young bodies. I used to exercise myself. I was not always as you see me now," the earl declared. He stared at her critically. "But at the dinner table, I like to see a woman in a bright dress, perhaps with a jewel or two about her throat." He turned to his son. "See that she has a pick from your mother's jewels."

Piers nodded stolidly. He had given up all pretense of eating.

Larne cursed softly, then smiled at his daughter-in-law. "Please send for a mount at any time. Ride as long as you like. We have grooms aplenty in the stables. Just be sure you do not ride after you've conceived. Too much danger of accidents." For his son he had only a sneer. "Right, m'boy?"

"If y' shay sho, Larne." Piers held out his glass for the footman to fill again.

"Heard of many a woman losing her baby, falling—" He went on and on.

By the time the butler served dessert, a lumpy pudding, unattractive and tasteless, Vivian's mortification on the subject of childbearing had subsided into disgust. Almost she prayed for the peace of the abbey. At least there, the conversation had been quiet, though dull, and the food well prepared, though plain. Here she had been insulted with every other sentence and served such food as would make convicts run riot. Such food should not be tolerated. Under no circumstances should servants be allowed to serve this mess.

She caught a glimpse of Mrs. Felders standing in the door surveying the scene. Vivian shot the housekeeper an accusing glance and spooned up a bite of the maltasting stuff, to let it plop back uneaten in her dish. The woman merely pursed her mouth even tighter.

Undoubtedly, these people were paid well, or they would not stay and work. Mrs. Felders wore black silk. She should oversee this house better. The servants should be compelled to perform their duties in a proper fashion.

If she were really the lady of the house—

"Shall we withdraw, Vivian?" Piers's slurred voice interrupted her smoldering thoughts. Listing distinctly to the left, he rose from his chair as the footman pulled it back. One hand on the edge of the table steadied him until he could walk stiffly around to her side. "I could do with a breath o' fresh air. P'rhaps the garden—"

From his seat at the head of the table, the earl let out a sarcastic bark. "Good! Good! Romance her. Take her for a turn in the moonlight. With snow on the ground. Don't be a fool! Take her right up to bed. You've fed her now. She won't pass out on you." He leaned toward her. His yellowed, gnarled hand crawled along the white tablecloth. "You feel better, don't you, my dear? I noticed you ate a portion of everything."

Flinging down her napkin, Vivian scraped back her chair and hurried to the end of the table where her husband waited to offer her his arm. He might be the lesser of two evils in her life, but at least he did not constantly embarrass her before the servants.

Outside in the drafty hall, they paused to send a footman for her cape to protect her against the frosty night air. As they waited, Piers leaned against the wall, his arms folded, one long leg crossed in front of the other. Vivian shifted uncomfortably under his bitter regard.

"Enjoy the sh-shtimulating conversation, m'dear? Not to shpeak of the sumptuoush repast? An' you wonder why I drink? You'll do it too eventually." His sarcasm was heavy, his voice slurred. He closed his eyes for a moment, then blinked them open.

She clasped her hands together at her waist and shook her head.

"Oh, yesh. Oh, yesh, you will. My father doesn't taste the food. Nor would he care, I dareshay. He doesn't care for luxuries. Money and power're his pleasures. Likes to give commands. I've been made to shee th' right o' things. My mother—" He swallowed. His voice broke. Then he spoke more loudly and more pointedly in the direction of the dining room. "My mother hated him and fought with him. He s-set that Felders bitch up over her."

The dining room door slammed behind them.

He grinned at Vivian. "It would be nice, I admit, to have jus' a few of the minor creature comforts from time to time, but probably more trouble than they're worth." He pushed himself from the wall as the servant descended the stairs.

Taking the soft material from the other man's hand, Piers draped it carefully around Vivian's shoulders allowing his fingers to play along the slender bones. He stood so close behind her that she could smell the wine on his breath as well as the cologne and soap he used on

171

his body. Gently, he tightened the grip on her shoulders until she was held quite still. His hand was inordinately hot. The wine must have set a fire in his blood.

A frisson of fear played across her nerve endings.

His lips nibbled at her earlobe, brushed the skin beneath it. "Ah, there'sh a delectable shpot," he whispered.

Again she trembled under his hands.

His lips moved down the column of her neck. "Don't you be 'fraid that this time'll be a repeat of this afternoon. Jus' put that experience right out of your mind. It'll never"—he shook her gently—"*never* happen again. I'll be gentle with you."

She squirmed and tried to twist out from under his hot-seeking mouth, but he held her firmly as he touched first his lips and then the tip of his tongue to the throbbing pulse at the base of her throat. She twisted her head to the side in an effort to push him away, but he only transferred his mouth to the other earlobe taking it between his strong white teeth.

"Be shtill," he commanded softly, "or bear conshequences." Chuckling, he closed his teeth a bit tighter on her quivering flesh. His hot breath tickled her neck. When at last his hard hands released her shoulders, they moved to encircle her, dragging her back against his chest. Unfortunately, her weight was too much for his shaky balance. He staggered back against the wall, tangling his foot in the leg of a heavy table. Cursing, he released her and caught himself against its edge as it rocked and banged against the wall.

He was so drunk he could not stand upright. Angrily she turned to face him. Eyes blazing, her stare swept contemptuously up and down him before she brushed past him.

"Wait," he demanded, righting himself with some difficulty. "Le's step out in the garden. Need a breath of fre' shair t' clear m' head. Come back here. Walk with me."

With one foot on the stair, she paused to look back over her shoulder at him. Taking no care to conceal her feelings, she drew herself to her full height. Her disgust was apparent as she stared at him sprawled drunkenly against the wall, feet spread wide, hips braced against the edge of the table. Haughtily lifting her chin, she turned to mount the stairs, leaving him to struggle alone.

"Damn," he swore softly as he shook his head to clear it. "Damn."

Behind him in the hall, Watkins appeared. "Milord, shall I assist you to your room?"

"NO!" Piers roared. "Wedding night, don't y' know?" He began to mutter to himself. With the valet's assistance he untangled himself from the table and headed for the terrace beyond the glass-enclosed doors. "Shtep outside 'n' clear m' head. Then go up 'n' do the hus-husband thing." Taking considerable care, he walked out to the doors and opened them. "Watkins," he called over his shoulder as the icy wind rushed in, "p'rhaps you'd better bring a bit of brandy to the terrace. Jus' have a tot and get a brace of night air. That'll set me up right and proper."

The dining-room door opened. The earl limped through leaning heavily on his cane. Mrs. Felders supported him on his other side. "For God's sake, man," he barked at the valet. "What's that door standing open for? Surely he didn't take her out there. It's a blizzard."

"No, sir. Milady has already retired. Milord merely stepped outside on the terrace to clear his head."

"The devil you say!" exclaimed the earl. He limped a few steps toward the doors. The wind blew a fine sprinkling of sleet over the dark hallway. "That idiot!"

173

Leaning on his cane, he stalked back to the house-keeper. The valet tried to maneuver past them. "Where are you going?"

"Milord thought a spot of brandy—"

The earl's language made even Mrs. Felders blush. "Watkins, forget that brandy and take him up to his room."

As the valet hastened to obey, Larnaervon made his way down the hall to his study. "The fool," he muttered. "The utter and complete drunken fool. Well-bred girl. Beautiful girl. Rich. And can't utter a word of protest or denial. He won't ever have to listen to her carping. Does he realize what he has, what I have arranged for him? Does he seize his opportunity?" He slammed the door behind him with exceptional force.

Outside on the terrace, Piers's head cleared some-what in the biting wind. Wretchedness and self-pity, twin results of the alcohol overcame him. Tilting his face into the bitter wind, he shivered. He was cold, but his stomach felt as if it were on fire. Too little food. Too many complaints. What would he give for a well-cooked meal eaten in peace?

Sinking onto an iron bench, he hung his head. His elbows rested on his knees and his hands dangled limply between. The brisk winds rushed around his ears and ruffled the hair on his fevered forehead.

"Milord?" Watkins' voice at his side made him stir wearily.

Groggily, he stared at his servant, unable to make sense out of what the man said. He had forgotten his purpose, forgotten why he had come out here in the first place.

"May I help you to bed, milord?" Watkins repeated.

"Surely." Piers nodded his head. "Glad of the help.

Good fellow. Must have drunk too much again. Did I ever tell you how I came to drink, Watkins?"

"No, sir."

"Taught to me." He nodded again, very gently. Snowflakes began to fall silently onto his bowed head. "By my tutor. You wouldn't believe that, would you? Old Fetterman. Man'd drink anything. Wine, brandy, Hollands, anything from the cellar. Whatever came in, he stole some. Can you believe that?"

"Yes, sir," Watkins shivered. "Please, sir. Don't you think—?"

"He'd hide the stuff in the schoolroom behind the books. Sit there drinking while I'd do my lessons. Started pouring me stuff. Like a good fellow. Didn't want to drink alone. You remember old Fetterman?"

"Before my time, sir." The valet wrapped his arms around his body.

"Most boys get sick, Watkins. But not me. I didn't get sick. Not once. Just happy. Happy, happy."

"Yes, sir."

Piers lifted a hand and stared as snowflakes settled on the back of it. "It doesn't make me happy any longer, Watkins," he said solemnly. "But neither does anything else."

He shook his head, stood, staggered, and finally righted himself as Watkins slipped a shoulder under his arm.

"Come, milord."

From her bed in her own room, Vivian tensed as she heard them pass down the hall. Fervent prayers to God for preservation slipped meaninglessly off her lips. Beyond them, she knew of absolutely nothing else to do.

If her husband came to her bed tonight, she must

175

submit to his lust. She had exhausted all avenues and closed all doors. She was married and her husband had the right to her body.

She heard the door next to hers open and close. Heard the rumble of her husband's voice, the valet's quiet murmurs. After a time the door opened and closed again and all was silent. Gradually she relaxed. She had had little experience with drunkenness. Still she guessed correctly that he had passed out and would trouble her no more for the night.

Her natural intelligence and optimism combined to override her fear. She was the Viscountess Polwycke. Others had been forced into marriages probably as undesirable as the one in which she found herself. If she retained her dignity and pride and schooled herself to remember all the behaviors of a lady, she should come through as good as any.

A groan seeped through the walls. She tensed. If his sleep were disturbed, he might remember that she lay in the next room.

But no more sounds came. The last red eyes of fire died in the grate. She exhaled a long, painful breath, conscious that she had lain without breathing or moving a muscle. Sternly, she berated herself. In all likelihood, most of her fears would be as groundless as that. She would dread it no more. When it came, it came.

Her last tutor, a liberal and intelligent man, had been impressed with her mind. She had written long essays on various subjects after reading literature and philosophy usually reserved for men. In a surprising move he had allowed her to read Voltaire's *Candide,* a terrifying and shocking book. Yet from her memory rose the words of Cunegonde, after being raped and stabbed by the captain of the invaders. "—but women do not necessarily die from that."

Voltaire through Cunegonde had told the truth. The worst that could happen to her had happened today and it had not killed her, only frightened and disgusted her. If fright and disgust killed people, then the length of life of mankind would be very short indeed.

In the morning she would begin her new life, she resolved tremulously. She was mistress of this house. True, Piers and Lord Larnaervon were her masters, but she was their mistress. She knew instinctively that whatever the earl might be, he was no liar. As for Piers, no matter what his other faults might be, he was not a cruel man. She smiled. He had always done what she asked him to do.

She would find a way to live. She would

The housekeeper came into the study to find the earl sitting before a dying fire. Efficiently, she added coal from the scuttle. "Will that be all, sir?"

He had been staring into the fire, scarcely conscious that she had entered. Her question broke the spell. He stared at her, his eyes narrowing.

She kept her own gaze turned to the work at hand, stoking the fire with inordinant care.

"Emma, what maggot infests your brain now?"

"Sir?"

"'Sir,'" he mimicked irritably. "Don't say 'sir' in that tone of voice to me."

"I don't know what you mean."

"Come here."

Reluctantly, she straightened. Instead of her coming toward him, however, he laid his cane aside and came to her. His hands slipped up round her neck to caress her cheeks. "Ah, Emma." He kissed her lips.

They remained unresponsive under his own.

He drew back and looked at her. She turned her head

177

aside, her lashes lowered. He grinned. His right hand found the pins in her hair and plucked them out, dropping them one by one with little tinny sounds onto the stones. With his left arm, he encircled her waist and drew her resistant body in against his. Leaning heavily on his good leg, he pushed his hips into her belly.

She shook her head, her expression angry, defiant. The cloud of dark hair swirled around her shoulders. He caught her chin and lifted it. His mouth was hard and demanding, his tongue driving into her, flattening her own tongue, touching the back of her throat. She made a tiny whimpering sound and squirmed futilely beneath the punishment. She pushed against him with her arms and fists.

His arousal grew as she fought him. At last he released her mouth. A couple of steps and he had dropped into the chair, his face dark, his breath rasping harshly. She stood above him, her face hidden in the shadow of her hair.

"Witch!" He twisted her wrist, gently. Down she came on her knees in front of him. "Witch." His rasp turned the word into the scratch of a fingernail through velvet. He tugged her lazily toward him, until her body slid between his thighs. "You would tease an old man."

Her face still in darkness, she unbuttoned the front of his pantaloons and moved aside his clothing. "This doesn't know you're an old man," she murmured.

His head drooped as she slid her hands in between the layers of clothing. "Witch," he whispered again. His fist knotted convulsively in her hair.

Chapter Eleven

Vivian awoke slowly. Stretching and yawning sleepily, she opened one eye. The early morning light strained to penetrate the grimy windowpanes. Rolling over, she buried her face in the pillow and tried to count her blessings.

The first blessing was the lavender-scented down pillow she clutched, its wonderful softness conforming to the contours of her breasts. The abbey had not had such comforts at the heads of their abominably hard cots. The three pillows she had brought with her had mysteriously disappeared one by one, leaving her to wonder at the people who had dedicated themselves to lives of poverty and obedience within the walls.

For several moments she lay still trying to think of other such small creature comforts. The second blessing was the warmth and softness of the bed. Reluctantly, she dragged her face out of the pillow and stared around her.

The third blessing hung on the wall beside the bed—a bell cord. With a smug little smile, she pulled it and slipped back under the covers to wait for whoever might come.

Her summons was answered with gratifying promptness. A young girl in a ruffled mobcap timidly opened the door and peered around the edge. "Will you be wanting your morning chocolate, milady?"

Pulling herself to a sitting position, Vivian smiled and nodded.

The maid bobbed her head and disappeared to return in minutes bearing a small tray. Vivian could not help noticing that the girl—besides being very young—walked with a pronounced limp. Nevertheless, she bore the tray with creditable skill. Setting it carefully down on the bedside table, she folded her hands and stepped back.

Vivian looked at her expectantly. When the girl did not move, Vivian pointed to the robe lying across the end of the bed.

A faint flush stained the already rosy cheeks as she muttered a hasty apology. When she helped Vivian into the warm garment, her fingers shook. At last the pillows were arranged, and Vivian's long braid was pulled around to hang over her left shoulder. Uttering a tiny sigh of relief, the girl stepped back again and smiled timidly.

Smiling in return, Vivian folded her hands. Since Mrs. Felders had seen fit to send an untrained maid, she would begin the girl's training immediately. Helplessly, the girl looked from her mistress to the hot chocolate.

Reaching for her pad and pencil, Vivian wrote the words, *You may serve me*. Unfortunately, when she passed the pad to the maid, the girl shook her head and burst into tears.

"Oh, milady," she quavered. "I canna read nor write. Mrs. Felders said I was to serve you and be your personal maid, but I said that I couldna because I was too ignorant. But she said I must. Oh, what shall I do? Now I'll be turned off." She moaned and threw her

180

apron up in front of her face.

Mentally condemning Mrs. Felders to perdition, Vivian shook her head in exasperation. Tugging the apron away, she pulled the girl's hands down from her face. Soothingly, she patted the rough, cold fingers.

"Oh, I canna. I canna." The little maid wailed harder and tried to pull away, but Vivian tightened her grip and shook the girl's hands sharply.

Immediately, the wailing stopped. Looking straight into her tear-streaked face, Vivian carried one reluctant hand to the handle of the chocolate pot and forced the maid to lift and pour. With that task completed, Vivian took her hand away and leaned back in the bed.

"Oh, I can. I can. Oh, thank you, milady, for showing me the way of it. If you was to just show me once. I could do. And I'd never forget." Sniffing noisily, the girl carefully passed the cup and saucer to Vivian.

While her lady sipped the warm chocolate, the maid pulled a scrap of cloth from her apron pocket and blew her nose. Efficiently enough, she moved to pick up the blue velvet dress and underclothing.

"My name's Adeline, milady," she volunteered. "But you can call me Addie. Not that you'd be usin' my name." Suddenly, she blushed beet red. "Oh, lor'," she gasped. "What I mean to say is, not that you'd want to. Oh, I canna. I canna." She began to wail again. "I told Mrs. Felders—"

Vivian clapped her hands together sharply. When the girl pulled her apron down in front of her face, Vivian smiled graciously.

"You're not put out, milady? Oh, you're that generous." Drying her cheeks for the second time that morning, she moved to the wardrobe. "I'll try extra hard. I promise. Now. What will you be wanting to put on this morning? Ooh! Where'd this come from?" She opened the oak doors to find only one garment hanging there—the nun's habit.

Vivian stiffened, the cocoa sloshing in the cup. Silently, she vowed that if she had to go naked, she would never don it again. The insensate piece of cloth had become a symbol of her helplessness, her inability to control any aspect of her life. Nuns were mindlessly obedient. She would never be mindlessly obedient again.

Get rid of it! she willed herself to scream. *Burn it! Bury it! Fling it into the ocean.* Silence. She closed her eyes as real pain streaked through her throat. Again as countless times before she willed herself to speak. She opened her mouth, she pushed the air out of her lungs—and nothing happened.

Opening her eyes, she saw the maid was staring at her. Probably the poor girl believed her to be mad.

Flinging back the covers, she hurried across the room. Jerking the garment out, she thrust it into the maid's arms.

"Do you want me to press this, milady, and bring it back to you?"

Vivian shook her head vigorously. She closed the maids hands over it.

"You're giving it to me?"

Vivian snatched the garment out of the girl's hands and ran to the door. She jerked it open and tossed the habit out into the hall.

"Oh." Addie's eyes sparkled. "You want me to throw it away."

Vivian flashed her a brilliant smile. Crossing to her trunk, she flung back the lid.

Addie broke into a smile. "I don't guess there's anyone that needs to tell me what to do with these. I'll get all your clothes unpacked as fast as may be. And pressed and hung too," she promised. "That's what I used to do below stairs, but I just came in two days a week and m' mum was right anxious for me to get more work cause—"

She continued to chatter amiably as she began to pull garments from Vivian's trunk. Feeling as though she had done a day's work, Vivian climbed back into bed to finish her chocolate. Before she realized what had happened, Adeline had limped out the door with an armload of clothing and no fire stoked in the hearth.

A year ago Vivian would have rung the bell again. Now she merely slid from under the covers and stalked gamely across the icy floor. Her training in the monastic life stood her in good stead as she began to stoke the fire and add coal from the scuttle. When a bright flame rose out of the grate, she scampered back for the second time to thrust her feet beneath the still warm bedcovers.

Mentally, she cursed Mrs. Felders. The woman had been her enemy from the minute she had entered the hall with poor Sister Grace. But why? The housekeeper obviously was privy to the earl's plans. And quite a lot more besides, Vivian thought nastily. Still it was not the housekeeper's place to approve of them?

If Vivian were truly mistress of the house, her first act would be to discharge Mrs. Felders. The cleanliness of the house, the condition of the furniture, the food, the service, all bespoke the woman's inefficiency if not downright neglect. But perhaps they bespoke something else. Perhaps her position was unassailable.

Vivian shrugged. A mistress had certain privileges. Perhaps Mrs. Felders was only nominally the housekeeper. She tried to picture Emma Felders lying beneath the earl doing what Piers had done to her. While she had little problem with that, the difficulty came in picturing the earl in Piers's place.

Best forget the idea of discharging Mrs. Felders.

Vivian shook her head and reached for the bellcord again. She could not lie here in bed all day.

The riding habit alone hung in the closet now.

She would take a ride. She glanced at the window. The sun was shining brightly. Never mind the cold. She had been determined to ride yesterday, when she had some thoughts of trying to escape. No more of that. She would put those thoughts away. Today, she would merely ride as the earl himself had said she might.

Yes, a ride. She had been pent up too long. She would let the winds, no matter how chill and strong, blow away some of the lingering fear and pain.

The effort to get a mount proved so difficult that she began to doubt the ride would be worth the effort. After almost half an hour during which time she had handed notes to three different people, she descended the steps in front of the house.

The light snowfall had stopped during the night, and while the lawn was covered in crystalline white, the snow was already melting from the drive and lane beyond. The horses waited in the company of not one but two sullen-faced men who bore little resemblance to grooms. Moreover, if the grooms looked like farm laborers, the horses were certainly their animals.

Vivian's mouth curled in disgust at the sight of the chunky gray punch under the sidesaddle. An appraisal of the other mounts revealed them to be equally unprepossessing.

The shorter man, a weasel-faced lout, shuffled forward and laced his fingers to toss her into the saddle.

Gathering the reins, she patted the horse's shoulder. Barely fifteen hands high, the animal was obviously a cart horse of such great age as to be nearly white. She tugged on the rein, but it did nothing beyond flick an ear back in her direction. When she touched it with her crop, it lifted its head and opened its eyes. By a dint of strength she managed to haul its head around.

The "grooms" climbed clumsily into their saddles, and they set off at an amble down the drive. At the gate Vivian's horse stopped dead and would not move until the weasel-faced man came up behind it and gave it such a cut that it whickered and actually trotted forward. When she tried to haul its head to the right, it proved to be iron-mouthed.

She almost turned it back and abandoned the idea of the ride, but the wind hit her face, carrying with it the salt of the sea. She lifted her chin and kept on going.

Out in the lane, the punch felt itself on familiar ground and moved along at a trot that jarred every bone in her body. With a sigh she pulled it back to a sedate walk. When she returned home, she wondered whom she might approach with the problem of a suitable mount. Surely these were not the only horses in the Larnaervon stable. If so, then the first order of business would be to send men to bring several mounts from her own stable at Stone Glenn. Provided that Sebastian had not sold them off. At the thought of her guardian, her stomach clenched. Where would she be now if not for the earl and her husband? Locked up somewhere, she did not doubt.

Suddenly, the wind switched around to the north. The sun paled, fighting a battle with the lowering clouds. Tears, not alone from its icy blast, started on her cheeks. Angrily, she wiped them away with her gloved hand. Even if she returned chilled to the bone, the ride was a necessity for her. Without the opportunity to get out of the house for a few minutes each day, what matter whether she was locked up by Dawlish or by Larne? Without some freedom, she would surely go mad.

The pounding sea began to call to her. She had not realized how close it was until she rounded a headland and saw it stretched before her. Her breath sighed softly out of her throat. It was so beautiful. So free and wild. Gray and white, the water foamed icily up the white sand and disappeared into an inlet. Awesome granite boulders guarded its entrance. Against them the waves shattered and sprayed high into the gray sky.

"It be fearsome cold," the groom called behind her.

She shot him a disgusted look and turned the punch off the lane and down a trail that meandered to the beach.

While the men shivered and huddled over their saddles, casting her evil looks, she led them up and down the beach. Only when her cheeks were red as fire and her hands were stiff in her gloves, did she turn the punch back up the trail in the direction of her new home.

Built within the foundations of an ancient Roman wall, the house had been added to by successions of occupants until it reached its present size. Against the burnished blue of the sky, it stood bleak and gray. To her unhappy eyes, it seemed to glower down on her.

Halfway up the trail, she pulled the mount to blow while she studied the house. The portion that faced the sea must be very old. Only a few narrow windows dotted its sides. For defense? In ancient times had men stood at those slits and fired arrows through them at invaders?

No portion of the rest of the house—not the gate, not the drive, not the wings with their gracious windows—could be seen. Every stick and stone of it hid behind the thick gray wall. No one approaching from the sea would see the hospitable home, only the forbidding shield of granite. A defense in itself.

Turning her face toward the roiling waves, she tried

to imagine those invading vessels seeing this sight and passing on by in search of easier pickings.

As the men behind her grumbled unintelligibly, she sucked the harsh air into her lungs. The wind blew against her reddened cheeks and brought more tears to her eyes. From here she could see inside the inlet where white froth poured like milk up to the white sand beach.

Gray gulls turned and circled and trailed each other in mewing turns. One dived into the choppy waves and rose with shining silver in its beak. Shrieking in envy, the others swirled around him. From high behind Vivian's head, a blue-gray streak plummeted down into their midst, striking one with deadly force. The gull collapsed in a burst of feathers. A seahawk flapped its wings to gain speed, veered away, and skimmed behind the rocks of the inlet, its prey clutched in its talons.

Vivian shuddered. The cold pierced her bones, and her heart shivered within her at the brute nature of the bird of prey. She was in the process of gathering her reins and hauling the gray's heavy head up when alien movement caught her eye at the edge of the inlet.

Barrels floated and sloshed in the ceaselessly moving water. Only partially visible, in the wash of the waves, they were covered by white foam a moment later. She rose in her stirrups, her eyes searching. Had there been a shipwreck? No other debris appeared along the beach stretching around the side of the inlet.

A hard hand grasped her bridle and pulled her mount's head around.

"We'd best be going, milady." The groom with the weasel face firmly tugged her reins from her hand and led her horse up the road.

The presumption of the man made her furiously angry. High spots of color stood out on her wind-reddened cheeks. Someday she would be mistress here in full, she vowed silently. The other man spurred his mount on ahead, and the weasel-faced one dragged her mount ignominiously behind him, letting her trail along like a dull child whose mount had to be controlled on a leading rein.

At the steps of the house the party halted. When the groom strolled back to assist her from her saddle, her eyes spoke volumes as they blazed at him.

He gave her a cheeky grin and bowed before lifting his hands to her waist to bring her down. "Them that don't see, can't be answering questions, milady."

Still furiously angry, she swept into the house as the butler opened the door.

The brisk wind of the morning combined with the poor food of the evening before had given her a ravenous appetite. With the butler in attendance she strode to the morning room and seated herself at the small table.

"What will you have, milady?" the butler inquired solicitously.

Drawing her pad and pencil from her jacket pocket, Vivian wrote his name Millard and her request in her firm hand. The butler did not even raise an eyebrow. Evidently, Addie had told her story below stairs. Taking her note in his hand, he positioned it for better light and read it quickly. Then allowing himself a small smile and nod, he folded it carefully.

"Very good, milady."

As he turned away, Vivian struck her glass with her knife.

"Will there be something else?"

She wrote again and handed him a second note. Did his eyes widen a fraction? She could not be sure. All she was certain of was a grave nod.

When the butler had bowed his way out, Vivian was left alone with her own thoughts.

A crystal pitcher of water stood on a tray on the sideboard. Rising, she poured herself a glass and drank it thirstily. As she returned to her chair, Mrs. Felders came stiffly into the room carrying the two notes in her hand.

"You sent for me, milady?" she inquired with cold politeness.

Nodding, Vivian picked up her pencil. With a look of grim determination, she wrote the word "Menus."

The woman drew herself up haughtily. "Lord Larnaervon has approved of my meal selections for many years, milady. We serve his favorite foods."

Vivian frowned, her pencil poised above the paper. At that moment the butler entered with a tray. While he served the breakfast, Mrs. Felders waited, pursing her lips. Two spots of high color flamed in her cheeks. Her hands crossed over her apron twitched nervously.

When the butler had withdrawn, Vivian wrote again on her pad and passed the note to Mrs. Felders.

"You must be mistaken, milady." She shook her head. "Lord Piers has never complained of the food. Why he hardly eats anything at all—" She broke off in consternation realizing what she had admitted.

Vivian nodded haughtily.

The notes rattled in Mrs. Felders's fingers as she folded them with fierce defiance. "Might I suggest that you would do very well to—"

Vivian laid down her fork and started to rise.

Mrs. Felders cast a look over her shoulder as Millard entered and stood by the door. "Oh, very well, milady. I'll bring you the menus in the drawing room after breakfast. If you want to do them, it'll save me the time and trouble. But," she predicted direly, "you needn't think you're going to come in here and make a lot of changes. This is Larne's house and he's the master here. Make no mistake about that."

189

Vivian shook her head and wrote again.

Mrs. Felders twisted her neck so she could look over Vivian's shoulder. "In your room? But—"

Vivian underlined the words with strong bold slashes.

"Oh, very well."

"Why, Emma Felders. I didn't know you could say 'very well.' Such a surprise. Millard, bring coffee. Hot and strong."

Both women started and turned at the sound of a masculine voice. The butler bowed and left.

Piers stood in the doorway, deep shadows beneath his eyes and his mouth set in a straight line.

"Lord Piers." Mrs. Felders's voice rang with shock. "Why you're up very early."

"My wife and her maid made so much noise next door that they disturbed me. I couldn't get back to sleep." He scowled at Vivian. "You did, you know?"

She started to write, but he put his hand over her own. "Spare me the apologies. It really wasn't you. It was your blessed maid. 'Milady' this and 'milady' that and banging doors open and closed. God!" He dropped into a chair. "Where is that man with the coffee?"

Mrs. Felders allowed a small smile to ease her mouth. "I'll see to him, sir. Ah, here you are, Millard," she said in a clear loud voice. "You took your own sweet time."

Piers groaned and pressed a palm to his forehead. "Bitch," he muttered loud enough for his wife to hear.

The butler came through with a tray. Smoothly, he removed Vivian's plate and set it down before her, whisking the cover off as he did so. From a silver coffeepot he poured Piers's cup and set it in the saucer.

Despite a green look around the mouth, Piers managed to look with some interest at her plate. He swallowed a mouthful of hot coffee. "Why, that looks good. A piece of toast and an egg. Hard to foul that, I collect." He looked at the butler. "I'll have the same."

"Very good, sir."

Vivian bit into a corner of the toast, too hungry to stand on ceremony or wait for him to be served and her food to become cold.

Piers took another swallow. "I should come down to breakfast more often," he muttered. "Evidently it's the best meal of the day. More likely it's easier to serve a hot meal in this room than any other room in the house." Resting an elbow on the table, he drank the rest of his coffee down.

Even as the viscount finished, Millard came bustling. "One egg and toast, milord." He set the plate before Piers, who held out his cup for more coffee.

"Looks excellent. My compliments to Cook."

"Cook does not get up so early in morning," Millard informed him coolly. "I prepared this myself."

He stepped back as Piers stared from dish to man, and Vivian gave the butler a warm, approving smile.

The butler poured more coffee and left.

Uncomfortable at being alone with her husband, Vivian directed her attention to her plate. She buttered the second half of toast and cut her egg with delicate precision. With each bite her appetite seemed to increase.

Piers watched her with something like envy, a sour smile curling his lips. "When Millard returns, perhaps you should order another plate," he suggested.

Blushing, Vivian shook her head. Her appetite had always been healthy, and she had not eaten any great amount of food in forty-eight hours. To cover her embarrassment, she laid down her fork and reached for her cup. Over its rim Vivian studied her husband.

For the first time she could view him in something other than an abnormal situation. When they had met, he had been consumed with worry and grief at his mother's illness and subsequent demise. When she had been brought back to be his bride, his father had angered and upset him to a frightening degree.

Now he sat at the breakfast table fresh from his bath. His dark-wine hair was combed damply back from his high forehead. Dark crescents under his eyes accentuated their darkness until the pupil seemed to fill the iris.

Tentatively, he took a small bite. His expression relaxed, then he turned his attention to her. His gaze slid over her clothing and her windswept hair. "You've already been riding."

Self-consciously, she smoothed several loose strands away from her temples.

"You should have waited for me." He looked at her critically. "Your hair looks quite all right. I like it curling around your face." He reached out a long aristocratic finger that trembled only slightly. It touched the ringlet in front of her ear and brushed the skin beneath.

Startled, she pulled away.

Instantly, he drew his hand back. "Don't be afraid," he murmured. "I'm not going to ravish you at the breakfast table." He smiled engagingly. "However, it's not a bad idea. Since we've done it in public once, it rather breaks the ice, don't you think?"

Embarrassed at his words, she glanced around hastily to assure herself that they were alone.

"Vivian," he said softly. "It doesn't have to be painful or unpleasant. Thousands of people enjoy it very much."

Her face flamed scarlet. Her cup clattered in the saucer. All interest in food and drink faded.

He caught her hand. "Tonight, dear wife. I will come to you and show you . . ."

192

She tried to rise, her chair scraping back, but he held her firmly. "Don't struggle. As I said, I don't mean to ravish you at the breakfast table. Here. Sit down and finish your food."

She shook her head, but he held her until she subsided in her chair.

"Take a bite of food," he commanded. "Get your appetite back."

Reluctantly, she pulled herself back to the table. He spread a piece of his own toast with butter and spooned some marmalade onto it. "Here now." He held it out for her to take a bite. "You'll need all your strength."

When she tried to take it from his hand, he drew back. "No, you'll just set it down. It's very good," he took a bite to demonstrate. "Good marmalade. Sweet with just the right amount of peel in it. Not too bitter. Come. Take a bite. Don't be shy."

She hesitated.

"Look at how sweet and golden," he coaxed, holding it closer. "Come on, sweetheart. Think of me as a father."

The corners of her mouth lifted in a reluctant smile. Daintily, she leaned forward and took a little bite.

"Excellent." He set the toast down on the side of her plate. "And from the same spot that I ate." He grinned at the flush rising again in her cheeks. "Don't start again. Just eat your breakfast."

He drank another cup of coffee, took a single bite of egg, and grimaced. "Not for me this morning." Throwing down the napkin, he rose. "Too bad you've already gone riding. We could go together. However—" Suddenly, he was very close to her chair, very close to her shoulder. His hand dropped onto it, long fingers caressing the velvet. "—we have a rendezvous tonight."

She looked up at him, fear in her eyes.

He bent over her. "Vivian, when you were a little girl,

you must have fallen from your horse."

She tried to look away, knowing and hating what he was going to say.

"No." He took her chin and lifted her face to him. "You will build horrible fancies in your mind. I don't want a wife afraid of me. The pleasures of the bedchamber are one of the few left in this old and very unpleasant world." He dropped his mouth onto hers, a light brush of lips, a flick of his tongue, and then he straightened. "Till tonight, sweet, sweet wife."

Chapter Twelve

The meeting with Mrs. Felders in the bedroom proved to be a pitched battle. Each dish Vivian wrote down was firmly and definitely rejected by the housekeeper. The earl did not care for that. His delicate digestion would not tolerate such heavy spices. The foodstuffs were unavailable at this time of year. Cook's skills were limited and could not be stretched so far.

At this objection Vivian angrily wrote down, "Get a new cook."

Mrs. Felders drew back. "The man has worked here for years. He was engaged by the late countess. To turn off a man at his age would be cruel."

"Helper with some skill." Vivian wrote.

Mrs. Felders shook her head. Her mouth pursed repressively. "You'd best speak to the earl about hiring new people."

"Recipes?"

The housekeeper tilted back her head. "I believe the countess had a book at one time or another, but—"

"Find it."

The older woman stepped back. "I shouldn't be surprised if it's been destroyed or sent away to a charitable establishment. Lord Alexander ordered all

195

of his wife's things removed. Didn't want to remind himself of his terrible loss," she ended, her voice flat. The corners of her mouth twitched as if she might have found the entire interview amusing.

Vivian could see that she was getting nowhere with the woman. The time had come to take a stand. Shaking with suppressed rage, her inability to speak driving her almost mad, she coldly set about listing dishes for the cook to prepare that very evening.

Mrs. Felders closed her mouth and swelled out her generous bosom. Her own color was high, her nostrils pinched with her indignant breathing. She sidled forward and looked over Vivian's shoulder. "He doesn't like green beans in the French style," she declared triumphantly. "Doesn't like anything in the French style. Cabbage is the vegetable for him."

Vivian shot her a warning look.

Mrs. Felders sniffed. "Only three removes. He won't like that. Insists on a formal dinner."

At the top of the menu, Vivian wrote the instruction that the courses except for the salad should be served hot, but the green beans in particular should not be overdone.

"Light French wine." Vivian underlined the first word and signed the bottom of the sheet with a flourish. With a cool smile, she thrust it into Mrs. Felders's hand.

The woman's eyes narrowed to points of angry light. The paper crackled between her fingers. Vivian expected her to wad it up or rip it across, but she finally thrust it into the pocket of her apron. Her voice was hoarse and breathless. "You'll live to regret this," she prophesied. "Just mark my words."

Rising in the face of the woman's ire, Vivian realized that she had created an implacable enemy. Reasoning that the woman could be no angrier, Vivian swept her fingers across the surface of the table at which she sat and then showed their tips. She crossed to the window and shook a drapery that discharged a cloud of gray dust and lint into the crackling air. She rubbed her hand down the wardrobe, its wood grain devoid of wax and dulled by many handprints never wiped away. As a final note Vivian pointed out the fireplace with its smoke-stain blackening the mantel and the ornaments on it.

Mrs. Felders color had deepened to a dull puce. "We'll see to this room as soon as I can free some of the staff, milady. Of course, we're short-handed and it may be some time. Winter is a hard time on the coast." Her breath hissed angrily between her teeth. Her expression foretold clearly that Vivian would not have a clean room before spring if she had anything to say about it. "I'll go and deliver this to Cook now, so he can get started on it. Of course the poor man may have a smothering spell. No one has ever complained about his skills before."

Before Vivian could dismiss her, the woman swept out, closing the door harder than necessary behind her.

Vivian wrapped her arms around herself, finding she was shivering with strain. Stumbling back, she sat down in the chair and held her cold hands out to the fire. A pitiful warmth rose from the bed of coals that was almost consumed. Shaking her head, she reached for the scuttle only to find it empty.

Damn! Damn Felders! Damn Sebastian! Damn poor old Sister Grace Hospitaler for bringing her here in the first place! Damn the earl and damn the viscount! And damn her lack of voice most of all! How could she continue to live her life like this? Perhaps Sebastian was right after all. Perhaps the abbey was all the life for which she was suited.

Tears started in her eyes. *Why go on against such odds?* She let her hands sink limply to her lap. They were dirty. She had handled the dusty draperies and filthy furniture, and now her hands were dirty. The sight infuriated her. She sprang to her feet. Suddenly, she wanted to drag Felders back by the hair of her head. She would make her—

A knock sounded at the door and then Addie's head came poking round the edge. "Oh, lor', milady, but you've set the cat among the pigeons." The girl giggled as she limped across the floor. "Mrs. Felders came stormin' down into the kitchen and fair threw that 'menoo' at the cook. She was slammin' around there and cursin' fit to scare the de'il hisself."

Vivian shivered at the draught that slipped in behind the maid. She handed Addie the coal scuttle.

"Right away, ma'am." The girl curtsied but did not stop talking. "Then Millard, the countess's old butler hisself, comes in and says, 'What's the meanin' o' this,' and she tells him to mind his own business and sails off in a huff." She grinned excitedly. "Lor', I wish'd I could read, so you could write me what you said."

Vivian patted her stomach and pantomimed eating.

"I figured you'd told her that the stuff she gets Cook to serve to his lordship ain't fit for hogswill."

Vivian started in amazement.

"Cook knows it, milady. He's tried to slip some things in, but the old earl, he don't taste too much, so with your husband"—she stopped and looked a bit nervous—"the way he is for near every meal, it don't really much matter."

At Vivian's expression, she shrugged. "I guess I shouldn't 've said that." She looked around. "It don't look real clean, now that I look at it."

198

Vivian waved a disgusted hand at the smoke stains that blackened the mantel and the painting above it. In fact the huntsmen and hounds pictured there were merely dim figures hunting perhaps unaccountably at twilight.

"Anyways, I've come to get started, for so she told me."

Vivian straightened up at this piece of news.

"I wanted to get out of that part of house anyway 'cause they was about to have a reg'lar mixup down there." Addie moved to the window and began to unfasten the swags that held back the over drapes. "You want I should start with these, milady? I can take 'em down and clean 'em and wash the lace behind 'em and have 'em back up by nightfall."

Vivian nodded. Curious as to what the "reg'lar mixup" might be, she left the maid to her work and walked downstairs. Angry voices rose to meet her.

"—time you got your comeuppance," Millard was saying.

"Jack!" Mrs. Felders screeched. "Don't you let him talk to me like that."

A deep voice rumbled unintelligibly, but the tones struck her as faintly familiar.

"—suggest you get some of your help together and get them to cleaning this place before—"

"You old fool, you don't—"

"Emma," the deep voice snarled, "don't raise such a stink. It's what you're paid for after all. Gawd almighty, don't queer a sweet deal like this with your—"

The epithet struck Vivian to stone on the stairs. Her hand clutched at the banister for support. "Gawd almighty" was the favorite expression of the man who had brought her here. Step by step she began her retreat. But not fast enough.

The door behind the stairs flew open and the burly man she remembered strode across the front hall toward the door.

"Jack!" Emma Felders ran after him.

Vivian tried to hurry, but her heel caught in her skirt and held her. She reeled backward, hanging onto the railing as she shifted her foot.

"Damn it. It's not like you have to do the work yourself." He turned back to the housekeeper—and caught sight of Vivian. With a mocking smile he swept off his hat. He took a step toward the foot of the stairs. His greatcoat flapped open revealing a horse pistol tucked into the broad leather belt at his waist. "Milady."

The sight of the weapon alarmed her so that she struggled even harder to free her skirt. She could not doubt that he was dangerous.

Emma Felders turned, too. All the hatred, all the venom in the world blazed from her eyes. She clenched her fists.

The door to the study opened. "What in the name of all that's holy is all the commotion about?"

"Lord Larnaervon." Emma's face smoothed immediately. That is, the hatred disappeared, to be replaced by an expression of extreme annoyance. "She's disrupted everything. This beadrattler." She pointed up the stairs at Vivian, who had finally managed to get her heel off her skirt and catch her balance.

"Indeed!" The earl glanced up the stairs, then at the man and woman. "Ah, Jack, back so soon. Good. Good. I need to see you. So long as you're here, you might as well come in."

Jack Beddoes nodded. Without another glance at either woman he followed the earl into the study and shut the door.

Emma Felders's face turned puce. Vivian stared in amazement then whirled on the staircase. Wishing she could giggle, she fairly ran back up to her room.

Before Addie left with the draperies and curtains, Jem had come to clean the fireplace. "And see that y'do a real good job of it," the girl commanded. "Don't just swish that broom around the edges and call it clean."

"Nobody's complained afore," Jem defended himself sullenly.

"That's as cause Lord Piers don't really give a care. You know how he is." Addie warmed to her subject. "Gone most of the time until the countess took sick and when he was here, being in his cups."

Vivian flashed her a look of warning and disapproval.

"Ooh, milady, pardon me." Stammering an embarrassed apology, Addie hastily gathered up the draperies and curtains and beat a hasty retreat.

The sweep ran his brush up into the chimney and was immediately covered with soot and ashes. It billowed out into the room accompanied by his curses and groans as he wiped it from his eyes. A glance over his shoulder in the direction of the lady and he lifted his broom and gamely burrowed on.

Unable to stay in the mess, Vivian retreated to the draughty hallway where she waited, arms wrapped around her.

"Milady." The valet Watkins called to her from Piers's room. "Come and wait in here. There's a fire in the hearth and the chimney draws well. I take care of it myself."

Vivian hesitated. Still, it was chilly standing in the hallway. She had been cold all morning. While she stood undecided, two maids came strolling down the hall. At least she assumed they were maids. Buxom and garbed more like farm women than attendants in an aristocratic household, they stopped short at the sight of her, then ducked their heads briefly before carrying their mops and pails into her room.

"You'd best wait in here," Watkins urged. "They'll do their jobs better without your watching them." He looked down the hall. "Here comes the one to oversee what they do."

Vivian glanced over her shoulder. Face like a thundercloud, Emma Felders bore down the hall. Without waiting for another invitation, Vivian hurried through the door that Watkins held open for her.

Piers's bedroom was warm and clean. Trembling inwardly, she looked around her, seeing his room and realizing that she had noticed nothing about it the day before. A cheery fire leaped in the grate. Naturally she gravitated to it and held out her hands.

"Just set yourself down, milady. I don't expect his lordship back before late this evening. Would you care for some refreshment?"

Relaxing slightly she seated herself and nodded eagerly.

"Tea, ma'am?"

A loud thump from the room next door made her jump. They exchanged knowing looks, then she rewarded him with a warm smile and a nod.

"It might take awhile. They are unused to giving service. Likewise, I can imagine the kitchen is in turmoil. I shall probably have to prepare the tray myself." He chuckled to himself as he strode out.

"Vivian. Viv-i-an."

Her eyes flew open. She heard Piers's voice calling her. Her whole body tensed. Her hands clenched on the

202

arms of the chair. She looked up, her eyes still half blinded by the light.

He laughed. "Dare I hope that you have come back for the same reason you came the first time?"

Where was she? What was she doing here? She must have dozed off in his chair. Horrified, she sprang to her feet. The sudden movement drove the blood from her head and she staggered. He caught her and gathered her in against his body. The dampness of his clothing chilled her as it drove the last bits of drowsiness from her brain.

"Having a wife might not be such a bad idea," he said thoughtfully, "if I could have you waiting for me when I come home." She tried to pull away, but he tightened his grasp. "A kiss. A kiss of welcome."

She pushed harder, but he shook his head. "Just a kiss. We've done it before. It's a natural thing. Not something to get so excited about."

Resignedly, she stopped struggling. He smiled. "Now, you kiss me."

Pertly, she rose on tiptoe and brushed her lips against his cheek.

"What a disappointment," he teased. "I don't kiss you like that. Come." He tightened his arms around her waist. "Kiss me properly."

She tilted up her chin and pursed her lips.

"That's not the proper way. Here, let me show you." The chill of his hands had seeped through her clothing, making her unmistakably aware of where he was holding her. One arm was around her back, the fingertips pressed against the side of her breast. The other hand curved over her buttock, its fingertips hooking upward. Fear slashed through her belly. She shuddered as he lifted her against his body.

He felt her response even as he touched his mouth to hers. Then his tongue came out and caressed her lips.

Ever so slowly, and warmly, he touched them, the hot, moist tip tracing their shape, the indentation at the top, the full swell at the bottom.

His whole mouth closed over them, laving them with the inner velvet of his own. Unconsciously, she relaxed, her mouth opened, and his tongue slipped inside her.

A heat began to curl in her belly. His hand at her buttock, no longer chill, but warm, squeezed her and lifted her more firmly against him. She could feel his arousal, a rod against which he pressed her.

Pain. Not the pain of hurt but the pain of longing, of desire began where the base of his rod touched her, began at the very top of her thighs, began at the swollen point of flesh until that time, buried untouched. She tried to move to relieve the pressure and the longing, but they only intensified.

All at once her thighs seemed too weak to bear her weight. Her calf muscles tensed then trembled as they too turned to water. Her very toes felt the acute sensations.

His kiss went on and on as incredible excitement swept through her body in waves. She began to shudder convulsively. Her hands came up to sink into the wine-dark mane and hold his head closer. She wanted more and more of the kiss, more and more—

"God," he breathed into her mouth. "My God, Vivian."

"Finding anything down there was something of a problem, milady. For the very first time cookfires are blazing, water is boiling. Oh, excuse me, milord." The valet stood in the doorway, a tea tray in his hands.

"Damn you, Watkins. Your timing is execrable." Piers released Vivian but kept his arm around her supporting her against his side.

She stared at the valet as if she had never seen him,

204

then looked up at her husband dazedly.

"I can well see that, sir. Refreshments took rather a long time to fetch, ma'am. The kitchen was in a furor, but no worse than I expected."

"And whose fault is that?" Piers chuckled. He guided his wife back into her chair, then moved away to unsling the greatcoat from his shoulders.

Vivian's face, already rosy from his kiss, blushed deeper at the information that she had upset the entire household. Embarrassed, she tried to push herself out of the chair.

"Stay, wife. After all, this tea is for you. Watkins, I'll have something stronger after you have served her. The dampness has seeped into my very bones."

"Very good, milord." The valet poured tea and milk into a cup, stirred in sugar and passed it to Vivian. "I hope this is satisfactory, milady."

Gratefully, she accepted it. Treats of this sort had been hard to come by of late. She drank it thirstily.

Throwing his long frame into the chair opposite, Piers propped his booted feet up on the bumper of the fireplace. "Ice cold," he murmured. "My damn toes are stiff."

His boots were indeed wet and muddy almost to their tops. Over the rim of her teacup, Vivian glanced at the window. The sun shone brightly. Surely the light fall of snow had melted. Where had he been that he should be so cold and damp?

Watkins handed the viscount a brandy. He sank back into his chair and raised his glass to his lips. As he stared wearily into its depths, the firelight reflected in his eyes. Suddenly, aware of her scrutiny, he raised his glass to toast her with a gesture and a look before he drank his first swallow.

She smiled a little tremulously, her body still humming from his kiss. Truth to tell, she had never expected anything like it, never felt anything like it before. Surreptitiously, she rubbed her palm along the outside of her thigh where the ache still lingered.

He watched her as she drank, glad she was here. He had stared down at her figure asleep in the chair, her head slipped to the side, her hands limp and graceful in her lap and thought how beautiful she was. Forgotten was his fear that she might be mentally impaired in some way. Having a wife might not prove to be such a bad thing after all. And, by God, she *was* his wife.

The second problem that he had foreseen had not materialized. She had been kidnapped after a fashion and treated roughly if not brutally. Still she seemed to bear no grudge. At least not against him.

She was behaving very well about all of this. After being forced into marriage, she might be expected to be sullen and resentful. She could be expected to weep like a fountain overflowing, or else to tremble and hide from him. Certainly, after her sexual initiation he would not really blame her if she did. But she acted in none of those ways. Instead he found her sitting naturally in his room.

"I invited Lady Polwycke to wait here in warmth and comfort while her room was being cleaned." Watkins supplied the information while he hung up the viscount's coat.

"Where else?" He sank lower in his chair. A sigh escaped him. "Good lord, never tell me that Felders actually ordered the servants, such as they are, to turn a hand to do some useful work."

Piers took another drink of brandy. He held it on his tongue, then winced as he swallowed it as if it burned more fiercely than usual. His voice was a bitter snarl. "I can't believe it. I don't think anyone has done anything in this sty since Mother took to her bed nearly a year ago. And before that, Felders did as little as she could possibly get by with. Housekeeping is not—after all—her primary duty."

"I believe Lady Polwycke insisted."

He stared at Vivian. "How did you do that?"

She reached into her pocket and pulled out her pad and pencil.

"Oh, of course. The notes. You must be a very talented writer." He looked around him. "Cleaning this pile. Really cleaning it would be akin to the cleaning the Augean stables." He toasted her again. "Forgive me, if you don't quite measure up to Hercules. Besides, I seriously doubt that this moldering wreck can be changed. Truly, it has been allowed to sink into a hopeless condition." He gestured to the room in which they sat. The lace on his sleeve swayed. "Hopeless and useless." His bitterness was palpable in the twist of his lips and the savage glint of his eye. "This is my—forgive me—*our* inheritance."

Vivian looked around her. The room did not compare unfavorably with Stone Glenn as she remembered it. It was merely distressingly plain; the furniture, old and not very well cared for.

The silence grew between them. Piers took another sip of brandy. His voice was alcohol warm when he spoke to Watkins. "Beddoes is below."

"Yes, milord. I believe he is with the earl."

"Damn him. Damn them both." Piers cursed evenly as he thrust out the glass for the valet to refill.

Vivian finished her cup of tea and rose.

"Don't go."

She shook her head. A heavy object was being dragged across the floor in the room next door. She pointed in that direction.

"I hear it. I hear it. For God's sake, use your head. Don't go over there in the midst of all that confusion. You'll only add to it."

207

"He's right, milady," Watkins agreed. "Have another cup of tea. Since you have arrived, milord, I'll bring more refreshments." He bowed and left them alone.

"I can't get over your doing this," Piers said when the door had closed behind the valet. "You must be incurably optimistic if you think you can make an impression on this place. Or foregoing that, are you one of those people who likes a fight? I've heard of such, but I've never met any man nor woman to equal the fortitude you seem to display."

Nervously, she interlocked her fingers and thought about his estimates of her.

Piers studied her expressive face, wondering what lay behind it. At last he cleared his throat. "And will you set them to this room when your room is renovated?" A glass object shattered on the floor next door. "Although from the sound of those renovations, they may be too expensive for us to afford many of them."

Vivian rose and crossed to the window that looked out over the terrace. Pulling back the lace curtains, she revealed the filthy windows. Although the sun was shining at that particular moment, its rays were split and refracted by the dinginess of the panes. Shuddering expressively, she dabbed her index finger across the glass and brought it away dark with soil on its tip. Turning back around to face him, she held up the slim member for his inspection.

He grinned as she pulled a handkerchief from her pocket and wiped her finger. "A labor of Hercules indeed. But perhaps you are Hercules in female form. What a unique thought. Hercules herself. Or Heraclea. My father calls you Boadicea. The Celtic warrior-queen. But I shall call you Heraclea. Which are you?"

She shrugged. Smiling faintly, she came to him and

took his free hand. In its palm she traced her name "Vivian."

"Ah, the sorceress who imprisoned Merlin. Magic, not might." He clasped her hand in his big warm one and brought it to his lips. His kiss on her naked palm drove a bolt of lightning through the soft part of her belly.

"Will you clean my room when you have finished with yours?" he asked with curious softness.

Hastily, she pulled the hand away, feeling color again mount in her cheeks. With an attitude of reverence, she brought her palms together. Bowing her head slightly so that her chin touched the third fingers of her hands, she bent her knee in a deep curtsy. As one before her lord and master, her hands parted and her arms spread wide in a slave's gesture of humble obeisance. Then in one fluid movement, she straightened.

He grinned sardonically. "You are no servant, no slave. No question of that." He put out a hand to catch her own and drew her toward him. His head lolled back in the chair so he could look deep into her eyes. The brandy he had drunk had begun to work.

"No, you'll never be any man's slave. But will you truly be my lady?" He shook his head. His eyes closed for an instant and an expression like pain flickered in his face. "Will you truly be my wife?"

Her glance flickering, Vivian stared down at the drawn face. Suddenly it looked infinitely older and sadder. What she read there sobered her. She bit her lower lip against a wave of sympathy. He was in deadly earnest. He wanted not just his right to her body, but his right to her soul.

"Take them, Pross." Larnaervon pointed to the

stacks of ledgers, the boxes of papers. "Close your entire office. Go down to Stone Glenn and go over the place with a fine tooth comb. Find everything. Or if it's not to be found, discover what happened to it."

"Yes, milord."

Larnaervon limped back to his desk and lowered himself painfully. His head sank between his shoulders, like an eagle brooding. "Get a writ," he said, "to keep Dawlish out. He is not to set foot on the place again. Do you hear?"

"Yes, milord." The solicitor's eyes glinted with excitement he could not quite suppress. The business would make his firm powerful. He would have to engage auditors. His efficiency, his dispatch would be remarked on in the City. Important men would seek his services.

"And not a word of this to my son," the earl warned.

Pross raised his eyebrows. "I—I'm not sure that—"

"Not a word. You will report directly to me." The thin skin stretched white over the knobby knuckles as the earl clenched his fists. "Drunken fool."

Pross hesitated. Good business did not require him to question prosperous clients, yet he knew himself to be treading on dangerous ground. "Perhaps responsibility is what the young man needs," he ventured.

"Responsibility!" The earl gave a short bark of contemptuous laughter. "He was hopeless from the very beginning. Never had a head for business or anything else."

"He spent two years at university," Pross observed mildly.

"He *wasted* two years at university," the earl snapped. "His mother was determined that he should go, but I was equally determined that he should not be turned in that direction. I have always had a use for his body here."

210

The old man canted his head up. His eyes narrowed, scanning Pross as if daring the solicitor to make any further remarks.

Pross dropped his eyes. His mind was troubled about what should be told the viscount who was, after all, the lady's husband. Still, the earl paid him handsomely. The man of business gathered up the records and ledgers and went away.

Chapter Thirteen

Addie hastened to answer the knock on Vivian's door. Piers stood there in a black coat and black buckskin trousers. His immaculate white stock was tied in a graceful waterfall. Addie's hands flew to her mouth, her eyes dazzled by his appearance. She dropped an awkward curtsy. "Oh, milord, do come in."

Vivian rose from her dressing table. An uncertain smile on her face, she walked to the center of the room. He was quite the most handsome man she had ever seen. In her heart of hearts she hoped he would find her beautiful. Perhaps they could both be a little bit glad that they had married.

He had seen her in nothing except a nun's habit or a riding dress. Moreover, he had seen her miserable, afraid, angry, hurting. Never had she been able to offer him a voluntary smile. With a conscious effort to please, she smiled for him now.

Before the terrible year of illness and virtual imprisonment, she had dreamed as any young girl would of a London debut. Desperately she wanted to see some hint of admiration in the eyes of the man who was her husband. She was not disappointed.

For the first time Piers saw her garbed in a dress

suitable to her station. Of heavy ice-blue watered silk, its high waistline was gathered just below her breasts with silver ribbons. The skirt fell in long shimmering patterns to a deep row of silver fringe. It parted to tantalizingly reveal slender, silk-clad ankles and narrow feet encased in slippers of the same ice-blue silk.

His admiration was evident in his slow smile. Not so evident was the potent warmth of desire he felt beneath the admiration. "Milady," he murmured. "I've come just in time, I see."

Her smile faded. She blinked and lowered her lashes. How silly to have wanted a less prosaic reaction. Still, she wished she could ask him how he liked the dress, wished she could tell him that this particular ensemble was to have been for her come-out. Because she had fallen ill, she had never gotten to wear it. Now the occasion was past forever.

He frowned as he took both her hands in his. What had he said? *Dolt! A compliment. Pay her a compliment. Have you been removed from polite society so long that you have forgotten how to pay one?* The girl expected a compliment. He cleared his throat. "That gown is exceptional, my dear. I fear if you had been presented in London society, I would have had to fight a half-dozen duels at least for even a dance."

Her lashes swept up. Her eyes shone with a terrible hope. And then a moment of alarm. How had he read her thoughts? The warmth of his hands began to play strange tricks on her body. Tension coiled in her belly. She tugged gently to free herself.

Piers felt her change of attitude though he could not understand it. One minute she had been a graceful form walking toward him, giving him her hands. Then she had become stiff and nervous. "What's wrong?"

She managed to tug her hands free and step back.

213

The resistance annoyed him. *What ailed the fool girl?* Perhaps she really was deficient in some manner. He caught her by the wrist and held her when she would have backed away. "Relax," he snapped. "We've been over this route before. Just because you're all tricked out, I'm not going to spring on you and ravish you before supper. I'm not a monster. I can control my lust for a few more hours."

At the word lust, she tried to twist her wrist away. Her own body was betraying her mind. While her memories fueled her fear, his touch created a heat which she found herself unable to control. Yearnings for she knew not what played havoc with strange places in her body. The tips of her breasts hardened beneath his admiring gaze, and warmth and moisture gathered between her thighs. She looked at him from under her lashes, wishing he would go away, yet wishing he would stay.

"By God, Vivian, I'm a man just like any other. If we had met in society, who can say but that we might have been attracted to one another? Perhaps I would have been enthralled by your beauty had I seen you dancing at Almack's. Perhaps you would have picked me out from among all your other suitors. In any event our marriage was arranged not unlike almost everybody else's and for exactly the same reasons. We are of a class in society where land and money marry for land and money much more often than people marry the people they love." He snorted rudely. "Whatever that may be."

Vivian quit trying to free herself from his grasp and stared at him. Was he apologizing? Was he trying to excuse himself and his father for forcing her into this? Was he merely trying to make her see the way of things—at least from his point of view?

"As for the marriage bed. It was an unmitigated

disaster for you, a virgin. But I beg you again. Don't dwell on it. Tonight." He bent his head and kissed her first on the cheek. "Tonight"—he kissed her on the point of her jaw—"tonight"—and last on the lobe of her ear—"I will teach you what you are made to learn. I promise."

Vivian twisted slightly in his grasp. Her fear was evident again, for his breath, smelling of the brandy he had consumed, was fanning her cheek.

"Be still," he commanded. Insistently, he blew his hot breath in her ear and took her lobe between his teeth.

She trembled as chills ran up and down her spine and covered her arms. Another minute and she would be unable to control her excitement as her blood sang in her veins and her heart pounded. Desperate to escape him before he found out, she tried to pull her head away from his mouth.

His temper flared. With an oath he threw one arm around her waist pulling her tightly against his body. The other hand gently struck the cheek she tried to turn away from him. "Stop that."

Her eyes flashed in anger at the blow even though he had not hurt her. More like a pat, it had not even stung, but it had frightened her. "Don't stare at me like that, and don't struggle any longer. I've had quite enough of that." His low, deep voice exerted a hypnotic quality. She was helpless to move. "I mean to kiss you now and taste what I plan to enjoy tonight. If you let yourself, if you are indeed the sensible girl I believe you to be, you'll enjoy this, too."

Humiliation rode her hard. She felt the curling heat as his lips caressed hers, coaxed her mouth open, touched the inside of it with his tongue. She drove her fingernails into the palms of her hands in hopes that the pain would help her retain some semblance of control.

215

To no avail. The warmth grew, she could not get enough of the taste of him. Suddenly, she rose on tiptoes, her body pressing against him, returning his kiss avidly. Heat blazed between them, their clothes weak barriers to their desire. Her hands clutched at the sleeves of his coat, dragging him closer to her.

At last, dizzy with passion, he lifted his head to look into her face. The light revealed her with eyes closed, cheeks flushed, lips swollen with his kisses. Head tipped back, body pliant against him, she stood in the circle of his arms.

"Open your eyes," he whispered. "That's right. That's a good girl."

She raised her eyelids to see him through a mist of tears.

"Beautiful," he breathed, bending his head to her mouth once more. His lips barely touched hers, but so sensitized was she that she flinched. His tongue flicked out, touching, tasting, moving over and over the same spot until she thought she would scream with passion. The pulse at the base of her throat raced, her breasts rose and fell against his chest with her rapid breathing.

Finally, he withdrew his mouth, shaken to the core. His attempt to put on a cynical smile, failed miserably. Like a fool he had excited himself almost unbearably and now would have to sit through dinner in this uncomfortable condition.

Disgusted with himself, he released her and stepped back. Offering her his arm, he bowed stiffly. "Madam, shall we go down to dinner?"

She nodded weakly. Her face was flushed with excitement, and her chest heaved beneath her soft gown.

He swallowed hard. "Then let us be off, or in another minute I'll have you on that bed and all my good intentions for a long and leisurely lovemaking quite forgotten. As it is I'll have an uncomfortable dinner."

She put her hand on his arm. If she had had a voice, she would have told him that he had only himself to blame. And she blamed him because she, too, felt uncomfortable with the blood pounding in her temples and every sense throbbing almost painfully.

In the hallway, he sucked in a long cold draught of the chill air and glanced down at her appraisingly. "You look so cool. Silvery hair, white skin, ice-blue gown trimmed with silver. A veritable snow queen. The sorceress Vivian. But underneath all that snow, I begin to suspect hot blood flows. Does it?"

She glared at him and shook her head.

"Sweet liar." He laughed. And then he did a thing shocking only because they had reached the end of the hall and were beginning to descend the staircase. He reached across his chest and closed his hand over the mound of her breast. His fingers and thumb felt her, found the hardened nipple easily and pinched it through its fragile covering of silk and gauze.

Her breath escaped in a gasp. Almost painful weakness made her legs tremble. She tripped, tightening her grip on his arm to keep from falling on the stairs. Then embarrassed, she looked down at his hand and then at the empty hall below. Frantically, she pushed his hand away.

He only laughed harder as he let it fall back to his side. He was still laughing as they came to the bottom of the stairs.

Her nerves still vibrating, Vivian sat at the supper table staring across the space of white cloth at Piers's stony features. The food was immeasurably better, but

217

her husband had tasted nothing of the clear court bouillon nor the excellent fish served with a small side dish of tiny Brussels sprouts.

Millard stood at attention at the sideboard, his hands at his sides, waiting to give the signal to serve the next course. Mrs. Felders, her hands folded under her apron, her lips pursed in tight disapproval, lingered in the shadows beyond the doorway.

So far the housekeeper had been pleased to see the earl had torn a patch off his son for drinking too much. Still, he had made no comment about the meal. Indeed, apart from rejecting the clear soup with a wave of his hand, he had eaten liberally of the fish and fresh bread and butter. Then, his first hunger satisfied, he had resumed the furious tirade with which he had entered the dining room.

"You're not to drink again," the earl snarled at his son. "I've told you. Spirits mar the performance. You have a wife. A breeder by the look of her. When we get a little meat on her bones, she'll bear healthy children." He gestured rudely with his fork.

"Larne," Piers snarled. "I warn you."

"Warn me. Ha!" He looked at Vivian. "He warns me, but he doesn't do anything. Don't ever be afraid of him, m'dear. He only talks." He smiled and forked up another bite of food. "Wouldn't you like to have children, daughter?"

Vivian could feel the color rising in her cheeks. She shot an agonized look at Millard, whose face registered a flash of sympathy before he picked up the tray and left the room, shooing Mrs. Felders before him and closing the door.

The earl looked over his shoulder. "Ah, embarrassed before the servants. Nonsense. My servants have been hired for their discretion. Isn't that right, Piers?"

The viscount pushed back from the table and

218

stomped to the sideboard. Then he collared a decanter and a glass. He brought them back to the table with him and threw himself into his chair.

If a look could have killed, the earl's gaze would have burned him where he sat. When Piers defiantly sloshed the brandy into the glass, Larne turned his attention back to Vivian. "A little blue-eyed girl just like yourself, my dear." His voice changed to the silky-smooth seduction she had heard before. "A sturdy little red-haired boy. Did you know Piers was almost carrot-headed when he was child? A charming boy. Eager, intelligent, mischievous. Wouldn't you like a pair like that?"

She looked from one man to another. Taking a deep breath, she nodded.

The earl chuckled softly, never taking his eyes off his new daughter-in-law. "There, Piers. She's agreeable. What are you waiting for?" He leaned toward her. "My dear, you may have to help my tardy son. Now that you know the way of it, perhaps you could visit him?"

Her cheeks blazed. She crushed her napkin beside her plate, and started to rise.

The earl raised his hand. "Now, don't fly off in a rage, my dear. Finish your dinner. And think about it."

Piers turned white to the lips. He tossed an ounce of fiery liquid into the back of his throat. "Before God, Larne, you go too far. I will not tolerate—"

"With that in your stomach, you can tolerate anything," his father interrupted contemptuously.

During the serving of the next course, the charged silence grew. Vivian stared from one man to the other. *Was this to be the rule for the dinner hour in her new life? How could such hatred and contempt exist in the same household for much longer without violence erupting?*

The Earl of Larnaervon stared at the slice of roast

219

beef on his plate. From its faintly pink center to its crusty outer edge, he could find no fault with it. As the footman ladled a piquant sauce out beside it, he smiled again at his daughter-in-law. "I have heard reports of your doings, madam."

Vivian tensed. She could well imagine what sort of reports Emma Felders had brought him.

"Would you like to hear some of them?"

"Not if they're going to be lies, Larne," Piers interceded. He stared hard at the open doorway. Vivian could see that the housekeeper was back, listening in the shadows.

"Oh, I very much doubt them to be lies, my boy. Just differences of opinion." Larne took an appreciative sip of a fine Beaujolais that had been left to breathe for just the right amount of time. "For example, I understand you have been interrupting the regimen of the house to a disastrous degree. The servants it seems are quite exhausted by your incessant demands. You have, according to a source close at hand, criticized the cook until he has threatened to quit."

"No great loss," Piers gritted. "A farmer serves better swill to hogs."

Ignoring his son, Larne cut himself a bite of the tender roast beef and forked it into his mouth. "Fortunately, for my digestion tonight, he decided to wait. This seems quite edible, so perhaps he has reconsidered. I would appreciate your tasting the roast tonight."

Nervously, Vivian cut herself a bite. The beef was done to perfection, succulent and flavorful. The mild horseradish sauce complemented without overpowering the taste.

"Is it good?" the earl asked.

Vivian nodded, her expression puzzled.

"I'm glad you find it to your liking. I can taste

nothing, as you no doubt became aware last night. The accident that crippled me also smashed my nose. While a clever doctor was able to straighten it out to look quite like what it was before, he was not able to do anything about the nerves there. I can taste—salt, sugar, bitter, and sour—but the sense of smell which makes food distinctive is gone alas forever."

Vivian could almost pity him. Still something in the calculated way he looked at her made her realize he was gauging her reactions. She glanced across the table at Piers, whose mouth was curved in a sneer.

"We've heard it all before, Larne. No one feels sorry for you. You know why you're served the food you're served. Your whore—"

The earl gave a bark of laughter. "Watch your tongue in front of your bride's delicate ears. Wasn't that what you told me yesterday evening? Vivian, my dear, what shall we do with your husband? He seems almost beyond the touch of polite society."

The new Viscountess Polwycke had come to realize that she sat in the middle of a hornet's nest. Perhaps she was just as well off unable to speak. Neither man could demand that she take sides. Unfortunately, her stomach had clenched and unclenched so many times that she had completely lost her appetite. Swallowing hard, she stared down at her plate.

Piers took a long drink of brandy. No longer white, his face now appeared flushed with blood. Vivian observed the knuckles of his clenched and trembling fist as he sought to control his mounting anger and resentment. The other hand cradled the brandy glass and swirled it in a steady circular motion as if he sought to hypnotize himself with its contents.

Millard came to Vivian's side. As he topped off her wineglass, he gave a faint deliberate nudge of her elbow. Vivian glanced up and met his eyes, kind and

221

encouraging in his otherwise impassive face. A small warm spot of gratitude grew in her breast. A faint nod of his head and he was gone, but the compliment was delivered. The food was good. Evidently the cook and the butler, as well as Addie, were trying to please their new mistress. Even if they were doing so to thwart and anger Mrs. Felders, they were still pleasing her and making her a lot more comfortable.

Likewise, the earl had not exactly sided with Mrs. Felders. His comments with regard to the woman's tales had been neither positive nor negative. Heartened, she determined to adopt an eat-or-starve attitude. She would devote her attention solely to her food while ignoring as best she could the atmosphere of the room.

No sooner made than her resolution was interrupted by the earl. "Vivian," he said silkily. "My dear, I leave the subject of domestic activity which—albeit fascinating—is not a great favorite of mine with this one thought. Manage to give me a grandson and you can turn the house over and shake out the contents onto the beach for all I care. To that end I shall instruct my housekeeper. Do I make myself clear?"

She met his eyes and shivered at the steely look she read there.

"Do you understand?"

She nodded. Her cheeks were hot, but she was going to have to get used to the earl's personal questions. She took a deep breath and finished her food.

Across the table Piers still scowled from under his brows, but Vivian would not look at him again. Disgusted and more than half drunk, he ran his left hand through his hair. The thoughts he directed toward his wife were not pleasant. Although he could not blame his drinking on her, he had come to the inebriated conclusion that had she been more receptive, more cooperative, she would have accompanied him into the garden last night for a breath of fresh air. She should have waited while his head cleared and then taken him into her bed.

Tonight he had already promised her that he would come to her. Were it not for his promise, however, he would avoid her like the plague. His father would not tell him what to do. He had made love on demand once. He would be damned if he would perform like a prize ram for Larne's heir. His thoughts whirled and grew murkier with each passing minute as the brandy in his bloodstream depressed his spirit.

Perhaps he should eat something, just to keep up his strength. Leaving the empty brandy glass, he began to eat the excellent beef and Yorkshire pudding. His spirits lifted a bit with the ingestion of food, and he sat up straighter, paying more attention to his plate. Again he glanced across the table at his silent wife. Their eyes met as she raised hers from her plate to reach for her glass. His angry stare of a few minutes ago was replaced by a slight smile. He forked another bite of food into his mouth and she smiled at him.

No words were spoken through the remainder of the course. As the footman cleared away for the sweet to be served, Lord Alexander raised his head from between his shoulders and peered at his son. Piers sat with his shoulder turned away from the head of the table. One elbow propped him up; his eyes stared moodily into the heart of the candles. When the butler approached with dessert, he was waved away.

Larne's stare shifted to Vivian, who likewise had now presented him with a side front, her eyes carefully avoiding both of her dinner companions. One small white hand rested on the cloth where her fingernail traced the pattern in the damask.

Feeling pervertedly pleased at having cowed them

both, the old man cleared his throat in the manner of one making an announcement of great import. "Piers, the *Spanish Girl* comes tonight after midnight."

The long body stiffened. With a visible effort it turned and straightened in the chair. The viscount blinked, then raked all ten fingers through his dark red hair. "So," came the wet slurred whisper. "So. Tell me, Larne. Do you wish me to bed my lady before or after I handle the family business?"

"Insolent bastard."

"Ah, but I'm not a bastard," Piers pointed out. "And you don't wish I were. Do you, old man?" The alcohol had roughened and numbed the vocal cords. He coughed hoarsely.

"Millard!" the earl called.

"M'lord."

"Prepare a pot of strong, black coffee. Send for Watkins. He'll have to get his charge sober enough to ride. That is"—he turned to Piers—"if you're to be gone and back before the morning tide."

"By that I take it I am to ride my horse first and my wife later." Piers rose from the table, staggering slightly. His mocking bow to his father overbalanced him and he had to catch himself with his palm on the table. "My apologies, lady wife. But, you see, the Earl of Larnaervon has spoken. Does the *Girl* land in the inlet?"

"Beddoes is having her brought in farther up the coast. The garrison commander has been asking questions in the village."

"Ah. A long ride indeed." Piers swayed and belched softly. "Hope I'm up to it." He reached for the brandy glass and drained it, staggering backward and knocking over his chair.

Larne pushed himself to his feet. His yellowed knobby knuckles pressed against the tablecloth. "Give me a grandson," he muttered to Vivian. "A grandson."

Mrs. Felders had come into the dining room behind the butler, now she hovered behind the earl's chair, a contemptuous smile on her face as she watched Piers's swaying figure.

"Where in the hell is that valet?" the earl growled over his shoulder. "See what's holding him up."

Vivian too rose from her chair and threw down her napkin. Whoever the Spanish girl was, she seemed to have put a cap on the dinner. Without speaking to either of her dining companions, Vivian sought to slip from the dining room.

Her husband's hand fell on her shoulder. The hot, moist fingers scorched the skin over her collarbone. He staggered slightly. For a moment she felt more than the weight of his hand and put out her own to steady herself against the paneling. She did not turn but stared down at the hand on her shoulder and then back up at him.

His dark eyes, glowing like anthracite, hardened as he correctly read her disgust of him and his condition. He straightened but did not let go of her shoulder. "Madam wife," he spoke steadily in a whisper, "as you've heard, duty calls. And when the earl speaks, a man can do no more than obey."

Millard and Watkins entered at that moment.

"Get him off her," the earl barked angrily. "*Now* he wants to make love. Fool."

Watkins came to the viscount's side. "Milord—"

"In a moment." He moved his hand to clasp the side of her neck. He could feel the pulse throbbing there, feel her contempt despite his intoxicated state. "When I return, Vivian, I promise to come back to join you in your bed. Be warm and willing for me. I assure you a ride in the icy air will sober me up amazingly."

Her heart pounded in her chest. He was very drunk,

had deliberately made himself so. Thank God for the reprieve, whatever it might be. She nodded.

With a mocking smile to her and then to the earl, Piers released her shoulder and allowed the valet to lead him out.

Vivian slipped out of the dining room behind them. In the hall she caught her skirts in her hands and fled as though pursued by demons. She had set her first step on the foot of the staircase when she heard his laugh, a low, menacing sound devoid of humor.

Looking back over her shoulder, she felt her heart pound more violently than before. Piers was standing outside the dining-room door, his form lighted from the side by a branch of candles. His wine-red hair and velvet coat glowed in the muted light. One side of his face was in darkness; the other, a study in light and shadow. A high pale forehead, a shadowed circle beneath the eyebrow, a curving jut of cheekbone above a hollowed cheek, a straight, determined line of jaw. The singular impression on her sensitive nerves was one of fierce implacability.

With a terrified gasp, she hiked her skirts even higher and ran up the stairs.

"The tide's changing, Captain."

"It shouldn't be much longer then. Check your weapons, men." Rory MacPherson sat his horse on the headland. His men had deployed themselves on the road less than a mile below Larnaervon castle. From his vantage point he could see the stretch of white sand beach clear beneath the ice-ringed moon.

"Shipments at regular intervals," Dawlish had said. And department information had reported a flurry of activity aboard at least two of the seedier sloops in Le Havre.

226

Of course, they could have been legitimate merchants making trade voyages, but the nature of their cargoes—brandy, silks, and laces—the very items guaranteed to make a quick turnover among the English gentry had all but confirmed that they were smuggling vessels.

As MacPherson watched, a lantern flashed in the Larnaervon stables. A few minutes later a couple of horsemen came galloping down the road. At the trail to the beach they turned off and began to descend.

"Move down the cliffs, men. Quietly, now, on your life. We want to be on the sand by the time they reach it, but not so close that they can see us and signal the ship to pull out. They've got to be unloading the goods. If they offer any resistance, shoot. They mustn't get away." MacPherson dismounted, tied his horse, and selected a path of descent.

The gale blowing from the water cut his face and made his eyes water. Coast patrol was a terrible job. The sort of thing a Scotsman would get stuck with. If he managed to nab this smuggler, he might expect a promotion and a better position. His boot slipped on a wet rock and he slid a couple of yards through the clay and bracken. With a mild curse, he stopped himself and moved on more cautiously.

On the headland the soldiers had just vacated, another lantern flashed once, twice.

"Now." The viscount ducked his head as he guided his stallion out of the stable. He and a half-dozen stalwarts loped their horses across the meadow and up to the road above the castle. "Far enough, lads," he called. "Whip 'em up."

The band of men galloped up the coast to meet the *Spanish Girl.*

Chapter Fourteen

Tucked beneath the covers, the upper half of her body propped up by several feather pillows, Vivian stared into the fire still burning strongly on the hearth. Her silver braid lay over her left shoulder outside of the covers, for all the world like a princess in a medieval painting from the Book of Hours.

She lay just as Addie had arranged her when she had helped her mistress into bed. But Vivian's stillness was false. Every nerve in her body sang with tension; her ears were tuned for the slightest sound. Her hands nervously plucked at the lace edge of the sheet.

Midnight tolled and then one and two. The fire died, and with it the tension changed to exhaustion. Several times she had thought she had heard footsteps on the stairs, once in the hallway outside, but no one came to her room, nor to the room next door. During the long hours she had reasoned with herself and lectured herself about how she must remain calm, and that she really had nothing to worry about.

After all, hundreds of women had gone to their marriage beds without knowing, much less liking, their husbands. From queens to peasant girls the whole great sisterhood of married women had all faced the inevitable first time and most had not had any say in their husbands. She would endure as they had done and bear children whom she could love and cherish.

Over and over she told herself that the terrible experience of a couple of days ago—had it been only a couple of days—was not at all how it would be. He had been rushed. She had been unprepared for any of it.

He had promised it would be different. When she had burst into his room and demanded that he make love to her— She could feel herself growing hot with shame. After it was all over, he had wanted to continue and do it the proper way.

He had always been kind to her. He was an unhappy man who would not hurt someone who had never done him any harm. Only when he had been drinking . . . She pushed that thought firmly away. His kisses were not unpleasant.

Despite her own council, her thoughts kept returning inexorably to the pain she had suffered that first time. How could he know he would not hurt her? He was not a woman. Presumably he would have no idea if she would ever be big enough to accommodate him. Perhaps they would never fit. Perhaps he was too big?

Nervous rigors shook her body. Her forehead felt hot as fire; her feet and hands, cold as death. To keep from crying out, she gritted her teeth until her jaws ached. The wind soughed against the windows.

"So, you've returned." The earl leaned on his cane, his face gray. Deep grooves bracketed his mouth and divided his eyebrows.

"Frozen but alive." Piers's throat was so raw that he had almost no voice left.

The yellow light from several lanterns threw the men's shadows onto the cellar walls. Heavy burdens on their shoulders and in their arms distorted them into monstrous shapes. Mentally, the earl counted the pieces of cargo.

"It's all there, Larne," Piers rasped painfully. "Some of it we had to swim for, but eventually it was all unloaded and stowed in the wagons."

"And the Riding Officers?"

"Will and Jamie led 'em a merry chase for miles. down the beach." This from Jack Beddoes, who had come up behind the viscount. "Finally lost 'em in the headlands. They'll be searching the caves for weeks, maybe months."

The earl nodded. "Good. Good. They'll be off our backs."

Beddoes grinned maliciously. "MacPherson'll have trouble getting his superiors to let him order another night like this."

"Excellent."

"I wouldn't be too sure." The viscount wearily mounted the stairs toward his father. "He's smart and stubborn. He's dedicated to his job. And unfortunately he's honest. He won't take a bribe and he won't take tonight's wild-goose chase as more than a momentary setback."

"Then perhaps we will just have to bribe someone higher up the line," Larne muttered speculatively.

Piers halted two steps below his father. "You'll keep on until you'll bring the whole thing down on us." He coughed deeply. "It gets more dangerous every time we go. MacPherson can search those caves for a month or more; but when he finds nothing, where will he come? Back here where Will and Jamie started from."

"And we'll lead him in a different direction and land the *Spanish Girl* in the headlands." Jack Beddoes slapped his gauntlets against his thigh. The wet leather cracked like a whip.

Larne stared down at the smuggler, but Piers did not so much as glance around. Wearily, he brushed by the earl. "And that greedy bastard is going to get himself killed," he murmured. "Unfortunately, we'll all probably go down with him."

At the cellar door stood Mrs. Felders, her face illuminated by the lamp she held to guide the earl's feet. At the viscount's remark, her face suffused with anger and her breath hissed in through her pursed lips.

Vivian started awake, jerking upright, the covers falling from her shoulders. She must have fallen asleep and allowed the fire to go out. The room was icy cold and dark except for a few red eyes of coals glowing faintly beneath the grate.

Slipping on her night robe, she hurried across the carpet to pile on more coal from the scuttle. Toes curled, teeth chattering so hard her jaws ached, she bent over to stir the bed into new life.

Suddenly, she distinctly heard the grating of the lock mechanism and the creak of hinges as the door to the viscount's room next to hers swung open. Like a hunted animal she whirled. The poker clattered from her hand. With a deafening noise it struck the fire tongs and whisk setting them to swinging and clanking in their stand. Fearfully she cowered against the mantel dreading what must come.

At first, silence greeted her confusion, to be broken by a murmured conversation between Piers and Watkins. She heard the door to Piers's room open and close again.

At the sound of its closing, Vivian fled breathlessly to her bed. Flinging out of her robe and burrowing

231

under the covers, she pulled them tight up to her chin. The bed curtains had been tied back on one side and the foot. Between the posts she could see the door.

He was coming. So late. Surely he could not expect that she would be waiting for him. Surely he must be too exhausted after meeting the Spanish girl, whoever she might be. Watkins had probably come out the door and gone on quietly to his own much deserved rest.

Even as Vivian framed the thought, the handle of her door began to turn. Staring at the softly glowing brass in the light from the newly made fire, Vivian's eyes burned as she caught her breath and held it. So it was to be tonight.

Silhouetted in the doorway, tall and black, a light behind him, stood her husband. He wore a full-length robe of quilted velvet. In his right hand he carried the crystal carafe of brandy. His shadow falling before him made him appear incredibly tall before he stepped inside and closed the door. Slowly he walked across the room to the foot of her bed. Deliberately, he contemplated her across its length.

Now that he was really there a curious calm settled over her. The waiting was over. Her hands relaxed over the top of the covers. Slowly, she straightened out of the tight ball she had drawn herself into. She let out a long breath.

The fire hissed and spat sparks. The flame leaped high bathing the bed in red light. She was sure he could read trepidation in her face, although his was still hidden in shadows.

She felt a need to say something, but what? Where had he been? Why did he come so late? Wouldn't it be better to wait until another time when both of them were not so nearly exhausted? If only she had the power of speech, she could say so many things, offer so many alternatives.

232

At last when her nerves were stretched almost to the breaking point, he moved around the end of the bed. Her eyes followed him as he came between her and the fire, as he put his hand around the bedpost. They watched in a sort of trance as he set the carafe on the table. Wearily, he dropped down beside her, the mattress sagging beneath his weight. His face was visible now in the flames that flickered up as the fresh charcoal caught.

Her hand flew to her mouth at the sight of his ravaged countenance. He looked more gaunt than ever. Watkins had combed the wine-dark hair starkly back from his forehead where deep lines of strain and exhaustion crossed above his eyebrows. Dark smudges underscored his eyes. His mouth, set in a tight, mirthless smile, only deepened the creases running from the sides of his nose almost to his jaw. He might have been as old as his father.

Enigmatically, he stared at her for a full minute before reaching for the carafe. With practiced fingers he held the stopper and neck in one hand and poured a liberal tot into the water glass. Lifting it to his lips and tipping back his head, he tossed the fiery liquid down his throat. Bracing himself, he shuddered slightly and set the glass back on the table.

Raising one dark eyebrow, he spoke in a voice that rasped painfully out of his throat. "Vivian, dear wife, how kind of you to remain awake for me. I really hadn't expected it. And a warm and welcoming fire, too? You've gone to too much trouble."

Even as he spoke, his hand reached out. He rested its fingertips on her smooth cheek. "I expected you to be sound asleep."

His touch was so cold that Vivian flinched. Noticing her movement, Piers drew back instantly. "Sorry. I didn't realize." He tucked his fingers into the palms of

233

his hands and lifted them to his mouth to blow on them. "I should have remembered." Rising wearily, he stalked to the fire. "The wind from the sea tonight was an icy knife. In fact more than my fingers are chilled to the bone."

Leaning up on one elbow, she watched him as he bent to the fire rubbing his hands briskly above the flames. Suddenly, she was glad she had lighted it, glad she had waited up even though she had done so out of fear rather than concern. A lock of his long, dark hair almost dry now swung forward to bisect his cheekbone. He turned his head to look at her with a wan smile.

He looked as she had first seen him, sitting beside his dying mother. Then as now his face was gaunt. Then as now he looked miserably unhappy and tired to death. A pang of sympathy tore at her heart. A pang of pity. A pang of tenderness.

He warmed his hands to his satisfaction, straightened and stretched, groaning as he did so. "That will have to do," he murmured. "I hope I don't cause you too much discomfort."

At his approach, she clutched the bedclothes to her neck and stared wide-eyed into the shadow of his tall form. Sighing softly at the expression he read there, he resumed his seat on the bed facing her. His right hand, now warm, but terribly rough as if it had been exposed to the most inclement of weather covered both of hers and gently pressed the coverings down.

"You have nothing to fear, my lady," he murmured softly as the palm of his left hand gently caressed her shoulder pushing aside the silky braid resting on her breast.

Vivian drew a deep breath. Inwardly trembling, she kept her eyes on his face, watching his expression, seeking to read his feelings toward her. As she stared, his eyelids closed and his head sank to his chest.

Sightlessly, he continued to caress her shoulder. Just when she had begun to relax at that presumption of her person, he slipped his palm lower to find, as he had once before, the mound of her breast this time covered only by the thin lawn of her nightdress. "You feel beautiful," he sighed softly as he moved his hand in a circular motion, rubbing the warm flesh beneath the material. His hand was still quite cold. Perhaps the fire had only warmed the surface of the skin so the chill still seeped from his bones.

Nevertheless, the friction and the coolness caused her nipple to harden in his palm. Strangely disturbed by the peculiar feeling, she sucked her breath in sharply.

"Dear wife," he whispered as if he had been waiting for some response. "Does the rest of your body feel as warm and pleasant as your breast? Let me just—" Without finishing his sentence, he slipped both hands down to clasp her rib cage. At the same time, his thumbs circled the nipples of her breasts, circling, pressing, circling, pressing.

Vivian caught her lower lip between her teeth, afraid of the strength of her body's responses. Twisting under the gentle ministrations, she caught his wrists in her hands.

"No," he breathed. "Oh, no. Don't try to stop me. Be still. Better still, lie back." Gently he pressed her back into the bed before he took his hands away.

Rising stiffly, he unbelted the quilted robe. As he slipped it off, she caught her breath, staring at his body in utter fascination. He was naked underneath, his skin very, very white. Although she had seen his loins, they seemed somehow more than naked. As if the whole spectacular male creature were greater, more dominant than the parts. The dark hair arrowed up his belly and spread out in a light pelt across his lean, muscular chest.

In the dim light she could not tell whether it was the same color as the hair on his head. The thought of the dark red hair curling lightly on his white skin made liquid heat curl at the base of her belly. Involuntarily, she drew up one leg beneath the sheets and twisted onto her hip.

Recognizing the sensuous movements as the beginnings of sexual excitement, Piers tossed his robe across the foot of the bed. The very sight of him warmed her, whereas he—he was tired to death. Although the touch of her had excited him, he could not sustain the excitement.

His throat was so sore, he would be lucky if it did not turn putrid. His legs fairly trembled with exhaustion and his head pounded. He had not the strength for a long bout tonight. Certainly he did not have the strength to woo and bed a frightened demi-virgin.

Mentally, he cursed Larne. What was he doing here if not obeying the earl's command? He had ridden for hours through the icy night, stood beside and finally waded into the tumbling surf. The skin of his cheeks and nose had been freezing in the icy wind that literally froze the very breath an inch from his nose. A part of a human chain, he had passed dripping bundles and crates up a line. Now he had no physical reserves left. His body ached from toe to crown with exhaustion.

He looked at her face, the eyes wide with alarm, the pupils filling the pale iris. As he stared, she moistened her lips nervously. He had promised her no pain when he should come to her again. Certainly, she did not deserve a quick thrust and then oblivion.

Instead, she deserved a long, slow lovemaking with kisses and caresses. Yet here she was, waiting for him, her body stirring in nervous excitement and dread beneath the covers, her eyes like a haunted child's.

He slipped between the sheets and drew her to him. As he had expected, her untutored body was stiff and awkward. He had to lift her arms and put them around his shoulders. Then, he parted her thighs and lowered himself onto the bed.

Only the finest of lawn nightdresses separated their bodies, and hers felt on fire with embarrassment where his touched. He must be able to feel every bone, every curve, every— She shuddered at the intensity of the wave of feeling that started with her toes and flooded upward. Thank heavens, he could not see her face in the dimness.

"Oh, God, you feel so good," Piers murmured. "So incredibly warm. I had begun to think I was going to die of the cold." Her belly and breasts fairly radiated heat against his chilled skin. The insides of her thighs closed like warm silk about his flanks. He shifted and groaned in pleasure.

Pressed against him, Vivian hardly dared to breathe. How could he be not only unconcerned but positively luxuriating in their closeness? Her muscles were paralyzed by the smell and feel of him. His clean male scent, only slightly tainted by the brandy he had consumed, filled her nostrils.

And he was so cold. The expression "chilled to the bone" must describe his condition. Suddenly, his limbs and body began to shiver and his teeth to chatter as if he had allowed his tight controls to succumb to the cold that permeated his entire being.

Without thinking what she did, she wrapped her arms and legs tight around him and began to chafe his back with her hands.

"Umm-m. That's good. Ohh-h. Ohh." He pressed his forehead into the side of her neck. "God. I must be

237

freezing you to death. Oh, that's good, that's good."

Gradually as she continued to warm him, he relaxed his limbs. The warmth of the bed and her body enclosed him. Gradually the shivering decreased in violence and finally stopped altogether. At last he lay still, his breath tickling her neck. She felt him tremble with weariness. Then he resolutely stiffened and raised his head off her shoulder.

"Kiss me," he whispered, his mouth hovering over hers.

Obediently, she met his lips with hers.

He lifted his head after only a brief pressure and sighed. "I know you're inexperienced, but at least open your mouth." He rested his forehead on her shoulder before he went on talking. "You kiss the way children kiss, and we're not children."

He kissed her again with better results. His tongue delved into her mouth, caressing her tongue, and running along the edge of her teeth. When she shivered and squirmed, he made a soft sound that might have been a chuckle.

"Did you like that?" he asked when he drew away for breath. Again his head dropped to her shoulder. Beneath his cheek lay her braid. He stroked it feeling its texture and shape with his fingers. He wound it around his hand and tugged at it gently. "Vivian," he whispered, "run your hands up and down my back slowly. A man likes to be touched, too, as well as warmed."

Embarrassed where she had not been before, she spread her hands awkwardly and pushed her palms down over his shoulder blades, then back up to clasp his neck. Her hands came together at his nape and pushed upward through his hair. It curled over her fingers, heavy and coarser than hers, like the hair on his body. She could hear it crackle with electricity as it slid beneath her palms. His skin beneath it was very warm.

Against her neck he groaned softly, exhaling his warm breath over her bosom. "God! Your touch, Vivian." He kissed the tender spot below her ear.

Since her action pleased him so much, she reasoned she would be foolish not to do it. Steadily, gently, she continued to stroke him, casting spells of her own to tame the devil who lay between her legs. First, her fingers roved through the hair on the back of his head. Then, shyly, she began to knead the heavy muscles of his naked shoulders.

His body relaxed against her; his weight pressed hard on her breast and in the cradle of her thighs. Despite his heaviness, she slid her hands along his shoulders and down along his spine to the middle of his back.

Suddenly, his breathing evened. She froze, then smiled. He had drifted off to sleep. Stopping her stroking, she sought to wriggle out from under him.

He stirred fretfully and muttered. His hands at her breast and hip clutched her as if she were his favorite toy.

The fire began to die and the room to darken. If she could continue to stroke him until he was deeply asleep, then she could postpone the violation of her body for one more night. If he fell asleep and remained asleep, she might slip away from him and he would never know when she had gone from his side. Where she would go, she had no idea. Perhaps into his room?

Long minutes crept by. His slumber deepened. His weight pressed heavier and heavier upon her torso. Her right hand began to tingle unpleasantly and go numb. She could not feel his skin beneath her fingers, but still she dared not move for fear of waking him. As the fire began to die, she could finally bear his weight no longer. Cautiously, she pushed at his shoulder. He muttered and shifted over to his side. As he moved, she breathed a silent prayer and dragged her upper body and right arm from under his chest.

She was free!

With a soft grunt he settled deeper into the bed. She started up but then fell back covering her mouth to suppress her gasp of dismay. He had wrapped her long braid around his hand and now clutched it in a loose fist. When she tried to unwind it, he muttered and tightened his grip on it.

Exasperated, Vivian sank back against the pillow. Helpless, she turned her face toward her tormentor. By the light of the dying fire, she stared at him. His long eyelashes fanned his cheeks, the harsh lines smoothed out around his mouth. His finely chiseled lips were firmly closed. His long hair fell over his forehead.

As she watched, he turned more onto his stomach and pushed the right fist up beneath his chin. Her braid wrapped around it was beneath his lips as if he were about to kiss it.

Even as she gazed at his face in the light from the dying embers, her own weariness settled on her. She was beyond trembling; her limbs were merely leaden. Her eyelids drooped wearily then flickered open in fear. Her husband had not moved. With a sigh she closed her eyes. This was her bed and it was warm and snug. Her body sank into slumber.

Later as the fire died down on the hearth, the two bodies moved closer, huddling together, their limbs entangled, as each drew warmth from the other against the encroaching chill.

"The whole thing's going to blow up in our faces, love. We'd best be moving on."

"Don't be such a coward, Emma. We've got a sweet arrangement here. It's got a lot more time to run." Jack Beddoes tipped back in his chair, his booted feet propped on the open door of the oven.

She handed him a steaming mug. "But if that captain—"

"He's a fool. And if he comes a-sniffin' around here too many times, then one dark night, a stray bullet'll find him."

Emma shuddered. "And we'll be running for sure."

He laughed nastily. "There's always more arrangements. And them that stays here can take the blame."

"That bead-rattler will queer the deal."

He cocked his head upward at her. "You're really tetched on her, ain't you?"

She wrapped her arms around her body and dropped onto the bench beside the kitchen table. "She's the one who's tetched. Creeping around without making a sound. A woman who doesn't talk is a crazy woman."

"So is a woman who talks," Jack sneered.

"She's always watching. Always listening. And the men go out of their beans about her. That old stick Millard started treating her like she was somebody the minute she came in with a dress on. Even Larne himself . . ."

Beddoes put back his head and hooted with laughter. "Emma, m'darlin', the bird's made you jealous."

She flared up at him, straightening from her slumped position and throwing out her ample breasts. "What do I have to be jealous about?"

"Not a damn thing, m'darlin'." He leered at her. "Not a damn thing."

"Right you are." She lifted her chin, her dark eyes glittering. "Bloodless bitch."

He drained the steaming mug and set it down on the

241

floor beside the chair. His boots hit the floor at the same instant and he pushed himself upright. "Sometimes I get right jealous though."

Her lids drooped. She moistened her lower lip with a flick of her tongue.

"I'm the one who's sleepin' alone." He pushed back his greatcoat from his waist. A belt buckle fully four inches high cinched in a thick belt of black leather. Reaching across his body, he drew from it a volley gun with four barrels and laid it on the table beside her shoulder.

She dared him with a look. "And whose fault is that?"

His belt buckle was within a couple of inches of her chin. He ran his hands through her hair, hurting her with his violence and scattering the pins. "I just wonder how good that old man really is."

She whimpered, the pain making her eyes tear. "As good as any fifty-five-year old can be."

"And how good is that?" He pulled her hair gently.

"He falls asleep a lot."

Beddoes laughed. "Before or after?"

She shrugged. "Sometimes during."

"Poor Emma." His voice carried not a hint of sympathy. "So you're sleeping alone, too. Do you still taste the same, Emma? Do you still not wear any drawers?"

She pushed herself up. "You talk too damn much." Catching his face between her hands, she glued her mouth to his.

He grunted as he butted his hips forward. His fists fastened in her skirts and began to pull them up. Even before he had the petticoats bunched around her waist, he had discovered the answer to his question.

His hard fingers sank deep into her naked buttocks. She cried out against his mouth, but he was inexorable. Roughly, he lifted her, tilting her pelvis as he pleased, uncaring of her person. She fought against his handling, but he pushed his knee between hers and set his booted foot upon the bench. Her feet no longer touched the floor, but she rode his thigh. Her back arched as he plunged his tongue into her mouth effectively, stilling her protests.

Roughly he began to jog his thigh up and down and rock her from side to side. After only a minute, she stiffened. Her nails dug into his cheeks. She screamed again in his mouth.

For a minute more he held her until her spasms had ceased, then he pushed her back until she fell sprawling across the table. Ruthlessly, he unbuttoned himself and thrust into her. She opened her mouth to scream, but he slapped a hand over it and pistoned harder.

Her eyes were open above his hand damning him silently. Fierce as any vixen, she sank her teeth into the fleshy pad at the base of his thumb.

With a yell of pain, he climaxed into her body and jerked his hand away. Her head slammed back against the table, as he cuffed her across her mouth then collapsed on her.

They lay unmoving for a time, their bodies satiated. At last, she spoke. "Get off me, Jack. Your belt buckle's cutting my belly."

He shrugged and pushed himself up, his hands on either side of her shoulders. "And how you love it."

"I'd like a little kindness and softness once in a while," she complained, sitting up and rubbing the back of her head.

He snorted as he rocked back to his feet and jumped nimbly away. "That'll be the day. When Larnaervon gets through with you, I'll bet you lie on your back and stare at the ceiling."

"I'll have you know—"

243

"I do know." He buttoned himself and reached for her skirts. With a jerk he pulled them down and lifted her to her feet. "Ah, Emma. What a fortune a man could earn with you in a house of your own."

"Damn you, forget that, Jack Beddoes. I don't whore for no one."

He laughed as he stuck the duckfoot back in his belt. "Got to be goin', Emma, m'darlin'. And thanks. I've been warmed up real nice now."

Chapter Fifteen

The Viscount Polwycke breathed in the clean fresh odor of lavender-scented linen. As he emerged from a dreamless sleep, he became aware of smoothness and softness. The side of his face was pressed against a pillow that did not stink of sweat and brandy. Where was he?

Although he was still tired, his head did not ache as it usually did in the morning. His stomach did not churn. Instead, he felt a sharp pain in his vitals. Hunger. He was hungry. Rolling over on his back with a groan, he opened his eyes. Above him a strange canopy stretched before his puzzled eyes. And then he remembered.

He lay in his wife's bedchamber. He raised his head and looked around him warily. Where was she?

In the darkest hours of the night, he had come to her exhausted, his body aching with his exertions and half frozen from exposure to the elements. He could not remember anything after he had crawled into bed beside her. Dropping his head back onto the pillow, he closed his eyes in an effort to summon up some recollection of what had happened next. He remembered settling himself on her belly. Her thighs had wrapped warmly around his waist.

He remembered—he remembered her hair in his hand. He raised his right hand and opened his eyes. Rubbing his thumb speculatively across the tips of the other four fingers, he recalled the soft skein of silk wound around his palm.

Hesitantly, he lifted the covers and stared at the sheet on which he lay. Too smooth by half. Unstained. Moreover, his own loins did not feel the delicious lassitude he associated with satiation. He wiped his palm across the lower half of his face.

"Damn!"

The word vibrated with equal parts of embarrassment and disgust. He must have climbed into bed with her and fallen asleep. What had she thought? He grinned mirthlessly. Probably she had sung songs of heartfelt thanksgiving to send herself to sleep.

Clenching his fist in the bedclothes, he sat up and stared around him. The draperies at the window were still drawn, but a fire burned in the hearth. He had no idea of the time. No doubt Vivian had slipped away hours ago, eaten her breakfast, and gone to see how many servants in Larnaervon House she could lift off their lazy rumps and set about their duties.

Disgusted with himself and irritated with her, he yanked at the bell cord.

He was still sitting in fulminating silence, his knees drawn up, his forearms resting on them, when his valet entered with a tray bearing a decanter, a coffeepot, and a cup and saucer. Setting it down on the bed, he dragged the bolster into position against the headboard.

Piers watched him, a sour expression on his face. "What time is it, Watkins?"

The man paused in the act of fluffing the pillows and arranging them behind the viscount's back. "Past

246

noon, milord. Close onto two, I believe."

Piers's scowl darkened. He felt a complete fool sleeping late in his wife's bed while she was up and about. Undoubtedly, the entire household knew where he was. And they were probably sniggering about him.

In his experience he had always left the bed first. A lady did not quietly steal away from a gentleman. It was damned embarrassing.

"Brandy, milord?" Watkins interrupted his thoughts.

"Yes. No!" He stopped himself, realizing that he had no headache. Actually, he felt quite good all things considering. "Just coffee. And breakfast, Watkins. Eggs and some ham. I'll eat and then have a bath."

"Very good, milord." Watkins took care to conceal his amazement as he handed the viscount the cup and saucer. The sherry-brown eyes were uncharacteristically clear. Although Piers's face was fine-drawn with dark circles under the eyes from the night's activities, he appeared singularly alert and well. Only the scowl boded no good for someone—probably the viscountess. The valet went to prepare the bath.

"Pull back the draperies before you go, Watkins." The viscount caught his man at the door.

"The draperies, sir?"

"I wish to see what kind of day this has turned out to be."

"Oh." The valet swept them aside. "Bright sunshine, sir. Clear and crisp. I believe the wind has died."

"Excellent. My compliments to my wife. I should like her to ride with me this afternoon at, say, half-past two."

"Ride, milord?"

"Yes, Watkins, ride."

"Very good, sir."

247

His face expressionless, Piers settled himself more comfortably in the bed and let the warmth of the coffee flow through him.

After an excellent breakfast, the second one that Piers remembered really tasting in one week, he rose from his wife's bed and followed his valet into his own bedroom where a steaming tub awaited him behind a screen. As he lowered himself into it, he heard the door to his wife's room open and close. Had she perhaps been waiting down the hallway for him to leave?

"Is my wife dressing for our ride?" he asked Watkins.

The valet paused in scrubbing the viscount's back. "I believe so, milord. When I invited her to ride with you, she—er—readily agreed."

"Did she now?" Piers raised one mocking eyebrow. "Good. Good." He thought about a brandy but relinquished the pleasure. He needed a clear head to deal with her.

Tingling with anticipation of the confrontation, he pulled himself from the bath and began to towel himself dry with unaccustomed vigor. In the act he paused to grin at himself ironically. After riding miles last night in bitter cold, he was actually looking forward to a ride with his wife.

Why? If he were interested only in setting the record straight about his sexual prowess, he could merely request that she meet him in the bedchamber. But no, a ride together would do much to establish the relationship on a pleasant footing. In a way he owed her an apology for his drunken behavior during dinner. And the night before.

He would entertain her today and when he came to her bed tonight, she would be warm and willing to be taught. With that thought in mind, he allowed Watkins to dress him in his buff breeches, fine cambric shirt, dark wine surcoat and simple stock. Stamping into his boots, he took up his hat and riding crop.

When he tapped on Vivian's door, she answered it immediately. Though she smiled, her eyes were watchful. She wore a different riding habit, this one in heavy black velvet. Her pale hair was bound up in a knot at the back of her head and a tall black hat with a floating veil was pinned securely on it. Over her shoulder he caught a glimpse of her little maid tidying industriously around the dressing table.

"Vivian." He inclined his head. "Shall we?"

She hooked the trailing skirt over her arm and preceded him. A step or two behind her, he studied the neat trim figure in the unexceptionable garb. Although she might be mute, her other attributes shone. The fact that she possessed two riding habits indicated that she had never been locked up in her own home for her own protection. Damn Sebby! Her guardian was turning out to be more of a villain by the minute.

Once in front of the house, Piers gaped at the gray punch. "My god, Tyler, what is that?"

The weasel-faced groom shifted uneasily from one foot to another and shrugged. "Lady Polwycke's horse, sir."

"What?"

The groom jerked his head and walked a couple of steps down the drive.

"Excuse me, Vivian." Piers followed him.

"Your lordship, Lord Larnaervon put out that she was to have a slow horse, so's we could catch her if she tried to run away."

Piers shook his head in disgust. "She's not going to run away. She's married to me."

"Beddoes said—"

"Damn Jack Beddoes!" Piers exploded swinging round and striding back to Vivian. He gestured to the unoffending punch. "Take it away and bring her a decent mount. Good god! I didn't know we had such a beast in the stables. I assume you can ride something with a little more fire than that."

She nodded vigorously.

"Take Lady Polwycke's saddle off that cart pony and put it on Barbary. I notice you have him saddled for yourself."

"I'm exercising him, milord," the one called Tyler explained. "He's a lot of horse for a lady. Better let me go back and get Lady Georgina's mare."

"My mother's horse is fifteen years old, Tyler." He put his hand on the flank of a gleaming chestnut gelding, fully sixteen hands high, with a white race down its nose. "What do you say, Vivian? Think you can handle him?"

Eagerly, she stepped forward, her whole face lighted with animation. Her black-gloved hand stroked the white nose. The gelding, entranced with the petting, dropped its head and nuzzled her palm. Over her shoulder she smiled at Piers as she patted the horse's face.

She had a lovely smile. Even white teeth flashed and a dimple curved in her right cheek. The viscount felt a tightening in his groin. He had not anticipated such a powerful and instantaneous reaction to her innocent sensuality. It doubled his resolve to bring her to his bed tonight and teach her how to be a woman.

When the groom hesitated, Piers impatiently slapped his crop against the top of his boot. "Tyler, I'm riding with my wife. I'll assume responsibility for her. I am sure that she can manage this horse. You no longer need to fear for her safety. And," he added with an ironic nod in her direction, "Romany Prince can catch Barbary any day."

Muttering under his breath, the groom made the exchange. Piers tossed Vivian into the gelding's saddle. Both men watched as she gathered the reins and settled herself tightening her leg comfortably around the horn. Satisfied that she indeed knew what she was about, Piers vaulted into the saddle of the shining black stallion he called Romany Prince.

When the groom started to mount, Piers stopped him. "No need to accompany us today. Just take that thing back to the stables or to the knackers."

Under a light touch of the crop both mounts cantered down the drive side by side.

The sun warmed the riders' bodies through the dark materials of their coats. The wind was a gentle breeze, cool but not yet chilly. Piers led them away from the sea beyond a grove of trees with thick, twisted trunks and branches barren of leaves.

The yellowed grasses rolled away under the horses' hooves as he called to her. "Will you gallop, Vivian?"

For answer, she touched Barbary's rump with her crop and shifted her weight forward in the saddle. The chestnut surged forward and stretched out with a will, his nose splitting the breeze. Vivian balanced gracefully in the saddle. Her veil and skirt whipped out behind her.

Spurring his stallion, Piers easily overtook her. Across the meadow they thundered, enjoying the heady rush of air and the powerful muscles beneath them. At the end of the park rose a hedgerow, some three feet high and perhaps as thick with another meadow beyond. Whipping a glance in Vivian's direction, Piers assured himself that she was balancing herself to take the jump and had no intention of slowing her horse.

251

At the same instant black and chestnut rose from the ground and sailed over the barrier with feet to spare. Across the adjoining meadow they tore until Piers recognized that particular section of ground. Remembering the stony area toward the end, he raised his crop to signal a halt. Reluctantly, Vivian pulled her mount and wheeled to face the way they had come. Piers did the same with the stallion, circling around to pull up beside her.

"That was well done. You have an excellent seat." He smiled thinly at the pink-cheeked girl who smiled back at him as she leaned over to pat the neck of her mount.

Her pale hair had come loose. Silvery tendrils curled charmingly across her cheeks. How ingenuous she was! Before the family fortunes had fallen to such a depth, before his mother's illness, he had spent a season in London. His title had gained him entrée to the outer circles of the ton where he had seen quite a few beauties at play. No other woman with whom he was acquainted would have patted her mount before she smoothed her hair, adjusted her hat, and generally ran an inspection of herself to be sure that her appearance was undisturbed. He watched his wife in some amazement.

Suddenly, aware of him, Vivian grew hot. Flustered, she straightened in the saddle.

"Relax, Vivian," he murmured. "I'm only looking."

His words alarmed her afresh. Her free hand flew to the neck of her blouse to find the linen stock disarranged. With trembling fingers, she smoothed it back into place.

He looked away; his mouth curved mockingly. "I'm no lovelorn rustic swain. I've never had a taste for a roll in the grass. Just imagine how uncomfortable that must be. And despite the sunshine, I suspect portions of the anatomy would get quite chilled."

She blushed furiously and made a motion to pull Barbary's head around, but Piers caught her wrist. The ride had freed her mind briefly. Now the tension returned full strength. She could feel her stomach clench and her breath come short.

"Don't ride off," he warned. "Remember I promised Tyler you'd ride with me. I can't break my promise."

Reluctantly, she eased up on the reins.

"Good." Piers allowed the stallion to drop its head to crop a mouthful of the dry meadow grasses. He stared at the gray clouds scudding in from the sea. "The day is going to turn off cold after all. We'll have to be returning soon. But I wanted to speak to you far away from the house. I seem to remember my father giving you permission to make whatever improvements you wanted in that mausoleum back there on the cliff."

She frowned. Somehow she had not expected he would want to talk about housekeeping.

"With his voucher you certainly don't need mine," he continued, "although you have it and welcome. Tear it down to the ground for all I care."

She looked at him quizzically.

He smiled. "But I have an idea that may please you more. I've made up my mind that in the spring we'll be moving to Stone Glenn."

She swung round in the saddle, her face lighting with wild hope and happiness. Reaching across the space that separated them, she caught at his arm and stared deep into his eyes.

"I don't know why you're acting so amazed. Surely, you didn't think that I loved this moldering pile with Larne presiding like the demon king over every dinner."

She shook her head and pulled his hand over palm up. Patiently, he allowed her to make the letters "Thank you" in his palm.

"No thanks necessary," he replied.

Reluctant to break the communication, she wrote, "Now!"

He shook his head. "For now I have business obligations that must be seen to. But very soon we are going to be ending the business."

She tossed his hand back into his lap and shook her head.

"Do you think you know what the business is?"

She hesitated, then nodded.

He shrugged. "You'd have to be stupid not to have figured it out. You must also know that marriage with you makes the 'shipments' from France unnecessary so far as we are concerned. By spring I shall be able to put all these illegal ventures to rest."

She shook her head and made a slashing motion across the saddle horn.

He laughed bitterly. "No, my dear. I cannot simply cut them off right now. Not and come out with a whole skin. Smuggling is a way of life here on this coast. It's not considered a crime but a profession. And quite a few men as well as their families depend on our business for their livelihoods. We can't simply abandon them."

During his confession he had watched her reaction. The play of expressions across her face intrigued him at the same time it frustrated him. "I wish you could talk," he complained. "I want to hear for myself what's going on behind those blue, blue eyes."

His words cut her like a knife, all the more dreaded because of its familiarity. The pain, the frustration stripped the skin off and left her raw and bleeding. Her hands clenched on the reins jerking the gelding's head up and making him back.

"Here!" The viscount raised his voice. "Don't get upset. I don't care if you can't talk. I just meant that—"

254

She turned the horse back the way they had come.

He spurred his mount alongside her. For a few minutes they rode in silence. "I only want to know what you're thinking," he told her. "When we get back, let's go somewhere quiet and you can write down what you think about all this. For instance, whether or not you like this horse better than the one you rode yesterday."

Her mouth curled in a sneer.

"Or," he continued smoothly, "whether or not we'll have a good meal tonight from Cook."

She allowed herself a faint smile. He was teasing her. She had begun to realize that he actually had a sense of humor and teased her more often than not. Unfortunately, neither one of them had had much to laugh or joke about in their short acquaintance.

He was watching her mouth. "Oh, Lord," he cried. "Can it be? Watch out. Oh, no. Her face will crack."

She could not help herself. She flashed him a full smile.

He smiled in return. "Good. Now, come on. The day is going to close down on us before we know it. A quick gallop along the seashore and then back up along the high trail."

The plans were abandoned in a moment when Tyler came thundering up. "Beddoes needs to see you real quicklike, sir."

Piers's face turned dark in an instant. "Oh, he does."

"Yes, sir." Tyler's face glowed red from the wind and from his own embarrassment. "Said it had to do with a change in plans."

"Change in plans?"

"You'd best come, sir."

Piers cursed feelingly. Without apology, he turned to her. "You'll have to excuse me. I'll have to be riding fast. Tyler will escort you."

She nodded with a shrug.

"Maybe she'd better come with us," Tyler suggested. "Jack ain't at the house. I'm to bring you to him."

"Damn him. Vivian, you'll have to come."

She shook her head, pointing toward the beach and the winding trail that led up to the back of the house.

"A lady can't ride alone."

"She don't have no business—"

Piers cut the groom off sharply. "I shall decide what is Lady Polwycke's business, Tyler." He turned to her. "Are you sure?"

She nodded, placing her hands together in a prayerful attitude.

"Will you come straight home?"

She nodded again.

"Very well. Lead on, Tyler. This had better be important." The two men galloped off leaving Vivian alone to pick her way down to the sand.

The whitecaps whipped the waves into great chopping canyons. The wind was icy cold. Vivian soon realized she was not enjoying the ride as she had imagined that she would. Still the moments of freedom were precious despite the discomforts.

How many bundles and barrels had floated in here? She shuddered. And how many lives had been lost in bringing them in? If she thought very much about her marriage, she would start to weep and weeping did nothing except make the eyes red and swollen.

Her guardian had been a thief; her solicitor, an accessory; and now her husband, whom she had married to escape their clutches, had confessed to being a smuggler.

Yet all was not completely and irrevocably gloom. Besides his confession, he had told her that he intended to quit and take her home.

256

At that thought her eyes did fill with tears. She had not been home in over a year, not slept in her own bed nor walked in her own garden. What had happened to her garden last spring? What had happened to the house itself? Had Sebastian looted it? Were the furnishings and paintings, the silver and crystal, in short, her inheritance still there?

Pain knifed through her, so intense that it bent her over in the saddle. Through a film of tears she could see the entry hall—the diamond tiles, the crystal chandelier, the Persian carpet, the—

"Miss Marleigh!" A man was hurrying toward her across the sand!

She straightened in the saddle and lifted her crop. Though the tears still wet her cheeks, she had mastered the pain. The gelding felt the grip tighten on the reins and threw up his head. He laid back his ears at the approaching stranger and shied.

"Miss Marleigh. That is—Lady Polwycke!"

She hesitated.

"Milady."

Captain Rory MacPherson came to a halt several yards from her, drab seaman's garb flapping in the wind. His face was all rugged concern, his eyes kind.

Where had he come from? Her eyes swept the rolling waves empty of vessels of any kind. He could not have been boating. If he were fishing, where was his gear?

And then she knew, knew with deadly certainty why he was dressed as he was here in this inlet. He was spying on incoming vessels. He was out to catch the smugglers and with them her husband. The realization threw her into turmoil. What was she to do?

She wiped at her cheeks with the back of her gloved hand and managed a tremulous smile.

"Lady Polwycke." Hand extended, he came up to

her horse's head and laid a hand on the rein. "May I be of assistance?"

His warm words uttered with such heartfelt sympathy touched her tender feelings again. A pair of crystal tears started down her cheeks.

"Milady," he whispered.

She turned her face toward the sea while she struggled for control.

"May I be of some assistance? Any assistance at all?"

The sea wind swept her tears away although it left her cheeks feeling cold and tight. She looked toward the heights. More and more clouds were rushing in. A storm was blowing toward them. She had promised that she would return to the house directly.

He took another step closer. The toe of her right boot almost touched his chest. "I only want a minute of your time."

She did not want to refuse him. Yet did she dare stay? What if she told what she knew? But what did she know? Really?

He held out his hand. "Please."

She gave hers into it and lifted her leg from around the horn. He stepped closer still and then his hands went to her waist as she left the saddle. Her hands came to rest briefly on his shoulders as he lowered her to the sand.

He was much taller than she, a little taller even than her husband. His red hair was the true Scotsman's fire-in-the-thatch. His eyes were blue as a spring sky and as gentle. They stood staring into each other's eyes measuring each other, the blue-blooded English lady hardly out of her girlhood and the garrison captain, almost twice her age, with lines deeply grooved around his firm-set mouth.

"I'll not beat about the bush, milady. I meant what I said the other day. It didn't take much of a brain to figure that you were caught between a rock and a hard place. And now I come upon you and find you—" He stopped. His big hand rose as if impelled by something beyond his ken. One long rough finger reached out to touch her cheek. Feather light, he traced the path her tears had left.

Vivian felt her skin prickle. A warmth spread as blood rushed into the spot. Her lips parted slightly to breathe in more of the bitter air.

Startled, he dropped his hand. "If you want to come away from that house, I'll keep you safe," he promised, his voice slightly hoarse. "I'll be happy to escort you wherever you want to go."

At first his words made no sense to her bemused mind. Then sadly she shook her head. Stooping, she wrote in the sand with her crop, "Where would I go?"

He dropped to one knee to read and then looked into her face almost at a level with his own. "Why, home! Your home. You must have relatives."

"None," she wrote.

He wiped the words away with a swipe of his big hand. "Friends? People who've known and loved you all your life?"

"My guardian." She wrote, her mouth curled.

"Friends. Friends of your family, your father."

"Father dead. Mother dead. No friends."

"But everyone has friends." His eyes were wide, incredulous, and very, very blue.

She shook her head.

"Then I'll be your friend. It won't be easy, but I have a small house, a housekeeper, a"—he hesitated biting his lip—"son. My wife is dead. Years ago. There's only me and Reiver. But he's a bonny little boy. We'd be honored."

She put her gloved hand over his mouth to stop the river of words. Her smile was brilliant and tear-filled.

Cognizant of the honor he did her, she would not have had words had she had the power of speech.

His mouth moved against her glove. His eyes above it were agonized. She took down her hand. Their eyes spoke to one another as she lifted her lips and fitted them to his.

Only the briefest of instants. Then she pulled away, faltered back across the sand into Barbary's shoulder. Her heel caught in her skirt, almost throwing her, but she grasped the stirrup and instead of straightening dropped down to her knees.

When he would have put his arms around her, she waved him away. With the crop she began to print. "You can't. Ruin you. Ruin your life, your son's. Married." She looked up at him with pleading eyes. "Married. Forever."

"I love you," he whispered. He went down on his knees before her. "I loved you the first minute I saw you, so proud, so white-faced. And I knew what had just been done to you."

She flushed and dropped her eyes. For a space she had forgotten that terrible afternoon.

"When I saw—what I saw—it made me sick. For you. I'll do whatever you want me to do. We can go away. To America. There's nothing here in England for a Scotsman anyway."

"NO!" She wrote it in great capital letters.

"But—"

"I made a vow." At those four simple words, he seemed to collapse. Then without looking at her, he rose. His feet turned unsteadily in the sand, but he righted himself and put his arm around her shoulders as she, too, rose and shook the sand from her skirt.

"Then there's nothing more to be said." He put his hands together to toss her into the saddle. "I do respect

260

you for your vow, milady. I hope your husband respects you, too."

She nodded as she settled herself and gathered the reins. Then she looked down at him. The tears were back on her cheeks, he noted. Then she reached for his hand. Turning the palm up she wrote three words.

"The truest friend."

They were not the words he wanted to hear, but he closed his fist over them to hold them against his heart.

She touched her heel to the gelding's flanks. The sand spurted as she galloped up the beach. When she came to the foot of the cliff trail, she looked behind her. He had disappeared.

Chapter Sixteen

"Forget it, Beddoes. We can't take the cargo out of here tonight. The beaches are crawling with riding officers. For all we know, the roads leading north are, too."

The smuggler swept his greatcoat apart and hitched up his wide leather belt. The hilt of his volley gun protruded ominously only a couple of inches from his hand. "That's what I'm tryin' to tell you, yer lordship. We *need* to get the stuff out of here. Sooner or later, they'll find the entrance and then—" He made a rude sound with his mouth. "You've got to give the word."

Piers ran his hand through his hair. He knew himself to be right in his estimate of the danger. But he also knew—as Beddoes did—that he had ordered shipments moved in more dangerous circumstances than this. Ordered them and gloried in the danger. For the first time since the smuggling had begun, he was not eager to be gone from the house.

Likewise, he acknowledged, his reluctance—evident by the vehement objections he was making to Beddoes—came from his desire to stay with his wife. He wanted to climb up the ladder and through the winding passages into the cellar and from there into the house and his own bedroom. He wanted to bury himself in her. His whole body tightened suddenly as a wave of heat swept through his loins.

With the physical surge came an equally emotional surge of anger that he had to clamp his teeth together to contain. The entire enterprise was a stupid and totally unnecessary risk for him now. He no longer needed the revenue to support that pile of rotting gray granite above him. He could go to Stone Glenn tomorrow. His wife would probably cry for joy if he went upstairs and made such a suggestion.

He swung around glaring at the great mound of goods, a veritable caravan of French contraband worth thousands of pounds. He could move to wealth and comfort, but his men could not. Divided among them, the money meant enough to live on through the winter. Otherwise, they would have great difficulty feeding their families. If his responsibility were only to the men, they could take their chances. Criminals, even smugglers, did not expect a steady income. But these men had wives with babes, old mothers and grandmothers, all of whom had no part in this, no say in who their menfolk were nor how they made a living. Innocents would undoubtedly starve to death if he abandoned them.

His brows drew together in a heavy frown. The sea roared and ebbed, filling the caverns beneath the cellar with its eternal noise. Because of it the oldest part of the house had become virtually unlivable. Therefore, subsequent owners had built wings where the bedrooms were located and an entire new front. In one of those bedrooms his wife would be waiting for him.

A breaker stronger than its fellows flung spray across the piece of sail that covered the mound. Droplets of it wafted to him, wetting his face. He shivered.

"Goin' a little bit soft?" Beddoes sneered. "Just say the word and I'll take it myself."

Piers threw him a disgusted glance. "And just where would you take it, Jack? To some old sailor's rest in Bristol? Or some whore's crib in Cheapside? You'll get good prices for it there."

"Give me the names of the connections," the smuggler whined. "I'll meet them."

"They wouldn't come within a mile of you and you know it. The Larnaervons have always had exclusive custom. It's why we can make double and triple what others make. And why we purchase quality goods in France."

"God damn it!" Beddoes whirled away, kicking at the remains of a barrel half buried in the sand of the cave. The staves went flying. One of the hoops spanged apart. Another rolled crazily away to end up against a rock.

Piers made no effort to disguise his contempt. Jack Beddoes had been the thorn in his side from the first trip. The man had no sense of caution. No thoughts passed through his mind beyond ways to obtain instant gratification for his body.

Part of Piers's contempt, however, was directed at himself. How could he ever have looked forward to the expeditions on "family business?" Now, not only did he not want to go, he dreaded going. What had once been an adventure now seemed an onerous chore, sour at the onset. He no longer felt the need to exorcise grief, frustration, and anger in intrigue, in wild midnight rides, in danger. Now with his wife's money and holdings combined with his own, the whole thing seemed silly, a waste of time, and, certainly in the light of Beddoes's rather garbled intelligence, an unnecessary risk.

In the spring he would leave the entire thing regardless of what Larne wanted. He glanced upward to the roof of the cave on which by accident or intent long ago builders had constructed the cellars of the house. Somewhere above him hunched the earl, his eyes gleaming beneath drawn white brows.

Say what you will, old man. I'll never be down here again. To Beddoes, Piers sneered. "You're a damned idiot, and the sooner I'm done with you, the better. We'll leave tonight after midnight. Send Tyler and Jenks ahead with the word."

"Right you are. Now you're talkin'." The smuggler whirled and started for the back wall of the caverns. As he went, he rubbed his hands, grinning in evident delight.

"If we're caught on the road," Piers called after him, "you'll be singing a different tune. Someone might be putting a load in a musket for you right now."

Beddoes came to a halt, his smile turning into a smirk. "Not bleedin' likely, your lordship. More 'n' likely they'll be looking for you. You're the jakey who married the bird and brought the London swells down here snoopin' around. If we meet anyone, they'll be aimin' for you so's they can get her back."

Piers waved him on. "Just send Tyler and Jenks and keep your mouth off my wife."

"Right y' are." Beddoes whipped off his hat and tugged at his forelock in a mockery of subservience. "Oh, right y' are, y' bleedin' sir." He sprang for the ladder and scaled up it and out of sight agile as an ape.

Piers started to follow him, then stopped. A grin spread across his face. Back he went to the piece of sail and tossed it aside. He tossed several bails aside before he found the one he sought. Pulling a knife, he used its tip to pick the knot on the bindings and opened the oilskins.

Tyler helped Vivian down at the front steps of the

house. When she looked at him quizzically, he shrugged in his cheeky way. "I got 'im there fast, ma'am."

She nodded graciously. The wind whipped her veil and tugged at her skirt. She gathered the heavy velvet over her arm and hurried in through the door that Millard held open for her.

"Ah, back in good time before the storm. Did you have a pleasant ride, milady? Your tea will be served"—he looked at her for confirmation—"in your room. Before the fire."

She smiled as she made a definite motion with her hand, a twist of the wrist with two fingers extended.

Millard watched her, his brow wrinkling. Then it cleared. "For two? Yes, milady."

Time to start using her hand signals. They would have to begin to learn them for the remainder of her stay here. Buoyed by Piers's promise to leave Larnaervon and take her with him, she intended to assume her rightful place as Piers's wife. She was the Viscountess Polwycke and her rightful place was as mistress of his household.

In the hallway at the foot of the stairs, Vivian pulled her notepad from her skirt pocket. Hastily she scribbled more specific instructions for Millard, who accepted them with a smile. As she mounted the stairs, she met Mrs. Felders coming down. The woman's expression was glacial, but Vivian pretended not to notice. She would not let this woman destroy her good humor. Anything could be endured for a few months.

Vivian had hardly removed her hat when Addie came panting into the room having run all the way up the stairs.

"Oh, you've done it again, ma'am. Mrs. Felders is in a taking because Millard is having Cook fix your tea with all the things you ordered. She says we've never had tea before. Nothing except a tray taken up for Lady Georgina, and since she's gone—God rest her soul—there's no reason to start up again."

Smiling at her own reflection in the mirror, Vivian unbuttoned her jacket and slipped it off her shoulders. Without missing a word of her monlogue, Addie took it from her and hung it in the clothespress.

Answering a knock on the door, the maid ushered in a footman carrying a bowl and pitcher of hot water. "I thought you'd be wanting this," Addie said proudly. "Since you'd been ridin' and all. You like to smell good, you do with clean hands and face. And so I told Millard. Him and me, we put our heads together ever so often now. Mrs. Felders don't like it a bit, but she can't do nothing but suck on a pickle."

Vivian grinned at the allusion to the housekeeper's pinch-purse mouth. Reflected in the mirror, the maid bustled around the room, chattering amiably. Addie had certainly gotten full of herself. As well as a servant, she had become a loyal supporter.

"Here now, ma'am. You just come and wash, so you'll be all sweet and clean when his lordship comes back. Watkins is havin' the same brought up for him." Her conspiratorial smile made Vivian blush.

The earl limped out of the library as Piers started up the stairs. "Dawlish is still in the vicinity. The Singing Herring has a 'secret' guest in the special parlor."

"Special parlor." Piers snorted. "You mean the one where they only sleep two to a bed."

The earl grinned. "Perhaps he has the solicitor with him. At any rate he bears watching. He'll not let the fortune like the one upstairs slip through his fingers without a fight."

The viscount shrugged. "He's probably just sulking

and drowning his sorrows. He'll leave soon enough. Sebby never had any staying power."

"You remember him from childish games," the earl replied dryly. "For wealth and property such as he was very close to possessing, he might be more determined."

His son glanced upward toward the head of the stairs, then sighed. "There is little he can do."

"Except create trouble for us. I believe he has already set in motion the activity that is plaguing us now."

Piers shrugged impatiently. "Possibly. But only by accident. Sebastian never thought to plot anything that carefully."

"He had her locked up," the earl reminded him.

"Ah, but if he had had any sense at all, he would have courted her and married her." Piers started up the stairs.

The earl's voice rose behind him dripping with mockery. "What a change of tune for you, my boy. Can this be the man who only a few days ago was wondering whether he was being married to a half-wit?"

Piers did not bother to answer. He had little enough time before his rendezvous with Beddoes. Little enough time to do what he wanted to do with surprising urgency. He gave a little shiver of anticipation. He would go and make this last run. Thereafter, the earl could find someone else to do his dirty work. His son would retire to Stone Glenn with his wife and live a life of bucolic respectability and, with any luck at all, domestic bliss.

As he strode by the door of her room, he thought about how he would approach her. Perhaps a drink first to ease her perfectly reasonable semi-virginal trembling. Then a series of kisses and caresses calling upon his not inconsiderable experience. A gradual sensual softening.

Watkins awaited him. "I've brought water for washing, milord."

Piers's brows drew together. "Water?"

"Yes, for washing. I thought you'd want to freshen up before tea."

"Tea?" Had the man gone mad?

"Well, yes. Millard reported that her ladyship has ordered tea to be served in her room."

Piers grinned. "Oh, she did now. Well, I'll drink it with her and gladly, but I'll need more than tea to take the chill off my bones. Pour me a brandy like a good fellow."

He could not fail to catch the regretful expression on Watkins's face as he poured the potent liquor into the glass and brought it. Piers lifted it to his mouth. "Now, I didn't say I wouldn't wash. And I'll go next door and have her damned tea with her. But for now I need something stronger."

He had barely finished his ablutions before a knock came at the door. A female voice requested that he come next door for tea. He drained the brandy and set it down as Watkins tied a fresh stock around his neck. He cast a quick glance at himself in the glass. The valet had had the right idea about washing. A man should always put on his best appearance when seducing a lady even when she was his wife.

"Pass the word to the Monk. We'll be movin' the stuff tonight."

"In this weather?" Tyler's weasel nose twitched. "Coo. We'll freeze our friggin'—"

"If you wanted to work in the sunshine, you should've stuck to farmin'." Beddoes cut the little man off with such a vicious tone that Jenks stepped back warily. "The longer we keep the stuff stored below, the

269

more chance that some nose coast guard'll find it."

Jenks ducked his head and reached for the tack, but Tyler tried again. "Who gave the order for this?"

"His bleedin' milord Polwycke, that's who."

"This afternoon, he sure looked like he was goin' to be stayin' the night with his lady."

Beddoes pushed aside his coat. "I'm tellin' you to climb on that horse and get on up the road. If you want to argue, go roust the old devil out and I'll send Jenks by hisself. One less split'll just makes the pot that much sweeter."

Jenks had got the bridle on his horse and was tightening the girth. "Come on," he muttered. "What difference does th' night make?"

"The whole damn coast is crawlin' with law," Tyler protested. "We'll be spotted before we've gone a mile on the road."

"Then take 'em over the fields," Beddoes snarled. "Stupid sod." He turned and stomped out of the stable.

Tyler shot him a look that would have melted brass but followed Jenks's lead. In a couple of minutes, the two galloped out together.

Her hair was freshly combed; her cheeks glowed softly pink; a hesitant smile lighted her face. She sat in a chair before a leaping, flickering fire that glinted softly off sterling silver and fine French porcelain. He stopped speechless in the doorway, the decanter in his hand.

Behind him Watkins held the door. Addie slipped through with a tiny knowing simper hastily tucked into her shoulder.

"Vivian." He recovered himself and smiled brightly, then set the brandy down on a side table near the door. "Quite a charming picture. I appear to have brought unnecessary refreshments."

270

With a smile she indicated the chair opposite her and waited with her other hand on the teapot.

He seated himself, crossing one long leg over the other, and leaned back to drink her in. Her hair had been freshly brushed back from her face and released from its tight chignon to fall in waves down her back. Again he was struck by its silvery color. Light gleamed off her crown as she bent her head.

The room was warm and peaceful, silent except for the spit and crackle of the fire. He felt tension begin to ease from his muscles.

Then she was smiling at him as she extended a plate with a cup of sweetened tea and a variety of delicacies.

His coloring was the most beautiful thing about him, she decided. His hair was the color of fine French burgundy as it poured from the bottle. When he looked out from under his dark brows at her, his eyes were fathomless with points of light reflecting up from their depths. Heat and liquid swirled at the bottom of her belly. She tried to control the feelings by tightening her muscles, but the effort only added to her excitement.

He was staring at her, his long-fingered hands cupped one over the other beneath his chin. She would not shift in her seat. He would know what was happening with her, that he made her uncomfortable.

As she passed him the plate, their hands touched, his shocking her with its heat. She could not help herself. She shifted, squeezing her thighs together. In an effort to conceal the reason for the movement, she reached for her pad and scribbled a note.

He read it and laid it back on the table. He took a sip of tea managing to control his grimace at the taste. "In answer to your question, I must leave tonight. As soon as it is full dark, I'll be away."

She wrote again.

"Yes, before supper. Although that's scarcely a loss.

271

Even though the dinner was much better last night, it still has a long way to go. I'll leave the efforts in your hands."

By way of comment, she edged a plate of small sandwiches toward him.

"I don't often eat," he said flatly, setting the plate down and rising. "Brandy's the thing to get me through this. The wind's a knife and the sleet hits you in the face until you think you don't have any skin left."

She watched him walk across the room to retrieve the decanter. Her face must have reflected sympathy because when he turned back to her, he smiled.

"Don't worry. It's uncomfortable, but not particularly dangerous. On clear nights the coast roads are crawling with eager troops all primed to catch the evil smugglers that deprive the good, kind king of his taxes. But when the temperature drops and the horses' eyelids freeze shut, they stay home safe and dry."

A vision of MacPherson clad in seaman's clothing searching the rocks below the great house rose in Vivian's mind. MacPherson would not shrink from a night in the fierce elements. Instinctively she knew that the Scotsman would do his duty come storm, come dark, come freezing rain and snow.

She made a movement to her pad, then pulled her hand back. MacPherson had offered her his help. She would not jeopardize his future. If he could catch the smugglers, so be it. Besides, she was sure that her husband knew about MacPherson. If he chose to ignore the man, then her warnings would be superfluous.

Piers resumed his seat and sloshed brandy into his teacup. "Use my own stuff to make this brew palatable."

As he drank deeply, she looked away into the fire letting it mesmerize her.

The silence grew between them. The draperies stirred as a particularly strong gust of wind found its way in despite shutters and sashes.

"Vivian," he whispered softly. "There is one thing I want more than brandy or food."

Her hands had been clasped in her lap, but now she pushed them flat against her thighs as tiny darts like pain shot through her muscles. She took a deep breath.

He rose and came around the table. She did not look up, did not dare. Her body began to shake. The tall columns of his legs clad in black buckskin and black leather boots came between her and the fire.

"Vivian." He held out his hand.

Still without looking, she put her own into it. Not just one hand but two. He must pull her up. Her legs were so weak; she did not think she could summon the strength to push herself to her feet.

"Come. You've no need to be afraid. I promise you. Sometimes, this is the only comfort in this whole damned uncomfortable world. Believe me."

She lifted her eyes to his face then. In the firelight, he saw they were moist, but whether with tears he could not be certain. "You're not going to cry, are you?"

She shook her head.

"Good." He gathered her in against him then, by the simple expedient of straightening his arm down in front of him, and pulling her hands with it. Her skirts billowed between his widespread legs. "Feel me," he urged.

She started and tried to fall back, but he held her fast and guided her. The maleness that had hurt her almost more than she could bear a few days ago was swollen and ready again. Terror came in a wave that made her fling herself backward against his hold.

"Here, stop that." He wrapped his arms around her and dragged her in against him. "Vivian. Vivian."

273

She was panting, her heart pounding, her body shaking.

But he held her fast, whispering to her, his lips warm, caressing her ear with every word. "Beautiful girl. Beautiful hair. Beautiful body. No need to be afraid. No need. Let go of your fear. Let it leave you. Sweet girl. Beautiful."

Gradually, she was able to master herself and stand trembling and sweating in his arms, sweating and twitching like a horse that had been run hard. The blood that pounded out of fear began to carry totally different sensations beneath her skin.

Still whispering beautiful compliments, Piers lifted her in his arms and sat down in the chair before the fire. One arm went around her shoulders, the other across her thighs. "We won't go to bed just yet, my love. We'll just sit here in the chair where it's warm and light. And I'll touch you."

She pressed her lips together and turned her face into his neck.

"That's right. Close your eyes." He stroked her shoulder. Gently, he gathered her skirt in his hand and slid it upward.

She twitched, but he continued to stroke her shoulder. His other hand at last found the hem of her skirt and slipped beneath it. The thin lawn of her drawers was no barrier to his heat. She stirred restively and raised her head to look.

Seizing the moment, he tilted his head to kiss her. Instead of drawing back, she waited. His lips gentled. His heart pounded as he felt her soft breasts lift in agitation against his chest. As part of the same movement, she shifted her bottom in his lap.

"Vivian," he exclaimed with a groan. "Sit still. You've got to help me in this."

She drew back, a frown on her face.

He grinned. "Yes. Don't look at me like that. Good lovemaking only happens when two people help each other."

She smiled uncertainly, but she had forgotten his hand on her thigh. It took her by surprise slipping into the slit in her drawers and finding the warm mound at the apex of her thighs.

Her response was electric, she jerked her hips back, sliding across his lap, rubbing herself roughly against him. He groaned at the excruciating sensation and caught her more tightly.

"Don't buck and pitch around like that."

His hand followed her inexorably. His thumb brushed the secret lips, spreading them.

Dizzy with sensation, she let her head fall back across his arm. Her mouth opened in a silent cry as he pushed and flicked at the pearl of pleasure that throbbed there. She tried to writhe her hips to escape the exquisite torment, but she had wedged herself into the chair, so she could move no further.

He must stop. The sensations were tearing her apart. Her eyes opened wide. At the same time, she realized she had hands that she was not using. One draped limply across his shoulder, the other hung useless at her side. She tried to clench them, but as she did, his fingers slid down between her slack thighs to the opening of her body he had violated only a few days before.

"How I must have hurt you," he whispered. "Here you're like velvet. And soft, so soft. Vivian, forgive me."

One of his fingers slid into her, slid out, and joined by its fellow slid in again.

She gasped soundlessly. Her hands clenched, but she made no move to pull him away. Her eyes closed as sensations rocketed through her body.

"Vivian," he whispered. "Can you feel that? Feel how

good that feels. You're made for more. There's more. And better. More."

His thumb pressed hard against her, rotating on the spot from which spurts of white hot pleasure rocketed up to the crown of her head and down to the tips of her toes.

Her whole being seemed compressed within the semicircle formed by his thumb and his index and third fingers. They were pressing and sliding ceaselessly building a painful fire that drove her higher and higher.

"Now, sweetheart," his voice called to her from out of the red fog. His powerful fingers squeezed and thrust.

She exploded outward, propelled by his force whirled and drowned in indescribable sensations that seemed to go on and on until finally her flesh could stand no more.

The tapping of the earl's stick swung the housekeeper around. "Eavesdropping, Emma?"

"Of course not, sir." She pulled herself up haughtily. "I merely came to supervise that silly girl. She's never served any tea before, let alone such an elaborate meal as that woman wanted brought up."

"Leave it be." The earl directed her down the hall with a sweep of his stick. "They'll work it out by themselves."

"But the incompetent little fool will make a mess of it."

"If she's such a fool, why did you assign her to my new daughter-in-law?"

Emma Felders flushed. Her tight lips barely released the words. "The girl is good enough with dressing. I didn't expect a bead-rattler to put on such airs."

"Of course not." The earl waited, his hands crossed

276

over his stick while Emma opened the door to his room and ushered him in. "I find I am in need of a restorative, my dear."

She raised one eyebrow. "Are you?"

"Emma, leave my son and his wife to their own devices. We have business of our own." He came toward her, pushing her back against the door.

Chapter Seventeen

Vivian's mouth gaped open; she stared sightlessly at the ceiling, hearing only the sounds of her own breathing. Dimly, she was conscious that he lifted her as he rose to his feet. Kissing her on the forehead, he moved with her to the bed. "Time for myself," he murmured, standing her on her feet and letting her skirts fall.

She swayed finding the bedpost with her shoulder and wrapping her arm around it. In a bemused state, she slid her palm along its smooth oak. Her temple and then her flaming cheek rested against it. Eyes only half open, she stared at him.

"Steady now?" he asked.

She swallowed, restoring some liquid to her dry throat, and nodded. Her eyelids drooped. Taking a deep breath, she caught her lower lip between her teeth as he shrugged out of his jacket.

Her eyes opened wide as he did not stop with that but stripped off the rest of his garments with an economy of motion that was almost frightening. When he was naked, he bent over his coat and pulled a length of silk from the inner pocket.

In splendid nudity he walked toward her. His fine

white skin was almost translucent, with faint shadows of blue veins across the hipbones. The male organ thrust out toward her from a halo of dark red hair. A dark fire flickered in his eyes. His voice was a sensuous rumble, deeper than she had ever heard it. "Vivian, did you enjoy what I did to you, the way I touched you?"

Her fingers splayed around the thick smooth wood. Her tongue slid out to moisten her lower lip. Her blood was pounding in her ears as her eyes scanned him fearfully. He wanted her to make love to him. She knew he did. But how? He was not shaped at all like her.

"A man feels the same things if he is touched and kissed as I touched and kissed you."

Heat rose in her. She had never thought that she would ever look at a man's body, much less touch it. Yet—

He held out the material, letting it ripple from his fingers in a column of pale silk and lace. "He also gets a great deal of pleasure from the sight of you."

With an effort she tore her eyes away from him to look questioningly at the material. Her hand moved of its own volition, reaching out to take it from him.

"I want to bury myself in your sweet body."

She shuddered at the words. Her belly quaked as liquid weakness wet her between her legs. His voice poured over her with much the same heat. Her nerves responded, creating exquisite sensations in her belly, in her nipples, up her spine. Was that what lovemaking was? Nerves responding to nerves. Would she be aroused by this man every time he spoke to her?

"Please allow me to enjoy you as you have enjoyed me."

Their fingers touched as she allowed him to drape the material over her hand. It was silk, the color of white wine. It slithered down her wrist until she held it by a pair of lace strips. It was a gown, a nightgown. She

279

had seen fashion plates of the like in dressmaker's shops. But she had never considered having one made for herself.

Now her husband was handing one to her, a request implicit that she don it. She shivered again. A blush rose in her cheeks.

He took a deep breath and let it out slowly as if he fought for control. Without another word he stretched himself full length on her bed, one hand behind his head. The other rested lightly across his belly only an inch or so from the tip of his organ. The dark fire in his eyes flamed higher.

Beneath the burning eyes, her fingers rose to the neck of her own gown. There they performed their tasks mechanically. The dress fell open. She pulled the sash loose, pushed the shoulders down, stepped out. Bending, she snapped her garters and rolled down her hose.

He groaned faintly. She lifted her head inquiringly to find him staring at her breasts, bare to his eyes where the chemise fell away from them.

When she straightened up, suddenly shy, he shook his head. "Please go on. You're very beautiful."

She nodded, her face pink, and bent again to her task. When her feet and legs were bare, she straightened, clad only in her chemise and drawers. Her nipples were turgid, her breasts hard. They pressed against the soft material, their aureoles dark.

"God," he whispered. His hand had moved; his fingers played up and down the length of the swollen staff. "You are so beautiful."

She was trembling, having trouble pulling enough breath into her lungs to keep oxygen to her brain. How could she possibly take such a monstrous thing inside her? She was terrified. Yet she slid the straps of the chemise to the points of her shoulders. Her vision misted and swam. She was cold and hot by turns.

"Let me see you," he beseeched. "We're husband and wife. The sight of you will give me pleasure."

Closing her eyes, she slid the straps down her arms and pushed the garment to her waist.

"Go on," he whispered, "take off everything."

A tug at the ties and both those garments fell from her.

His eyes scanned her figure, caressing her pointed breasts and the pale curls at the top of her thighs. "I've never seen anyone more beautiful. Never seen such silvery hair," he murmured. "It's almost a sin to cover it up, but there are other pleasures."

Their eyes met as she lifted the hem of French silk, and then she slipped it over her head.

Its cool draperies slithered over her curves, its lace appliqués scratching faintly. The combination of textures made her shiver. Her blood simmered in her veins, yet her skin felt chilly, and she set her teeth to keep them from chattering.

Piers leaned up on the bed. When she swayed before him, he held out his hand to her. "Come here."

The French silk sliding icily over the heated flesh of her limbs, Vivian moved to the edge of the bed.

His fingers brushed her cheek, her neck where the pulse throbbed against his hand. They trailed down her breast, caressing the nipple until she trembled from head to toe. "I can't believe you're so beautiful," he whispered. "I can't believe you're mine. Come to me."

Without knowing exactly what to do, she put a knee on the bed beside his leg.

"Oh, yes." He caught her other thigh at the back and pulled her across his hips. She was dragged down to sit astride the throbbing, swollen length of him. The intimate contact with heat and velvety hardness acted like an electric shock. She instantly shifted her weight.

"God!" He set his teeth. "Wait a minute!"

She started at his vehemence and shifted again.

He clutched at her thigh and at her waist. His hands were so long and strong that they frightened her. She was a toy to him. He could twist her, use her, break her. Her own thoughts frightened her. She tried to raise herself away from his hips, but he pulled her back.

"Don't move," he grated. "I'll get control of myself in a minute and then I'll—"

She could not help herself. Knees and toes digging into the mattress, she pushed herself upward.

Acting like a creature with a will of its own, his staff sprang up. His hand guided it to her entrance. "Don't be afraid," he whispered through set teeth.

Hot liquid poured from her, wetting his hand and the creature at her gate. Desire fully as hot flooded her. The woman in her knew what she wanted. She wanted to be filled. She wanted the feeling. Wanted him inside her. Wanted him. She let herself down, felt herself surround him, felt herself spread, felt the pain, the good pain.

She threw back her head and arched her back, thrusting her hips forward, unconsciously, instinctively accommodating herself to his shape. Then weakness, the weakness of submission, a part of the elemental female makeup, filled her. She slid farther down the staff until she was resting on his belly and thighs. Her head fell forward, her upper body tilted.

His hands found her breasts, squeezed them. Through half-closed eyes, a prey to the sensations of fullness and exquisite stretching, she nevertheless could mark his face.

His eyes were closed, his head thrown back. His

white teeth clenched as if he fought a battle he had no chance of winning. "I— I— My God!"

His hips bucked upward, thrusting him into her, pushing higher into her, driving her breath from her lungs in a silent scream of pleasure. He bucked again. His hands slid around her waist, holding her tight against him.

And it was happening again. The hot flooding of pleasure, the explosion of sensation. Her eyes opened wide, then closed as she slid weakly forward to lie upon his chest.

"Not bloody likely, yer bleedin' lordship." Jack Beddoes slapped his hat on his head and pulled the ends of his muffler together under his chin. He strode to the door, his coattails switching.

"Keep a civil tongue in your head there." Sebastian Dawlish, face red with anger, brandished a heavy walking stick at the man's retreating back.

"Be seein' you."

"Mr. Beddoes, hold on." Dawlish hauled himself to his feet. The dampness of this wretched seacoast had settled in his gouty foot. He was miserable and angry at having to lodge at an establishment with so ridiculous a name as the Singing Herring. To cap the climax, he now was having to deal with this riffraff. For two cents he would chuck this whole thing and return to London. Except then he would have to give up all that lovely money and those beautiful properties. "I'm sure we can reach some sort of a compromise on this."

"Naw, we cain't." The man actually swung open the door and stood there, letting his voice carry down the hall. Rowlings' face turned from red to dead white. Beddoes grinned evilly. "You'll do what I tell you to do,

283

and when the time comes, she'll be a widow. Then you get what you want, and I get what I want."

"For God's sake, close the door," the solicitor bleated.

Dawlish kept his eyes on Beddoes's face. "Which is?"

The smuggler grinned, revealing stained and broken teeth. "You ain't above turnin' a trick here and there. The way the earl's always done it. He's been the connection with the gentry. That's why we've made so much money. You'll be the connection."

"Absolutely not," Rowling declared. "We're here merely to rescue a poor unfortunate girl whose wits have been addled since she was nine years old. Everything is strictly legal. What you're demanding is simply not possible."

Sebastian moistened his fat lips.

Beddoes raised his eyebrows and cocked his head in Rowling's direction.

The solicitor looked from one to the other. "Impossible," he said again. "Absolutely impossible."

Sebastian made up his mind. "And in exchange?"

Beddoes closed the door and stalked back across the room. "You get the bird and not only her money, but a share of a real sharp business deal."

"For God's sake, we're talking murder and smuggling. We're talking about breaking the law. I can't believe this. You can't be serious."

The smuggler swung on the mewling solicitor. He swept his coat aside to expose his duckfoot volley gun stuck in the left side of his belt and a horse pistol stuck in the right side.

Rowling squeaked at the sight of the arsenal and backed against the wall. His fist pressed to his mouth.

"That's right. We ain't serious," Beddoes sneered. "We ain't serious at all. So just shut yer yap and back out if y' want to. But just remember you had your chance. Don't come pantin' around us when we got plenty and the business's goin' good."

"Rowling, it's the perfect solution," Sebastian urged. "When she's a widow, we can move to regain control of her estate on the grounds that she's incompetent. You can surely fix up those papers."

"But what about the law?" Rowling was white to the lips. He looked at the door and then at the pistol butts glinting in the flickering light. Never had he seen so much firepower on a single man. "Dawlish, you're talking about breaking the law."

"Yer friend here's sure got a yeller streak," Beddoes sneered.

"Not yellow," the solicitor objected. "I'm not a coward. But neither am I a criminal."

"Oh, an' I suppose lockin' a woman up and stealin' her money's right and tight with the Parly-ment?"

"She's incompetent."

"So you say."

Sebastian brought his cane down hard on the floor. "Gentlemen. We are getting nowhere. Sit down, Rowling, and keep your mouth shut. You're in this up to your neck and you know it. You can't go back without the Marleigh estate to manage. Old Barnstaple will fire you even if you are his partner's son. Remember his *late* partner, so loyalty can only extend so far." He turned to Beddoes. "How can we trust you?"

Beddoes laughed. "Well now, you can't. But I can't trust you neither. Look, you bleedin' fools. It ain't like we're goin' to be friends. We're business partners just once in a while. So we don't see much of each other. That way we don't get into each other's hair."

"I think—"

Dawlish nodded his head. "Shut up, Rowling. You haven't even started to think." He tucked his cane under his arm and walked across the room to Beddoes extending his hand. "To à mutually profitable partnership."

Beddoes stared down at the swollen white fingers, then up at the pudgy face. He grinned onesidedly. "Oh, it'll be profitable all right. For ever'body."

When the smuggler had gone, Rowling rounded on Dawlish. "Have you lost your mind? We can't get mixed up with an operation like that. I absolutely refuse. Do you hear me? Absolutely."

Sebastian re-seated himself propping his gouty leg against the firedog and sighing heavily. "Of course, we're not going to get mixed up in some petty smuggling operation, my dear Rowling."

"We're not?"

Sebastian threw the solicitor a withering look. "Why should we? With Polwycke dead, we have her and her estate as well as his when the old man turns up his toes which, by the look of him, should be any day now. Don't you agree?"

"Both estates?"

"Marleigh and Larnaervon. Can you imagine administrating both of them? Even though the thing has run into the ground, I happen to know that the old demon has never sold a single dirty acre off. Not one. Vast. Vast."

"Vast?"

"Could be sold off in parcels."

"But what if—?"

"Why don't you go round and find a promising-looking ostler, if there's such a beast in the Singing Herring." Sebastian's face expressed a world of martyrdom. "While you're gone, I'll compose a suitable missive for that very enterprising Captain MacPherson. Even though he was incredibly rude to us both, he'll not turn up his nose at a chance to catch smugglers. A big catch, especially with a man like Polwycke among the dead, and he can't help but get the promotion he's been seeking so arduously."

Rowling stared at Sebastian for a minute. The man's plump cheeks were quite red from the heat. A little smile played about his features. He looked like nothing so much as a chubby cartoon of a happy-go-lucky, feckless Englishman, only concerned about a pint of porter and a joint of mutton.

At that moment, Sebastian turned his head and caught the younger man staring at him. "I've given you an order," he murmured.

Rowling whirled and all but bolted from the door. Outside, he looked wildly around. His scalp prickled as he remembered that his partner was the man who had plotted to kidnap, drug, and then lock a young mute woman away for the rest of her life in an insane asylum. Sebastian Dawlish was quickly revealing himself to be a man who would stop at nothing, and he, Roderick Rowling, was a party to his schemes. He felt the trap closing around him.

And, God help him! He could not seem to find his way out.

The fire flickered over their still figures. Dreamily Piers had reached for the cover and pulled it over them, wrapping them in its cocoon rather than making any effort to crawl beneath it. Nor had he turned on his side, but kept Vivian lying atop of him like a contented cat.

Her even breathing stirred the hair on his chest and

287

titillated his nipple. Piers felt himself hardening inside her. He wanted her again. He smiled as he ran his hand up her spine. He had never known such pleasure. Her body had been perfect, exciting him to the point that he had lost control.

She stirred and shifted her hips. The folds of hot, velvety tissue inside her body caressed him. He set his teeth to suppress a moan of pleasure. As he did she murmured something.

He froze, his pleasure almost forgotten. She had made a sound! He raised his head, listening with his whole body. Gently, he stroked her back with a tender touch. For a long time her quiet, even breathing was all he heard. He was just about to sink back onto the pillow when she moved again. Her little hand caught at his shoulder and she spoke again.

Three little words unintelligible uttered in a childish voice.

His hands clutched at her body. She made a tiny movement of negation.

Instantly, his hands relaxed. Frowning, he stared down at the form sprawled so delightfully upon him. Somehow he knew that if he woke her, she would be unable to duplicate the sounds. He put his arms around her and hugged her to him. When this was over, he would take her straight to London to the best doctors. She would speak again. He was certain.

For now, he had to waken her gently and bid her good-bye.

He sighed with pleasure at the memory of their lovemaking. She had been willing enough to be taught by him. And every movement had been exquisite and yet ingenuous. He had never received such pleasure. He felt himself twitch at the thought of the silk slithering over her slender white curves.

She must have felt him, too, because she murmured a third time and stirred. Her hand slid along his chest. Her fingers curled, the nails scratching him. Then she raised her head.

He saw she was still more than half asleep. Wondering if she were unconscious enough to answer him, he asked "Was it good for you?"

A slow, lazy smile started. She flattened her palm against his chest, pushing up. Her mouth opened.

He caught his breath, when suddenly there came a knock at the door.

"Damn!"

She looked over her shoulder, her face suddenly fearful.

He hugged her tight against him. "No need to fear, my dear. I'm certain that's not Sebby come to check on our marital progress again."

She looked back at him and smiled uncertainly. The knock came again.

"Who is it?"

"Watkins, milord. It's time."

"Damn! Give me a few minutes."

"Yes, sir."

Piers sighed heavily. "You heard the man. Business calls."

She let her head sink back to his chest. He would have liked to see her face, judge by her expression how she felt about his leaving her.

"You'll have to roll off me."

For an answer she hugged him closer, her hands slid around his ribs, her fingers insinuating themselves under his shoulder blades.

"Don't want to lose your couch, I suppose."

Her grasp tightened. At the same time she tightened the muscles of her belly.

"Vivian!" He caught hold of her shoulders. "Be careful."

She did it again.

"Stop it." He sat up, pushing her up to face him. Their bodies were still locked, and his needed little urging to spring to life. "For God's sake."

She smiled silkily. Her hands locked together in the center of his back.

"Witch." He could not help himself. Let Beddoes be damned. He rolled her over.

Her eyes widened in alarm as she learned that he was even bigger when he came down on her then when he thrust upward. She caught at his back with her nails. Her legs wrapped around his hips.

Damn! She was doing it again. He had meant to take her with exquisite care. But that wasn't so. He knew he had no time. He was rushing this. Plunging into her, thrusting again swiftly, satisfying himself.

He caught a glimpse of her set teeth, her eyelids half closed, her eyelashes veiling the blue. And then he was rocketing out of control, exploding inside her with a great cry of satisfaction.

As he slumped forward, he felt her drag him closer, her heels pushing him down against her until she too arched shuddering before she fell away.

Watkins waited outside the door, shifting his weight uneasily in the cold hall. He was dressed for riding as well. Piers's great cape collared with many small capes was thrown over his arm. "You're going to be quite late, milord. You may not make the meeting place even if you leave now."

Piers nodded to his valet who was also his friend. He allowed the great enveloping garment to be adjusted

290

around his shoulders. He could feel his smile, the warmth, the well-being leaving him. From the hall table Watkins handed him his whip and hat.

Turning back to Vivian, he bowed ceremoniously and made an ostentatious leg. "My dear wife, will you accompany me to the door, there to bid me a safe journey and a swift return?"

Willing to play any part he assigned to her, she swept a deep curtsy to match his bow. As she rose, he offered her his arm so they might descend together.

In the dingy hall at the foot of the stair, the Earl of Larnaervon waited. At the sight of his son and daughter-in-law arm in arm, he smiled his most handsome smile. "Ah, the happy couple with fatuous looks on their faces. My heart is filled with hope that you have created my grandson today."

Affronted, Vivian stiffened. Her movement communicated itself to Piers, who glanced at her and then glared at his father. "If we have, Larne, we did it for us, not for you."

"To be sure. To be sure. But surely I may be allowed to share in the gains. A voyeur's share perhaps, but a share." He grinned at Vivian. "My dear, you look radiant."

Vivian lifted her chin and gazed straight ahead at Millard standing beside the door. Hurrying ahead to see that the horses had been brought up, Watkins now appeared framed in the doorway. Mrs. Felders's dark-skirted form lurked beside the staircase, her hands folded under her apron.

Midway down the hall, Piers turned Vivian to him. Gently, he placed his hand beneath her chin and lifted her face to his. "Larne," he said loudly and clearly, so that all might hear. "My countess has pleased me in every way. She is the Viscountess Polwycke and the lady of this house as well as her own. I expect that the servants will obey her and see to her comfort. I'm certain you will support her in my stead in whatever will make her happy in this house."

The earl raised his eyebrows, then shrugged the crippled shoulder. "Whatever she wants. To be sure. I told her that. Just give me my grandson and she can tear every stone down and move it three feet to the right."

"—and Felders will cooperate."

The older man's eyes slid to the figure hovering in the shadows. "She's done well for years. No reason why she shouldn't do well now."

"She will do better," Piers insisted. "Not as she did for my mother."

They all heard the angry hiss of breath from the stairway.

He smiled mirthlessly down at Vivian, his eyes cold.

"Do you hear, milady?" Her vulnerable mouth was close to his lips, her eyes were luminous in the flickering candles. She smiled faintly and nodded. Her hand pressed warmly against his. "Then you are now the mistress of this house."

He bent to place his warm lips against her own. When she trembled, his own passion heated again. Damn! He had to get away or carry her back upstairs. When he returned, he vowed he would take her on an extended honeymoon immediately.

He drew her in against him, her breasts pressed against his chest, her thighs against his thighs. His mouth moved against her lips, parting them, tasting her.

Her tongue responded instantly, to touch the tip of his, to follow his into his mouth. Her small hands slid along his ribs under the folds of his cape.

292

He was the one to pull back. Sighing, he drew his mouth away from hers. Raising his head, he smiled down into her face again. Then abruptly he sobered. One last run, he promised himself. This is the last. In a swift movement his head dipped again and kissed her full on her mouth, his lips hard, a salute and farewell. Dropping his arms, he stepped back from her, turned on his heel, and strode out the door. His cape billowed behind him like great black wings in the cold night wind.

Chapter Eighteen

Vivian awoke with a sense of physical contentment. Beneath the covers the muscles of her thighs protested only faintly when she moved them. Hesitantly, casting a surreptitious glance at the door to her chamber, she slid her hands down her belly. Her fingers parted the curls at its base and touched herself. She felt swollen, the skin oversensitive. A definite soreness in the delicate tissues at the edges of the entrance that Piers had used three times to her surprised delight. With her index finger she traced the area. Despite his use of her, she was still small. Very small.

And he was very big. She blushed at the memory of his rampant maleness thrust toward her like a lance. The heated blood spread through her body even heating the skin beneath her fingertips. Suddenly, moisture slicked the flesh.

Vivian snatched her hands back. The memory of her husband was almost as powerful as his presence. If he were here beside her, he could slide into her with ease. And she would feel the pleasure that she had felt last night. With a start she realized she was smiling, her lips parted as she remembered his kisses.

When he came back today or tonight, she would be

glad to see him. The physical part of their marriage made her shiver with anticipation.

But he did not come back that day, nor that night, though she waited in her bed with the fire blazing so the room would be warm for him to undress.

Early the second morning, Millard brought Vivian a notebook and pen which he placed beside her breakfast plate with some show of ceremony.

She looked at him inquiringly.

"I thought you might care to set down instructions for the day, milady."

She raised her eyebrows, then wrote at the top of the page. "Felders" with a question mark after the name.

"Mrs. Felders has not come down this morning. She spent the evening—er—seeing to the needs of Lord Larnaervon."

No longer an innocent, Vivian could easily imagine what needs Millard alluded to. She repressed at the thought of the earl's body with its crookback and knobby brown-spotted hands.

"If you'd like more time, milady, I could come back."

Snapped back by Millard's question, she shook her head. At the top of one sheet, she wrote "Menu." Then set it aside. At the top of another she wrote "Housekeeping."

Millard looked over her shoulder. "Very good, milady. The house hasn't really been properly taken care of since the old earl was alive. Not Lord Alexander, you understand, but his father. It was a happy house. And well kept. I was a boy myself then, taken into my first service as a footman.

"Lady Larnaervon was a stickler for service. The furnishings she bought were elegant, and the house bustled keeping them shining."

Vivian looked up into his sad, serious face. "What happened?" she wrote.

He shook his head. "Ah, milady died, and the old earl was in a bad way for a long time, drinking hard and heavy. Then Lord Alexander, who was Viscount Polwycke at the time was thrown from his horse. The fall broke his back and shoulders. He wasn't expected to live. And the old earl couldn't face anything more. He went into the library less than a month after it happened and shot himself."

Vivian sucked in her breath in horror.

"The bloodstains are still on the floor, beneath the carpet." Millard sniffed and swallowed. His forehead wrinkled as he struggled to retain his façade of imperturbable dignity.

Vivian wondered suddenly if he had ever told this story to anyone before. She put out a hand, but he lifted his chin and resumed his formal demeanor.

"Everyone thought Lord Alexander was going to die. When he didn't, they thought he was going to be bedfast for the rest of his life. The creditors came and looted the house. Lady Georgina hid some things away, but she couldn't do much. And young Piers was just a lad of four. He kicked and bit, but they knocked him down and told her if she wanted to keep him, she'd better hold him off."

He shook his head sadly. "I think rage was what brought Lord Alexander out of his bed and put him on his feet again. I've never seen a man so mad. But he never forgave her for not driving them off. In his own way I don't think he ever forgave his son either. So since then, milady, it's been a sad house, and a bad house. With Lord Alexander wild to recoup what was lost—and not caring how he did it."

Vivian looked around her at the darkened and stained woodwork and wallpapers. She shook her head faintly. "But the house," she wrote, "it's so neglected."

Millard looked apologetic. "I suppose his lordship hasn't had much success."

Vivian nodded. If a fortune was being made by the smuggling, it was certainly not being spent here.

Piers had said they would be moving in the spring. She could go back upstairs to their rooms and save herself the trouble. But Millard had such a hopeful expression on his face. The task, as Piers had said, was roughly the equivalent of cleaning the Augean stables. Still, she knew much about the running of a household. Likewise, during her year at the abbey she had been drafted into doing much actual work herself.

She shrugged and dipped the pen into the inkwell. At the head of the paper she wrote, "All floors to be scrubbed and waxed. Where necessary, stained floorboards will be taken up and replaced."

Millard inclined his head to read over her shoulder. He smiled. "Yes, milady. I think that's an excellent place to begin."

Emma Felders caught up with Vivian in the hallway, where she was overseeing the cleaning of the mirrors on either side of the entrance to the dining room. The housekeeper's face was brick red. "You will stop all this immediately."

The fury in the woman's voice frightened the footman into dropping his sponge. It fell into the bucket of vinegar water with a splash. Vivian stared pointedly at the hand that clutched her forearm.

Felders followed her eyes, then allowed her tight mouth to curve into a sneer. Far from releasing Vivian's arm, she tightened her grasp and shot a furious look at the footman. "Carry that mess back to the scullery and go on about your usual chores."

The man tucked his head down. His eyes skipped from one woman to the other. He shuffled his feet.

"Go on, I say!"

The woman had joined the battle here in the front hall. If the footman were allowed to go on about his business, his business would be to carry the word. Whoever would be mistress of this house would be decided today.

Vivian twisted her arm out of Felders's grip. She made a slashing gesture to the footman and pointed to the sponge floating in the bucket.

He hesitated.

Her finger stabbed the air again.

"Yes, ma'am." He resumed his work though he kept a wary eye cast over his shoulder.

"I told you to stop that." Mrs. Felders spaced each word with furious emphasis.

Vivian stepped between her and the man.

"You've no right—" the housekeeper began.

Vivian seized Felders's arm and twisted her around.

"What are you doing? Let go of me."

Vivian pushed her shoulder into the woman's back and hustled her down the hall, behind the stairs, and into the butler's pantry. On the table lay the lists she had made with Millard's suggestions and approval. Catching them up, she stuffed them under the housekeeper's nose.

Felders shook herself free and stepped back. "I might have known you and that cold fish were in this together. You've turned them all against me. But it won't last. You won't last. So take your hands off me."

Her protests ended in a grunt when Vivian pushed her down into a chair.

When Felders tried to spring up, Vivian pushed her back down again.

Infuriated, the housekeeper came up with nails

curled like talons, making for Vivian's hair. Her scream of rage echoed down the hall. Millard came on the run from the dining room, and Addie raced to the top of the stairs.

The Earl of Larnaervon came out into the hall from the library. A mocking smile played about his mouth as he thrust out his cane to prevent Millard from bursting into the pantry.

"Milord!" Millard all but brushed the cane aside and plunged on. "She may be injured."

"Indeed *she* may be."

He had to raise his voice to be heard above a scraping and a heavy thud as a piece of furniture fell. The floor vibrated beneath their feet.

From the kitchen Cook came out through the dining room; his moonface twisted in anguish. Another scream and a shatter of glass made him clap his plump hands to his cheeks. "Lord, love us all."

"Sir—"

"Millard, the ladies have the right to settle this between them without our interference. I shouldn't think that we will have to wait much longer for a victor."

At least ten people now stood in the hall to hear another crash immediately followed by a cry of pain that ended in a filthy name.

The earl grinned. "From the sounds I would say that the Viscountess of Polwycke is asserting her authority."

"But how can you be sure?" Millard was wringing his hands and practically dancing from one foot to the other in his anxiety.

"I have seen Lady Polwycke in action once before. She has a most impressive right cross."

"But Mrs. Felders might be hurting her."

"Not at all. Emma's the one doing all the yowling."

The earl hobbled a few steps down the hall to give himself a clear view of the door to the butler's pantry.

Another cry and then the door burst open. Emma Felders charged out, her hair wild about her shoulders, her face contorted with pain and fear. A great bruise was already swelling on her forehead and another on her jaw. She saw the earl and fled sobbing into his arms. "She'll kill me."

He put one arm around her shoulder and gathered her in against him. "Yes, I suspect she will, Emma, if you don't do what she tells you to."

"You can't let her treat me that way. You've got to send her away."

He laughed softly. "I'm afraid that I can't do that."

At his words she pulled away from him. She stared up into his face, reading there his amusement and his lack of sympathy for her condition. Her expression turned sullen. "You'd let her treat me that way?"

"She is the Viscountess Polwycke and my son's wife."

"She hurt me."

"But I'm sure you were able to defend yourself creditably."

"I was only trying to keep peace in your house."

"And succeeding admirably." His eyes moved away to the pantry door.

Vivian stood in it, her hair down around her ears, her face flushed, her eyes flashing with anger.

He raised his cane in salute. "Ah, the victor."

Vivian came down the hall, her ice-blue gaze directed at Emma Felders. The servants fell back in awe before her progress. Her jaw was set. One sleeve was ripped out of the shoulder of her dress. A line of bloody scratches ran down the arm. Her fists were clenched. As she neared the couple she raised them.

Emma Felders screeched and Larne passed her behind him. "That will do."

Vivian glared at him. A vein throbbed in her temple. Her chest rose and fell with her quickened breathing.

"That will do, I say," Larne repeated mildly.

For the first time she appeared to focus on her surroundings and the awed people who watched her. Slowly, she lowered her fists.

The earl turned to his cowering housekeeper. "Perhaps you'd better go to your room, my dear. You look a sight."

She flashed him a look of obdurate hatred and fled, skirting wide around Vivian, who watched her with narrowed eyes.

"Perhaps you'd better go after her, girl," he called to Addie, who had halfway descended the staircase. "She will undoubtedly need some assistance."

"I serve Lady Polwycke," she retorted saucily.

"You will serve who I say, or you will serve no one at all." Beneath the bristling white eyebrows and cowl of white hair, his dark eyes were fierce as an ancient eagle's.

Addie's mouth snapped to, her face paled, and she came down the stairs at a run to follow Mrs. Felders.

"The rest of you must have work to do." He did not look at anyone specifically. The half smile still curved his mouth upward. Indeed his eyes were still directed to Vivian's stiff figure. "If you do not, then those of you with no jobs are dismissed. Or better still, I will unleash Lady Polwycke among you."

The hall was instantly emptied except for the footman who dipped his cloth into the bucket of vinegar water and began vigorously cleaning the beveled glass of the mirror.

"My dearest daughter." He took Vivian's arm.

301

"Please come into the library with me and have a glass of warmed brandy."

His request made her suddenly aware of her condition. Ineffectually, she pushed at the mass of silvery-blond hair sliding down onto one shoulder.

"It looks charming, my dear. I quite see how my son has grown so enamored of you that he does not want to leave your side."

Vivian looked around her in sudden amazement. Her blood still pounded madly through her veins. Fighting color still flushed her cheeks. Nevertheless, she began to feel the pain in her scalp where Mrs. Felders had pulled her hair. Likewise, she was becoming aware of bruises on her body and a stinging on her arm.

"Come."

She followed the earl, moving a bit unsteadily on her feet. At the door he took her elbow and guided her in. Ordinarily, his touch would have offended her and made her pull away, but this time she was glad of it. He led her to a leather chair and steadied her as she lowered herself into it. Its arms felt wonderfully solid. She clutched at them as a wave of dizziness assailed her.

He left her to pour them each a drink. His he set over the warming candle, but hers he brought immediately. "I'll warm the next one," he promised, "but for now drink this."

She accepted it, staring at nothing as her heart began to slow and her breathing to even. After a moment she drank it, letting the liquid bite her throat and send its fumes into her brain. She winced and sucked in her breath.

He lifted his own from the hoop and carried it to a chair opposite her. "I take it you and Emma had a disagreement about who should run the household."

She nodded wearily. Glancing down at her torn sleeve, she turned her arm inward to see the scratches oozing tiny stipples of blood. The wound stung. Ignoring it, she drank another swallow of brandy.

"You should take better care of yourself," he said. "You could be carrying my grandson."

She shot him an angry glance.

He held up his hand. "Don't attack me. I beg you. I'm an old man, crippled and in ill health. No match for the champion battler of Stone Glenn." He laughed a little, then drank a sip of warmed brandy. His hand sought the mound of his belly and he pressed hard against it.

Vivian became aware of a pain in her shin where a chair had fallen on her. If the earl had not been sitting across from her she would have pulled her skirt up and inspected her leg. She really must get upstairs. She started to rise.

"Stay a minute." He took another sip of brandy and shifted in his chair. A tiny groan slipped out, quickly covered by a cough. "I wanted to pay you a compliment."

Her eyebrows rose. She pushed her torn sleeve back up onto her shoulder. It fell immediately smearing the blood oozing from the scratches.

With approval he noted that she neither winced nor trembled. "I was immensely proud of you today. I kept Millard from bursting in to 'rescue' you, you know. A fight between you and Emma was inevitable. She is a very jealous woman. And very possessive. At the same time I saw a second demonstration of your proud spirit. It pleased me very much."

Vivian smiled faintly. At the same time she shuddered inwardly. What kind of man would foresee a fight and do nothing to prevent it? What kind of person would stand outside while women he professed to care

303

about tried to injure themselves? She slipped a hand into the deep pocket of her skirt and drew forth pad and pencil. With them she wrote, "Glad you enjoyed the show."

He read and shrugged insofar as his crippled shoulders allowed him to do so. "As I told you before, I don't care what you do to this house. All I care about is that you conceive and bear a healthy son. Whatever you want to do and are strong enough to do, you have my permission. If funds are required in your little beautification project, you have a limited amount at your disposal."

Her mouth curled upward. She stabbed a thumb at her chest.

"Yours?" He grinned. "Well, yes, I grant you, you do bring certain funds with you, but as yet they have not been turned over to us. Your solicitor and guardian are still lurking around the neighborhood hoping to spirit you off. Does that frighten you?"

She took a deep breath, then nodded her head.

"Good. A sensible woman. Not one of the proud ones who thinks that her dainty aristocratic hand will stand between a man and whatever it is he wants." He took another drink of brandy. "I think you will have no more trouble with Emma Felders. She was beaten fairly before the entire staff. They'll all look to you for instruction from now on."

She passed him another terse note. "Dismiss the housekeeper."

He read it and shook his head. "You must have been quite a trial to the nuns in that abbey. Whatever happened to Christian teachings like forgive your enemies?"

She shot him a look heavy with meaning.

He chuckled. "Sorry to disappoint you in this, but Emma stays. She's very necessary to my comfort and well-being. And I have almost no comforts in life anymore. Ask for something else."

With a shake of her head, she rose and set the glass on the desk. Inclining her head and sweeping back her skirts, she sketched a formal bow of withdrawal.

"I mean what I said," he called after her. "Do anything you want so long as it does not—"

The library door thudded behind her.

"—damage my grandson."

Chapter Nineteen

Icy rain pelted Piers's cheeks and nose. With his hat pulled low over his brows and the collar of his great cape upstanding, he presented a perfect picture of hunching misery. His hands in his soaked leather gloves ached with the cold. He could not feel his fingers where they crossed over the pommel of his saddle. He clenched and unclenched them. They might have been sticks for all the tactile sensations they sent to his exhausted brain.

Romany Knight, own brother to Romany Prince, shifted wearily under him as water beat down on the big black's drooping head and neck. The movement tilted Piers's stiff body, and more water cascaded down before his eyes from the brim of his hat. He cursed mildly and then coughed. A harsh hacking sound tore out from deep within his throat. His body was suddenly convulsed by chills that further unmanned him as the cough bent him over the saddle. Again he cursed— monotonous, sobbing, wheezing curses to vent his disgust and weariness.

A burly figure strode out of the rain. The bearded malevolent face raised itself to Piers's and squinted belligerently at the sick man. "No sign yet? Here now, are you sure of yer meetin' place? We've been waitin' five nights now for this bloke and every night a different place. Maybe you're the one makin' the mistake."

Piers looked down at his henchman with real hatred. "Beddoes, I've explained for the last time the precautions we have taken to ensure that we are never caught. The meeting places are changed by prearrangement. Both parties have the list. If there is a mistake one night, it won't be made the next night. The only reason that they're not showing is because they've gotten a tip that the meeting is too dangerous."

"Bunch of lily-livered pansies."

He bent closer to Beddoes to be sure the man heard every word. "And you're a greedy idiot. For tuppence, Jack, I'd blow you to hell and gone and go home and forget the whole thing."

The henchman fell back a step, ducked his head, and fell to muttering.

Piers looked around him again. The blackness was inpenetrable. His face contorted in a grimace as he straightened himself in his saddle. His whole body alternately burned hot and icy cold. His forehead throbbed painfully against the constriction of his hat band.

"See anything?" Beddoes's question came in a much more subdued tone.

"In this blackness who can see anything? It can't be much blacker than this in hell." Piers looked around once more, then dropped his head to stare at the upturned face.

Millard's beard and hair were so thick and so tangled that the eyes and nose that protruded from the middle of them seemed scarcely human. Indeed for the fortnight, the smuggler had behaved like a wild man, ranting, raving, cursing, hindering the expedition more than he helped.

"Look again," Beddoes urged. "And this time open yer bleedin' eyes, yer bleedin' lordship. There's gotta be a signal tonight."

"Beddoes! Damnation! With this storm, no one can see a hundred yards in any direction. They could be out there signaling till dawn and we couldn't see them. We might as well give it up for tonight."

The smuggler grabbed Romany Knight's bridle. "No. Look again, I tell you. We've swived around with this long enough. Let's get this stuff on its way and get our money."

Piers's hand went to the pistol holstered on his saddle. "Get your filthy hands off my bridle and shut your mouth. Or I will shut it for you—and permanently."

The smuggler subsided again, his face contorting with rage. For an instant he looked as if he would spring at the man on horseback, but he clenched his fists and ducked his head.

Suppressing another cough, Piers stood in the stirrups and looked around him in every direction.

Nothing but howling wind and pelting rain in a blackness like the lower circles of Dante's *Inferno*. Particles of ice struck his cheek and clung there in the beard stubble. They likewise began to crust in his eyelashes and eyebrows.

Another bout of coughing bent him over the saddle. As pain knifed through his chest, he swore if he could only get himself under control, he would abandon the vigil and disperse the men. Nothing was worth the agony of waiting under these conditions.

A half-hour's gallop would take him back to the inn where he could slide from the saddle into a hot bath and a warm bed. In his mind he fantasized a glass of warmed brandy. But he would not be greedy. Merely to be dry and away from this cursed rain and cold would seem heaven to him at this point.

"Don't suppose you've got the wrong spot?" Beddoes had moved back so he stood at the viscount's knee and in the lee of the horse's big body.

Piers shook his head. "I've spoken to the contact each time, Jack. And each time the meeting place has had to be changed to avoid the Riding Officers. We've almost been caught three times."

"So they say. Maybe they're standin' us up, tryin' to bring the price down?"

"Not a chance. It's taken a long time to build this organization. They have more to lose than we do. Still if we don't get rid of this cursed cargo tonight, I cannot but believe the whole enterprise to be futile." Again Piers coughed, as his long speech seemed to drain the strength from his body. Privately, he thought the whole business to be damned. Bright specks danced before his eyes as he stared out into the rain.

"Look again," the henchman urged in a wheedling tone. "It'd be a damn' shame to wait this long and come back empty-handed."

Again the bright specks. Piers blinked and wiped his hand across his eyes. Was he delirious? He dropped his hand onto the shoulder of the man beside him. "Look yonder! Can you see a light?"

Beddoes spun around and stared in the direction Piers pointed. Instantly, the tone of his voice changed from servile to belligerent. "Sure, it's right there in front of us. The bloody fools took their own sweet time about gettin' here." He slapped Piers's thigh jubilantly. "They sure better have their money in hand." He slogged rapidly away through the rain. In a moment a lantern was uncovered. Its light streamed as a beacon

Piers's senses strove for alertness as he straightened painfully in the saddle, grasped the reins, and tugged the horse's head up. The lantern was before his eyes in the distance, blinking, then disappearing. He could not count the times. Had it blinked twice as was the signal, or was it simply bobbing and waving? Just as suddenly, it disappeared. He pulled the horse around.

Beddoes's voice growled through the darkness. "Damnation! What in bloody hell did they do that for?"

"Douse your light, man!" Piers's hoarse command barely reached the smuggler's ears. "Wait for the signal to come again. We can't be sure that the man behind the lantern is who we hope it is."

"Has to be," Beddoes argued. "Nobody else'd be fool enough to be out on a night like this swingin' his light around. Show them again, boys. Bring them in."

"No! Wait!" Piers's command rang through the frozen darkness. Unfortunately, it ended in a rasping cough that doubled him over the saddle.

"No!" The burly smuggler lost his temper. "No, your damned lordship! We stand out here and freeze our bloody bums off and you tell us to wait when we saw the signal? Throw off that blanket, Twitch, and let's get this business over with."

The light flashed out from under the blanket. Its directed beam stabbed through the pelting rain.

"No! You fool!" Piers reined the stallion across the light. "Beddoes! You idiot! You could destroy all—"

A shot rang out! The stallion screamed like a woman and plunged sideways bucking wildly in pain and terror. Its huge body and flailing legs scattered the men gathered around the lantern. Up it reared, its iron shod hooves smashing into the back and shoulders of the unfortunate Twitch, driving both man and light into the muddy oblivion.

"Easy, boy. Whoa up there!" Piers sawed on the reins, fighting with hands and voice to regain control of the animal, but the horse was too far gone in pain and fear to respond. With a savage twist it swung its head around to bite at the tormenting bullet.

In horror Piers jerked his leg from the stirrup to avoid the teeth. With one leg thrown over the mount's rump and his weight canted to one side, his seat was destroyed. The next plunge of the stallion threw him onto his back in the mud.

The breath whooshed from his lungs. Light exploded into darkness behind his eyes. Less than a minute and then the icy rain pelting his face woke him to a cacophony of curses and cries punctuated by gunfire. Freed from the man in the saddle, the stallion plunged away, twisting its great body in pain and terror. Straight at the line of approaching men it tore. Their disciplined ranks were broken as the maddened beast skidded to a halt and reared high above their heads.

"Catch that damn thing!"

"Watch out!"

"Shoot it!"

A volley of gunfire followed what could only have been a command. Romany Knight screamed again, but the thunder of hooves faded into the rain leaving behind curses and cries of pain.

Piers was fortunate that he lay paralyzed in the mud. Muskets and pistols spat mayhem and death in the air above his prone body. Flashes from the exploding firearms as well as from lanterns created a kaleidoscope of light against the inky blackness.

Drawing in a breath as deep as his shocked, infected lungs would allow, he rolled halfway over. A boot stumbled over him and knocked him flat on his face. A man fell across him, climbed to his feet, and ran on.

311

Piers cursed. He could not direct his panicky men, not that he would have said anything except "Run for your lives."

"Close ranks. Fire." A deep voice called.

Another volley. And more screams.

"Throw down your weapons and surrender. You're surrounded!"

Close by his ear, a shrill scream of a man in mortal agony roused Piers to full consciousness. He tried again to push himself up on his elbow. This time a booted foot struck him viciously in the side. Rolling over, he pushed himself up on hands and knees. A mighty blow to his shoulder slammed him back into the mud.

"Stay down, ye blackguard!" a guttural voice snarled.

Piers twisted about, blinking upward through the icy rain. A uniformed man reversed his musket to bring it smashing down butt first into the upturned face.

With a shout, Piers threw up his good arm to ward off the blow. It never fell. Instead a shot rang out. The man's body arched. The musket sprang from his nerveless hands. Momentum projected him forward, his booted feet crashing painfully into Piers's hip and ribs. Overbalanced, the man crashed to the ground.

"Up ye go, milord."

"Watkins. Thank God."

"We're in deadly danger, milord." The valet crouched low, placing a firm hand under the viscount's injured shoulder.

At the man's touch Piers clamped his teeth into his lower lip to suppress the cry of agony. Close in his ear beneath the sounds of the fighting came the popping and grinding of broken bones. Using every ounce of determination he possessed, he staggered to his feet leaning heavily against his smaller companion.

"This way, milord." Watkins tugged at the wounded arm eliciting a moan from the depths of the younger man's throat.

At a stumbling run Watkins half dragged, half carried Piers across the field. The ground beneath their feet was a sucking morass. Rain pelted them, but the sound of the fighting grew fainter as the pursuit moved in another direction.

In the elemental darkness, the pair blundered into a hedgerow. With an agonized shriek, Piers sank to his knees beside it. The left side of his body felt paralyzed. But worse was the pain in his chest. His congested lungs labored to draw breath down his raw throat. He coughed and the agony bent him over, his forehead resting in the mud.

The valet bent over him, grasping his shoulders trying to pull him upright. "We can't stay here, milord," he whispered urgently. "So help me God, I don't know where we are. Can't tell one bloody direction from another, but we've got to get out of the field. They'll be sending out parties to pick up stragglers before long. Then when first light comes, they'll be beating the bushes."

"Go on," Piers gasped from his knees. He crouched on the ground, waves of pain washing over him with each agonized breath he drew. "Hide me here. I can crawl in under the hedgerow and wait. Get away. Save yourself. Tomorrow hire a carriage and come back to get me."

"Leave you here in the rain with you half sick and hurt! You'll be dead by morning. Frozen to death." Watkins's voice sharp and pleading. "Not likely, Lord Polwycke."

"I can't go on. Leave me."

"You have to. You can't stay here. You'll freeze to death."

The rain seemed to slacken for a moment. A cry came out of the dark and then a musket boomed.

"Watkins." Piers began to cough as he drew his breath into his already raw throat and aching lungs. "Watkins. You must. I cannot go . . . far . . . Too slow . . . You . . . get away now. Leave me."

"But, milord." The man bent low, placing his arm under Piers's shoulder.

"No!" Piers howled in pain. Falling over onto his hip, he braced his neck and shoulder against the prickly bush. "You see . . . I'm finished." He slumped down on his side. Another fit of coughing forced his knees up to his chest. "Go on, man! Hurry."

Suddenly, lightning jagged down to strike the field in a ball of blinding light and steam. Directly overhead thunder clapped with a boom to waken the dead. The rain poured down with renewed fury. Watkins shrank lower, racked by indecision. Above the noise of the storm, a musket cracked off to the right.

"They'll be here in a second. Run, man!"

Another musket exploded. Watkins jerked his hat down over his face and ran.

Piers rolled his body half over beneath the hedgerow. The rough-trimmed ends of branches tore at his face, his clothing, his hair. His hat hooked on one, and his scrabbling movements pulled it from his head.

Beneath the hedgerow the ground was awash with freezing water. Thinking that he would be lucky not to drown, Piers turned his face into his good arm. Lightning split the sky and thunder boomed again, but not directly overhead. The rain no longer pelted. Rather it sluiced down among the leaves and branches onto his prone body and unprotected head. The clothing beneath his coat was soaked. Like a leaden mass it encased him in ice. Then amazingly, the painful cold ceased. Instead he felt fiery hot. He seemed to be

314

floating in the water in which he lay. No longer could he feel the rain, nor the sharp thorns stabbing into his flesh.

In a moment of lucidity he heard footsteps approaching; boots slogged through the mud toward his hiding place. He must have been moaning. Viciously, he clamped his teeth down on his lower lip. The pain awakened him to a sort of distorted reality. The dragoons were all around him searching for stragglers. He must suppress all sound.

When a fit of coughing struck him, he closed his mouth over the muddied sleeve of his coat. The boots stopped beside the hedgerow. For several seconds the only sounds in the ears of the sick man were the pattering of the decreasing rain and the peculiar ringing noise inside his own head. He held his breath, his body rigid against his shuddering.

Then a harsh, unintelligible order came from farther out in the field and the boots moved on.

Piers began to shiver again, his body shaking with the intense chill. More dead than alive, he lay helplessly waiting for the valet to return. So miserable was he that he was tempted to surrender to the dragoons. If they arrested him, they must surely imprison him in a dry cell.

The pain in his chest and throat mingled with the pain in his shoulder to distort his surroundings. Gradually a red haze began to glow before his eyes. Again his body burned. He felt as if he were floating, spinning, swirling up and up toward terrible blackness closing down. His last conscious thought was a fear that he might pass out and drown if his face dropped into the water beneath his arm.

A few faint streaks of dawn broke through the

lowering clouds. The young lieutenant saluted smartly before his commander. "There's five dead, Captain MacPherson. And two wounded so badly they'll likely die."

"How many did we lose?"

"Only one. Shot in the back."

"Poor fellow. Take him up on a litter."

"Yes, sir."

"Pull the bodies together. I want to inspect them as soon as there's enough light."

"Yes, sir."

MacPherson turned as a dragoon led the big black stallion limping and whickering in pain across the field. "The leader was riding this horse, sir."

"Was?"

"Shot out of the saddle, we're guessing, sir. The horse has been shot twice. Seems likely he got the brunt of a volley."

MacPherson felt a start of excitement. He ran his gloved hand down the stallion's barrel. Even in the dark, he recognized the big black as one he had spied Polwycke mounted on. Blood still trickled sluggishly from a bullet hole where a man's leg would have been. If the viscount were among the dead, or the wounded—he did not care which—Vivian Larne was a widow and a free woman. He patted the horse with unusual attention. "Had a hard time of it, have you, old fellow? We'll see to you. It's not your fault who owned you. We'll take him back to quarters and let the farrier see to him."

"Yes, sir."

The lieutenant slogged up. "We've pulled the dead altogether."

MacPherson hurried across the field. He stooped to scrutinize each face, washed clean by the rain. Piers

316

Larne was not among them. A dragoon pushed the two wounded men forward.

"Where's your leader?"

One man shrugged. "Last time I seen 'im, 'e was flat on 'is back in the mud. 'Orse threw 'im. Guess 'e broke 'is neck."

"He's not among the dead."

They looked at each other. "Can't 'elp y' then, gov'nor."

MacPherson looked around him angrily. "Send out the men again, Lieutenant. Scour the fields. We've got a few small fry here. But the big fish got away. Send men to the neighboring inns. Find out if a nobleman is staying in any of them. If he's hurt, he can't hide very long."

Piers screamed in pain!

"Try to keep quiet, milord. Sound carries in the fog." Watkins's tired voice penetrated the agony as the valet tried to drag him out of the mud.

Piers's body roused to flaming agony and blistering heat alternating with chills. A heavy fog hung over everything. Both sky and earth were a uniform smothering gray.

Finally, on his feet with his valet's shoulder beneath his, Piers staggered dizzily along beside the hedgerow and finally through a gate. As he came out from behind the thick protection, a vagrant breeze touched his face and froze his sodden clothing to his body. His teeth began to chatter uncontrollably.

Beside the road a coach waited, a hired hack with the curtains drawn. Brushing Watkins's help aside, he swayed determinedly while the valet opened the door. The step seemed a long way up when he tried to lift his leg. Dead game, he grabbed the sides of the door and pulled with all his strength. Only the toe of his boot caught while his fingers slipped pitifully from their grip. Ignominiously, he tumbled headlong into the coach, the lower half of his body still hanging out.

"Sorry, sir." Watkins unceremoniously placed his shoulder against his master's rump and boosted him inside. A cry of pain stifled by a curse sounded from the dank, musty interior. The door slammed behind him. Watkins mounted to the box and whipped up the horses. The coach jolted away.

Piers pulled his body onto the leather seat and tried to brace himself against the sway and jerk as the horses made slow headway through the ruts and mire. The effort to keep himself upright bathed his body in perspiration which immediately chilled him.

He groaned as violent ague shook him. He had been so miserable so long that he prayed for unconsciousness, but even that was denied him. Lifting his benumbed hand to his mouth, he pulled off his sodden leather glove with his teeth. The hand was stained blue where the dye in the leather had faded. The skin was wrinkled and puffy from the overnight soaking. Incredulously, he stared at it in revulsion as if it were not a part of his body. Shutting his eyes tightly, he spat the glove from his mouth and blew on his cupped fingers. His breath was the only thing hot and dry about him.

A particularly hard jolt threw him to the left side of the coach against his injured shoulder. Too weak to control himself, he set up a howl.

"Sorry, milord!" Watkins shouted from the seat above him. "The road is all but impassable. Shall I slow down?"

"No." Piers wondered that his teeth did not chip, so hard were they chattering. "No. Carry on."

In the coach's interior he nodded grimly to himself and clenched his teeth. Still his nerves quivered, and his muscles jumped. Neither rest nor sleep was possible to his overstrained body, broken and chilled as it was.

The odyssey of agony seemed everlasting. Finally, another lurch flung him against the side of the coach with such force that he banged his head. Flesh and blood could stand no more. His body slumped unconscious. At the next jolt it slid off the seat into a heap on the muddy floor.

When Piers next knew himself, two hostlers stinking of manure were clumsily extracting him from the depths of the coach. One clutched his booted legs around the ankles and dragged his body unceremoniously across the floor. The second reached in and grabbed hold of the wrist of his left arm.

Loosing a mighty curse, Piers kicked brutally with all his strength at the hands that held him. In surprise he realized that his struggle, instead of sending the man reeling away as he had intended, only resulted in the slightest inconvenience to the man who held his ankles.

The curse, so vituperative in his mind, had come from his lips as a dull, low croak of pain. Chained by his own body, he could only submit helplessly to the agony they inflicted on him.

Like a bag of wet laundry, they bore him between them, one carrying his legs, the other his shoulders. The tails of his coat trailed ignominiously across the muddied straw of the yard of a delapidated inn.

Watkins's voice could be heard alongside cautioning them. "In the name of God, handle his body gently. He took a bad fall from his horse."

"Sorry, sir, but he ain't no lightweight, y'know."

The sense of the words faded as Piers experienced

wave after wave of pain, accompanied now by roiling nausea.

Uncaring, the stable hands swayed his body back and forth as they mounted the stairs. Finally, they heaved him onto a surface somewhat soft but redolent of mold and mildew.

"Send hot water and towels and brandy."

"Comin' right up, sir." Even as the door slammed behind them, he felt Watkins's familiar hands working at his throat.

With practiced skill the valet drew the clothing from the injured body. Sometimes when a particular portion was removed, such as his coat and shirt, Piers roused himself to grit his teeth and swear. Otherwise, he lay as one dead. After what seemed like an eternity of suffering, the valet had him undressed and slipped beneath the covers. The bed itself was damp and cold. Piers began to shudder immediately.

"Watkins." His voice trembled and shook with rigors so strong that his body convulsed. "Get me something to warm me and this bed, or I will die." His words slipped out in hot whispers blowing over his parched lips. When a fit of coughing struck, he doubled over on his side to try and ease himself.

"Immediately, sir." Watkins brought hot bricks wrapped in rough cloth and slipped them in beside his legs and feet. Gradually the ague abated to a steady shivering.

"Milord." Watkins' voice sounded from a long way off. "Milord Piers, can you drink this posset? I've had the innkeeper prepare it, and I've added a little laudanum to dull your pain."

"Mustn't drink that." Piers's voice was a dry whisper. "Must leave in the morning. Rendezvous. Some men might have escaped. Return to Larne." He licked his lips. Their surfaces were dry and scabbed

320

from being bitten in his agony. Strange. He did not recall biting his lips. His head spun dizzily as he shook it.

"Listen, milord. You'd best drink this and forget about everything. You can't help them."

"Beddoes?"

"Jack won't keep that rendezvous. I talked to one who's headed back as fast as he can fly. He told me Beddoes's was shot and killed."

"Killed?" Piers choked.

"I wouldn't count it," Watkins said wearily. "Only the good die young."

Again Piers groaned. "God's mercy."

"Drink, milord."

"Yes." Piers allowed the valet to hold the cup to his lips. It was hot and powerful. It tasted like heaven to his sore throat. When he had drained it, he lay back.

His eyes were already closing as the bricks began to heat the bed. But he roused. "I owe you my life."

"Don't think about it."

"But I do. And I promise you . . ." He faltered. "I promise you. This foul business . . . Over and done with. Forever." His voice strengthened for a moment. "I'll have no more of it. Forever."

"Yes, milord." The little man nodded. "Now go to sleep."

"No!"

"Milord Piers, there is nothing you can do tonight. The horses can go no farther, and I have no money to hire more. Sleep is the best thing for you, milord. Besides, we can't go home for a time."

Rousing, Piers rolled his head on the pillow. "Why not?"

"Your horse, milord. The Riding Officers caught it. They think it's Romany Prince and he's a very famous stallion. They'll be waiting for you if you go home

321

wounded and sick. We have to hide until your father throws them off the scent. When they approached me early yesterday morning, I told them that you were spending a discreet time with a certain lady and would not return for some several days. Then I cleared out after they'd gone."

Piers groaned in anger and apprehension. "You are the most loyal of men, Watkins. I shall never be able to repay you." He coughed and the sound tore through his raw throat. "We will never go again," he promised. "I swear."

"Yes, milord," Watkins replied wearily. "Here's a bit of quinine for the fever."

Obediently, lifting his head, Piers swallowed the bitter stuff. As Watkins supported the wine-dark head back onto the pillow, the Viscount Polwycke flung his good left forearm over his eyes. A sob broke from his throat.

Chapter Twenty

"I am highly insulted that you should come here with vile accusations, Captain MacPherson." The Earl of Larnaervon's voice was icy with affront. "My son has gone to Scotland to take care of some estate business there for his new wife. Isn't that so, my dear?"

Vivian felt a thrill of fear trickle down her spine. Two weeks. More than two, closer to three had passed without a word from Piers. While the earl said nothing about his absence at the dinner table, Millard had told her that he had sent a rider out with instructions to follow certain roads and ask questions of certain people.

"Lady Polwycke?" Rory MacPherson prompted softly.

She nodded hastily. On her pad she wrote. "Scotland."

"Then how does it happen that his horse, the famous Romany Prince, was found wounded in a field where a smuggling operation was foiled?"

"I don't know anything about horses," the earl growled. "A horse did the damage you see today. I can't abide the beasts. If a horse is missing from the stable, he

323

undoubtedly was stolen in my son's absence. Don't you agree, Vivian?"

She put on what she hoped was her most gracious smile as she wrote. "Romany Prince was in the stable this morning. I rode him."

MacPherson read the note, his face disbelieving. "I'm afraid you're mistaken, Lady Polwycke."

She shook her head emphatically.

"The way to solve the problem is to call for the damned horse," the earl suggested in a bored tone. "Then you'll be satisfied and can be on your way finding who the horse you have in your possession really belongs to. How you hope to do that I have no idea," he added nastily. "One horse looks remarkably like another."

"But—"

"See here, sir. I'll send for the horse immediately." He waved his cane toward the door. Millard bowed and left.

"Smugglers?" Vivian wrote.

"Yes, a large band of the scurvy fellows. Quite a few killed, several wounded. Not many escaped, I'm proud to say. Although the leader did manage to elude us. But he was badly wounded." His eyes never left the earl, gauging his reaction. "Probably crawled off to die somewhere."

Vivian could feel the color draining from her face. Quickly she bowed her head over her note pad, trying to think of something intelligent to write.

"And so he should," Larne enjoined loudly regarding the leader of the smugglers. "Damned scoundrels every one of them. Create unemployment for good workmen here in this country. Refuse to pay their lawful taxes. Every one of them should be shot or hanged."

"Oh, you can be sure those whom we captured will

324

be," MacPherson told him. "We caught them with the goods. Their contraband in wagons waiting to be traded."

"And how did you happen to be there at the right time?"

MacPherson looked uncomfortable. He shot a glance at Vivian. "An informant among them. Sometimes the government has to resort to bribes in the right places."

"Fight fire with fire," she wrote.

He smiled, his humor restored. "I'm glad you see it that way."

"The horse has been brought up, milord," Millard informed them from the doorway.

"Take the captain and show the animal to him," Larne ordered Vivian. "Can't stand the damned beasts myself. Never want to be near one again."

Together they went down the steps to the drive. There Tyler held Romany Prince, who whickered softly at the sight of her. When she came down to him, he pressed his nose into her hand for a treat.

"You've quite ruined that horse, milady," the weasel-faced groom remarked. He cast the captain a long-suffering look. "Every morning she brings him a treat."

Tilting her head on one side, Vivian looked inquiringly at the man as Romany Prince thrust his black nose insistently into her hand snuffling gently.

With his cheeky grin, he informed MacPherson. " 'Tisn't right to be always bringing sugar. Makes him fretful when she doesn't come. Now he's got his mouth all set for more and he's disappointed." And indeed the horse tossed his head up and down, jingling the halter rings.

Vivian stroked the blue-black face and smoothed the forelock.

"He certainly seems to know Lady Polwycke," MacPherson remarked weakly.

"Knows her and loves her. When Lord Piers gets back from Scotland, he'll have a time climbing onto this black devil's back. As it is he gets fractious under anyone else who tries to ride him. Milady, he thinks he's your horse and nobody else's."

Enjoying the fantasy, Vivian patted the blue-black arched neck. Romany Prince nuzzled his velvet nose against her shoulder and pricked his ears forward.

MacPherson's neck was quite red. "Obviously, the horse we found must belong to someone else. I do apologize for bursting in here with wild stories. Still this horse looks enough like the one we have to be his own brother. I wouldn't have thought there was another one in the country."

Vivian nodded graciously. She cupped her pad in her hand and wrote, "You must do your duty."

"I thank you for your understanding."

Tyler tugged at his cap. "Shall I take the horse back to the stable, milady?"

She gave Romany Prince a final pat and nodded.

"When do you expect your husband to return?" MacPherson asked as they watched the horse being led away.

Vivian shrugged. "When business is finished."

"And you are satisfied that he is taking care of your best interests?"

She looked away toward the door of the big, brooding, gray house. A curtain moved at a window. She was sure that behind it her father-in-law spied upon her. Or perhaps Emma Felders? She heaved a sigh.

"Milady?"

She flashed him a brilliant smile and offered him her hand.

He took it between his two and lifted it to his lips. "I am not convinced, milady," he murmured. "I, too, see the curtains moving. Why won't you trust me?"

She drew back quickly.

He sighed. "Then, milady, I'll wish you greetings of the season and a Happy New Year."

She started.

He regarded her sadly. "You did not remember that it's the day before Christmas. Then I am more than pleased to wish you joy." He bowed formally. "I bid you good day."

With a sinking feeling, she watched him walk away.

At the end of Christmas Day, she sat staring exhausted into the flames flickering in her grate. She was alone as she had been every Christmas for the last ten years and as in the past ten years she felt the familiar depression of loneliness. Added to this was her concern for Piers. Where was he? Had he been wounded and perhaps lay dying somewhere? Tears welled in her eyes. She tried to put the thought away quickly.

Watkins had been equally silent. But what if Watkins had been among the men killed? More tears.

Stop! She pressed her hands against her temples. Thoughts like those would drive her insane.

A light tap sounded at the door. While she was considering ignoring it, the door opened. Millard entered, bearing a tray with a silver cover, a crystal wineglass, and bottle of wine wrapped in a heavy white napkin.

"I do not wish to disturb you, Lady Vivian," he intoned respectfully, "but the staff, that is, Cook and myself, thought you would enjoy a bit of dessert. He has baked a plum pudding especially for you in honor of the season."

Vivian turned her head to wipe at her cheeks. When she turned back it was with a brilliant smile.

"We are all aware," Millard continued, "of how hard you have worked to set things to right. Likewise, we have noticed that you have not always had the cooperation you should have had."

Maintaining an impersonal façade, he set the tray on the table and unwrapped the bottle, revealing the gold foil top of a bumper of champagne.

"We thought you should enjoy a bit of a celebration," he explained, "since the house looks more as it should than we can remember it. We look forward to your redecorating in the new year when you shall have time to order new papers and materials."

She stared at him as if she could not believe her eyes nor her ears. The champagne cork popped into the fireplace. In her gratitude she could not stop more tears that left shining paths down her cheek.

The pale gold liquid foamed into the glass. Millard presented it to her. With a flourish he removed the cover from the pudding. He thrust a straw into the fireplace and with another flourish the rum blazed up. When it had died, the butler served a piece and set it on the small table at her right hand.

"Now, milady, you buck up your spirits. We below stairs wish you a Merry Christmas and the very happiest of New Years. And may you have many more pleasant evenings in your new home."

With a smile he bowed respectfully and left.

Sipping the delicious cool sweet wine, Vivian was left to smile at the thoughtfulness of her friends.

The viscountess curled her feet beneath her and stared out her bedroom window at the last of grim January on the terrace below. Between the gray flagstones, snow collected in the fissures. Frozen and twice frozen moisture made treacherous patches in low places in the granite.

She thought of the gardens at Stone Glenn. Had they been allowed to run back as those beyond the terrace? Here a boxwood garden surrounded what must surely have been rosebeds. Over the seasons the roses had gone wild, and their canes were a tangle overgrown with high brown volunteer grasses. As for the boxwood, it had been allowed to stand untrimmed until its shapes had been obscured.

Sighing, she turned her face away and gazed around her sunlit room with pardonable pride. Her eyes rested on the newly upholstered blue velvet chaise lounge before the fireplace. Above the freshly cleaned mantel an antique mirror removed from the late countess's suite reflected the room and its furnishings. Only in this haven did she feel secure away from the conflicts and unhappiness of the lower house.

She looked again at the mirror. If she had sought to remove it one day later, she would not have been given permission to do so. On that day she had awakened to discover that she had not conceived the earl's grandson. Her condition would have been impossible to conceal from Emma Felders even if she had tried.

The housekeeper had seized upon the news and run to the earl with it. His disappointment had been keen. He had not appeared at lunch. At dinner his eyes had bored into her belly, stripping away her clothing, her very skin, seeking a reason for what he deemed her failure to conceive.

Since that night he had seldom spoken. His drinking had increased at dinner where he habitually muttered to himself. But he would not allow her to dine in her room, so the unpleasant interlude marred her days.

Resting her chin on her hand, she gazed out the

window again. When the weather warmed a bit more, she would do some things with the garden below. The roses could be easily pruned, the grasses weeded out from around their roots and fresh soil piled up. The boxwood could be trimmed into a simple hedge.

But she did not really want to oversee any of the work. She was tired of working with this huge gray pile of rock with its filthy and neglected furnishings, tired of working where her labors went unappreciated by most and resented by some. She longed for her own home to expend her energy on.

Piers had promised that they would go to Stone Glenn in the spring. When he returned— She shook her head. If he returned—for no word of him had come. For almost eight weeks despite the earl's inquiries, nothing had been heard of the Viscount Polwycke. He might have dropped off the face of the earth.

Loneliness made her sigh softly. Piers had just begun to be important in her life when he had gone on that doomed smuggling expedition. Who knew what accord they might have come to had they more than one ride together, more than one night of fiery passion?

A blush stole into her cheeks at the thought of their lovemaking. Not since her mother's death had she been held against another warm body. Starved as she was for human companionship, for touching and holding, kisses and caresses had turned her into an animal. An adoring creature who clung with all her secret heart to the possibility that her new husband might treat her well, even come to like her.

What was more, she wanted him again. She wanted him to return to her as soon as might be. She had even been disappointed when her monthly courses had begun. The prospect of a baby, even the earl's grandson—she grimaced at the thought of Larnaervon—to shower with affection was not without its attractions.

Nervously, she sprang up and began to pace the length of the room clasping her arms about her body. The passion she had felt had racked her, too. Cravings she had never felt had come to her in moments of solitude. Fantasies had woven themselves into her dreams around the terrific explosion of feeling she had experienced in Piers's bed.

She stared at herself in the mirror. Her cheeks were pink, her eyes sultry. She longed for her husband, a lawbreaker, a criminal, a smuggler. She shook her head ruefully. The Christian teachings of the abbey seemed to have been totally cast aside.

A knock at the door spun her around. Excited and smiling, Addie burst into the room. "Oh, milady, I ran all the way up the stairs to tell you." She paused, placing her hand over her bosom to suppress its heaving. "He's home! He's downstairs now in the hallway. Lord Piers!"

Vivian felt a spurt of wild excitement; her face flushed with color. She had been standing here wanting him and he had come. She whirled and stared at her reflection in the mirror.

"Come, milady, let me tidy your hair and slip you into something with a bit more color just to make him feel like he's really home." The little maid's voice was shrill with excitement. "My mum always says that a man loves a woman to look pretty."

Vivian shook her head. Intuitively, she knew she should go down the stairs to meet him immediately. She gave her silver-gilt hair a quick pat, and bit her lips to heighten the color which had already flooded them.

"Oh, please sit down, Milady Vivian," Addie fluttered behind her.

But Vivian was already hurrying from the apartment. The hall at the foot of the stairs was empty, but she could hear the sounds of Lord Alexander's voice raised in anger in the library.

Running swiftly down the stairs, she caught Mrs. Felders stooped over, her ear close to the keyhole of the library door. So intent was the housekeeper on her eavesdropping that she neither saw nor heard her mistress's approach. Angrily, Vivian dropped her hand onto the black-clad shoulder.

The woman bobbed up as if she had been stabbed and swung around. Her startled expression quickly changed to sullen embarrassment.

Eyes cold with disapproval, the viscountess stared the woman up and down.

The housekeeper dropped her eyes. A hot flush mottled her neck and cheeks.

With a fierce peremptory gesture, Vivian dismissed her. Unable to offer any excuse, Felders scuttled off down the hall, ducked behind the great staircase and vanished into the shadows.

Through the library door the earl's voice raved on and on. One particularly loud bellow stayed Vivian's hand where it poised above the paneling to knock. She dropped her hands to her side and stepped back.

Larnaervon was furiously angry. Did she dare interrupt the harangue? Yet her husband was behind that door and, from the sounds of it, would welcome her interruption. Her courage coupled with avid curiosity triumphed over her fear. Wiping moist palms on the sides of her skirt, she took a deep breath and rapped on the heavy oak door.

Silence answered her. No inquiry nor order to enter sounded from the room beyond. After only a moment's hesitation Vivian stepped into the dim library.

It was as she remembered it with its pervasive musty

atmosphere. It was still a room too long shut up without clean fresh air to blow through. The dusty, fetid odor assailed her sensitive nostrils particularly since the rest of the house had been so improved by her thorough cleaning.

Her eyes swept the room. The old man sat hunched in his leather chair behind his huge desk. The light fell over his knobby, spotted hands clenched tightly around his cane.

She did not immediately see her husband. Could Addie possibly have been mistaken?

The Earl of Larnaervon lifted his head. "What do you want?" he barked. She stared at him shocked. His normally cynical demeanor, the lips crooked in a humorless smile, was gone. In its place pure rage empurpled his face. A vein stood out in his hollow temple throbbing even as she watched it.

"What do you want!?" He repeated, louder and angrier than before. A bead of sweat trickled down his face. One hand let loose his cane to disappear behind the desk. He bared his teeth in pain.

Hesitantly, she advanced until she was even with the two wing-back chairs. Slumped wearily in one, his right palm supporting his bearded cheek, one booted foot drawn up on the knee of the other, sat her husband.

When he raised his head to look at her, she gasped at the sight.

If the father had worked himself into a black rage that changed his appearance, the son was hardly recognizable. She could find almost nothing of the handsome young man who had strode out into the blackness of the December night, his cape swirling around him.

His eyes burned in the dark hollows of his gaunt face. Staring hot and unnaturally bright, they rested on her dully, only vaguely comprehending her presence. The pain groove between his eyebrows deepened. He opened his mouth to speak, but Larne commenced his harangue again.

"What are you doing here?" he growled at Vivian. "No one sent for you. Get out!" When she did not move he raised his voice until his shout rang from the oak beams above them. He lifted the cane and brandished it in her direction. "You can have him to fawn over when I get through with him. Get out, I say!"

Her husband was a sick man. Indeed, he seemed largely unaware of his surroundings, incapable of responding or defending himself against the rage that his father poured on his head. In this very room she had seen Larne strike him. Keeping an eye on the earl, she bent and gazed into Piers's face. Her eyes brightened with sympathy as she saw the dazed expression slowly give way to recognition.

He tried to pull himself upright. His foot dropped to the floor with a tired thud. The noise drew her attention to the boots, for the first time becoming aware of them as a symbol of his own condition. So caked with mud were they that they were unrecognizable as the beautifully tanned leather that he had donned the day he had gone away.

Instead of elegant clothing, he wore no stock, his throat bare above a coarse wrinkled shirt. A soiled filthy coat had a sleeve ripped out at the shoulder. No carefully tanned buckskins fitted his well-muscled legs like a second skin. Instead, he wore rough wool trousers such as a peasant might wear.

His face was a skull over which the skin stretched tautly. Its color was whitish-gray apart from two spots of bright color that rode his cheekbones. As he leaned toward her, she discerned heavy padding over his left shoulder and detected the unmistakable odor of fever.

Shifting uncomfortably under her stare, he clutched his left arm protectively in his right.

"—not even pregnant." Larnaervon's harangue continued unabated, rolling over them like waves. While his words no longer shocked her, they still had power to irritate her with their harshness and crudeness. Vivian shot a furious look at her father-in-law.

"Don't you look at me like that, you ignorant bitch. You don't know what he's done." He hoisted the cane from the desk top. "He's failed! Failed. My son. That wretched half-dead lump in that chair. Just like he's always done and his mother before him."

Here he brandished the heavy stick, waving it over the desk and reaching out as if he would strike Piers. Spittle sprayed from his lips. "He's lost it all. Everything. The cargo of the *Spanish Girl*. The men. Scattered, killed. No profit. Not a thing to show for months of work. And who's to know when we can make another run? No way of knowing whether we'll ever be able to make another, whether we even have a business anymore."

Unwilling to listen further to his madness, Vivian turned away from the ugly face spitting hatred. Her scalp prickled as she heard the whish of the cane through the air. "Don't turn your back on me, girl! Don't you dare! Next time I'll smash this stick down across your shoulders."

Breathing defiance in every pore, Vivian planted herself between the desk and Piers's chair. If necessary she would defend them both against this insanity.

"Larne." Piers's voice sounded weak and rasping, unlike the strong, deep voice Vivian remembered. He bowed his head drawing the strength from a well that was almost dry. "Larne. Listen to me. The Riding Officers were everywhere. MacPherson was a bulldog. Sebby must have bribed someone because they knew our every move. They knew when and where we were trying to make the connection."

"Coincidence! Stupidity!"

"Five times. Five!" Piers rocked forward, smothering the pain, his head hanging only inches above his knees. In his disheveled hair, threads of white shown clearly. Vivian felt her own heart contract.

"Someone must have given them the times and places," he insisted. "But we kept trying until finally, we rode into a trap." He had talked too much and set off a fit of coughing. Deep hacking spasms tore at his throat from deep in his lungs. Helplessly he coughed, the force of the painfully expelled air bending him over until he drew his knees up against his chest to try to suppress pain. Tears spouted from his eyes as his throat closed ever tighter from the punishment it endured.

The agonized explanation only drove the earl's rage further. *"Look at him!* Damn him and his mother that bore him! A weak woman produces a weak son! Failed! Failed!"

Cane in one hand, the other hand pressed to his belly, the earl lunged up out of the chair. Suddenly, he choked. Abruptly, he tottered backward. One brown-spotted hand dropped the cane and tugged loose his stained neckcloth. He sat down abruptly. The cane clattered to the floor beside the desk. His face turned from dark purple to yellowish-white as anger gave place to fear for his life.

Vivian looked from one to the other. The time had come to end this confrontation. From the looks of them neither could survive much longer. Waiting until Piers's coughing had ceased and the earl's breathing seemed to have evened, she slipped her hand under her husband's shoulder and helped him to his feet.

Swaying, Piers glanced at his father, sitting hunched in his chair, eyes hooded like an old eagle's. Slowly, he shook his head as if to clear it. His long, dark locks swirled lankly. "I'll leave you, Larne," he announced, sarcasm discernible even in his whisper. "My thanks for your well-wishes as regards my health. My good wife will see to my care."

Staggering slightly, he turned. Vivian placed her arm across the small of his back and grasped his arm. Firmly she pressed against him to strengthen him and steady him as he walked. His body burned hot through his rough garments, and she could feel him trembling with weakness.

As she opened the door, Mrs. Felders darted past them. "Larne. What have you done to him? Larne!"

Ignoring the housekeeper, Vivian guided the viscount out into the hall. Together they slowly mounted the stairs.

Watkins came halfway down to meet them. "I've got him, milady," the valet said, but he could not catch hold of Piers's bad side and Vivian dared not release her husband for fear he would topple backward. Panting beneath his weight, she managed to get him up the stairs.

"We've got a nice hot bath prepared for you, milord." Addie dropped a curtsy from where she waited on the landing.

Piers made no response as his breath rattled in and out of his chest. His red-streaked eyes were bent on the steps before him; his head swung back and forth doggedly as he clung to consciousness.

"Let him go, milady." Watkins reached out to try again as they came up to the top step.

Shaking her head, Vivian waved them on.

The small procession made its way to the viscount's bedroom. There Watkins helped Piers out of his coat and opened his shirt before seating him in a comfortable chair in front of the fire. Addie pressed a snifter of brandy into his shaking hand before turning to see to the preparations for his bath.

Watkins knelt to remove the muddy boots. At the first tug, Piers groaned. Draining the brandy in a single gulp, he spoke for the first time to the silver-haired girl bending over him. "If I'm going to get through this, I'll have to have some more brandy."

Smiling encouragement, Vivian took the glass.

Watkins got one boot off and then the other. Piers cursed, then coughed. The valet glanced apologetically at Vivian as she brought the drink back.

Piers accepted it gratefully.

"Maybe you'd better lie down, sir?"

"Not until I bathe," came the moaning reply. "These clothes are sticking to my skin and I smell worse than a pig. Your pardon, Vivian. I'll see you this evening. Or perhaps tomorrow."

She shook her head. Gently she unbuttoned the shirt.

"No."

"Your wife was a nurse, sir," Watkins reminded him. "I think she needs to see this."

"But—"

Mouth set, Vivian began to unwind the shoulder.

"It was broken deliberately, milady," Watkins informed her. "Chap was aiming another blow for his lordship's face when someone shot him. Milord ought to have had a doctor, but he wouldn't let me call one."

"We couldn't take the chance."

"I'm sure I didn't set it right. It was so swollen. And then I didn't want to unwind it, since he wouldn't let me send for anyone. I thought it was better to leave it alone than hurt him more." He shrugged helplessly.

"It's been under those wraps to give it support and padding while it heals. God knows, he's suffered. We've

338

been on the run, moving and hiding for more than a month now."

Piers looked up into her face. The gold rings around his pupils seemed to burn brighter with a feverish light. "All anyone would have done," he rasped. "I suspect it'll be all right."

Nodding her reassurance, she finished unwinding the bandage. The sight drove the color from her cheeks. Not one but two lumps pushed upward against the skin of the shoulder. What must surely have been extensive bruising had faded, but she was practically certain that it would have to be rebroken and set properly. He must have a doctor.

She pulled her pad from her sleeve and wrote to Watkins. "1. Bath. 2. Bed. 3. Doctor."

To Addie, "1. Send for Tyler. 2. Bath for Watkins." The maid bent over the note. "Ss-e-nd—"

Watkins read it to her. When the girl had gone, he smiled wearily. "I thank you, ma'am, for your thoughtfulness."

"Help me up, man," Piers begged hoarsely. "Let's get this over with, so you can get to your rest. You're not much better off than I am."

"No, sir."

As he stood, Piers attempted to straighten his arm. The pain almost overwhelmed him.

"Easy, sir."

Vivian slipped the shirt off his shoulders. Suddenly, she realized both men were watching her. With gentle concern, her hands touched his wide shoulders, the hard muscles of his upper arms. His eyes widened in his pain-wracked face; his body trembled with chill and weakness. He looked so ill and yet so brave.

An impulse was born. A mad, wild impulse that she made no attempt to control. Disregarding the presence

339

of the valet, she rose up on tiptoe. Her palms pressed against his cheeks and turned his face to her. Smiling timidly, she kissed his cracked and bleeding lips.

He moaned, but this time not with pain.

She dropped back on her heels and backed away. Turning to Watkins, she cupped her hand at her mouth, then pointed to herself.

He frowned. "Yes, ma'am. Do you mean for me to call you when I've gotten him in the bed?"

She nodded.

"I'll do that, milady."

She smiled at them both as she hurried out.

Piers watched her leave as if he could never get enough of her. His tongue licked out across his dry lips hoping for the taste of her.

"Come on, sir," Watkins urged. "It's cold out in the hall. We mustn't keep her waiting long."

"Has the horse been found, Vivian?"

She nodded. "Captain MacPherson has him," she wrote.

"Damn."

"When he came here, he saw Romany Prince," she wrote again.

Piers grinned. "I'll bet that put a spoke in his wheel."

She nodded. "Your horse?"

"Romany Knight. Romany Prince's own true brother, two years younger, but the same sire and dam. Identical. Poor Knight. He was shot twice."

Vivian shuddered. "I've sent for the doctor."

"No. You didn't."

She nodded emphatically.

"Damn it. I can't have a doctor. He'll ask questions."

"You had accident," she wrote. "In Scotland."

"But the arm's about healed."

She took his good hand and lifted it, indicating that he should do the same with his injured arm.

Sweat broke out on his forehead as he tried. "It needs more time."

She shook her head. Her jaw set, she wrote. "Has to be rebroken and reset."

"Damn." His face lost all color. "You're sure."

She shook her head slowly.

"But you think so? And you were a nurse." He lay back on the bed staring at the canopy. After a minute he threw his good arm across his eyes.

Addie entered with a tray. "Everything's ready, sir," she addressed Watkins.

As the valet excused himself, Addie set the tray on the bed. "Will that be all, ma'am?"

Vivian nodded.

Alone at last, she seated herself by her husband and gently touched his arm. He lowered it and looked at her, his eyes burning. She put pillows behind his back and propped him up.

"I can feed myself," he said irritably when she would have dipped the spoon into the soup.

While he ate halfheartedly, she sat back to watch him. Because of his weakened condition, Watkins had not taken time to do more than comb the long hair and beard.

That he had suffered terribly was apparent. The ravages of his ordeal were clear. His wine-dark locks brushed his shoulders. Here and there strands of silver glinted in the firelight. Deep grooves outlined his mouth and creased his forehead between his eyes. His lips were dry and bitten where he had gnawed at them in agony or clamped them tightly with his teeth to still cries and moans of pain.

341

Except for the beard, his face might have been a tragedy mask with dark hollows around the eyes and below the sculptured cheekbones. The fires of the gods might have burned away all traces of softness.

"Does my appearance offend you?" Piers's voice was stronger for the food.

Instantly, she shook her head. Her eyes reflected nothing but her pity. The terrible physical agony of the past weeks was not over yet, particularly if the doctor should decide to reset the arm when he arrived.

Moreover, her husband had been subjected to a painful and vicious confrontation when he had arrived home. Gently, she laid her hand on his crippled left arm where it rested on a pillow.

Evidently, his mind was on the homecoming as well. His speech was heavy with cynicism when he spoke. "The failure of my expedition seems to have upset Larne inordinately," he drawled. "For a minute there, I thought he might have a stroke and shuffle off this mortal coil. But no such luck. Still, it's an ill wind, and so forth. Jack Beddoes hasn't been heard of since that night. No loss to anyone."

He sighed. When Vivian would have removed her hand, he reached across his body and caught it. "Don't take your hand away."

He did not tell her why he wanted it to remain. Instead he studied the food remaining on his tray. "I suppose this is to help me sleep." He lifted the warm milk to his mouth. "Here's hoping I sleep forever."

No sooner had he taken a drink than he was struck by a fit of coughing. The milk slopped over the lip of the glass, but she rescued it before it spilled more than a few drops.

"Damn!" he gasped between the dreadful bursts that shook his frame. He fumbled for the napkin and pressed it to his face. It failed to muffle the cry of agony.

Vivian could do little to help him beyond throwing her arm across his back and offering him a brace to support his ribs. Finally, when he fell back exhausted, she held water to his lips to wash away the tickling. As he sipped it gratefully, she saw that sweat had broken out on his forehead. Extracting her handkerchief from her sleeve, she wiped him dry.

Tears stood on his sunken cheeks. When he could speak, he lay back weakly against the pillows and muttered his thanks. His head rolled wearily as Vivian hovered over him.

At last, he opened his eyes, staring upward into hers. When he could speak, his voice was a raspy, angry whisper. "Dear God, Vivian. What are you doing here? I'm a failure. A crippled, incompetent who can't even deliver the goods as a smuggler. You heard that foul-mouthed old man downstairs."

She tried to cover his mouth with her fingers, but he pushed her away.

"Why don't you call for the gallant Captain MacPherson? He'll be glad to take me away. And you'll be free."

His bitterness was a tangible thing slapping her across the face, seeking to drive her away from him. She shook her head helplessly, wondering at the attack on her innocent self.

"Men have died because of me," he continued. "My father is right in his estimate. I deserve his calumny. Not the sweet sympathy of your blue eyes." He tried to raise his arm and push her away, but it would not work. Angrily, he sank back and fell to cursing. "Damn you! Get away! Don't wipe my brow like a ministering angel and hold water to my lips when my own father curses me. I'm not worthy of your care. I'm not worthy."

He was a suffering human being whose agony of spirit was worse than his agony of body. Mentally donning her black habit, she left his side to fetch warm bricks for the bed.

"No. Don't! I don't deserve—"

Sliding them beneath the covers, she wrung out a cloth and bathed Piers's face and lips. As she slid it over his forehead, he closed his eyes and kept them closed. His skin felt hot enough for him to be sliding in and out of a delirium dream.

As she began to arrange the covers, he caught her wrist with his good hand.

Uncertain what he might do, Vivian twisted her hand gently.

"No," he whispered. "The fit is over, I swear. I'm not going to hurt you, Vivian. My God! I'm so tired. I don't know what I'm saying, or what I'm doing." After a moment's silence, he rolled his head on the pillow. His eyes bright with fever found her face. "Do you think it will really have to be broken again?"

She folded the cool cloth and laid it on his forehead. With her thumbs she massaged his temples. His eyes closed without seeing her answer. He sighed and his breathing seemed to even.

She thought he had fallen asleep when he spoke. "I dreamed of having you beside me in my bed. For weeks, I've dreamed of nothing else. Don't leave me. Please."

Vivian smoothed the hair back from his hot forehead. His breathing deepened again as he slid back into sleep.

She looked down at him. Mentally, she doffed her habit and hurried to her room. Throwing off her garments, she pulled on her nightgown and hurried back to his bed.

Lifting the covers opposite his bad shoulder, she climbed in and lay down beside him. A blush suffused her cheeks when he smiled. His eyes remained closed, but he patted the bed beside him until he found her with his hand.

"Vivian." He put his hand on her hip, then slid his fingers between her thighs.

Hastily, she pulled his hand up and gathered it between her own.

"Pity," he whispered as he drifted off again.

Basking in the heat from his body, she could not sleep for the fantasy.

Chapter Twenty-One

Piers's scream drove Vivian to her knees.

The cries of pain in the infirmary of Shaftesbury Abbey had been nothing when compared to the pain of a person for whom one cared. She clasped her hands together at her forehead, driving her knuckles against the bone. Gradually she eased off the pressure when no more cries came. God in His mercy must have allowed the suffering man to lose consciousness.

Upon his arrival the old doctor had looked at the pitiful wreck of his patient's shoulder and complained that he should have been called immediately. When told that the viscount had been in Scotland on business when the accident occurred, he had changed his attitude. Calling in a Scots doctor, he averred, would have been worse than leaving the body alone.

Reassured and at the same time alarmed by the stretching silence, Vivian pushed herself shakily to her feet and recited a paternoster. When it was ended and the tremors in her hands had ceased, she was certain she had given the doctor time enough. Her husband would need nursing, and this she could do for him.

Shoulders braced, jaw set, she flung open the door into the hall and froze. The Earl of Larnaervon stood just outside his son's door. Her sudden appearance must have startled him, for he jerked awkwardly and lost his grip on his cane. It fell to the floor with a clatter and rolled away to come to a stop against Vivian's shoe.

She jerked her foot back, staring at the long black rod as if it were a snake, then raised her eyes to its owner's face.

Violent emotions played across the ravaged features. He took a step, tottered back, and clenched his fists helplessly. Another one might bring him crashing down. His balance was exceedingly precarious, for he had depended so long on the cane's providing him with a third leg.

His face whitened as he recognized his predicament. His eyes shifted up and down the hall, but no help appeared. No butler nor footman stood at attention to do his bidding. No Emma Felders lurked in the shadows of the upstairs hallway.

As she too recognized his condition, Vivian's face must have reflected her pity, for his lips curled back in a snarl. "Don't feel sorry for me. I don't need nor want your pity. I've lived with this body for a quarter of a century. I don't even think about it anymore."

Nodding in agreement and reassurance, she stooped to pick up the cane.

"Leave it!" he commanded hoarsely. "Damn you. Leave it, I say. I can get it."

Somberly, she swept it up and held it out to him.

He hesitated for a fraction of second; his hand clenched into a fist. The fury in his expression made her believe he was going to refuse. Then he shrugged in the odd way he had. His smile was suddenly affable; his demeanor switched from rage to cool cynicism. "Ah, what fools we mortals be. Pride is surely the most deadly sin of them all. I thank you, my dear daughter."

347

With an insouciant twirl he set the cane's tip to form an equilateral triangle to his feet and leaned into it with the ease of long custom. "When I was informed, quite by accident I might add, that the doctor had been sent for, I naturally came to ascertain the reason. From the sounds, I can only guess that he is—as was his wont with the late lamented countess—again 'practicing' medicine." He grinned wolfishly at his poor joke.

Vivian pulled her pad from her pocket. "Left shoulder broken. Doctor resetting it."

As he read the words, he grimaced. "Damned uncomfortable. Why wasn't it set properly when it happened?"

"Hiding!"

His fingers clenched around the note. He closed his eyes, the crease between his brows deepened.

When he asked nothing more, Vivian started past him. His eyes flew open. His cane swept up to bar her way. "Is he very bad?"

She looked at him in some surprise. This man had poured fury on his son's ill and defenseless head. She shrugged. By way of description she slowly lifted and lowered her bent arm some six inches from her side pantomiming Piers's crippled shoulder.

His eyes took on a speculative look. "Will he be crippled?"

Only then did she remember that the earl's own shoulders had been crushed and broken years ago. Was he weighing his own pain against what his son must be enduring? She put her palms together in an attitude of prayer.

"Oh, of course. Prayer. Works wonders. My own condition is a result of prayer. I am given to understand that my own dear wife spent hours at my bedside. So easy to do. People use it as an excuse to keep from doing really difficult things." His eyes flashed.

348

A chill prickled across Vivian's skin. Meeting those eyes was like staring into great volcanic pits of anger.

"I supposed Piers's condition to have resulted from being forced to live without the usual pampering to which he has become accustomed. That, along with a chill, would be enough to put him down. Especially when he's probably spent the last few weeks at the bottom of a brandy bottle." The dark eyelashes swept upward. "And then I heard his scream. I was naturally concerned. But if the doctor is with him, everything will be all right."

She stared meaningfully down at the cane.

He followed her stare. Again his cool courtesy returned. "It's good that you are on your way to his bedside to nurse him. I remember you nursed the countess. And made a good job of it, or so I was led to believe."

Vivian acknowledged his approbation with a nod.

He let the cane fall but as she walked by him, he caught her arm. "Vivian Marleigh, your silence has made you a listener and an infinitely better listener than most. You know our secrets. If you could, you would use them against us. But you can't. Don't think you can run to the law with what you know about the operation. Remember, your mental capacity has been doubted. That can always be invoked."

Her jaw went rigid with her anger. She clawed at his skeletal fingers.

He only tightened his grasp and shook her harshly. "Stand still and listen to me. What you can do is turn this disaster to your advantage."

She twisted her arm succeeding in bruising herself.

"Don't fail to seize this opportunity," her captor hissed. "If you're halfway clever, you can get him to fall in love with you. When he's thoroughly besotted, you can seduce him to give us the heir we need."

349

Color flooded her cheeks. Her heart set up a thrumming at this old man's inference that he and she were somehow in collusion, plotting against Piers for the use of his body. Equal parts of rage and disgust shook her. If only she could voice her feelings, release her anger to the heavens. Her lips parted. She took a deep breath, framed words. Nothing. Frustration added weight to her arm as she struck at his wrist and hand once, twice.

Wincing, he opened his hand.

Free, she sprang away and darted to the door of Piers's bedroom.

His dark chuckle followed her. "If I were you, my dear, I wouldn't commit this conversation to paper. If you do, I'll be forced to relay my version to poor Piers. Also your friendship with the estimable Captain MacPherson."

She froze, her hand wrapped around the doorknob. Her fingers tightened until the knuckles showed white.

His laugh was triumphant. "Believe me, my dear, Piers won't like that. He'll think that you were the one who betrayed him. At any rate, he'll never trust you again. Think how depressed and bitter he'll be. Poor boy!"

Throwing him a look of unutterable hatred, she yanked open the door and closed it loudly behind her.

The doctor reported that after all, he had not had to rebreak Piers's shoulder. A deft manipulation of clavicle, scapula, and humerus had been accomplished. The humerus had been returned to its socket with a strong pressure and then the clavicle had been slipped back into its proper position.

Vivian turned pale as the man lectured on and on. Of course, the patient had had the good sense to faint

350

at that point. All three bones, in his opinion, had been fractured; but all seemed to be knitting well. Exercise would probably restore mobility, but only time would tell whether he would ever regain full strength.

The main problem with the patient was the fever which the doctor diagnosed as pneumonia. And from this—he spoke very frankly and seriously—the patient was in such a weakened condition that he might die. In his opinion it had all but overwhelmed the viscount's strong constitution.

He left Vivian with laudanum for pain and quinine for fever. The rest would be up to her and to God.

"I'll collect my fee from the earl," he told her with a wink that told her he understood more than she imagined.

For almost a week, Piers did little but lie in his bed. For hours he would sleep as one dead only to wake wringing wet with stinking sweat, weakly tossing about in his covers. Moaning, cursing, struggling, he would twist his body under Vivian's soothing hands.

In his sleep the nightmare would wrack him. He straddled the wounded stallion that bucked and pitched like a demon and sought to tear off his leg. When his struggles became too violent, Watkins would wrap sheets around him to keep him from reinjuring his partially healed shoulder.

Wrapped like a mummy at the beginning of the second week, he began to weep. He did not weep loudly nor to attract attention to his plight. The tears were those of despair. His body and the sheets swathing it were soaked with his perspiration as his fever broke for the last time.

His was an overburdened spirit entrapped within a pain-wracked body and unable to move an inch. Even though he made no sound, Vivian, keeping watch by his bedside, became aware of the charged atmosphere.

351

By the light of the fire, she saw the tears sparkling on his cheeks. At the sight of her bending over him, he gulped hard and closed his eyes. His head rolled away from her in a vain effort to conceal his weakness.

Her woman's heart contracted. In an outpouring of emotion she pressed her lips to his forehead.

"Vivian."

Gently, she bathed his face, lifted his head, and held water to his lips. He drank greedily and then sighed as she lowered his head to the pillow.

Conscious of his eyes following her intently, she stripped the binding sheets away and brought warm water from the fireplace.

He wrapped his hand loosely around her upper arm as she washed the stinging salt from his neck. When her soft, competent hands guided the cloth across his chest and shoulders, he moved his hand to her breast, pressing his knuckles against the nipple.

She stiffened. Not just her breast, but her whole body tightened in anticipation. Color rose in her cheeks as she sought his eyes. Sunken in shadow, their expression was unreadable. Surely he was too weak to make love. If he were merely torturing her, then he was cruel, for an ache had already begun in her thighs.

Trembling, she folded down the covers and moved out of his reach. His hand fell limply to the bed. She dipped the cloth and began to sponge his ribs and the curve of his belly.

"Vivian." Her name came on a quick intake of breath.

She felt her cheeks turn pink as she tried to tell herself that she was a nurse and he, her patient. His body was no stranger to her. She and Watkins had taken turns performing all the necessary ablutions. He was no different awake or unconscious or out of his head with fever. His body was the same.

352

With a show of control, she left him to go for a clean sheet. This she spread over his chest, while she brought the covers down to his knees.

"You have strange ideas of modesty, Vivian," he croaked, surprised that his voice was so weak. "Lord!" he exclaimed as the warm rough cloth moved across his lower belly. Then again as a warning, "Vivian."

Her hand froze. Like a snake uncoiling, his manhood began to move with a will of its own. Her eyes flew to his face.

He chuckled. "I'd say I'm feeling much better."

Face fiery red, she gave up and jerked the clean sheets down over him.

"Not a very efficient nurse. Not washing her patient below the waist," he complained.

She dropped the washcloth into the pitcher and drew the blankets up to his chin. When she met his eyes, they were laughing at her.

"I'm hungry," he whispered plaintively.

Thankful for the normal request, she rested the back of her hand against his cheek, satisfied to find that he seemed free of fever.

"Not just for food," he added, his eyes kindling.

She placed her index finger against his lips.

He smiled to himself as she left his bedside. A feeling of weak well-being spread through him. How pleasant to lie still and quiet and be served by such a beautiful woman. And when he had eaten—

Back in a few minutes with a tray that she placed on the bedside table, she leaned over him to make him comfortable. Reaching across his chest, she pulled a pillow from the other side of the bed and fluffed it vigorously. With her help he raised himself slightly so she could stuff it behind his head. Again his weakness surprised him. He had barely enough strength in his right arm to lever himself up. When he pressed his left against the bed a twinge of pain shot through his upper arm and shoulder.

When he had slipped back with his head raised, she adjusted the covers across his chest and sat down beside him on the bed. For several spoonfuls of soup, he was silent, accepting her ministrations like an obedient child.

All too soon he turned his head away in disgust. "Enough," he whispered, his voice stronger than before. "I can have a drink of wine now."

She frowned, then shook her head.

"Lord, Vivian." His voice was gaining in resonance. "A man can't live on soup. I need red wine and meat to get my strength back."

With a smile, she dipped the spoon into the bowl and offered it to him.

Angrily, he turned his head away.

Shrugging, she replaced the bowl on the tray.

Irritably, he rolled his head on the pillow. "How badly am I stove up?"

On her pad she wrote, "Pneumonia."

"What about my shoulder?"

"Lucky. Just out of place. Doctor popped it back."

"So I don't have another broken bone to heal. Thank God!" He tried to raise it. Sweat broke out on his forehead.

She put her forearm under his hand and helped him bring it back down.

"It's going to be weak a long time," he murmured.

She nodded solemnly. "Exercise," she wrote. "Heat. Rubbing."

"I look forward to your rubbing it."

She flushed again. With hands that shook she measured out his medicine into a glass of water and held it for him to drink.

He grimaced then lay back watching her as she moved about the room with her beautifully elegant walk. At the door where she balanced the tray on her hip, he called sleepily, "Are you going to get me some wine?"

She paused with her hand on the doorknob. With a slight smile she shook her head.

"Cruel," he whispered. "Vivian," he called as she opened the door and stepped through, "at least come back and sit with me until I can go back to sleep."

But she closed the door and left him alone. Within minutes, he began to feel drowsy. His attention was barely distracted when she returned to sit beside him. Again he felt her cool palm on his head. A cool wet cloth bathed his lips. He touched it with his tongue. Above his head her face hovered; her expression, tender; her eyes, soft. "Good of you," he muttered. "It's good to have a wife. I'm glad you're my wife." He was asleep.

Vivian sat beside him for some time. A shiver of pleasure vibrated in every part of her body. He was glad to have a wife. And she was glad to have a husband.

He muttered and turned on his side, resting his palm under his cheek like a boy.

Emotions swept through her body in waves. Pity for his pain, admiration for his courage, and above all, sensual response to his maleness. She glanced around the shadowy bedroom lighted only by the candle beside the bed and the leaping flames from the hearth. She did not feel alone in it. For the first time in ten years she was not alone. Her heart full, she bent forward and touched her lips to his.

Warm and soft, she enjoyed the texture and temperature of his mouth. Her hand rested on his hip beneath the blanket. Heat spiraled in her belly, and her breasts tingled.

When she drew back, she saw his eyes were open. "Vivian," he whispered. "Do you want me so much?"

Although he did not stir, she drew back as if burnt and retreated hastily. His face was turned toward her in the firelight. He smiled gently, but his eyelids were already closing. She tugged her rug around her and huddled in the darkness of the big chair.

A week later when Vivian entered, Piers was sitting up in bed, a robe thrown around his shoulders, a smile on his face. Watkins presented her with a cup of hot chocolate. Gratefully, she accepted it and sipped it. Over the cup she studied her husband.

Each day Piers had gained strength. Today he looked almost normal. Though he still used his arm gingerly, he could lift it shoulder high and straighten it out. He demonstrated his accomplishment for her. Holding the arm straight out in front of him. It trembled and he set his teeth, but around them, he grinned at her. His strength was beginning to return. "Good job, right?"

She smiled and nodded.

"Another few weeks and it'll be practically well."

She lifted her arm straight over her head.

He tried to imitate her action, but the pain was too much. "That's for later," he insisted with a groan. "I'll keep trying. Vivian, let's go for a ride this afternoon."

She shook her head aghast.

"My lord," Watkins protested, "you're not strong enough."

Vivian pulled her pad from her pocket. "The reins need a left hand."

"I'll use my right."

"Milord. I really think you're—"

"Endangering yourself," Vivian wrote.

"Nonsense! I've ridden since I could walk. It'll be like taking a walk. I need exercise."

"Let's go for a walk," she wrote.

"But, milord—"

"No. Send to the stables for Barbary and Romany Prince."

When Watkins began to protest, Vivian laid a restraining hand on his arm. Glancing down at her, he caught her knowing wink and the shake of her head. His face became appropriately bland. Without further objection he moved to help the viscount from the bed.

Vivian curtsied elaborately and left.

"Wear the black velvet," he called after her.

The mere effort of standing while Watkins dressed him completely and tied his stock left Piers weak. He had lost flesh and his legs trembled under him. A fine dew of perspiration stood out on his forehead. However, he was able to accompany Vivian downstairs.

There she insisted that they walk to the stables.

When Tyler led out Romany Prince, the big black ignored his master and nuzzled Vivian.

"That used to be my horse," Piers mourned. "So dangerous that only I could ride him." He patted the sleek neck, while Vivian put her hand on the horse's cheek and held her palm for him to lip up his treat.

Tyler laughed. "What did I say? Spoiled him, she has. Spoiled rotten. He'll probably savage you, milord, if you try to get on him. He wants her ladyship here."

Piers was feeling decidedly light-headed. The idea of a ride had been foregone when he had had to sit down on a bench midway from the house. He laughed ruefully. "I doubt I shall have anything to call my own when she gets through with me."

Leaning heavily on her, he allowed her to lead him back to the house. There he offered to teach her to play chess. With a slight smile she sent for the board and pieces and proceeded to trounce him thoroughly. On the third game he tightened his grip and managed to battle her to a stalemate.

Although his comments to her about her deception were sour, he smiled grudgingly. "Poor incompetent little thing," he remarked sarcastically. She flashed him the very sweetest of smiles and poured them both cups of hot tea.

A couple of days later, the afternoon turned sunny. Piers was able to dress and ride with Vivian. At her express orders he had not been given Romany Prince. No matter how much the black liked treats, he still required great strength and two good arms and shoulders to handle his characteristic high spirits. Instead, she ordered a tall dapple-gray mare for Piers and Barbary for herself.

The sun was warm on their shoulders as they faced the sea from the top of the cliff. Piers pulled the mare in and sat gazing out at the blue water pensively. "There were several times when I thought I'd never be back here."

The whitecaps tumbled in and foamed on the beach in the cove below them. With a slight shiver, Vivian recalled the barrels she had seen floating in the water. Hopefully, they would never intrude upon this peaceful place again.

Not waiting for Piers to take the lead, she turned Barbary aside and let the chestnut pick his surefooted way down to the sand.

Piers followed behind her, and soon they were

358

together on the beach. "The sea air cuts like a knife," he commented. "But at least I'm alive to breathe it."

She reached over and patted his hand, then tapped Barbary's rump and sent the sand spurting up. The tide came in beneath their hooves, spattering the riders' boots and the hem of her skirt. Along the beach they cantered, the wind and sun in their faces. The gray mare took the line along the sand, but Barbary plunged through the surf almost to his belly, liberally wetting Vivian as she laughed silently.

All too soon, they reached the edge of the small inlet and pulled their horses round to start back at a more sedate pace. An outcropping of rocks separated them from the beach at one point.

As the waves broke against their gray surfaces, Piers pulled up his animal. "Let's dismount, Vivian. I want to show you something—if it's still there."

Obediently, she slipped off her horse and reached for his bridle as Piers swung down more laboriously. His body was stiff, and already he was feeling the effects of his long inactivity. His shoulder ached even from the mare's soft mouth. Flexing it, he winced in disgust at his weakness.

Vivian gathered the reins of the two mounts and came to his side, ready to slip her arm through his and give him support. He grinned down at her as he noted her action. "Taking care of me?"

Smiling her response, she rubbed and kneaded the muscles covering his shoulder blade with practiced familiarity.

He groaned and flexed his back. "Ah, that feels good."

Anxious to prolong their easy companionship, she looked around. Here the expanse of sand was narrow with rocks on either side.

"Come with me." He took her arm to lead her toward

359

what seemed to be a solid rock wall.

As they approached, the gray rocks covered in patches with clinging lichen appeared to move and assume new perspectives until an opening appeared before her amazed eyes.

In surprise she looked up at him for explanation.

"I found the cave when I was a boy. I hid away in it many a time. It was a great place to play pirates." He grinned ruefully. "Now I play smugglers at the other end of the beach."

Like a shadow across the sun, the word "smugglers" wiped the smile from her face.

He hugged her against him and dropped a light kiss on her temple. "Larne would send someone to find me, but I'd disappear. The footman could pass along the beach within ten yards of this place and never see it. Once the sea came up into here, you see. And undercut all this. Some of the cliff fell down and dropped these big chunks that blend so well together. Part of the overhang is still there and keeps the whole thing in shadow. It's wonderful. I doubt that anybody knows of its existence except for me—and now you."

He took the reins from her hand and tethered the horses to a piece of driftwood, the gray and withered remains of a large tree undoubtedly washed far up on the beach in the terrible winter storms. Taking her hand, he led her to the entrance of the cave. Stooping low, they entered what was really more of a hole among the rocks. Inside when her eyes became accustomed to the dimness, she stood up and gazed around her. The floor was covered with sand. On a natural shelf some three feet up was a collection of childish memorabilia. Dropping down on one knee before the shelf, Piers shook his head in wonder. "It's still here. I can't believe it."

Leaning over behind him, Vivian looked, too. In the

360

dim light she saw a boy's pleasure spread out before her. Curious shells from the beach, a gull feather, a very small, very rusty knife, and two books so blue with mold that their titles were obscured. Flipping the cover back on one of them, Piers revealed the title of a seldom-performed play by William Shakespeare, *Measure for Measure*. On the flyleaf across from the title were inscribed the words, *Piers Larne, His Book* and underneath the name the quotation.

> *Death for death.*
> *Haste still pays haste,*
> *And leisure answers leisure,*
> *Like doth quit like, and*
> *Measure still for Measure.*

He stared at the words. Through the fingers she rested on his shoulder to steady herself, she felt his tension. Sympathetically, she squeezed the tightly bunched muscles. Vivian could not have said how she came to respond so to him. She only knew that he was sharing his secret hideaway and refuge from the world with her. In sharing it, he also shared the most secret part of his inner being.

"Bloodthirsty young thing, wasn't I?" He jeered at his own intensity. "All ready for vengeance against pirates or parents. Who knows? It was all so long ago."

Vivian's heart turned over at the thought of the four-year-old boy who had fought to defend the treasures of his home. Fought until his very life had been threatened. And his efforts had earned him nothing but his father's enmity. Both hands smoothed gently over his shoulders.

"It wasn't my fault," he whispered. "Nor my mother's. But we'll get it all back."

Again her hands massaged his back and shoulders.

She was weeping without knowing that she did.

He gave what might have been a groan and returned the book to the shelf. Rising and brushing the sand from his knees, he led her out into the sunlight. The sands on the beach glistened white as the sun sank low enough to shine in under the cliff. Her eyes were dazzled by their brightness.

Blinded, she swayed as soft sand slipped under her boots.

Suddenly, he pulled her into his arms, surrounding her slim body, holding her soft length against him. When he tilted her face up to his, the sun struck her full in the face, so she had to keep her eyes closed against it. Staring down at her, his jaw clenched, his brown eyes searched every feature, every eyelash bared naked before him in the incredible light.

"You're the most beautiful thing I've ever seen. And the dearest. You've made me abandon what I'd vowed to do in spite of everything." With a groan he loomed over her. The sun was shaded by his head.

Her eyes flew open to see his face descending, his mouth coming nearer. Fierce passion engulfed her as his lips opened against hers. His tongue caressed her lips, thrust between them.

She welcomed him. Her arms went around his waist beneath his coat and pulled them tight together. She began to tremble and then to shudder. The thunder of the waves rolling into the inlet was echoed and re-echoed in her own body as waves of heat and tension carried her higher and higher.

His tongue moved silkily across her teeth, then slid farther in to caress her soft interior and touch the tip of her tongue.

When he lifted his mouth away, she swayed against him, her limbs weak. Dimly, she was conscious of his turning her body away from the sun.

"Vivian, sweet wife, let me love you."

Her eyes opened and she dizzily glanced upward. The blue sky cut by gray crags swung above her. He wanted to make love to her. And she wanted him to with every breath in her body. For answer she rose on tiptoes, fitted herself against him, and kissed him with open mouth and thrusting tongue.

Chapter Twenty-Two

Deliberately holding her eyes with his own, Piers unbuttoned his coat and spread it on the ground. His carefully tied white stock followed it, and the strings of his full white shirt hung loosely down his chest.

Throat dry, Vivian moved her hand over his half-healed shoulder by way of warning.

"I won't hurt myself," he assured her. "But the past week has been exquisite torture. Your hands have touched every part of my body. Every time you've bent over my bed to wipe my brow or give me a drink, your scent has enveloped me. The pain and the fever were nothing compared to the everlasting nearness and all the time I was too weak to touch you."

The sand was surprisingly warm and dry; rocks and the face of the cliff formed a rough chamber, roofed by the sky and lit by the sun. The wind did not blow in this sheltered spot. The waves pounded and rolled a hundred yards from where they stood.

His description was so evocative of her own experience that she felt a blush begin to rise from her throat. Her hand slid off his shoulder and down over the curve of his bicep.

Cupping her face between his hands, he kissed her

forehead, her cheeks, her chin, the tip of her nose, and last her lips with sweet drugging tenderness. "I love you, Vivian Larne," he whispered. "I love you, wife. For a long time I've thought I'd never say that."

Feeling her tremble in response, he caught her wrists and raised her hands. Turning them palm up, he kissed them one at a time, lingering over them, breathing on her fingertips, licking them with his tongue, and nipping her index finger with his strong white teeth.

At his infliction of this tiny pain, she gasped. The fingers of her other hand curled round his cheek. Her fingernails scratched lightly at his skin.

He grinned, his teeth still imprisoning one of her fingers. "Have we reached a stalemate?"

She could feel a curling heat in her belly and an ache spread in her thighs. Involuntarily, she pushed her hips against him.

He gasped, freeing her finger and pushing her hands down to his chest burying the fingertips in the crisply curling hair above his masculine nipples. "Touch me," he begged softly. His lips tickled her cheek as he punctuated his words with kisses. "That's what lovemaking is, Vivian. Touch me and take me out of this place and time."

Excited as much by his deep voice, as by the warmth of his mouth, she kept her hands where he put them. His heart pounded against her palm, his skin warmed her fingers, and each crisp hair tickled.

Releasing her wrists, he began to unbutton the black velvet riding jacket. Her fingers roamed idly over his chest, finding his nipples and caressing them until they tightened and stood erect. The tender touch drove a groan through his set teeth. "Vivian. You learn fast."

His own hands trembled slightly as he continued his work of undressing her. At last the jacket was open and the shirtwaist beneath it. Pushing the lapels aside he framed her breasts before bending to kiss the tips of each one in turn through the sheer chemise. This time her fingers arched and her nails grazed his skin.

Instantly, he exacted retribution by taking one engorged darkened point between his teeth and biting her gently. When she gasped, he raised his head with a smile. "Pleasure comes in unexpected forms, Vivian."

Under the blue sky he pulled the straps of her shift down to expose her swollen white breasts. Gently, he stroked them with his open palms while she shivered in pleasure. "God. You're so beautiful. You should never be made love to except in the sunshine."

His words made her blush, at the same time she felt the tingling ache in her breasts. She pushed his shirt off his shoulders and set her mouth to the point of his shoulder.

"Beautiful," he whispered as he took the engorged tip in his teeth. Holding it firmly, he moved his lips around it.

She threw her head back, her mouth open to the sky, a silent cry of delight rushing from her throat. Dimly she thought that if she were ever going to speak again, she would shout her exquisite pleasure.

Then the sky and cliffs whirled above her and she lost all sense of time and place. No longer even remotely embarrassed, she felt only a dizziness, a light-headed floating feeling as excitement heated the blood in her veins.

When she swayed, he caught her in one arm and stripped the jacket and blouse from her body. She gasped at the sudden rush of cool air on her fevered skin, but he covered her mouth with his own and lowered her to the sand to lie on his coat.

Easing himself down on his side, adjusting his weight so it rested more on the sand than on his arm and shoulder, he continued to kiss and stroke her breasts with sensual sureness. At each new exploration with tongue or hand, she writhed and shivered.

"Open your eyes," he groaned against her breast, but the sun stabbed them and she could only blink before she closed them immediately.

He lifted his head to see her predicament, but she caught him in her arms and drew him back to kiss her nipple again and again. Her long slender fingers stroked his nape and curled in the short locks of his hair.

His need pressed hard, throbbing against his breeches. With clumsy fingers he tugged the heavy skirt up around her waist and placed his hand on the smooth flesh of her thigh above the wool and lisle stocking. As if he commanded, her thighs fell open and she tilted her hips upward.

"Why, Vivian," he murmured. "You've missed me every bit as much as I've missed you."

She shaded her eyes with her hand and stared into his face, trying to gauge his feelings about her eagerness, her lack of restraint. His expression was as pleased as it was loving.

"We're very lucky. Many people, forced to marry as we were, loathe their mates, but you don't loathe me, do you?"

She stirred. Ripples ran over her body radiating from the hidden spot between her thighs where his fingers were working their magic.

"Do you?"

She dropped her hand and clutched at the sand, lifting great handfuls in fierce ecstasy.

"Do you!?"

Her back arched, her booted heels dug into the soft sand. Her mouth opened in a silent cry of pleasure.

He rose on his knees and flipped the buttons open on the front of his buckskins. His good hand splayed under her buttocks and lifted them until he could bring the tip of his eager staff to the opening of her body.

Even as the ripples were dying, she fought their weakening effect. He wanted her. He had seen to her pleasure. She must give him the same. Her elbows and feet dug into the sand, lifting her torso. Setting her teeth with the effort, she rocked forward impaling herself.

He groaned as she sheathed him, groaned as he rocked back on his heels, lifting her, carrying her upward.

Her hands went over his shoulders and then she was clinging to him as he rammed upward again and again. His eyes only inches from her own glazed, a muscle jumped and clenched in his jaw. He rammed with all his strength.

Somewhere in her mind pain pierced her as he touched a place inside her that she had never known existed, a place that had waited for him alone, but then the pleasure began again, rippling, rippling. And she could no longer think. Instead came the waves of dizziness and excitement. Light-headed and breathless, she jolted like a doll, her legs wrapped tight around his hips. Her hair fell down around her shoulders.

It was going to happen again. And how could she bear it? The intense pleasure. The climbing higher and higher. The explosion.

A roar of pleasure burst from his lips. His strength sent her spinning off into space. His hoarse shout of triumph became the expression of her own voiceless cry. Shuddering, he collapsed, slipping to the side, careful not to fall on her, rolling over on his back to lie gasping in the sand.

She lay beside him, her hand trailed across his hot, damp chest, her body weak and boneless, her mind emptied of all thoughts. At last she reached across him and lifted his hand.

He opened his eyes.

"Love you," she wrote in the palm. "Love you." And kissed the spot she wrote in.

"Why don't you say it?" he whispered.

She looked at him sadly.

"You don't know it, but you can talk. I've heard you."

She shook her head.

"Yes, I've heard you. You talked in your sleep."

She started up.

A horse nickered somewhere close by. She looked around fearfully. A cloud scudded across the sun, and she shivered at the sudden chill.

Piers rolled over and sat up, catching her and turning her back to him. "Don't be upset. I didn't mean to upset you. Maybe I dreamt it."

She sat back on her heels and lifted her hands to her throat. Her lips opened and shaped words. Tears started in her eyes.

"Don't." He put his hand over her mouth. "Don't try now. Just believe that you can do it. Now smile for me." Slowly, he took his hand away.

"Beautiful," he whispered. "Beautiful wife. I've never known a partner more loving, Vivian. No woman has ever done for me what you've done. I can't describe the pleasure."

Barbary neighed again.

"Someone's coming."

They climbed to their feet together. He helped her pull up her straps and adjust her undergarment over her swollen breasts. As he covered them, he could not resist dropping a kiss on one. Response lanced through her. She felt a not-quite-painful tightening in her

369

abdomen. She shifted and looked around nervously.

He grinned as he closed her blouse and handed the jacket to her.

As he adjusted his clothing, he smiled to see her watching him. "Do you like what you see?"

She nodded and put out her hand to knead his thigh only a few inches below his crotch.

"Stop that," he growled, but she only smiled sweetly. He caught her wrist and pulled her to her feet with a chuckle. "You can't believe how fast you'd be on your back again," he warned. "Whoever is coming would find his fishing trip more interesting than he ever imagined it could be." He shook the sand off his coat. "Of course, we could get very good at putting on public shows. Charge money and so forth. Certainly the most pleasant work in the kingdom."

She cuffed him on his good shoulder.

"Here." He shook out his cravat and handed it to her. "Be so good as to tie this into some semblance of a fall, sweet wife."

With fingers that shook slightly from weakness and reaction, she tied the cloth and slipped the ends inside his jacket. Then she had to kiss his cheek, and he had to clasp her waist and tantalize himself with her willing softness all along his length.

Neither could keep from smiling at the sight of the other's rumpled clothing. Piers adjusted her hat at a jaunty angle. "Beautiful face," he commented. "But we look like we had a rough ride."

Out from the shelter of the rocks and mounted, Piers looked around him. "I don't see a sign of anyone. Maybe Barbary was just impatient."

Vivian patted the arched neck. The wind blew her silvery hair across her face. She pushed it back and tucked it behind her ear. Beside her, Piers worshipped

370

her with his eyes. The big gelding threw up his head and led the mare up the trail.

That evening they dined with the earl for the first time since Piers's return. The table glittered with polished silver, sparkling crystal, and the opalescent gleam of fine china.

Piers looked around in amazement as he entered with his wife's slender white hand resting lightly on his velvet-clad arm. "My god, Vivian! If you can accomplish all this without a voice, the mind staggers to think what you could accomplish if you could but speak."

His pleased eyes swept her from toe to crown. She dropped a tiny graceful curtsy and inclined her head.

She had not really done so much as order its thorough cleaning and the maintenance of its furniture. The neglect of twenty years had been deep, but now fine objects reflected the light with a new life.

The Chippendale pieces glowed with massive elegance—their brass polished, their curlicues cleaned and waxed. Millard waited proudly to serve what was certain to be one of Cook's best efforts.

Vivian blushed with pleasure as Piers's extravagant compliment warmed her.

At that moment the earl entered the dining room, Mrs. Felders at his shoulder. He moved more slowly than usual, his hand pressed hard to his abdomen. As he sat down in the chair, his left eye twitched once, twice. Then it steadied, and his contorted mouth lifted in a smile.

Piers seated his wife with a whispered, "He looks just the same—angry."

Vivian braced herself to endure the cynicism of the

371

evil old man who hunched like a smiling demon at the head of the table.

The viscount had not settled into his chair before Larne fired the first salvo. "You're looking quite well, both of you. An afternoon in the sea air does wonders for the complexions."

Vivian in particular had acquired a pink tint to her fair skin. She looked to Piers, who nodded. "Clears the head, too, Larne. There were some days this past month when I thought I'd never get out of bed."

"But here you are, hale and virile, I don't doubt."

"Yes, hale and virile. Your concern has been most gratifying."

The earl shrugged. The left eye twitched violently. He batted at the air beside it. "I don't visit sickrooms as you remember."

"Not unless someone is dying in one."

The footman filled the earl's glass with red wine. Vivian allowed a small amount in her glass. Piers covered his glass with his hand.

The earl looked at him suspiciously.

"I seem to have lost my taste for it," Piers informed him. "My . . . nurse refused to let me drink while I was taking medicine."

"Nonsense."

"Nevertheless, there's no point in starting it again." Piers smiled across the table. "My wife doesn't like me to drink. From now on, I abstain."

Before the earl could think of anything to say, Vivian signaled to Millard to serve the first course. The butler turned to the footman. Instead, Emma Felders came from the pantry with a tray.

Vivian flinched as the tureen of hot soup came over her left shoulder, but recovered herself quickly. She refused to allow the woman's presence to mar the

372

feeling of happiness that rose in her. He had made her a pledge not to drink again. He had declared that he loved her. He had made wonderful love to her in a place that was now special to them both.

Tasting the clear soup, she eagerly glanced in Piers's direction. He had already tasted it and was smiling at her, waiting for her to catch his eye. "Good," he complimented her. "This is really good."

Larnaervon regarded them from beneath his white eyebrows. "Besotted, are you?" He chuckled. "Good job, Vivian. I told you he would fall in love with his nurse. Weakness makes fools of men."

She shot him a terrible look.

At his back Emma Felders allowed her pinch-purse mouth a small smile.

"Good job, this afternoon," the earl went on. "White sand. Blue sky. Glad to hear you've started working again on my grandson."

She could have killed him at that moment. Her fingernails scored the tablecloth on either side of her plate.

"Larne. What we do," Piers said, his eyes wintry, "we do because we want to, not for your satisfaction."

"To be sure. To be sure." The earl regarded her with satisfaction. "She's not stupid, you know. For all you were worried about her. She knows that she needs to produce the heir as soon as possible."

Piers regarded his father impassively. The aura of pleasure generated by his afternoon on the beach began to evaporate beneath the fire of his father's evil conversation.

"If you were honest with me, you would fall down on your knees, both of you, and thank me for bringing you together." He winced. His left shoulder dipped badly. He tried unsuccessfully to raise it. "I brought her here,

373

you know. Delivered her to you like a procurer. Brought you your perfect bride. I did it. My plans, my plots."

His gnarled spotted hands trembled as he reached for his wine. "A toast to plans and plots." The corner of his mouth sagged. His eyes twitched again. "A toas'."

The wineglass was in his hand, but he seemed to lose the direction of it. It wavered until he clutched its stem with both hands and leaned forward stiffly. With terrible slowness he was able to turn it up to his lips. A trickle of red slipped out of the side of his mouth.

Vivian and Piers exchanged worried looks.

Every bite and every sip thereafter seemed to require a conscious effort to partake. The old man's stock as well as the tablecloth became spattered with drops of soup and wine which fell from the spoon as he carried it to his lips or dribbled from his slack mouth.

Piers had given up eating to watch his father in horrified wonder. "Is he always this bad?" he mouthed silently to Vivian.

She shook her head.

In the shadows Mrs. Felders drew in her breath with a vicious hiss at which Millard rolled an eye in her direction and smiled coldly.

Lord Larnaervon gave no sign that he was aware of either his son's comment or the sound of the housekeeper's response. Instead he twitched his left shoulder irritably and swung his head to the side as if some bothersome insect tormented him.

They finished their soup in silence. After the footman carried away the plates and served the fish and vegetables, the earl seemed to recover and eat almost normally.

Piers looked around him with satisfaction. "I still can't get over how fine everything looks. Why paintings now are revealed to be actually renditions of some person or thing rather than shadows writhing in the dark. Mirrors cast true reflections and lamps cast light."

She smiled, a sparkling smile of pure and unalloyed pleasure that limned her features in radiance.

He blinked at it. His desire which he had thought sated in the afternoon quickened in him, and he shifted in his chair as his loins tightened.

"—*Spanish Girl* again in the month," Lord Larnaervon announced. "Piers!" Suddenly, he slammed his stick against the dining table making his son jump and his daughter-in-law cover her ears.

"Larne! Calm down!"

"*Spanish Girl!!*"

"Let's discuss this tomorrow," Piers suggested, struggling for calm. "Vivian doesn't want to hear about the business."

"Besotted idiot!" the old man screamed. Spittle flecked with bits of food dribbled from the left side of his mouth. "Damn you! What? You dare to go weak and soft over her."

Anger gave him strength. He staggered to his feet. Millard moved back out of his way, but Mrs. Felders darted forward to offer her support. "Larne. Larne. Please, don't be so—"

Furiously, he swung his arm at the side of her head. As she stumbled back, he staggered around the table toward Vivian. "Georgina! You let them take it all. All that was to have been our substance. Damn you to hell, Georgina."

"Larne!" Piers's chair toppled back as he sprang to his feet.

"I'll punish you. I'll not have you destroy our son." He raised the cane above her head. "By God! I swore I'd beat you till the blood ran."

Piers vaulted onto the tabletop, knocking flowers,

375

utensils, service aside. The tablecloth slipped beneath his feet, but he managed to leap down in front of Larne and catch the uplifted stick as Vivian flung herself sideways from her chair to avoid it.

The old eagle eyes blazed with maniacal fire as he struggled to wrest the stick from his son's hand. "You dare! You dare! Damn you! Damn you! You'll not take my father's house. I'll—"

He stiffened; his hand dropped to his side. Irritably, he twitched his left shoulder again and tossed his head. Puzzled, he stared hard at Piers and then turned away letting the stick fall from his hand.

"Larne." Felders pleaded in his ear. "Larne. Is it your side? Shall I get some soothing syrup? Tell me what's wrong."

He looked at her also as if he did not know her, then stumbled back to the head of the table to slump into his seat. Staring fixedly ahead, he rested his forearms on the edge of the table.

Bending to lift Vivian to her feet, Piers threw an outraged look over his shoulder in his father's direction. Something was definitely wrong. The old man had called Vivian Georgina. Tomorrow he must have a doctor. He pulled her chair away from the table and helped her to sit down. "Are you hurt?"

Quickly, she shook her head.

"Thank God. Clear away this mess, Millard."

"Yes, milord."

The servants hurried about their business, but the earl seemed oblivious to them.

"He hasn't finished his supper," Mrs. Felders objected. With trembling hands, she picked up his napkin and placed it across his lap. "Larne. Wouldn't you like some pudding?"

He paid her no heed.

Emma began to wring her hands. "Larne. Speak to

376

me. Tell me what's wrong so I can help you?"

"Lord Larnaervon," Millard said softly.

The earl did not blink. His left eye no longer twitched although his mouth still hung slackly.

The butler looked helplessly at the viscount. Piers stared at his father then glanced at Vivian. She rose from her chair and cautiously approached the head of the table. Again the butler spoke.

Nervously, Vivian passed her hand back and forth before the staring eyes. They remained unblinking.

Emma Felders screamed.

Piers hurried around the table on the other side to speak to his father. At his son's touch the earl slowly slid to the side and slipped toward the floor. Piers caught his arm and saved him. Millard stepped forward exclaiming in horror. Vivian grasped the other arm and lent her strength to maintain the earl in a sitting position. His head fell back against the top of the chair.

"No. You'll hurt him. Don't touch him! He'll be all right in just a minute. He's just dazed. Larne!" Mrs. Felders tried to shoulder Vivian aside to reach her lover.

"Brandy, Millard!" Tearing open the old man's neck cloth, Piers gave the withered throat space to breathe. A footman at the sideboard poured a glass from the decanter. The man handed it to Millard, who held it for Vivian to moisten the blue lips with her handkerchief.

"Oh, Larne, Larne!" Mrs. Felders's shrill hysteria dinned in the ears of the four people working over the Earl of Larnaervon.

"Millard, shut that woman up!" snapped Piers as he bent over the old man who as yet displayed no signs of stirring.

But when the butler reached for her, her cries of

anguish changed to screams of rage. "You all want him dead. I'm not leaving his side. Never. Never. Take your hands off me."

Millard grasped her by the shoulders.

"No! No! He needs me. That bitch! Bead-rattler! She caused every bit of this. Brought it on. Upset the routine of this house, changed the food. It's just his stomach. It's been bothering him." She twisted in the man's grasp and sought to fly at Vivian, who steadfastly ignored her as she bathed the earl's sunken temples with brandy. "Don't touch him."

She pulled away from the butler and grasped Piers's arm. "I know you don't like me, but I-I care about him. Don't let her near him. She'll kill him if she gets the chance."

Millard finally managed to get a good grip on the hysterical woman and swing her around. He pushed her toward the door that had been thrown open by the kitchen maid who had been alarmed by the noise.

"No! Ow!"

Pushing Mrs. Felders screaming through the door, Millard followed her out. The door slammed behind them.

"Summon his valet," Piers said to the footman, and the man left on the run.

A dribble of fluid ran down the side of the earl's mouth, and Vivian wiped it away with her handkerchief. Her touch was tender.

"Is he swallowing any?"

She shook her head no.

"We have to get him to bed," Piers said when the footman returned accompanied by the valet. Together the three men lifted the limp body while Vivian supported the earl's head in her hands. The somber procession mounted the stairs to the earl's bedroom. When his body was stretched on the bed, Piers took

Vivian's arm and pulled her to the door.

Taking her shoulders in his hands, he drew her close. "Go on to your room."

Her expression mutinous, she took his hand in hers and wrote the word "Help."

He kissed her forehead. "Thank you, but none of us can really help him. We'll get him undressed and make him comfortable. There's no real nursing to be done until the doctor has seen him. I'll send someone immediately, but the doctor won't be here until morning. We'll handle what needs to be done tonight."

He glanced over his shoulder at the valet and footman hovering over his father's still body. "He's so still. It doesn't look good."

Her eyes reflecting her sympathy, she pressed her hand to his cheek.

He turned his mouth into her palm and kissed it. "Thank you."

As she walked down the hall, he turned back into the room. "I didn't realize he was ill."

The valet looked up, his face grave. "I think he's had some kind of fit, milord. He's been very worried about you."

"Larne?" Piers stared down at the still figure. It barely seemed to breathe. "Not Larne."

The valet shrugged. "If you say so, sir."

Suddenly, the earl made a guttural noise. Unintelligible words poured from his mouth. The crippled body arched up and twisted wildly. One arm thrashed knocking the footman back from the bed.

All three men sprang upon him to keep him from throwing himself to the floor.

Chapter Twenty-Three

The Earl of Larnaervon was sick to death.

"He awoke an hour ago as if he were waking up in the morning. Only he doesn't recognize me," Mackery, the valet, reported to Piers and Vivian. "He just lies there on his back barely breathing. His left eye doesn't move, but his right wanders around the room. He doesn't find anything he knows."

Vivian wrote a question. "Does he seem to hear?"

The valet nodded. "His eye moved in my direction when I spoke to him."

"Can he use his hands?"

"His right hand and arm stray around, but his left is stiff."

"Who's with him now?" Piers asked.

Mackery hesitated. "Watkins. But Mrs. Felders wants to come in."

"No," came the viscount's instant reply.

Vivian caught him by the arm. "Yes," she wrote. "Let her stay. She must talk to him constantly. Tell her to talk about everything. Hold his hand."

The valet looked skeptical. Mrs. Felders had gone to the bedside, weeping and praying fervently. The earl had gazed at her in a puzzled, tired way. Then his attention had wandered. The housekeeper had caught up his paralyzed left hand, pressed it to her mouth, and then burst into hysterical tears.

Thinking the earl would not want such a display, the valet had dragged her away from the bed and pushed her out the door, despite the housekeeper's curses and struggles. Now the viscountess was saying to let back in. With the expression of one who had been hard-used, he looked at Piers.

"Do as she says. She's the nurse."

"Feed him," Vivian wrote as an afterthought. "Talk to him. Move his legs and arms."

When the valet had gone, Piers took her in his arms and pressed his lips to her forehead. "What would this family do without you?"

"You have a visitor, milady. A Mr. Barnstaple requests a private interview with you."

Vivian raised her eyebrows. The earl had said that he would take over the management of the Marleigh properties. She had been in no position to object. In fact, she would not have objected. Rowling's betrayal had been a very near thing. Had the earl not sent Beddoes to abduct her, she would undoubtedly be locked away in some private institution for the rest of her life.

"I have no wish to see him," she wrote.

Millard bowed and went away but returned almost immediately. "He is most insistent, ma'am. He says he's come all the way from London to apologize and make restitution." The butler hesitated. "He seems like a nice enough old man and very tired."

Vivian let out her breath on a sigh. Picking up her pad and pencil, she allowed Millard to usher her into the newly cleaned and refurbished parlor where a fire was kept lighted during the daylight hours.

"My dear Miss Marleigh." Worthing Barnstaple was indeed an old man. His portly belly sagged and his florid complexion was mottled around his sagging jowls. Still he stood six foot six and though his hands shook they were warm and engulfing.

She nodded frostily as she freed her hands from his moist grasp.

He drew back his pudgy fingers. "My dear Vivian, if I may call you by your first name?"

She pulled out her notepad. "Of course, Worthing."

He frowned and cleared his throat. "That is, I have always looked on you as a daughter."

"Rowling handled my business."

He ran a finger around inside his neck cloth. "Well, that's not entirely correct. It is true that my late partner August Rowling did most of the paper work required to keep the estate up to date, but I had much to say about its administration."

"Roderick Rowling was stealing money," Vivian wrote underscoring the word "stealing."

"And has left the firm. In fact, he has been discharged from the firm that his father founded with me." Barnstaple pulled a huge handkerchief from the pocket of his old-fashioned knee breeches and wiped his face. "When I received the letters from the Earl of Larnaervon, your estimable father-in-law, and from his solicitor, I was aghast. I took young Rowling to task immediately. He hemmed and hawed, but at last admitted all."

"Prosecution!"

Barnstaple's already florid complexion darkened until his jowls turned reddish-purple. "He lost his job with his father's firm, Vivian. Surely the shame and embarrassment, not to speak of loss of income, are harsh enough."

His voice trailed away as Vivian began to write, her pencil stabbing at the paper. "Theft of funds, unlawful detention, attempted kidnapping. He drugged me."

Barnstaple sank down in a chair that creaked beneath his weight. "My dear Vivian—"

She shot him a murderous look.

"—Miss Marleigh."

"Lady Polwycke!" she underscored.

"Yes, Lady Polwycke." He tried again offering an ingratiating smile. "Perhaps you are right, but I didn't think you would wish to testify. The scandal after all."

"His scandal."

"Well—"

"What did you come here for?"

He looked around him desperately. "I came to speak to you in private."

She looked around them in withering mockery.

"I was given to understand that this—um—marriage was not to your liking."

She started to rise.

"Wait! Wait. I beg you." He wiped his sweating face again. "I was given to understand that this was a desperate measure on your part. On the part of a gentle lady"—he leaned forward to pat her hand where it poised over her pad—"who was offered no real choice."

She wrote again and thrust the paper viciously into his hand. "I chose."

"In a manner of speaking. Your land and your money have been transferred from one unsavory connection to another. Is that not the way of it?" He leaned forward to whisper his last question only a few inches from her ear.

She shrugged. "My husband is Viscount Polwycke."

"My dear lady, a good solicitor could make a case for declaring the marriage to have been made under duress. A legal separation could be arranged. You could return to your own home. Your own lands could be managed by a firm that is, ahem, familiar with them."

She drew away from his stale, fishy breath. She could not believe the man's presumption. However, curious, she wrote, "Sebastian Dawlish?"

"That blackguard will be banned from polite society if I have anything to say about it."

"Barnstaple and Rowling supported his legal guardianship," she wrote.

"Well, yes. But believe me I had no idea— He seemed unexceptionable. His family—"

She held up her hand. When his flow of explanations stopped, she began to write. "I will never consider engaging Barnstaple and Rowling again."

He was reading over her shoulder. His voice broke as he began to plead. "My dear lady, we will do everything in our power to make up for our mistake. I understand that you were looking forward to a London debut before your illness. This can be arranged. It can all be arranged. I personally will handle every stage of the delicate negotiations."

She shook her head, her smile rueful. "I do not choose to leave my husband."

"But his reputation is most unsavory," he hissed.

Vivian rose and crossed to the door. Opening it, she signaled to Millard, who waited in the hall at a discreet distance.

Barnstaple had risen, too. His pleading manner became nasty. "Your innocence does you credit, but you're making a terrible mistake. It could even be fatal. Don't forget the earl's wife died just recently. A woman in her prime."

Vivian stared at him without comprehending.

He caught her by the elbow and snarled in her ear.

"You don't know that her death was from natural causes. These are desperate men."

She jerked her arm away from him. Again the awful frustration. Words boiled in her mind. Blistered her tongue. She opened her mouth, framed them, but nothing came out. She clenched her fists, then slashed her hands across her body.

Barnstaple smiled unctuously. "My dear young lady, above all else you need a spokesperson."

"And she has one in me." Piers strolled down the stairs.

The solicitor gasped and jumped guiltily. He rubbed his sweaty palms on his handkerchief and held out his hand. "I take it you are the Viscount Polwycke."

Piers locked his hands behind him. "Yes."

With a nervous laugh Barnstaple returned to crumpling his handkerchief. "I have been Miss Marleigh's solicitor since she was born. I have always looked after her best interests."

"Was it in her best interest that she be locked away from her home for over a year?"

"I— She was ill."

"For—a—year." Each word was evenly spaced and accusatory.

Barnstaple tried to put his arm around Vivian. "This poor girl—"

She hit him in his portly belly. The breath exploded from his mouth as he staggered back.

With a hoot of laughter Piers vaulted down the stairs and caught her around the waist before she could hit the man again. "Millard!" he called, "Help the man on with his coat. I suggest, Barnstaple, that you be on your way."

The portly man rocked back and forth, his hand on his belly. "You've made a bad mistake, Vivian," he insisted. "I forgive you because you've been too

385

protected. You don't understand the way of things."

His unctuous forgiveness further infuriated Vivian. Baring her teeth, she clutched at Piers's hands and tried to pry them away from her middle. Her feet slipped out from under her and she kicked at Barnstaple.

"Better get out while you can," Piers called. "I can't hold her much longer. Bad shoulder, you know." His grin spread across his face. "Spitfire," he whispered in Vivian's ear. "Hellcat. Vixen."

Millard pushed Barnstaple's hat and coat into his hands and shoved him out the door.

Piers released Vivian who swung round on him, her fists clenched. He pointed over her shoulder. "He went that way."

She clenched her fists and shook them in front of his face.

"I take it that he made you angry."

She gaped at him, then reached for her pad and pencil. She had left them in the parlor. Suddenly, her frustration boiled over. She burst into tears.

"Here. Here." He gathered her into his arms and held her tight until she stopped crying. "I know. I know. You want to say all the things inside you and you can't."

In her heart, she knew he was coming to understand her better than any other single person in the world. Consequently, she held onto him for dear life. Finally the weeping stopped. She patted the lapels of his coat where she had wet it with her tears, and looked up at him. Her eyes were drowned aquamarines begging his pardon for her outburst.

He kissed her on the forehead and the mouth. His kiss warmed and deepened. Her hands slipped up around his neck. A shudder went through him. He turned her in his arms and led her toward the stairs. "Come up and lie down for a few minutes," he suggested softly "I promise you'll forget all about this."

Caleb Pross presented himself to Piers during the first week after the earl's attack. "I have the honor to be your father's man of business. I would hope that you would engage me to be yours," he added hopefully. "However that may be, I believe we should go over certain affairs. It is always wisest to be prepared in these cases."

Piers shook his head. "Perhaps you are not aware, Mr. Pross, that Larne and I do not have a warm relationship."

The solicitor nodded impassively. "Nevertheless, you are your father's heir. The will of which I am in possession leaves everything to you. Indeed, this entire estate is entailed to you. Therefore—"

"As you wish, but he may not be pleased."

"Who will tell him?" Pross allowed himself the tiny suggestion of a smile. "If he recovers, you will merely pretend that your ignorance remains absolute. I will continue as before." He waited a moment. "Now, as I was about to say, your father had already begun the accounting of your estate. I have only preliminary figures at this time, but Sebastian Dawlish, your wife's cousin, seems to have been a surprisingly good administrator of the business interests of Stone Glenn. Everything seems in good order, nothing missing."

"I'm not surprised. His plan was to live there after the true owner, my wife, had been locked away forever," Piers rejoined bitterly.

"I had heard that to be the case." Pross hesitated. "When will you wish to take possession?"

Piers glanced around him uncertainly. "I had planned to take my wife there in the spring—say the middle of April. Now, with Larne's illness, I cannot be sure."

"Of course. Of course. Duties are pulling at you. However, rest assured that our firm will handle everything at Stone Glenn with unparalleled efficiency."

Embarrassed color tinging his cheeks, the viscount cleared his throat. "I may need funds from Stone Glenn to operate this estate."

Pross's eyes narrowed. He cleared his throat noisily. "You have more than sufficient funds available here."

"I beg your pardon."

"Your father is a very wealthy man, milord. This is one of the most prosperous estates in the south of England."

Again Piers glanced around him—at the dim, dusty room, the rotting carpet beneath their feet, the books with blue mold on the spines, the inkwell black with tarnish, the desktop scarred and stained. "Pull the other one."

The solicitor smiled gently. "I suggest, milord, that you sit down and go over the books yourself. You will find much to interest you."

Piers shook his head dazedly.

The solicitor mistook his movement for negation. "As you wish, milord. However, I should like to make an observation. In my business I have seen many men who have lost their fortunes and remade them. I have noticed that they behave in one of two ways."

The viscount waited, his shoulders tensed, his breath still in his chest.

"Some happy ones treat their wealth as a thing of the moment and throw it about carelessly, confident that since they have regained it once, they can regain it again and again. Others—a most unhappy lot, I might add—clutch every farthing to them, amassing more substance and more, piling it away as a dike against another flood. They become very reluctant to lay out for even the most basic creature comforts."

When he had finished speaking, the silence grew in the room. Pross sorted several pieces of paper and arranged them in an order known only to him. When they were as he wished, he pulled out the earl's chair. "If you will look here, milord," he suggested softly, "I think you will find this most edifying."

Within an hour the solicitor had gone. The Viscount Polwycke found himself sitting behind his father's desk in the dark, dusty library. He stared at the pile of papers and the stack of ledgers. Beside him on the floor was the estate strongbox and in his hand was the key.

He hunched his shoulders against a draft that seemed to blow from somewhere on his unprotected neck. Guilt and a sense of intruding where he was forbidden made his hand shake so that he had to clutch the key with extra strength.

Childhood memories flooded the room. How many times had he stood on the other side of this desk in fear and shame? He could picture himself trembling as his father cruelly upbraided him for his faults. Somewhere around here in a dark corner behind the heavy draperies was the switch that he had cowered beneath until he had been deemed sturdy enough to sustain blows from the cane.

He clenched his fist around the key. His father was not dead. He was not even a particularly old man, not nearly sixty. Piers felt like a ghoul. Yet in another sense he felt the rightness of being there. He went down on one knee and inserted the key in the lock.

*　　　*　　　*

He was hard at work among ledgers and correspondence of all kinds when Vivian knocked softly on the door to summon him to his lunch.

"Sweetheart." As if they had been man and wife for years, he came from behind the desk to put his arms over her shoulders and buss her lips. With her smiling up at him, he wiggled his hands behind her and groaned, "I'm dusty and inkstained, or you'd get a kiss to remember."

She ran her hands up under his coat and clasped his shoulders. Her soft breasts pressed against his chest. Her hips tilted forward to match his. He caught his breath sharply as her mouth fastened on his and her tongue thrust against his teeth.

Abandoning his own restrictions, he pulled her against him and kissed her deeply. His excitement rose to meet hers. When finally she slipped back on her heels, his lips followed her, lingering on hers, drinking their sweetness. Since his recovery, he had come to her bed every night, or taken her to his, holding her beside him, caressing her, teaching her to respond to his desires.

Now the pupil performed for the master. To finish the kiss, she let her tongue slide sensuously across his open lips. A hot thrill of desire shot through him at the caress. With a tantalizing smile, she put her fingers over his mouth.

Finally, reluctantly, he put her at arm's length. "What am I going to do with you? If you kiss me like that very much longer, I can't be responsible for getting us to lunch in time for the food to be edible."

She freed herself from his embrace and stepped back. With a slow smile, she allowed her eyes to roam over his strong thighs clad in superfine trousers that revealed all too well his arousal.

With a groan he caught her back in his arms. "If you

don't watch out, you'll find yourself stretched full length over the earl's desk satisfying the devil you've awakened."

Silent laughter answered his threat.

"Temptress," he growled against her throat. "If you won't be warned, then you deserve what you get. Seducing a man from his labors." Leering, he dragged her toward the desk. She hung back, pretending reluctance, fearfully glancing over her shoulder at the door and trying to twist away.

At the desk he stopped, scratching his head. The oak top was littered with papers and pens; two ledgers lay open, one stacked on top of the other. He looked over his shoulder at the door unlocked behind them. With much show of disappointment, he let go of her arm.

"You'll escape this once, Vivian, but rest assured that tonight you'll pay a heavy price for trying to seduce me this way."

She shivered, her eyes bright with excitement. Catching up a pen, she wrote, "Promises."

"Only for now," he sighed. He let go of her hand and picked up two papers on which he had jotted columns of figures. "I've made some discoveries that affect us both." He handed her one sheet. "Look here. You're a very rich woman who in turn makes her husband rich since he controls her estate."

He waited while she scanned the sheet then passed her the second. "As you'll see here, I, after my father, am equally as rich. The rents from lands and mines are producing princely sums of money. In fact, I can't believe the amount of money that we together are worth."

Grinning saucily, she caught up a pencil and scribbled another message.

As she wrote, he read over her shoulder. "Why, yes, I suppose I am. A catch, that is."

She nodded and wrote again.

He sobered instantly. "You're right. I don't need to go smuggling ever again. In point of fact, I don't understand why it was ever begun. I was brought home from university and told there was not enough money for me to continue. But there was." He leaned his head against her shoulder. On a sigh he repeated, "There was."

She turned and took his face between her hands. In it she read his unhappiness, his sense of betrayal. Gently she kissed his forehead, his cheek.

He would not be consoled. "These records go back ten years. Even before I was set to smuggling. Smuggling! For heaven's sake. This wealth was acquired long before. It is too vast to have been carried up the beach by ponies in the dead of night. Money like this came from crops and mines and a fishery. I thought I was breaking the law, risking my own life, to save my father and mother's home. But there was never any need." He massaged his half-healed shoulder. "All the suffering. All those men killed. It need never have occurred. I don't understand. Why did he send me?"

She turned back to the desk. The pen flew over the paper. "Greed. Fear of losing all again?"

"That's impossible. Not with this kind of substance."

She put her hand on his shoulder.

His words tumbled out. "Did he want to punish me for what I didn't do? For what he thought I should have done? This last time was the most dangerous of all. The Riding Officers were everywhere. Everywhere. Yet he sent me anyway." He looked down into her face. "Because he thought you were pregnant. He didn't need me any longer."

She slipped both arms around him and hugged him. Her cheek nestled against his chest.

His eyes blazed. "I can't tell you how many times—

times without number—I've stood here even as a small child and endured his rages because I believed I was somehow guilty. I and my mother had failed him. And we paid for it and paid and paid. My mother lived in hell for almost a quarter of a century. Death was a release for her. And now I find he was actually anticipating my death, too. He wanted—"

Vivian put her hand over his mouth keeping the bitter words from being spoken.

He turned his face into her palm and kissed it. She could feel the tears there. He turned and took her hand between his. "I'm going to make you a promise here and now, Vivian. No, I'm going to make you two promises. First, I won't go again. I'm done with the smuggling. I've enough wealth to take care of my tenants and yours. I'll become the Viscount of Polwycke in truth as well as in name, and I promise I'll manage our lands well."

Excited by his plans, she hugged him.

He kissed the top of her head. "And, secondly, I promise to take you to London for a come-out in society."

Her head snapped back, her face lighted with a wild hope.

He kissed her mouth. "We'll go to balls and routs and the theatre and the ballet." He danced her back into the center of the room and whirled her around. "You'll love it. We'll shop for beautiful clothes for you. We'll dance the night away. We'll give our own ball. Everyone will stare at your beauty." Laughing at his own picture, he kissed her hard on the mouth before setting her on her feet.

She put her arms around his neck and returned his kiss with her whole body, her breasts and thighs pressing tightly against him in warm agreement.

At last, dizzy for lack of air, he broke off the

embrace. His face bore a bemused expression as he stared into her radiant face. "Do I really make you *that* happy, Vivian?"

When she would have kissed him again to reassure him, he shook his head. "One more kiss and we'll not only get nothing to eat but nothing else done for the day." Putting his arm about her shoulders, he turned her firmly and walked with her to the door. "Tonight," he whispered in her ear. "Just wait until tonight."

As Piers opened the door, Mrs. Felders swept down the staircase toward them. Her face virtually quivered with malignant triumph. "He's himself again, milord, and asking for you. You'd best come immediately."

Piers threw up his hands to his wife. "Obviously, I wasn't meant to eat lunch today. However, I'll expect an early dinner—perhaps in your bedroom. Remember I'll be very hungry." Lifting her hand, palm upward, to his lips, he kissed her with lips and teeth and tongue. As she quivered to his touch, his brown eyes grew hot. "Go on, Mrs. Felders. I'm right behind you."

The tender smile remained on Vivian's lips as she walked into the morning room for lunch. He was a different man from the cynical hard drinker she had first known. She would never have believed when she entered this house only a few short months ago that such happiness as she felt now was possible.

She was sure she loved him and he loved her. They felt it together and apart. The heating of the flesh. Mutual accord. Caring for each other's hurts both body and mind. In her solitary life since her mother's death, no one had ever treated her with such attention, such courtesy, and such affection as her husband. From the very beginning, she had received nothing but support from him. In that moment she vowed she would never leave him.

In the morning room, Vivian called for a light

394

luncheon to be served since she was sure that she and her husband would be dining early that evening. A frisson of anticipation played along her nerves. She smiled, running the tip of her tongue across her lower lip, swollen from his kisses.

The door opened and Mrs. Felders strode in.

Vivian stiffened at the sight of the woman's angry face.

"He sent me out," the housekeeper snarled. "I brought his lordship back from the dead and that idiot sent me out."

A footman entered at that moment with a tray. Mrs. Felders swung on the hapless man and ordered him from the room. Her eyes glowed with her hatred.

"You!" The word exploded from her mouth. "You're going to leave here now. His lordship agreed with me that you were to go back to your own home. Don't look as if you don't believe me. When I told him the good news, he knew he didn't need you or that fool son." She lifted her chin, her bosom swelled beneath the heavy black silk.

Vivian looked at her narrowly.

"I'm going to have his son," she announced triumphantly. "So you might as well pack your clothes."

Even as Vivian froze in shock, Emma Felders caught hold of her arm and lifted her out of the chair. Left breathless by the woman's revelation, so bald, so shocking, Vivian allowed herself to be pulled and prodded willy-nilly to the door.

However, when the pair paused at the door for Mrs. Felders to fumble for the handle, Vivian's spirit of rebellion asserted itself. This woman might be carrying a second child of the earl's body, but until he married her, it was not an heir and she was not mistress of this house. Vivian was.

With an angry twist Vivian wrenched herself out of

the housekeeper's grasp. The delicate sleeve of her morning gown tore from the shoulder. Mrs. Felders's fingers slipped in the fabric. Vivian darted away to catch up the little silver bell and ring it vigorously.

"No, you come with me!" Mrs. Felders's voice was hoarse with strain.

Millard came bursting in accompanied by the footman.

The housekeeper backed away as they came at her from both sides of the table. "You'd both better hear this, too. Lord Larnaervon's recovering. He's regained consciousness. Soon he'll be himself again. Everything will be the way it was before."

"That's good news," Millard agreed cautiously.

"And there's more. I'm going to be the mistress here. Alexander has come to realize how important I am to him. And he's asked me to marry him."

Butler and footman exchanged amazed glances.

Mrs. Felders drew herself up. "The first thing that I'm to do as his wife is to send this person and her husband off to her own house." She pointed toward the door. "I expect you to go and pack."

Millard frowned. "Mrs. Felders, you must be very tired, sitting beside the earl's bed for all these hours. While Lady Polwycke eats her lunch, why don't you let me take you to your room where you can lie down and sleep. Perhaps Cook could fix you some food to be served there."

The housekeeper nodded her head. "I am tired."

"And upset."

"Yes, I am upset. And she's part of the problem."

"Let me show you to bed. You'll feel better after a lie-down."

"But she must go," Mrs. Felders insisted.

"Soon. You wouldn't want her to go until the earl was out of danger."

"He is out of danger. He's regained consciousness and knows everything. I sat and talked—"

The footman led her out.

"My lady!" Millard came to Vivian's side and so far forgot himself as to touch the material of her torn sleeve. "Are you hurt? Did she hurt you?"

Vivian shook her head.

"I can't imagine what possessed her."

Vivian could not either. Even if Mrs. Felders were pregnant, her chances of becoming the wife of the proud Earl of Larnaervon were not certain. Surely a good rest would clear her mind.

"Shall I send for Lord Polwycke?" Millard asked.

Vivian shook her head definitely.

"At least let me send for Addie."

"I'm here." The little maid limped hurriedly into the room and put her arm around her mistress's waist. "Come, milady. No need to bother your head about her. Oh, my, she tore your dress again. She must be crazy."

Suddenly, the effect of the argument asserted itself. With a trembling hand, Vivian pulled her sleeve up onto her shoulder.

"We'll go change your dress," Addie continued. "I don't think it's ruined. It looks like it's just torn in the seam. I'm sure I can fix it." Over Vivian's shoulder she directed a command to Millard. "You'd better see that someone keeps an eye on that old loon."

Chapter Twenty=Four

Larnaervon lay in his great bed, his enfeebled right hand plucking nervously at the counterpane. His left eyelid and left side of his mouth drooped. His left hand lay useless, twisted into a claw on the bed beside him. A dribble of spittle ran down over his grizzled flesh in the deep groove cut between chin and withered cheek.

His valet reached over to wipe it away. The blue-veined eyelids opened slowly. Behind them the eyes like those of a raging bird of prey glittered angrily. A muffled guttural sound issued from the throat and slackly open lips.

"Beg pardon, milord." Mackery leaned forward again, his ear close to the old man's mouth. "I couldn't understand."

"Pie . . . rs." The word came out in two syllables at the end of a halting garble. The old man had to gather his strength visibly to force the proper sounds from between his lips. The paralysis extending to the left side of the tongue impeded the formation of the consonants.

"He's coming, milord. I've sent for him." The valet soothed the invalid and held a glass of wine to his lips.

"Mus' see now. Go!"

The valet drew back and nodded gravely. His long years of habit forced him to obey this man whom he could barely tolerate. Unquestioningly, he went to speed the viscount on his way.

Alone, the earl marshaled his faculties. With trembling hand he touched the left side of his face, his eye, his mouth. The right side of his face contorted in a frightful combination of disgust and anger. Weakly, he clenched his right fist and released it, testing the strength remaining in him. Unintelligible sounds burst from his mouth, the sense of which could only have been curses.

For perhaps a minute he cursed, then subsided exhausted. His good eye closed. He lay there drawing deep breaths, checking the parts of his body, feeling his lungs expand, feeling the great weight that seemed to lie on the left side of his chest.

The bedroom door opened. His eye darted toward it searching for the sound.

Silhouetted in the light from the hallway stood his tall son. As Piers closed the door behind him and came to the bedside, the light of the fire blazed strongly in the overheated chamber. His handsome young features were clearly illuminated.

The earl cursed at the sight. Strong straight shoulders, unbowed body, and dark red hair. Never ill, never hurt until a few weeks ago. Even his broken shoulder had healed without a trace. A perfect specimen just as the earl had been before the fall from the horse that had crippled him forever.

If envy could have lifted him off the bed, Larnaervon would have risen and walked.

"Larne." Piers voice was low and gentle.

Again the mighty surge of emotion—of anger. The earl's heart leaped in his chest. Never had he seen a closer resemblance to the wife he despised than now.

The boy had grown into a man whose very face reflected the dignity and self-possession which had characterized Georgina. Never had she admitted to a fault. In the end she had walled herself behind ice that he had never succeeded in melting. He had never forgiven her.

"Glad to see you're more the thing, Larne. Felders said you wanted to see me immediately."

The earl swallowed. His mouth moved soundlessly in his initial effort to speak. Saliva drooled onto the pillow. His skewed ravaged face contorted. At last he managed to form the words. Piers bent forward to hear. *"Span—niss Gir-r—"*

The viscount's eyes widened. He shook his head, depressed and disgusted. Even in dire straits, perhaps dying his father was more concerned about the smuggling operation than anything else. Heaving a sigh, he draped an arm along the headboard and leaned over the earl. "What about *Spanish Girl?*"

"Span—iss Gir-rl."

"What about it?"

The earl lifted his right fist toward his son's face.

"Spaniss Girl." The words were stronger now, expelled with urgency. The last fire from the dying frame.

"All right! *Spanish Girl!*" the viscount exclaimed. "Larne, why don't you just forget about the family business. That's behind us now. You should concentrate on getting well."

Irritably, the earl stirred in his bed. "Not behin'. Go," he whispered. "Mee' Beddoes."

"Beddoes is dead, Larne. The business is finished."

The skull-like visage rolled from side to side. The long hair, yellow with perspiration, stirred lankly. "No."

Piers bent low until he could look directly into the

demon eye. "Larne. Jack Beddoes is dead. The Riding Officers trapped us. He was standing right by the lantern when they opened fire."

The earl's mouth twisted wildly. "Comin' in," he insisted. He could not hold his eyes open. The lids like sheets of lead slid down, shutting out the light, leaving him alone in hateful, pain-wracked darkness. He tried to scream for help, but he had no voice. No voice. *No voice.*

The burning eyes closed. Patting his father's twisted left hand, Piers shuddered. It was cold and blue, the nails purplish. Lifting it in his own, he tried to straighten out the fingers, but they were stiff, curled like the talon of an eagle. It felt like the hand of a man already dead.

"Larne," he whispered. Then to the valet, "Keep him comfortable and call me at any time."

In the hall outside the chamber, he drew a deep breath of cool air after the sickening heat and odor of the sickroom. What had Larne said when Piers's mother had died? *"Sickrooms develop the odor of the disease and the medicine to cure it."*

He could almost pity his father at this moment. What torment of spirit for his hell-bound pride! Weakness had always been anathema, and now Larnaervon was weak. In the past month Piers himself had had more than enough of lying helpless in a too-hot-sour-smelling room unable to move. He knew firsthand the indignity of being turned and bathed and wiped by a servant. The thoughts that burned in his father's brain could only be guessed at by the rage in the volcanic eyes.

Piers lifted his arm to test the shoulder joint. It still pained him, and he still could not raise it above his head, but movement would come in time. He had begun using it more and more, setting himself tasks to

401

gradually stretch the arm above his head. Eventually, the whole ordeal would be a shadowy memory.

The valet followed him out into the hall. Dark circles showed under the man's eyes. His face was gaunt with strain. "Milord seems a bit better today, sir."

Piers nodded, then stared at the man. "Mackery, how long has it been since you've been relieved?"

"Quite a while, sir. I leave the room for a short while when Mrs. Felders comes in. But I try to hurry back. For propriety's sake, y'know."

Piers laughed dryly. "The hell with propriety. When she's there, go and take your rest, man. Bathe, eat, take walks." He clapped the man on the shoulder. "Can't have you getting ill yourself. You're the mainstay."

The valet smiled. "Rather thought Lady Polwycke was that, sir."

"Indeed. She is that. She certainly is that."

Alone in the hall, the viscount found he could pity the earl. Even though he could not love him, he could pity the man alone, cared for only by servants. Bought and paid for. Without money, he would be deserted, left to die in a dark room.

Then he thought of the earl's command to meet the *Spanish Girl.* Now as never before he could believe his father was bent on destroying him.

Even the procuring of Vivian for his wife had been for the express purpose of getting another heir. At that time he, Piers, would become unnecessary. He shuddered at the thought of such cold-blooded manipulation.

Casting his gloomy thoughts aside, Piers strode down the hall toward his room where he would find his wife. She would be waiting for him there, her body warm and willing, her responses vitally exciting. If he were asked, he would say she was more exciting, more loving than a woman who could speak because she responded with her whole body.

With every breath she took, she communicated her pleasure and her desire to give pleasure. Her long slender fingers had learned the things he had taught her and had invented more.

This morning in the library, he had threatened her with love, and—wonder of wonders—she had tempted him shamelessly. Tonight. He felt his blood surge with excitement thinking of the dance they would perform together. He would love her as she had never been loved before. He would love her until—

Would they make a baby together? Would they make the heir his father wanted? The thought of a son—or a daughter sent a wave of incredible emotion surging through him. Heat coursed through his veins, his heart pounded. He wanted to make this baby. He wanted to put it inside her in a burst of incandescent passion. He wanted to watch it grow beneath her stark, white skin and to put his hands on her belly day by day and feel it kick and turn.

He came to a halt blinking, his breath coming fast. His fantasies were out of control and they were all her fault. He smiled. What a pleasant fault to have. All husbands should be so lucky.

He was halfway into the room before he realized something was wrong. His wife sat bolt upright in her chair. Her eyes were frightened; her mouth set in a grim line. Emma Felders hovered malevolently behind her, her hand curled around Vivian's shoulder.

"What the hell—?"

From the shadows behind the door a sneering voice interrupted him. "What kept y' so tardy from yer lady, yer bleedin' lordship?"

Piers spun around in amazement. "Jack Beddoes!"

"Well, now, ain't you glad to see me? I don't think."
The smuggler stepped out of the shadows. In his
hammy fist he clutched his duckfoot volley gun primed
and cocked. "Just sit yerself down in that chair while
we have a talk. I want y' rested for tonight."

Piers gathered his muscles to attack, but Beddoes
didn't miss the swelling of his shoulders. "Uh-uh! Don't
try it, yer bleedin' lordship, or the bird gets it."

He waved the vicious weapon in Vivian's direction.
"And I won't even have to pull the trigger."

Emma Felders smirked as she raised Jack's horse
pistol from behind the chair.

"Just put it right back down, Emma, me darlin'."
Beddoes grinned at Piers. "Don't figure that chair's
more'n an inch thick behind her lung," he commented
conversationally.

"Beddoes. You're a dead man." Piers separated each
word with peculiar emphasis.

"Everybody's got to die." The smuggler shrugged as
he directed the four ominous barrels back at Piers. "Y'
might jump me before I could do more'n just pink y'.
'Course with this thing, it'd most likely be a sizable
hole, with three bullets left over for her. On the other
'and, might be y'd kill me, and Emma might hit a rib
instead of a lung. Everything's chancy like that. But do
y' really want to take the chance?" He grinned
maliciously.

Piers slowly unclenched his fists.

"Smart. Didn't want 'er to get stuck, did y'? Real
smart. Bleedin' makes such a mess."

"What do you want?"

"Good man. Get right to the point. I figured y' didn't
want no trouble. So that's why I'm 'ere. Want to make a
little deal."

At the mention of a deal, Piers knew why the man
had come. A muscle jumped in his cheek, but other-

wise he managed to conceal his anger. Ignoring the menacing pistol in the other's hand, he strolled to the chair opposite Vivian and lowered himself into it. His eyes met hers, trying to instill some confidence in her.

She managed a small courageous smile though her face was white to the lips.

"Sorry to have these moments of inconvenience, m'dear. We will settle these people's grievances and send them on their way." Crossing one long leg over the other, he spoke as if they were in the room alone rather than both sitting with guns trained on them.

"Watch him, Jack," Emma Felders warned, her fingernails digging into Vivian's shoulder. "He's not as stupid as he acts."

The smuggler laughed. "Maybe not. Maybe so. What d'y' say to that, bucko?"

"I say, get to the point," the viscount grated. "My wife is tired and I'm still exhausted from the last expedition. I'm sure all of this could have waited until tomorrow."

Beddoes gestured coolly with the pistol. "No way, yer bloody lordship. *Spanish Girl*'s down in the cove. I talked to the earl real private like not more'n a couple o' hours ago."

Piers glared at the housekeeper. "So well you take care of your charge, Felders."

A dark flush rose in her cheeks. "It didn't hurt him to talk to Jack. He was glad to see him as a matter of fact."

"Yea. 'E was really 'appy t' see me. And from what I can tell, real un'appy with you."

"Then you meet the *Spanish Girl* and take the cargo." Piers made a dismissive gesture with his hand. "I give it all to you. My wife and I are leaving here as soon as the earl's health improves. The business is yours, Jack."

"Well, I thank y' kindly for that," Beddoes sneered,

"but the truth is I need yer connections, m'lord. If y' was to see yer way clear to make the run, leadin' us like. We didn't make no profit on the last run. Fact is, as y' know, we didn't make nothin'. Some of the boys didn't even make it back. We need to make one more. Sort of break even, don't y' know?" The man leered evilly, all mocking subservience in his turn.

Piers shook his head deliberately. "Sorry, old man. Not a chance. The game's up. If we went down there tonight, the Riding Officers would be all over us."

"Yer not thinkin' as usual, y' bleedin' coward," Beddoes snarled. "They think we're all dead. It's a sweet arrangement for another run. Hell, we might make a whole new start, bucko."

Piers shook his head. "Then start it somewhere else. I'm telling you, the operation is over. May I suggest that you men take what you want from *Spanish Girl* and then return her to her usual fishing activities?"

Mrs. Felders snorted. Beddoes's smile disappeared. "Well, now, m'lord, if y' don't do like I tell y', I'm mightily afraid I'll be forced to put a bullet in y' where it'd do the most good." He aimed the pistol threateningly at Piers's middle. Vivian started from her chair only to be pulled back roughly by Mrs. Felders's hand on her shoulder.

Beddoes swung the pistol in her direction menacingly. "Keep yer seat there. I ain't gonna 'urt 'im if he does what I tell 'im."

Piers waved a casual hand. "Don't be a damned fool. You're not going to shoot that thing off in here. You're just as liable to hit your accomplice as your target. Use your head, man."

His words uttered with such cool unconcern drove Beddoes to lower the pistol instantly. The smuggler reddened, then raised his pistol again, careful to train it on Piers, who continued.

"You, my friend, have reached a stalemate, as we say in chess. You cannot shoot me because dead, I certainly cannot make a connection. The earl can no longer order me to go because, as you have seen, he is ill—probably dying. If he survives it will still be weeks, even months before he can assume any kind of position as intermediary. Your rash— er—demonstration will leave many impoverished men unable to care for their families. Your best bet is to take the cargo and sell it for what you can get."

Beddoes wavered. Much as he hated to admit it, the viscount made sense. The volley gun sagged in his hand.

Furious as she felt the tide beginning to turn, Mrs. Felders leaned forward, her strong grip bruising Vivian's shoulder. "Don't let him talk you out of our profit, Jack. Remember this is the last haul."

Beddoes rallied. "M'lord, she's got the right of it. This one more run and we'll be leavin' the country." He shot a fierce look in Emma's direction. "The missus and I."

Piers said nothing, but his muscles tensed in anger. The scent of treachery and double-dealing was strong. Suddenly the origin of the earl's smuggling activities became clearer. Felders—as his sometime bed partner—had made the connection for the two men. Her relationship to Beddoes must have been a closely guarded secret.

"Make him take you, Jack. He can't do us no harm without harming himself. We need that money after all we've done for them." She set her mouth, her dark eyes blazing. "Tell him that if he doesn't do what we say, I'll make sure this bead-rattler doesn't ever have the heir the earl wants."

Beddoes hesitated, then lapsed into a relaxed grin as he recognized the solution to the problem. "Right y'

407

are, Emma. She's right more times than not," he confided to Piers. "And when she says she's gonna do somethin', by God, she does it. So, bucko, we need y' one more time. And we can't shoot y' t' make you lead us. But I'm thinkin' y'll do what we say with a pistol at yer wife's heart. How d' y' like this?" As he spoke, he glided across the room. Almost casually, he pressed the duckfoot against Vivian's breast.

She flinched aside, but the muzzle followed her and the pressure never slackened. Emma Felders stepped out from behind the chair, her pistol trained on Piers, her eyes lighted with unholy triumph.

Piers sprang to his feet, his face white with emotion. "Get away from her!"

"Ah, m'lord, that got y' off y'r bloody bum, didn't it? But don't come one step closer, or this pretty little bird gets it. Don't say much, does she?" He laughed and nudged her breast with his pistol.

Her eyes flashed fire and she clenched her fists on the arms of her chair.

"That's good, Jack." His wife jeered at the crude joke.

Piers cursed. He clenched his fists at his sides and spoke through gritted teeth. "I warn you. Take that pistol away from her person, or—"

Beddoes leered grimly and punched the barrel again. "Get y'r coat."

The viscount was pale with anger, his dark eyes burning like anthracite above his white lips. Vivian's peril had touched a nerve that destroyed his control. An icy fist tightened on his gut, leaving him trembling in pain. The sight of her body threatened by this vermin brought a taste of bitter bile to his mouth. He swallowed convulsively. For several seconds he could not move. He was held captive by his fierce desire to kill

408

the man who leered at him so callously. Coupled with that was the tumultuous emotion he felt for the slim, silver-haired girl, his wife.

"Now!"

The single syllable barked by the villainous Beddoes unlocked Piers from his frozen posture. Nodding coldly, he strode to the door. "Let's be about it then." He looked back over his shoulder at the housekeeper. "If you harm her, remember you won't have just me to contend with. Larne will destroy you as easily as he would kill a fly."

He had sounded the right note. The mention of the earl's power wiped the smile from her face.

"The earl ain't gonna t' do nothin'. Once we make the run, 'e'll be satisfied to live an' let live." Beddoes stuck the duckfoot in his belt and tipped his hat mockingly to Vivian. "Watch this bird until we get back, love. With 'is bleedin' lordship 'ere t' lead us t' 'is connection, we'll be back by noon tomorrow."

Piers opened his mouth to protest as he remembered the extent of the housekeeper's hatred of Vivian. A second later he closed it, realizing that any plea would be futile.

Beddoes chuckled. "Thinkin' about 'ow m' dear wife feels about yers, are y'? Best not be delayin' a minute then. Emma's finger might jus' get too itchy and that'd be a pity. Seein' yer wife s' young and pretty and all." He grinned at his wife who laughed in return. "Any trouble, love, and y' know what t' do."

With a hoot of laughter Beddoes pushed rudely against Piers's shoulder making him stumble into the hall.

Within the chamber Vivian faced her adversary, a cold shiver wracking her body. Never had she been in such deadly danger.

Felders did not have the easy, unemotional determination of evil action that motivated her husband. This woman hated her with a jealous hatred that bordered on the deranged. Her hand clasped the pistol with an eager caress. The pinch-purse mouth had spread into a gloating smile. In the silence that followed the closing of the door, Vivian knew that she would not leave this room alive unless she exerted all the wits of which she was capable.

Keeping the gun trained on her captive, Emma swayed across the room in an exaggerated imitation of a lady and lowered herself daintily in Piers's chair. "Now, my fine lady, we'll just get comfortable for the night. Later on I'll tie you up so you can't move a muscle, but for right now I think I'd enjoy having a drink from a fine crystal decanter and watching you pour it and bring it to me."

Vivian forced her fingers to relax their death grip on the chair arms. If she were allowed to move around the room, she would have a better chance of surprising her captor and escaping than if she were forced at gunpoint to sit in the chair all night.

Felders brandished the gun. "Get it," she commanded. "Get it right now and be quick about it."

Vivian had no trouble pretending to be afraid as she pushed herself up on trembling legs.

"I told you to leave here. I did everything I could to get you out of this house, but would you listen? Not you. Now it's too late. I'll have that glass of sherry," she mocked.

Stiffly, Vivian started across the room to the sideboard.

"Graceless chit!" the housekeeper barked, enjoying herself hugely. "You forgot to curtsy. Who has taught you, fool? You'll be back in the scullery before you know it."

Playing the deadly game for all she was worth, Vivian hastened back to drop an impeccable curtsy before the woman. She was rewarded with a frosty nod and a rude grunt. Scurrying to the sideboard, Vivian poured a crystal water glass full of sherry. If Felders drank enough, she might fall asleep or be so befuddled that she would be easily tricked.

"Idiot." The woman continued her acting. "You didn't set it on a tray. How dare you bring it to me with your filthy hands! Take it back and serve me properly."

Gritting her teeth, Vivian did as she commanded. When she came back with the drink, Mrs. Felders laughed nastily. Rising, her eyes icy with cruelty, she struck Vivian a savage slap across the side of the cheek. The glass, sherry, and tray went flying. The fragile crystal shattered.

Instantly, Vivian lunged for the older woman, her fists clenched, only to be brought up short by the horse pistol aimed for her heart.

Felders laughed in delight. "Now you'll pay for it. Ignorant, stupid, clumsy girl. Down on your knees and beg my pardon." She pointed imperiously at the floor.

When Vivian hesitated, calculating the chances of springing at Felders and wresting the pistol from her hand, the woman's mouth pursed angrily. "Down!" she snarled, gesturing with the pistol. Trembling, Vivian sank to her knees.

"Oh, my god. Don't you look sweet?" Felders sucked in a shuddering breath. "You don't know how good you look to me. You the fine lady." She pushed the pistol into Vivian's face. "Do you know I've been in service of one kind or another since I was a child? I've been kicked and whipped and sneered at. I've been pawed and fondled by drunken fools and raped, too, until I found out that I could get a little of my own back and have a softer time of it if I'd just give in and

411

give 'em what they wanted. Does that shock you?"

Vivian shook her head.

"I'll bet it does. You'd say anything now on your knees, but you don't know what it's like. God! The years I've had to endure this very thing from you bleedin' ladies and then your men come to my bed at night."

Felders straightened and stepped back. Passion had transformed her face until it was barely recognizable. "How does it feel? Do your knees hurt? Does your back ache? Well, just stay where you are."

Out of the corner of her eye, Vivian tried to track the woman's movements. The housekeeper was moving toward the door. Could she possibly be leaving? No. What was she—?

Transferring the pistol to her left hand, the woman caught up Piers's riding whip where it had been left on the table beside the door. "Too bad I can't have the pleasure of hearing you scream in pain. But I can at least see the tears run down." Striding back across the room, Mrs. Felders raised the whip high above her head and brought it whistling down with all her strength.

Even as she twisted to escape, Felders struck her across the shoulder. A band of fire arced across her shoulder blade. The weight of the blow knocked her aside, adding impetus to the movement she had already begun. Determined not to take another blow without a struggle, she rolled over on her hands and knees and came to her feet. With a grunt Felders raised the whip again.

A loud imperative knock sounded at the door freezing both women in their attitudes.

As all the servants did, Watkins waited for the space of twenty seconds before hurrying into the room

412

followed closely by Lord Alexander's valet. "Milord, the earl—"

"My God—" Mackery breathed.

To Watkins's well-trained eyes the scene was unbelievable. The lady of the manor, the dear, sweet, gentle girl whom they had all come to respect, held at bay by a whip and pistol in the hands of the Emma Felders.

Fortunately, the housekeeper seemed to forget that she held the pistol, for she let both drop to her sides. "Get out!" she commanded. "This doesn't concern you."

Mackery drew back, hands upraised, but Watkins rallied instantly. "Here now, Mrs. Felders," he began soothingly, "you mustn't—" One step. Two. And he flung himself upon her. Both his hands clamped around her wrist squeezing with all his might.

The woman's cry of rage turned to pain. Still she brought the whip down across his back. When she tried to strike again, Vivian caught her wrist and wrenched the whip away.

"Damn you! Damn you all!" A string of oaths streamed from her lips as she fought them both until finally Mackery also joined in to pull the woman's arms behind her and hold her.

"You'll be sorry for this," she panted when she had finally stopped struggling. "The earl will hear about this. You'll both be discharged."

Watkins sobered. "I very much doubt that."

Vivian caught up her pencil and pad and began to write, her scribbling almost illegible in her frantic haste.

"Piers captive Beddoes. Inlet below house. Save him." She shoved the note into Watkins's hand.

He read it. "Beddoes. Are you sure? He's dead."

"He is." Mrs. Felders chimed in. "You're right, of course. She doesn't know what she's talking about."

Vivian shook her head. "*Spanish Girl,*" she wrote.

"The earl told him about that," Mackery supplied uncertainly.

"Trap!" Vivian wrote.

"No. She's wrong. Don't pay any attention. Ask Lord Alexander," Mrs. Felders insisted.

"I can't do that," Watkins replied. He turned the pistol on her. "He's dead, Mrs. Felders. Just a few minutes ago."

Emma's face crumpled. "No. He can't be. He's not an old man."

"Even so." Mackery sighed. He took the gun from Watkins. "I'll leave you here to look after the lady, while I take this one away. What shall I do with her, milady?"

Vivian wrote her instructions instantly. "Lock her in her room."

"No," Emma Felders protested. "You can't do that."

Mackery motioned the pistol toward the door. "If you'll be so good as to move, Mrs. Felders. I think you've troubled this dear lady long enough."

414

Chapter Twenty-Five

Once the door closed behind them, Vivian tottered to the chair and sank down in it. Nausea roiled inside her. Closing her eyes, she tasted its bitterness and swallowed convulsively.

"Milady." Watkins bent over her, patting her shoulder, his own hand not quite steady. "Where is Lord Piers?"

Fingers icy and fumbling, Vivian tried to balance her pad and pencil on her knee. Darkness seemed to be closing her range of vision. Into it spun wheeling pinpoints of light. She could feel herself falling.

"Milady! Here, milady, steady there." Watkins's gentle hands caught her shoulders and pushed her back against the chair.

The contact of her bruised shoulder blade with the chair back hurt her, but the spark of pain brought her back to reality. She nodded as she patted his wrist.

"Shall I bring some brandy?"

While he got it, she tried to marshall her thoughts enough to write. When he returned, she clutched at the glass and tossed the fiery liquid down her throat. Her eyes watered and her breath wheezed out of her throat, but she welcomed the warmth that spread itself through her shocked body. Her trembling stopped almost immediately. Resolutely, she sat up and began to write.

Watkins hovered at her shoulder reading the incredible events of the evening. He commented in a shocked murmur at each revelation.

Vivian, once she was well into her story, found she had more and more difficulty concentrating. She felt detached and light-headed, as if she were floating behind a gauze that separated her from the room and the man beside her. Like a recurring nightmare the experience of this night blended with the night of her mother's death in the freezing coach and the terrible journey when Beddoes had brought her almost across the south of England. She began to shudder violently.

"Another, milady?"

She nodded.

Stubbornly, she caught her lower lip between her teeth and bit down hard. Reading over her shoulder, Watkins cursed softly as she concluded in hastily scribbled terse words the threats and danger that hung over the viscount.

At her written question, Watkins sighed. "Yes, milady. I'm afraid it's all too true. Lord Alexander is dead. He can be of no help to you or Lord Piers, even if he would. You are a countess and your husband is the Earl of Larnaervon."

But not if he did not live through the night. She and she alone could set in motion a rescue. As if a mantle had settled over her shoulders, Vivian wrote her orders. Watkins read and departed without question to summon Addie and to instruct Tyler to saddle Barbary.

By the time Addie came, yawning, her face swollen with sleep, Vivian had already stripped off her clothing

416

and was pulling on her riding habit. Within a couple of minutes, she was running down the stairs and out the front door.

Millard held a lantern for her, his face worried. "Lord Piers would not let you do this, milady. At night. In the dark and the cold. And what can you do?"

She met his eyes steadfastly as he held out a long black cape belonging to her husband. To her way of thinking, she had no choice.

At the step Tyler waited with Barbary and Romany Prince both saddled.

She caught hold of his arm and pointed toward the stable.

He grinned one-sidedly and tugged at his forelock before he held his hands for her to mount. Spurred by her own sense of emergency, she cantered the gelding away into the night. Behind her Tyler mounted Romany Prince and spurred the big black after her. When she realized he was accompanying her, she stopped and laid her hand on his to restrain him. At the same time she shook her head vigorously. He had been a smuggler. She could not allow him to betray his friends.

He patted her hand. "You don't ride alone tonight, milady. I know where you're going, but I won't let you go out there by yourself."

The moon did not shed enough light for her to read his expression. She pushed at his shoulder, trying to send him back. Surely he could not know that if her mission tonight was successful, the smuggling would cease, at least as the Larnaervons' and their people were a part of it.

He sat his horse like a statue. "Don't think me a fool, just because Jack Beddoes is. I ride all over this part of the country exercising the horses. Rory MacPherson knows the big fish got through his last net. And he's stubborn as they come. He won't give up until he's got them all, or until he's satisfied that they're dead."

Vivian shrugged. In his hand she wrote the word, "Boat."

She had to write it twice before Tyler nodded. "The *Spanish Girl* is sailing into a trap."

A band tightened around her heart. Piers—pushed by Jack Beddoes into leading his men—might be sacrificing himself to save her. She put her gloved hand on Tyler's arm in a gesture of fervent gratitude. Then she swung Barbary's head around and laid her crop across the muscled rump. The gelding sprang forward at a gallop, and the two riders tore out onto the coast road.

The night wind rushed past her ears, and the clouds raced across the moon. At one moment the road would be clear in the moonlight, then plunge into darkness seeming all the blacker by contrast. So dangerous was their pace that Vivian half expected Tyler to pull up or perhaps reach across to try and pull both horses to a more moderate gait. But the little weasel-faced man stuck on the back of the big stallion like a jockey at Ascot.

Uppermost in her mind surged the thought that the danger of a broken neck increased with each passing moment. Yet Piers must be warned. He was in more danger than even he knew. At any moment he might be caught in a cross fire between the ruthless Beddoes and MacPherson's soldiers.

The clouds bared the moon as the pair neared the trail to the beach. Without hesitation she set Barbary's head upon it.

"Wait, milady!" Tyler shouted. "Pull back! The clouds—"

She glanced overhead. A thunderhead huge as a castle edged onto the shining silver disc. She reined Barbary fiercely, hurting his tender mouth. The gelding neighed loudly and rose up on its hind legs.

Just in time, the big horse came down. The night turned dark—dark in the infernal darkness just before dawn. How many hours had slipped away since Jack Beddoes had first appeared in their bedroom? To Vivian's ears came the roaring of the sea below. The tide had turned. *Spanish Girl* must have already come in with her contraband.

Barbary stamped and whinnied again, sawing at the reins. Vivian patted his sweaty neck, leaning far forward in the saddle. Behind her, invisible in the cold, windy darkness, she could hear Romany Prince blow breath from his nostrils and shift his weight. The saddle leather creaked.

Holding her breath, Vivian strained to sort out other sounds carried upward on the rising wind. Far below her she could distinguish men's voices rising faintly over the sound of the surf. The smugglers were unloading the *Spanish Girl*. Piers must be below in the cove where she had seen the barrels the first day.

Would he be standing in the surf, forming part of the chain to bring in the cargo? Or would he be standing somewhere up on the beach, his back menaced by Beddoes's volley gun? The latter surely, for he might slip away in the waves and darkness and make his way back to her.

No, somewhere beneath her, Piers waited helplessly, forced to stand by as a watcher in this dangerous undertaking, a hostage for her life. If he only knew she was no longer in danger.

She could not send him a visual signal through the blackness of the night, and she had no voice to call out his name. The darkness frustrated her, wrapping her in its folds, preventing her from communicating even with Tyler. Never had her handicap left her more isolated. Only with Barbary did her extreme terror and nervousness assert itself. The chestnut stamped and snorted beneath her, throwing up his head, setting his bit to jingling.

Her dearest love was in danger in the darkness below her. Now, for the strongest reason in the world, she should be able to speak his name. She put her hand to her throat and opened her mouth. Willing the words to come, straining to call out, sweat breaking out on her forehead with the effort, she could not make a sound.

The rushing sea wind tore the thunderhead away from the moon face, illuminating the scene below. Black figures against pale sand stood out in sharp relief. A hundred yards out, the black hulk of *Spanish Girl* floated. A small boat was pulled partway up on the sand. Shuffling figures unloaded heavy boxes and barrels in the foaming surf.

Rising in her stirrups, Vivian stared at each figure, but they were so far away, small moving forms, indistinguishable except as men. She could not pick out which one was her husband. A line of dark pony shapes, more than half a dozen, waited like silhouetted sculptures farther up the sand.

She had to get closer. Vivian urged Barbary forward, leaning back in the saddle to counterbalance his weight. With only a second's hesitation, the big chestnut began to pick his way gamely down the steep trail. Rocks and pebbles rolled under his hooves.

"Wait, milady," Tyler called softly. "Look yonder!"

As Vivian stared where he pointed, the spill of rocks at the far end of the cove began to move. First, one figure then another detached itself momentarily then blended back into the dark mass. Keeping as much as possible in the shadows, a troop of men was moving down on the smugglers.

A chill tore up her spine. The Riding Officers. MacPherson's men. The Scots captain's tenacity would pay off tonight. Tonight he would crush this smuggling operation forever.

Beddoes and his men were well and truly trapped in the cove. They had no way out except the steep path where Vivian and Tyler waited and watched, a path which as they watched, the soldiers moved to cut off.

"We're too late. They'll be on them any minute."

Refusing to believe him, Vivian urged Barbary down.

"Milady," Tyler called vainly.

She had to help Piers somehow. She had to. If she could not warn him, then she must get to MacPherson to explain that her husband had been taken as a hostage. MacPherson must not attack and endanger Piers. If Beddoes realized that the game was up, he might think Piers had somehow betrayed him and kill her husband in a vengeful fury. With Beddoes on one side and the King's muskets on the other, Piers would be caught between two fires.

Tyler urged Romany Prince down the trail until he came up beside her and grasped her rein. "Too late, milady," he gritted. "You'll burst out onto that beach in the middle of them. They'll shoot you without knowing who you are."

She struck at his hand, but he held fast. "I can't let you be going down there until the game's played out. We both know who's led the smuggler's until this night. He'll have to take his chances with the rest of them."

Angrily, Vivian jerked on the rein, pulling it out of Tyler's hand. Barbary's head came up. Fiercely, she reined back at the same time she brought her crop down with all her might on the horse's rump.

With a shrill neigh the gelding reared and plunged forward, crashing its broad chest into the shoulder of the stallion. Pushed off the trail onto the uneven stones of the cliff top, the larger horse staggered back under the unexpected attack. Down it went to its knees, despite Tyler's fervent curse and valiant effort to pull its head up.

For a perilous instant, Barbary staggered, too, but managed to gather his legs under him. With hands and heels Vivian urged the chestnut down the steep path, praying that the moonlight would last.

The noise had alerted the smugglers and undoubtedly the King's men, too.

Below her, two figures detached themselves from the knot of men at the boat and strode toward the path. With a feeling of thanksgiving, she recognized the tall figure in the lead.

Piers's head was thrown back staring upward in the blackness. His white stock gleamed at his throat; his white lace, at his cuffs. Like a mirror, his pale garments drew the moonlight, making him a target for every musket on the beach, not to speak of the duckfoot volley gun.

Behind her, she heard Romany Prince coming down the trail. Tyler was still trying to catch her. She clapped her heels to Barbary's sides, urging him on down. The trail leveled off fractionally.

In front of and below her, she caught the gleam of metal in the moonlight. The soldiers already guarded the trail. She would be stopped before she could warn him. Tears sprang to Vivian's eyes, and she gasped for breath. He would be killed. Any minute they would open fire and he would be the first to fall. Killed right in

422

front of her eyes, as her mother had been. A sob of pure panic tore itself from her throat.

Piers could have no idea who rode to warn him. Her habit was black velvet; her mount, dark. If only she could call to him. A stone turned under Barbary's hooves making the horse stumble. Almost unseated, Vivian struggled to bring the heavy head up and save the horse from a fall to its knees or, more disastrous, a slide over the side of the trail.

The clouds drifted across the face of the moon, again shrouding the whole cove in blackness. Vivian was left blind, muffled in darkness. Barbary halted as if turned to stone. Unable to see the way, the chestnut balked.

Vivian's stomach churned; her chest heaved in an effort to draw breath into her agitated lungs. Fear and love. Memories in the dark. Terror so fierce that it gripped her by the throat as it had so many years ago when she could not let go. Another sob tore from her. And another.

Sounds! Carried on the rushing air.

When blood and death were all around her, a viselike pressure enclosed both sides of her throat. She opened her mouth. Cold night air rushed into her lungs past her immobilized vocal cords.

White rays bathed the scene again. Like a spectator in an arena she saw it all. The two figures halted facing each other, engaged in conversation. At the foot of the path some twenty yards below her, the soldiers deployed their ranks. They had moved under cover of darkness and now knelt with muskets at the ready. They would fire at command, and her husband would be the first to fall.

Her eyes widened. Her face by the light of the moon contorted as her agony of mind and spirit became physical. He was there below her, the husband she loved. The man who loved her. Aimed at his heart was a musket. Her mouth opened wide; she drew a deep cold breath to swell her lungs. With all the force she could muster, she propelled the air upward against her vocal cords in a scream of terror, of warning, of love.

"Fire!"

The end of her cry was lost in the volley of musketry and the screams of smugglers who fell to the sand, some to writhe in agony, some to lie still. But the tall figure staring up at her had moved when he had first heard her call.

"Gawd almighty!" Jack Beddoes threw himself flat on the sand.

"Fire! Fire at will!"

The muskets spoke again, their fire more sporadic this time as some men loaded and fired faster than others.

The men who were not down in the white sand were running. The men closest to the boat dropped their burdens and tried to launch it. One figure slid silently into the water. Another arched as a musket ball struck him in the back. His torso hung over the gunwale, legs trailing in the surf until his friends pulled him in beside them and began to row.

Some of their fellows leaped into the surf trying to catch the boat before it got into deep water. A hundred yards out, the crew of *Spanish Girl* leaped to raise the sail.

"Y' bleedin' cowards! Fight!" The duckfoot gun boomed again and again.

"Fire!"

Spinning, staggering, dropping to one knee, Piers clutched at his body. Above the sand on the path halfway down the cliff top, another shrill, childish scream echoed. No time to find where the sound had come from. He had to get away, get out of the line of fire or perish. Though his wounds burned, he crawled cross the sand on his belly, leaving a trail of blood.

Jack Beddoes lifted his eyes to the trail, just as moon cleared the clouds and the first faint rays of dawn lightened the eastern sky. By their light he reloaded the volley gun. "Bitch," he groaned as he recognized the Countess of Larnaervon. "Bitch."

Shouts and curses rang in the night air.

"Forward!" In response to a barked command, the dragoons ran yelling across the sand and into the surf, trying to overtake the boat and capture its occupants.

Beddoes rose to one knee to meet them. The duckfoot spoke, even as a musket ball slammed into his belly. He cursed and fired again, bringing down the dragoon who had shot him. He flung his empty gun at the line of men charging him, their bayonets aimed for his chest.

"Gawd almighty!"

Then they passed over him, slashing and stabbing, driving him flat into the sand.

To Vivian's horror, they raced on toward the struggling figure of her husband. Then another thick cloud sailed across the face of the moon blotting out the whole scene.

More shots boomed from the muskets. Confusion and curses rose to her straining ears, but nothing was visible. Trembling with suspense, she slid from the back of the gelding determined to make her way down the cliff face or die in the attempt. Dragging the reins over the tall head, she patted Barbary's nose and led him forward, her fist closed in the check rein under his chin. Several times her slender weight dragged heavily on the horse's head as stones turned under her feet. Below her the foot of the path was clear, for the men had all moved out to the water's edge, and the sound of their voices was muffled by the pounding surf.

The land wind turned as she finally put her booted foot onto the sand. The clouds blew away as the moon sank lower on the horizon and faint streaks of dawn began to appear in the night sky. The white sand showed plainly the effects of the night's passage. The entire expanse was churned up. Footprints crossed and recrossed one another as the soldiers had charged and the smugglers had fled before them.

Keeping Barbary on a tight rein, Vivian followed the soldiers' charge. Less than fifty yards from the trail, the body of Jack Beddoes lay stiff, its limbs extended like a stick doll. His sightless eyes stared up at the lightening sky above his chest, a gaping wound torn open by bayonets. Barbary shied violently at the smell of the blood, dragging her away from the sight.

Where was Piers? Did he lie somewhere ahead, in the same condition?

Trembling with apprehension, she stared at the dark red patches that splattered the area to the right. Kneeling beside them, her gorge rose in her throat. She was staring at her husband's blood. He had been wounded and had dragged himself away from the melee.

Behind her she heard the sound of approaching hooves. Tyler loped Romany Prince across the sand toward her. With a swipe of her gloved hand, she flung sand over the stain. As she rose to her feet, she tried to think of herself as the Countess of Larnaervon. From that position she would be virtually unassailable.

The groom dismounted to pick up Beddoes's wrist. Instantly, he dropped it. The body was already stiff and cold. No need to check for the pulsebeat. With a shrug, he looked away across the churned sand, separating them from the scene at the water's edge.

Vivian watched believing that she should say something appropriate or ask a question, but unable to think of the words. She ran her tongue across her lips. What did people say about dead bodies of smugglers?

Then Tyler looked at her, his face sad. "Milady, I believe the smuggling will stop now. MacPherson has broken the ring for good."

She nodded in agreement. In the strengthening light of dawn, the redcoats stood out brightly against the white beach. A small group of men in bedraggled clothing huddled together surrounded by soldiers with muskets and bayonets trained on them.

But no white stock and pale buckskins stood among the prisoners. A little of the pain about her heart eased.

As if he read her thought, Tyler looked around him inquiringly, but she had covered the bloodstains in the sand. Lacing his fingers, he tossed her into the saddle. "Will you return home now?"

With a shake of her head, she guided Barbary toward the sea where the uniformed men were regrouping. The longboat had pulled alongside the *Spanish Girl* and those left among the smugglers would be underway in minutes.

Tyler galloped his mount past her and conferred with a tall uniformed figure. Rory MacPherson looked in her direction. His tired face lighted with surprise and pleasure. In her black velvet habit, her white veil floating in the freshening breeze, she made a gallant sight. Smiling, she walked her horse toward them. Snatches of their conversation came over the pounding of the waves.

The groom pointed back up the beach to the body. "—Jack Beddoes. —tried it once too often. Greedy sod!"

Captain MacPherson left the groom and hurried to meet her. At Barbary's shoulder, he pulled off his tricorne and swept a gallant bow. "You shouldn't be here, milady."

She shook her head. Long habit kept her mute. She could think of nothing to say. Even as she tried to frame the words, Tyler spoke for her.

"The countess prefers to ride early in the morning."

"Take her away from here," MacPherson commanded. "You shouldn't have seen that man's body."

Acknowledging the truth of his statement, she gazed sadly into his face. Her gloved hands tightly gripped the reins as she summoned her willpower to open her mouth and attempt intelligible speech after ten years of silence.

"Since this is your cove," MacPherson began carefully, "perhaps I should make some explanation to the earl and to the viscount. Do I have your permission to call later on in the morning?"

Tension gripped her. The earl was dead. The viscount? She must find him before MacPherson came to the house.

Tyler must have had the same concern. "Best not come too soon, Captain MacPherson," he murmured under his breath. "The earl died last night."

"No." MacPherson started and looked up at Vivian. "Then you are the Countess of Larnaervon."

She inclined her head in acknowledgment.

In the manner of one making a report, he swept his hat across the scene on the beach. "We caught the rest of the smugglers, milady. At last. And I hope—that is I believe—we have caught their leader. I'll wish to make a final report to your husband, since this is now his beach and his responsibility."

She smiled briefly, then exchanged a meaningful glance with Tyler.

428

"I'll stay here and look after the needs of these men, milady," the groom assured her hastily. "Will you continue your ride?"

Graciously, Vivian nodded. She held out her hand to Captain MacPherson, who took it and lifted it to his lips. His blue eyes were worried. A subaltern came up behind him to make a report. He gave her one last smile before he turned back to the business at hand.

Vivian pulled Barbary's rein and headed him down to the water's edge. She would ride through the water to the rocks at the end of the cove. Piers would be there. The boyhood cave with its special memories would shelter him. If only he had had the strength to get there.

Apparently riding in a meandering pattern, Vivian trotted the gelding along in the surf, then turned him up the beach swinging him wide across the path most likely to have been taken by her husband.

Quickly, her sharp eyes found what she sought—a splash of dark red blood. A heavy body had left its impression in the sand, perhaps rested there while it rallied its strength for the next effort.

A stab of pain went through her vitals in sympathy for his agony. Guiding Barbary's hooves over the spot, she directed the chestnut down the beach. Her sharp eyes followed his trail now, smaller dots of blood, sand displaced by footprints that staggered and wove about drunkenly. Despite his weakness and probably his disorientation, he was heading directly for the rock face at the end of the cove.

She must not lead them directly to him. Realizing she was still in the sight of the men on the beach, she rode the horse straight by the rocks and galloped down again to the water's edge.

The nearness of her wounded husband tortured her. Suppose he were badly hurt, needing her? She wanted to be with him. Her fingers twisted nervously in the reins as she sought to steady herself for the oncoming scene she must play. The creamy surf rolled around Barbary's hocks, and the gelding dropped his head to snuffle at it. He threw up his head and snorted in disgust when the saltwater slapped his nose.

For a full minute she sat, appearing to gaze out over the tumbling waves and the brilliance of the morning. Silently, she sat, seeing nothing while she recited her prayers for his safety. Her heart pounded fiercely as she imagined the men watching her suspiciously.

Finally, as unconcernedly as a lady might who rode aimlessly for pleasure, she reined Barbary around and rode toward the cliff face at the back of the cove. There she would appear to the men to be picking her way around the back edge. In a few seconds she would be out of their line of vision. Just as she rode out of their sight, she glanced in their direction. They were busy about their business. MacPherson was not even looking where she rode.

Instantly, she spurred her mount behind the rocks and galloped across the intervening sand. Heart beating frantically, she reined to a sliding stop and slipped from his back on the run. Between the rocks she darted along the narrow expanse of sand. The perspective opened up as it had before. To her horror when she came to the rock where they had tethered the horses, she found a smear of blood as if Piers had staggered against it and righted himself by pushing himself away with his hand.

Climbing over the driftwood, she flung herself at the entrance of the cave. At first she could see nothing; but as her eyes became accustomed to the darkness after the light, she found him.

He lay pressed back against the wall of the cave underneath the shelf. His shirt was open; his chest bared. He had used his stock to make a compress which he held tightly against his ribs. Still blood trickled between his fingers and stained one side of his breeches.

As her silhouette darkened the cave, he looked up. His dark eyes, underscored by circles of pain and exhaustion, had the look of a hunted animal. He pressed back against the wall of the cave.

She swallowed hard against the tearing pain in her heart and in her throat.

Chapter Twenty-Six

As Vivian's silhouette filled the cave entrance, Piers started up. When he recognized her, he slumped back. Eyes alight, he held out his free hand to her. "Vivian. Thank God," he whispered softly. "You got away from Felders. If that bitch hurt you— How did you get here?"

Slipping into the cave, she sank to her knees by his side. Her slender hand closed over his bloodstained one and gently added her strength to his. Empathy for his pain made her lean her head weakly against his shoulder.

"It's not too bad, just a crease over the ribs," he reassured her. "It looks worse than it is. Believe me."

She would not be satisfied until she had inspected it and replaced his hand with hers to hold the compress in place. Pulling off her own stock, she passed its length around him and made a competent bandage.

Entranced, he stared at her absorbed face as she worked over him. Finally, she sat back on her heels, satisfied that he was in no danger of bleeding to death.

"Are you all right?" he asked her softly.

The tenderness, the concern, in his tone made her

shiver. She marshaled her forces to speak to him, to utter words for the first time in ten years. Not for a minute did she doubt that she could do so. Before she could speak, he threw his free arm around her and drew her against him, as if to draw strength from her strength.

"Oh, Vivian. You must tell me everything that happened the minute we get home. You can write for hours." Chuckling weakly, he tipped up her chin and pressed her mouth with his own. His kiss was a revelation of tenderness and gratitude. Sighing, he drank her like fine wine. Then, he raised his head but continued to hold her close against him. His heart thrummed strongly beneath her ear.

Finally, when he spoke her name, his voice was husky with emotion. Embarrassed, he paused, grimaced, drew a deep breath. "Vivian, when you were in danger, I couldn't bear it. Now that I can see you, I'm— She didn't hurt you, did she? I've been wild with fear. If Jack Beddoes managed to escape this time, I'll hunt him down until I find him and kill him. He'll never, never come near you again. You'll never have to be afraid of anything again. I promise you—"

Her finger touched his lips, closed them over his babbling. She smiled at him, her heart in her eyes. Opening her mouth, she drew in a deep breath. *"I— love—you, Piers."*

Incredulously, he stared at her. Silence stretched between them. At last he spoke, his voice a croak. "Vivian?"

She nodded. "Piers."

His hand trembled as it rose to her mouth. His fingers caressed her lips. "You spoke?"

"Yes."

"You spoke. Vivian. Love. Oh, my dear. You spoke." He began to laugh. Shakily at first, then

joyously. "You spoke." He caught her by the shoulders and kissed her lips again and again. "You spoke," he whispered. "You spoke."

"Yes."

"Say my name again." His own voice broke with emotion. He tipped her head back, staring at her mouth.

"Piers." Her voice had a light musical tone like a child's voice without the deepening that adult voices gain with age and usage.

He laughed again. "Tell me," he begged excitedly. "Tell me how it happened." He leaned his forehead against hers. The tip of his nose touched hers. He pursed his lips and touched hers in a tender brush of a kiss.

She could not think how to begin. She could only repeat stupidly. "Piers, I love you."

"This is a miracle," he whispered. He kissed her again. "I can't believe it's happened."

She raised herself from his chest and placed both hands to her cheeks. She had managed so long without words that they did not come readily to mind. "I saw you were in danger." She hesitated. "You couldn't see me. The night was too dark. I couldn't reach you. The path was too steep. I screamed."

"I heard the scream," he breathed. "I started forward. Just at that moment a shot slammed into my side. You probably saved my life." He caught her hands and kissed them. "You saved my life."

"I found where you fell." She shuddered visibly. "Beddoes is dead."

"No loss to mankind."

"I knew where you had gone. I remembered the cave." She put her hands on his ribs. "Are you sure you're not badly hurt?"

"A scratch. Really, it bled hardly at all. It's already healing."

She looked at him doubtfully remembering the splashes in the sand. Her hands spread over his chest. Fascinated, entranced with the texture of his skin, she caressed him, satisfying herself that he was alive.

His eyes darkened at her touch. With quite a different motive, he raised himself to kiss her on the mouth caressing her soft interior and touching her tongue tip with his. Joy turned to desire despite his ordeal. His hand found her warm breast to feel the beating of her heart through the fabric of her blouse and jacket.

A blazing fire warmed him from within. He had never felt such need and such inordinate desire for fulfillment. So close had they both been to death that he wanted an affirmation of life. Certain as of nothing in his life before, he believed they would create life between them. "Let me love you."

The unadorned words sent an electric shock through her own body. "Yes," she whispered. Now she could speak. Now she could tell him how she loved him. "Yes. Oh, yes!"

They needed no tantalizing touches, no slow awakening of desire. Neither wanted it. His chest was already naked. She pulled the front of her jacket from the buttons in one swift motion.

"Yes!"

The blouse beneath tore in her haste.

"Yes!"

Her whole being was suffused in blazing desire. She pulled her skirt and petticoats up about her thighs. "Yes!!"

"My god, Vivian," he whispered. He tore his own clothing apart and pushed her down into the sand.

435

Unconscious of any pain, he rolled above her and drove himself into her.

A cry came from her. High and keening, pain and pleasure so intense that she set her teeth against it.

He pulled out and drove in again.

"Yes. Oh, my love—"

"I—love—you."

"Yes!"

They exploded together and he caught her first scream of pure pleasure in his mouth.

The housekeeper was angry defiance personified. "You won't get away with any of this," she snarled. "Lock me up, will you? In this house that I've kept for years."

"You will leave here within the hour," Piers told her coldly. "I'll send you in the carriage to Exeter. After that you're on your own."

"The earl—"

"Larne is dead," Piers interrupted coldly. "I might feel kindly toward you for what you did for him if you had not treated my mother with such cruelty and contempt."

"Jack—"

"He's dead, too. Cut to pieces on the beach when he tried to fight the dragoons. Soldiers that he assured me were nowhere in the vicinity—I might add."

"I'm pregnant."

"You might be pregnant by Jack Beddoes's child. You and he were married after all. But you can't be more than a couple of months gone." He looked at her critically. "If you expect me to believe that my father in his condition was capable of impregnating you, you must take me for a fool."

She faltered, then her dark eyes stabbed at him. "The

436

Riding Officers will be interested in what I have to say."

"You can't say much without implicating yourself. And I doubt at any rate they'd attach much credence to the word of a disgruntled servant, turned off without a character."

"Piers," Vivian interposed softly.

Mrs. Felders stared at her. "You can talk."

"Yes. It's all coming back to me."

"Then tell him. He can't treat me like this."

"I can't tell him to do anything. I can ask him. And I do. Piers, give her some kind of reference."

He looked around him in distaste. "I remember the condition of this house when you came here. I can't say anything that would be of any help to her."

Felders's face flushed darkly. She clenched her fists at her side. "The earl was pleased."

Vivian nodded. "Then tell the truth, Piers. Say she served the Earl of Larnaervon until his death."

He shook his head angrily.

"Please, love."

He glanced at Felders. The color had drained from her face. She stood like a stone, her mouth pinched, her eyes narrowed. How could the earl ever have found this woman remotely attractive? "Very well."

She seemed to relax fractionally. Then she lifted her chin. "I've got some money coming to me."

"I'll see that it's taken care of," Vivian said.

Felders flashed her a contemptuous look. "I'm not talking about my pittance here. Jack had a share coming."

Piers shook his head. "The operation is over. The *Spanish Girl* is gone back to France with the few men aboard who survived. The last two expeditions have been complete and dismal failures. Whatever he gave you before was all he was entitled to."

"You're lying."

"Get out."

"You're cheating me!" she cried.

His anger quickened. He rose from behind his father's desk, leaning across it, his wounded side drawing and pulling painfully. "You'd better pack your things while my wife is still willing to pay your wages and write you a character. Say one more word to me, and you'll be turned out of the house in the clothes you stand in."

She opened her mouth. He raised his hand.

She took a deep breath then let it out slowly. Without another word she turned and left. The door to the library slammed behind her.

"Don't see her again, Vivian," he warned. "Write your letter and hand it and the purse to Millard to give to her. You don't have to listen to any more of her lies and vileness."

"You don't have to tell me," she agreed softly. "Now sit down and rest."

"Captain MacPherson, sir." Millard looked uncertainly from one to the other.

His face pale but otherwise composed, Piers nodded. "Wait a couple of minutes, then show him in, Millard." He adjusted his coat over the bandage beneath his shirt. "Does anything show, Vivian?"

She touched his shoulder. "Is this really necessary, Piers? Shouldn't you be in bed?"

He covered her hand with his own. "I should be. And I promise to go straightway after he leaves, but this is important. Let's dispel once and for all the idea that I might in some way have been mixed up in the smuggling."

"You're hurting."

"Yes," he told her simply. "But there's an end in

sight. One more effort and then we'll never have to go through this again."

She bent and kissed him on the lips. "I don't like this."

"As soon as he leaves, I'll let you take me up to bed and—"

"Captain MacPherson," Millard stood back from the door.

"Ah, Captain MacPherson." Piers rose and held out his hand.

The officer looked at him sharply, plainly taken aback at seeing him. "You're looking a little pale, Lord Polwycke."

"Kind of you to notice. I'm still not over that accident in Scotland. Devil of a thing breaking one's shoulder and then getting pneumonia in the bargain. If not for my dear wife, I might have cashed in my chips."

The blue Scottish eyes slid over her warmly. "You're a very lucky man."

Vivian rose and came to him as Piers stepped back and lowered himself wincing into his chair. "Captain MacPherson."

The sound of her voice staggered him. "M-milady."

"I can talk again. It's all come back to me. In one night."

He recovered himself. "Why this is wonderful. Wonderful."

"I can at last thank you for all you have done for us in capturing the smugglers. I told my husband when I returned from my ride today."

"Right, MacPherson. We are in your debt. They had been creating havoc among the local people. My father was too ill to do anything about them. But now that he's gone, they were to have been my first task. And now you've done it for me."

The captain looked from one to the other. The lady smiled at her husband with such sweetness, such pride. He returned her look with such tenderness. MacPherson felt their passion like a knife to his vitals. His last tiny shreds of hope vanished in the blaze of their love. He tried to clear his throat, but the lump remained making speaking difficult. "I'm glad to be of such service to you both. Think of it as a belated wedding present and allow me to wish you happy."

Vivian turned to him. Her own tender nature ached for him. They had met too late. She had found her love and he must go and find his. She put her hands in his. "We wish you good fortune, too, Captain MacPherson. You and your little son deserve it."

"Aye, Reiver. This is not the proper kind of life for a lad. My job's too dangerous. Perhaps I'll take this time to leave England. I've heard there's opportunity aplenty in America."

"You'll always be welcome here," Piers said generously. He slipped his arm around his wife's waist and drew her against his side. The currents between this tall Scotsman and Vivian were making him uncomfortable. "But, of course, if you must be on your way—"

"Piers," she chided.

"He's right, milady," MacPherson agreed. "Time to be on my way. God bless you both."

She held out her hands again. "The truest friend," she murmured. They were the words she had written in the sand that day on the beach.

Despite her husband's scowl, he lifted her hands to his lips and took the memory of their touch away with him.

The door was pushed wide open, driving Millard back against the wall. "You needn't announce us, my good man. She'll be glad we've come back to help her."

Worthing Barnstaple, all six feet six of him, huffed and puffed to keep up with the younger man. "Right you are, Sebastian. She will need financial advice."

He threw a contemptuous look over his shoulder. "Just so you don't forget that I'll be her guardian."

"Barnstaple and Rowling will continue to manage as they have always done in the past," came the affronted declaration.

Sebastian Dawlish surveyed the entry hall with some disdain. "This place doesn't compare to Stone Glenn, of course, but I'm sure that much can be done with it."

"Right you are. Right. Now that she's inherited everything as Countess of Larnaervon, those estates will have to be managed as well." Barnstaple's portly belly fairly jiggled with his eagerness to add to his business.

Vivian stopped midway down the stairs to stare at them in disgust and some amusement.

Sebastian looked up and saw her first. "My dear. We've heard the sad news about the death of your father-in-law. And the capture of the smugglers. And the death of their leader. Now I may tell you that I—and I alone—was instrumental in setting up that little coup. I have always had your best interests at heart, Vivian."

"Always!" Barnstaple interposed.

"Naturally, we knew you'd need help in settling all these problems with your estates." Dawlish started up the stairs toward her. His eyes were dark with menace, daring her to try to protest his guardianship. "I wouldn't want you to be burdened with anything that would undermine your delicate health. I'm prepared to resume my care of you."

"But I don't need you to care for me."

441

The words drove him back. He clutched the banister to keep from falling. "You spoke!"

"Yes. Isn't it fortunate? I recovered my speech in the course of all the danger and excitement of the smugglers' arrest. Shocking things happened. I believe that I needed only a shock."

Barnstaple pulled out his handkerchief. "How wonderful!" His tone was hollow. "How perfectly marvelous for you! But, of course, you mustn't strain your voice. It might not be permanent."

"I'm quite sure that it is."

Dawlish's eyes shifted from side to side. He dragged a handkerchief from his pocket and wiped at his mouth. "But you never can tell. And you say you've had a shock. Perhaps you need to see a doctor immediately."

"I have no need of a doctor. I never felt better in my life. However, I wonder how you came to have any information about smugglers. Did you perhaps have some inside information?"

Sebastian advanced menacingly. "I knew you were in danger here, my dear. That marriage was forced upon you when you were not in your right mind. I put my own money to work bribing one Jack Beddoes to supply information about a shipment of contraband goods. Many members of the band were caught that night."

"And then I, my dear girl, supplied—um—extra money to certain magistrates and high-ranking officers to order Captain MacPherson to patrol these beaches regularly." Barnstaple started up the stairs, too. "We've really had your best interests at heart, my dear girl. You should be overcome with gratitude."

"And so I am." She smiled slightly. "But I have to tell you that your trap last night resulted in the death of Jack Beddoes."

Sebastian sniffed. "No loss to the world. So long as the chief of the smugglers was killed as well."

"But he was the chief of the smugglers."

The two looked at each other. "I'm sure you are mistaken, my dear. Your loyalty does you credit, but we know otherwise," Sebastian sneered. "It's obvious to me that you are not in your right mind. You need to see a doctor immediately."

"If she needs to see a doctor, Sebby, I'll take her to one."

"Polwycke!"

"Larnaervon," Piers corrected softly.

"Larnaervon. You're alive."

"As you see."

Burnstaple, his sagging jowls quivering, stared at Piers as if he had seen a ghost. "I suppose this means that you'll be using another solicitor."

"My husband and I will decide upon one," Vivian informed him sweetly.

He nodded and turned back down the stairs. Shoulders slumping he walked to the door. With a superior smile Millard handed him his hat.

"This isn't legal." Sebastian tried one more time. "You're a criminal. You led the smugglers."

"How can he possibly have led the smugglers when he was in bed with me the whole night long?" Vivian asked.

"That's a lie."

"Come, Vivian." Piers turned her around and they started back up the stairs together. "Show yourself out, Sebby."

"You can't get away with this." He followed them a couple of steps.

Piers faced him at the top of the stairs. "Sebby, may I suggest you not follow us any farther unless you have developed a taste for voyeurism?"

"Vivian!"

She shook her head. "Sebastian. If I needed a guardian, it would not be you."

"Leave, Sebby," Piers advised. "And she won't sue you for all the money you've siphoned off the estate during the year you had her imprisoned in the abbey."

Vivian nodded. She slipped her arm around his waist. "Just leave."

He shot them a look of frustrated anger. "You've no right to her."

Piers smiled. "No, I've no right to her. But I love her and she loves me. So she's promised to stay with me. And if she doesn't like me after a while, she can leave. But I've no right to her."

Vivian turned in his arms. "And I've no right to you. But I love you."

"Vivian."

She looked at Sebastian's shocked expression. Then grinned. "Piers—" She put her arms around him and kissed him with mouth and hands and body. When she drew back, she laughed. "It looks as though he requires proof, Piers. Do you think we might provide him with some? We did it once before."

Piers laugh floated back down to the angry Sebastian. *"In flagrante delicto,* my dear. With pleasure."

Epilogue

Stone Glenn
April 1820

If you can find your way to the heart of the boxwood maze, you'll find your heart's desire.

Piers read the note again, a smile tugging at the corners of his mouth. "When did you receive this?"

"Her ladyship came down the stairs only a short time before you rode up, sir," the butler informed him. "I believe she watches from the upstairs window. She can see beyond the terrace to the stables. It's been her special trick since she was just a little girl."

"Watching the horses?"

"And the riders, as well, your lordship." The man hesitated. "May I say again, sir, how very glad we are to have our lady back. The months she was away, we sorely missed her. She belongs here." A satisfied smile flickered across his austere features, then vanished. He cleared his throat hastily. "And we welcome you as well."

"Why thank you, Smithers." Piers folded the note and slipped it into the pocket of his coat. "I'll just join my wife in the garden. You wouldn't happen to know the secret of the boxwood maze?"

The butler looked startled. "I, sir. Oh, no, sir. What goes on out of doors is not my business really. I don't know that anyone inside the house does. Jacob and his sons, the gardeners, you know, are very tactiturn. But her ladyship knows. It's always been her favorite place. No one ever had to look any further when she was lost. She learned it when she was—"

"—just a little girl."

Bunches of bright blue squills lined the gray flagstone path and, behind them, yellow daffodils. A warm breeze blew across the flowers, ruffling them and carrying their perfume to his nostrils.

He paused at the entrance to the maze, his fists on his hips, absorbing as he had never had occasion to before the scent and sight of a garden coming alive with spring, growing and blooming profusely.

The breeze brushed his cheeks and lifted his hair from his brow. He felt an almost overwhelming urge to bow his head. Stone Glenn was heaven. He knew because until he came here, he had lived in hell.

He turned first to the right, but less than a quarter around, he ran into a wall of hedge. This was going to be simple. More turns, more double backs, but always he pressed onward, going closer and closer, the circles getting smaller and smaller.

Finally, he heard her voice humming softly. He smiled. He could picture her—in all likelihood sitting on a bench, a wide straw hat shading her delicate skin. "Vivian."

The humming stopped. He guessed that she smiled. "Hurry, darling."

He rounded the end of the last wall and stepped into a green room, its ceiling the blue sky. No bench as he had imagined. Instead a pear tree with a cloud of white blossoms, and a blanket on the ground beneath it.

His wife lay stretched upon it. Her magnificent hair was unbound, her feet bare. She stretched out her hand. "Piers."

He stopped thunderstruck. "V-vivian?"

"I'm so happy, sweetheart. And I've had this dream for so long."

"Dream?"

"I'm home and safe, Piers." She smiled as tears welled in her eyes. "I'm so happy. This is the heart of Stone Glenn. I want you to love me here."

He crossed the ground in a rush and dropped down on his knees beside her. "Vivian."

The kiss he gave her was long and slow, melting and shaking them both. Desire grew swiftly as his own emotions made him tremble. He cradled her against his chest. "I'm happy to be part of your dream," he told her humbly.

"I want it to be yours, too," she whispered, her skin delicately flushed. Her lips slid along his throat, feeling the pulse that leaped and drummed.

She might have touched the pattern of nerves beneath the skin as well, touched them with a fire that heated the very blood in his veins. He lifted his head to facilitate her sweet torture. The blossoms of the pear tree swung against the blue sky as he sank back onto the blanket.

Her fingers loosened his clothing and her mouth followed her hands, coaxing him, torturing him until he could not endure another moment. Ecstasy rushing through his veins, he possessed her with long, deep, languorous strokes while she moaned and wept and praised him.

"Piers!"

At last she called his name in her sweet voice. He

447

gave her what she asked for in full measure. The shuddering began deep within her body, drawing him deeper, drawing the very life of him into her.

And throughout their lives whenever they walked the maze together, at first with the son they had conceived there, and later with their other children and grandchildren, he would take his hand in hers and kiss it. "Say my name," he would bid her.

"Piers," she would reply. "Piers, my love."